SQUAD UP

TO MY WIFE, BETH, WITH LOVE AND GRATITUDE
FOR THE HAPPY SQUAD WE MADE. —S.N.

TO ALL THE YOUNG READERS. DON'T TAKE YOUR
FRIENDS FOR GRANTED, CHERISH THEM. —D.J.

CLARION BOOKS IS AN IMPRINT OF HARPERCOLLINS PUBLISHERS.
HARPERALLEY IS AN IMPRINT OF HARPERCOLLINS PUBLISHERS.

SQUAD UP
COPYRIGHT © 2022 BY HARPERCOLLINS PUBLISHERS
ALL RIGHTS RESERVED. MANUFACTURED IN SPAIN. NO PART OF THIS BOOK MAY BE USED
OR REPRODUCED IN ANY MANNER WHATSOEVER WITHOUT WRITTEN PERMISSION EXCEPT
IN THE CASE OF BRIEF QUOTATIONS EMBODIED IN CRITICAL ARTICLES AND REVIEWS.
FOR INFORMATION ADDRESS HARPERCOLLINS CHILDREN'S BOOKS, A DIVISION OF
HARPERCOLLINS PUBLISHERS, 195 BROADWAY, NEW YORK, NY 10007.
WWW.HARPERALLEY.COM

ISBN 978-0-35-851287-5 PAPERBACK
ISBN 978-0-35-851288-2 HARDCOVER

THE ILLUSTRATIONS IN THIS BOOK WERE CREATED DIGITALLY.
TYPOGRAPHY BY PHIL CAMINITI
COLOR ASSISTANT: JAKE HILL
PHOTO CREDITS PAGE 228: ANCIL MCKAIN AND DARNELL JOHNSON
22 23 24 25 26 EP 10 9 8 7 6 5 4 3 2 1

FIRST EDITION

SQUAD UP

A POWER UP GRAPHIC NOVEL

WRITTEN BY
SAM NISSON

ILLUSTRATED BY
DARNELL JOHNSON

CLARION BOOKS
IMPRINTS OF HARPERCOLLINSPUBLISHERS

CONTENTS

THE STORY GOES . . .

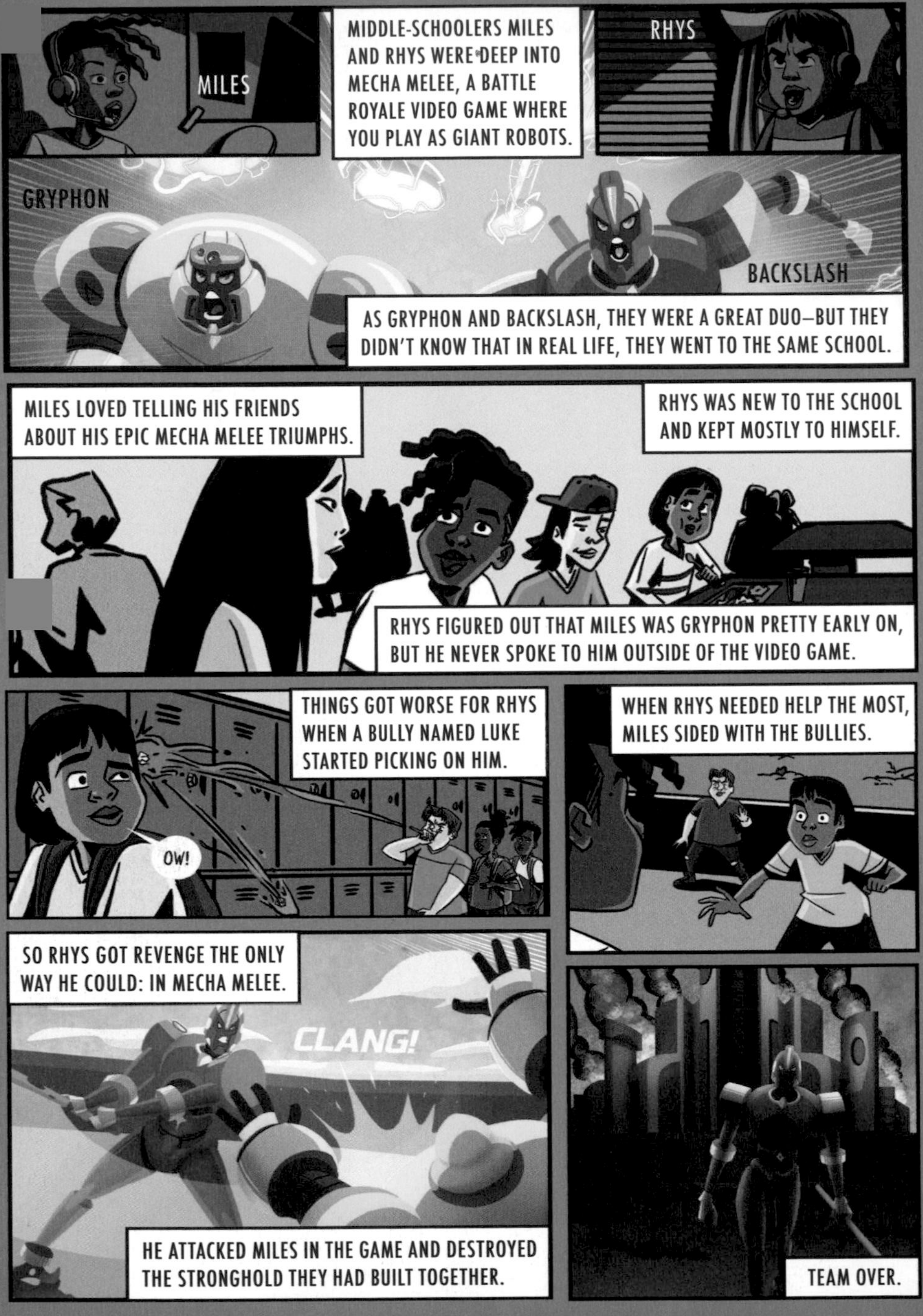

MILES
MIDDLE-SCHOOLERS MILES AND RHYS WERE DEEP INTO MECHA MELEE, A BATTLE ROYALE VIDEO GAME WHERE YOU PLAY AS GIANT ROBOTS.
RHYS
GRYPHON
BACKSLASH
AS GRYPHON AND BACKSLASH, THEY WERE A GREAT DUO—BUT THEY DIDN'T KNOW THAT IN REAL LIFE, THEY WENT TO THE SAME SCHOOL.
MILES LOVED TELLING HIS FRIENDS ABOUT HIS EPIC MECHA MELEE TRIUMPHS.
RHYS WAS NEW TO THE SCHOOL AND KEPT MOSTLY TO HIMSELF.
RHYS FIGURED OUT THAT MILES WAS GRYPHON PRETTY EARLY ON, BUT HE NEVER SPOKE TO HIM OUTSIDE OF THE VIDEO GAME.
THINGS GOT WORSE FOR RHYS WHEN A BULLY NAMED LUKE STARTED PICKING ON HIM.
OW!
WHEN RHYS NEEDED HELP THE MOST, MILES SIDED WITH THE BULLIES.
SO RHYS GOT REVENGE THE ONLY WAY HE COULD: IN MECHA MELEE.
CLANG!
HE ATTACKED MILES IN THE GAME AND DESTROYED THE STRONGHOLD THEY HAD BUILT TOGETHER.
TEAM OVER.

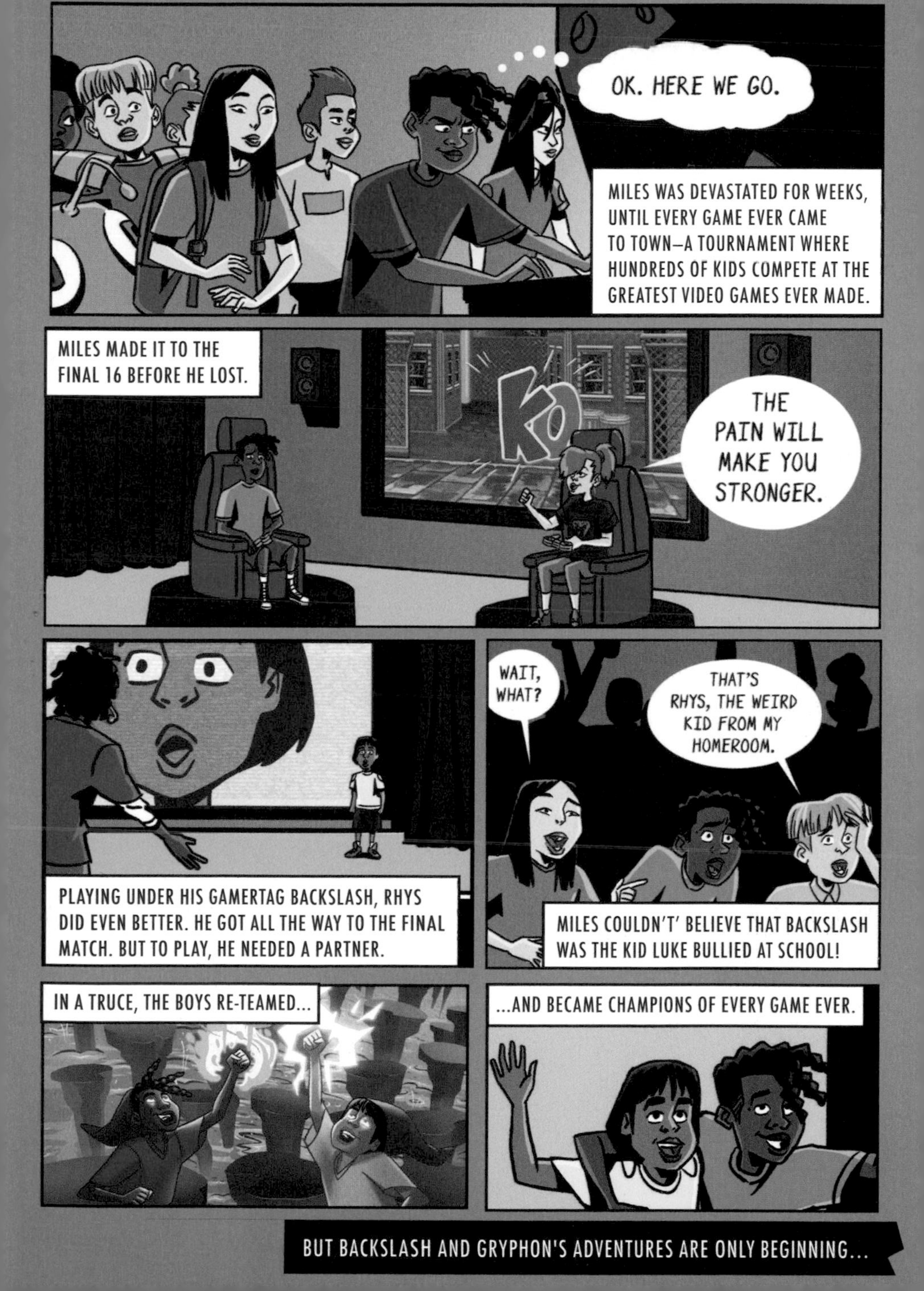
OK. HERE WE GO.
MILES WAS DEVASTATED FOR WEEKS, UNTIL EVERY GAME EVER CAME TO TOWN—A TOURNAMENT WHERE HUNDREDS OF KIDS COMPETE AT THE GREATEST VIDEO GAMES EVER MADE.
MILES MADE IT TO THE FINAL 16 BEFORE HE LOST.
KO
THE PAIN WILL MAKE YOU STRONGER.
PLAYING UNDER HIS GAMERTAG BACKSLASH, RHYS DID EVEN BETTER. HE GOT ALL THE WAY TO THE FINAL MATCH. BUT TO PLAY, HE NEEDED A PARTNER.
WAIT, WHAT?
THAT'S RHYS, THE WEIRD KID FROM MY HOMEROOM.
MILES COULDN'T' BELIEVE THAT BACKSLASH WAS THE KID LUKE BULLIED AT SCHOOL!
IN A TRUCE, THE BOYS RE-TEAMED...
...AND BECAME CHAMPIONS OF EVERY GAME EVER.

BUT BACKSLASH AND GRYPHON'S ADVENTURES ARE ONLY BEGINNING...

CHAPTER 1
QUEST

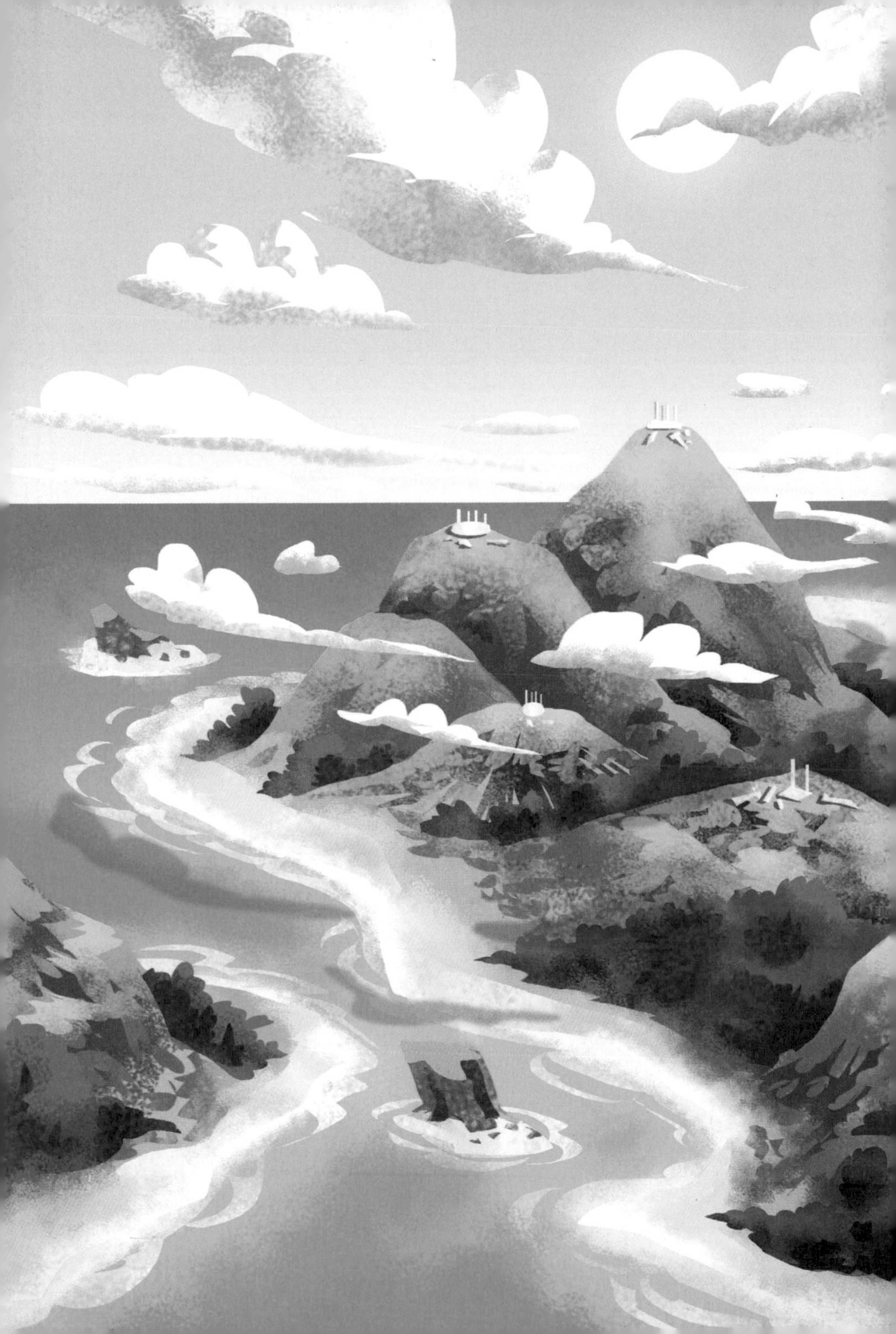

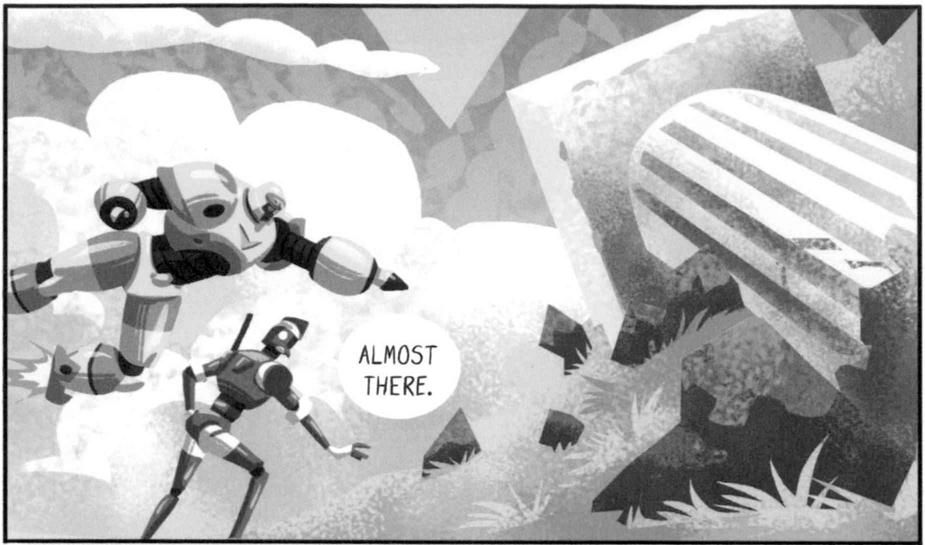
ALMOST THERE.

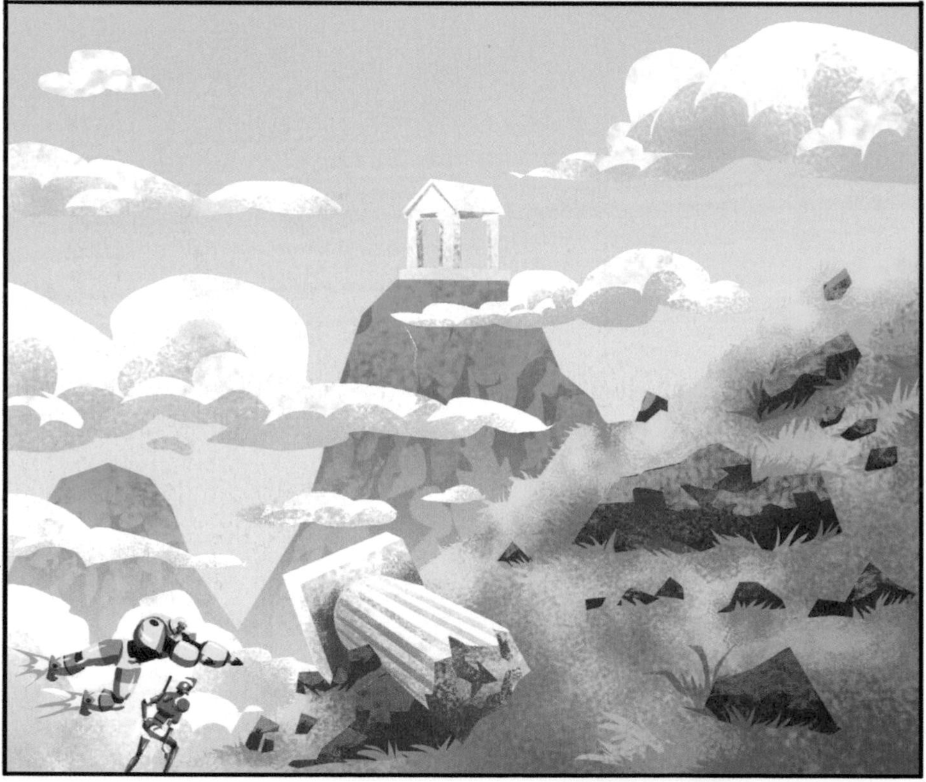

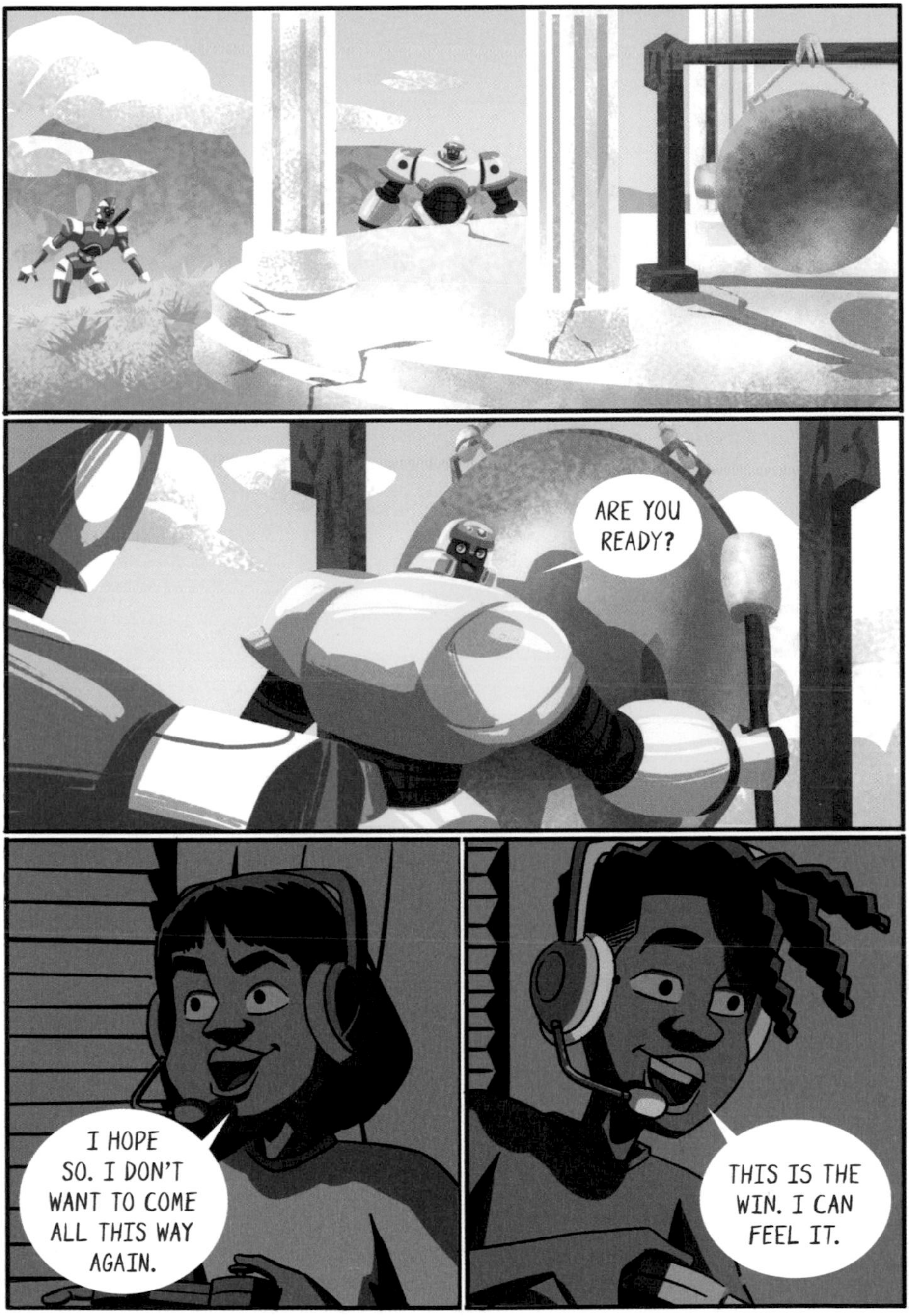
ARE YOU READY?
I HOPE SO. I DON'T WANT TO COME ALL THIS WAY AGAIN.
THIS IS THE WIN. I CAN FEEL IT.

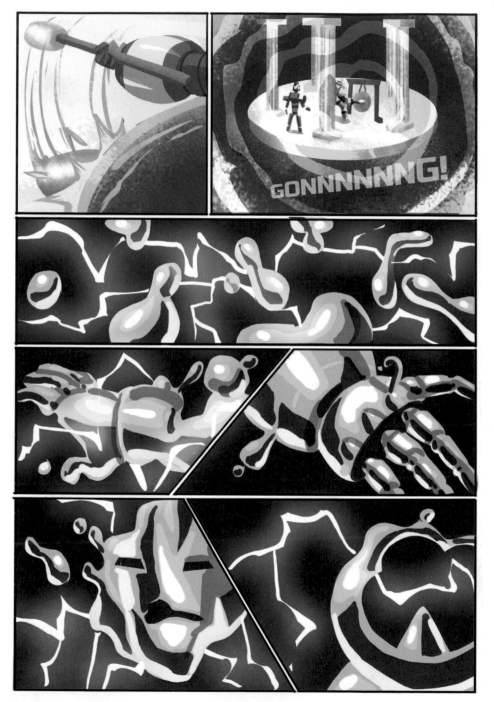

GONNNNNNG!

4

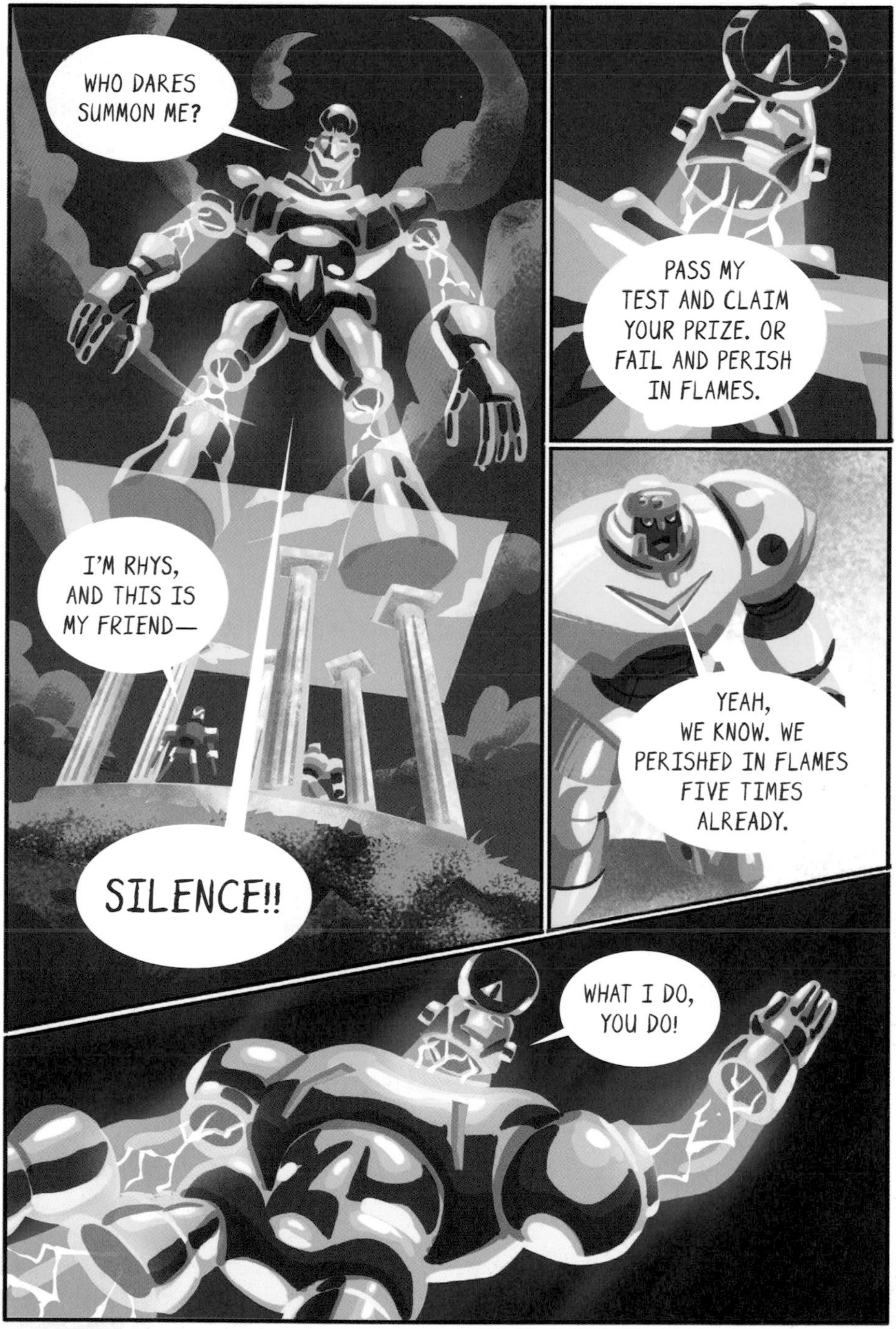
WHO DARES SUMMON ME?
PASS MY TEST AND CLAIM YOUR PRIZE. OR FAIL AND PERISH IN FLAMES.
I'M RHYS, AND THIS IS MY FRIEND—
SILENCE!!
YEAH, WE KNOW. WE PERISHED IN FLAMES FIVE TIMES ALREADY.
WHAT I DO, YOU DO!

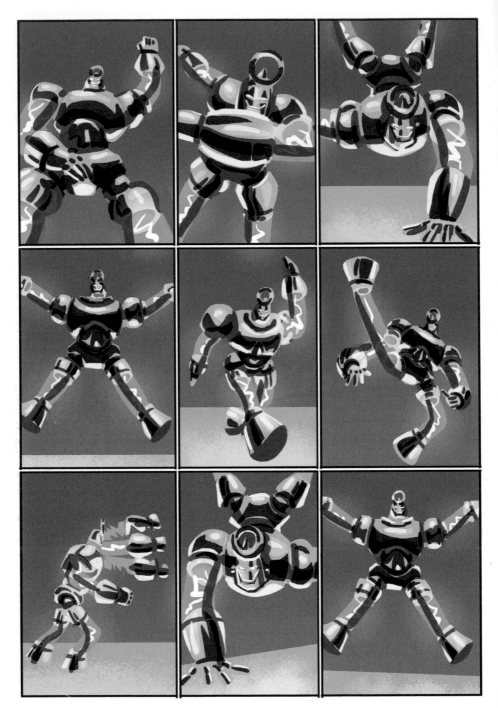

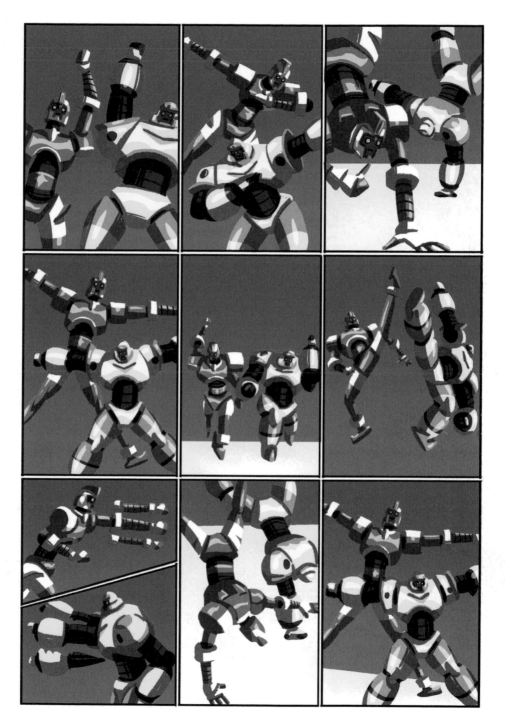

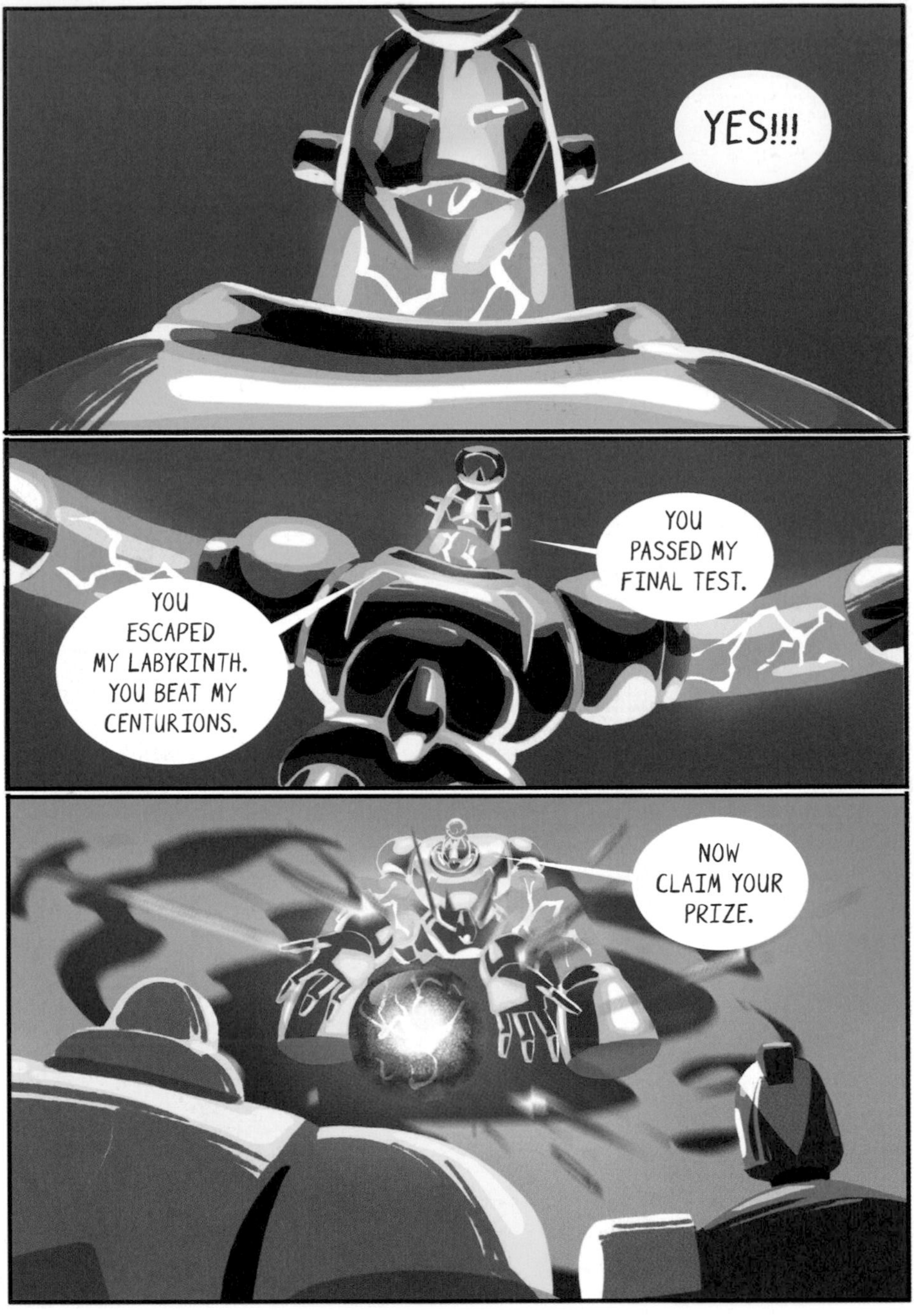
YES!!!
YOU PASSED MY FINAL TEST.
YOU ESCAPED MY LABYRINTH. YOU BEAT MY CENTURIONS.
NOW CLAIM YOUR PRIZE.

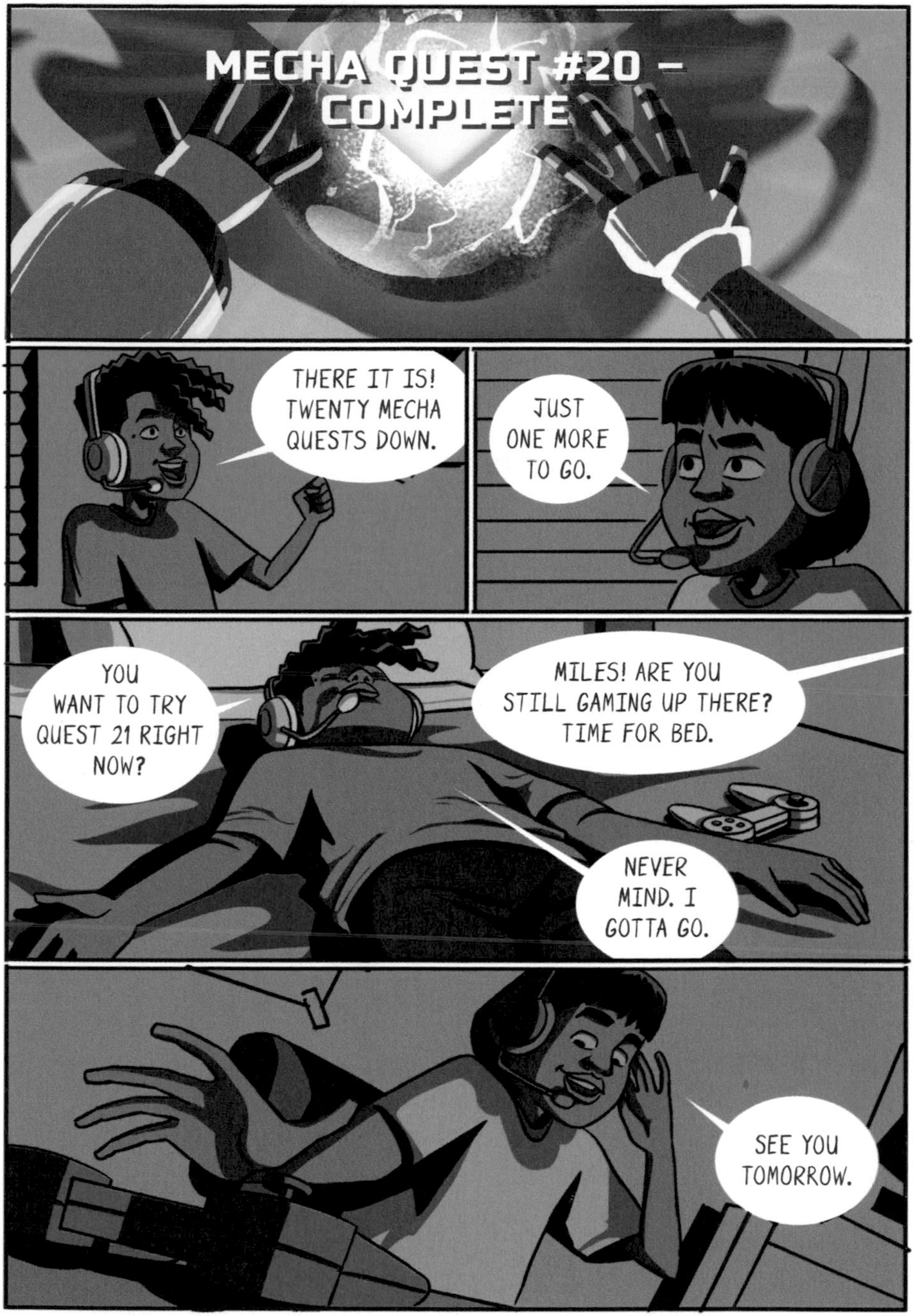
MECHA QUEST #20 – COMPLETE
THERE IT IS! TWENTY MECHA QUESTS DOWN.
JUST ONE MORE TO GO.
YOU WANT TO TRY QUEST 21 RIGHT NOW?
MILES! ARE YOU STILL GAMING UP THERE? TIME FOR BED.
NEVER MIND. I GOTTA GO.
SEE YOU TOMORROW.

CHAPTER 2

GAMER FAMOUS

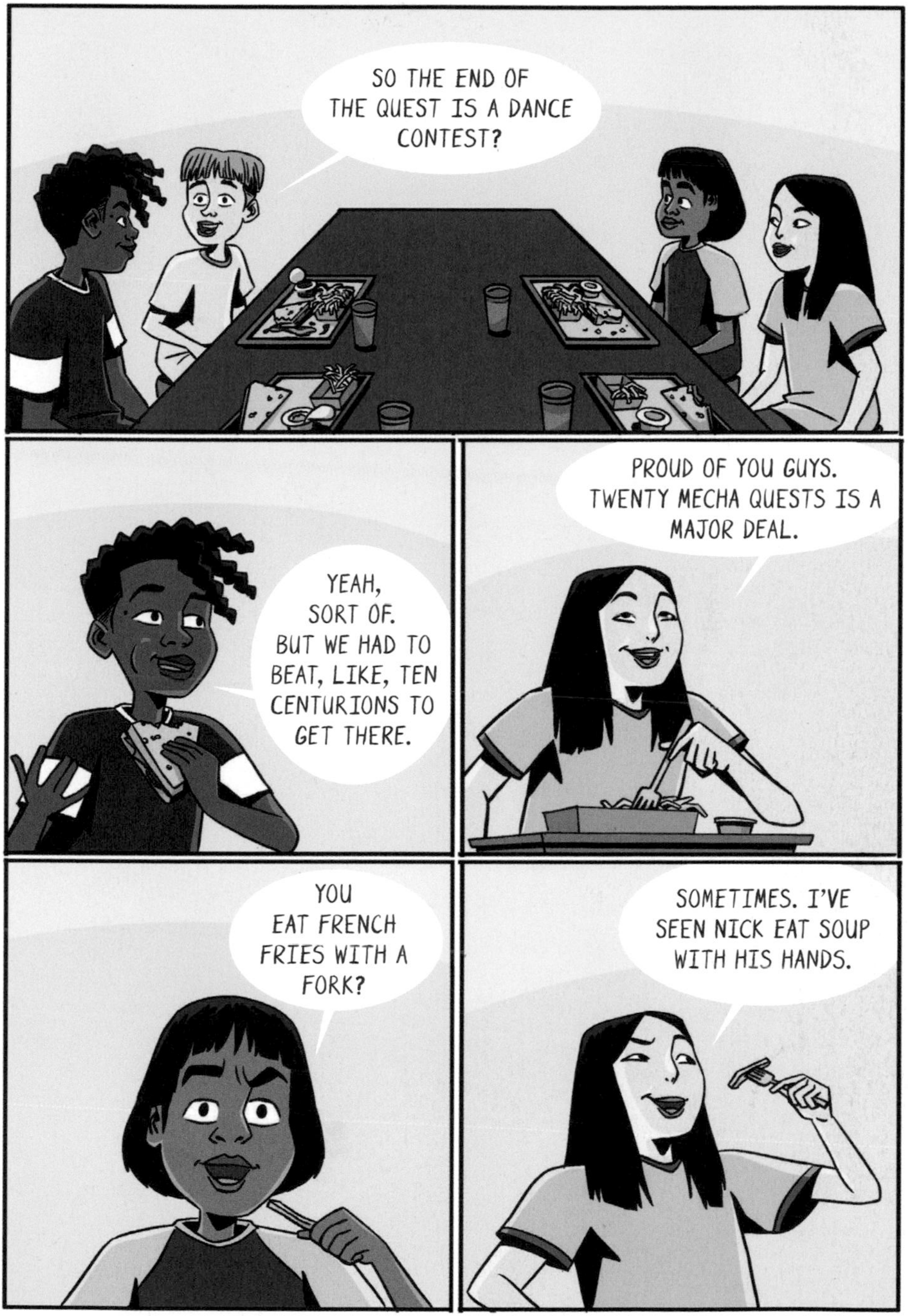
SO THE END OF THE QUEST IS A DANCE CONTEST?
YEAH, SORT OF. BUT WE HAD TO BEAT, LIKE, TEN CENTURIONS TO GET THERE.
PROUD OF YOU GUYS. TWENTY MECHA QUESTS IS A MAJOR DEAL.
YOU EAT FRENCH FRIES WITH A FORK?
SOMETIMES. I'VE SEEN NICK EAT SOUP WITH HIS HANDS.

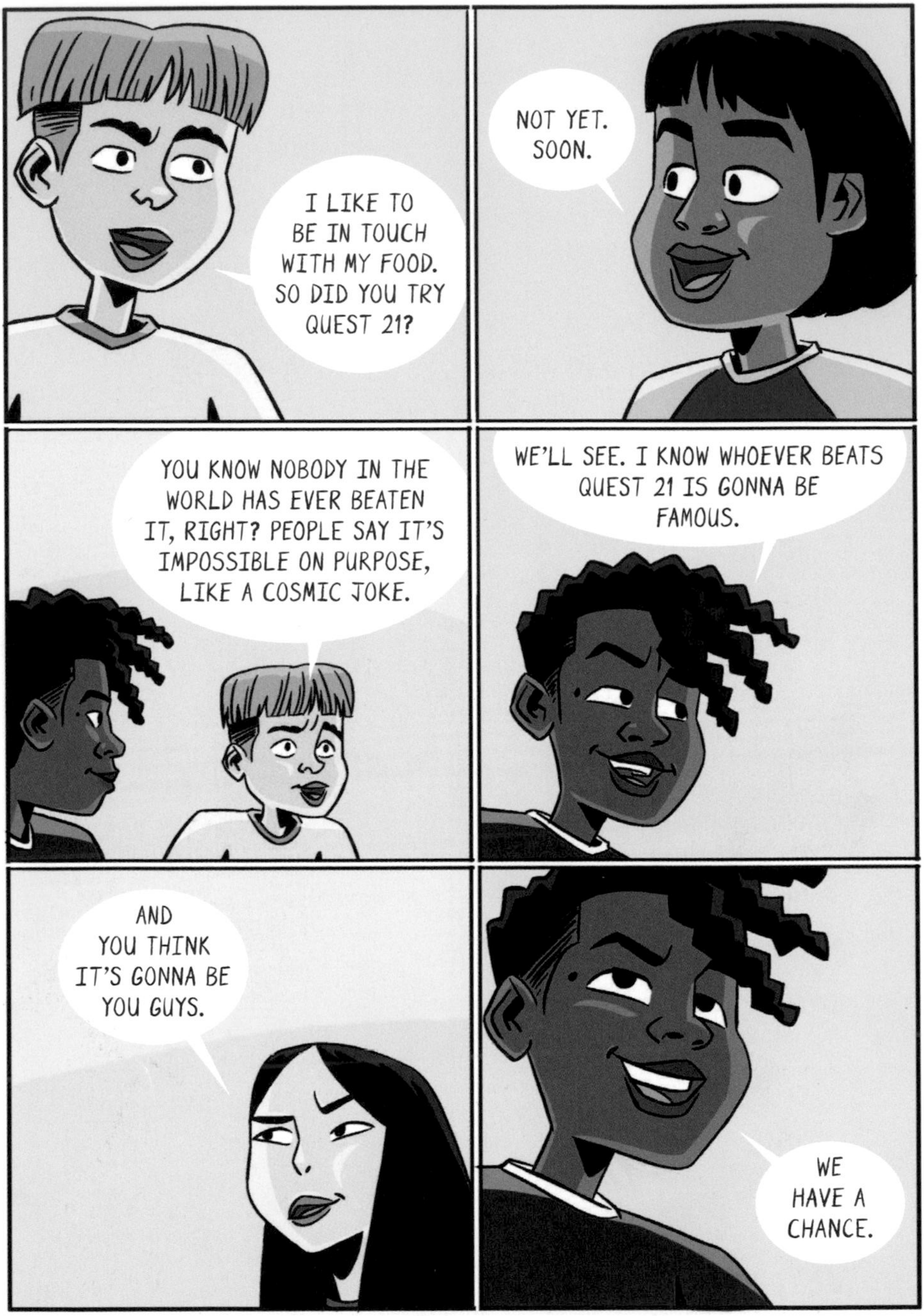
I LIKE TO BE IN TOUCH WITH MY FOOD. SO DID YOU TRY QUEST 21?
NOT YET. SOON.
YOU KNOW NOBODY IN THE WORLD HAS EVER BEATEN IT, RIGHT? PEOPLE SAY IT'S IMPOSSIBLE ON PURPOSE, LIKE A COSMIC JOKE.
WE'LL SEE. I KNOW WHOEVER BEATS QUEST 21 IS GONNA BE FAMOUS.
AND YOU THINK IT'S GONNA BE YOU GUYS.
WE HAVE A CHANCE.

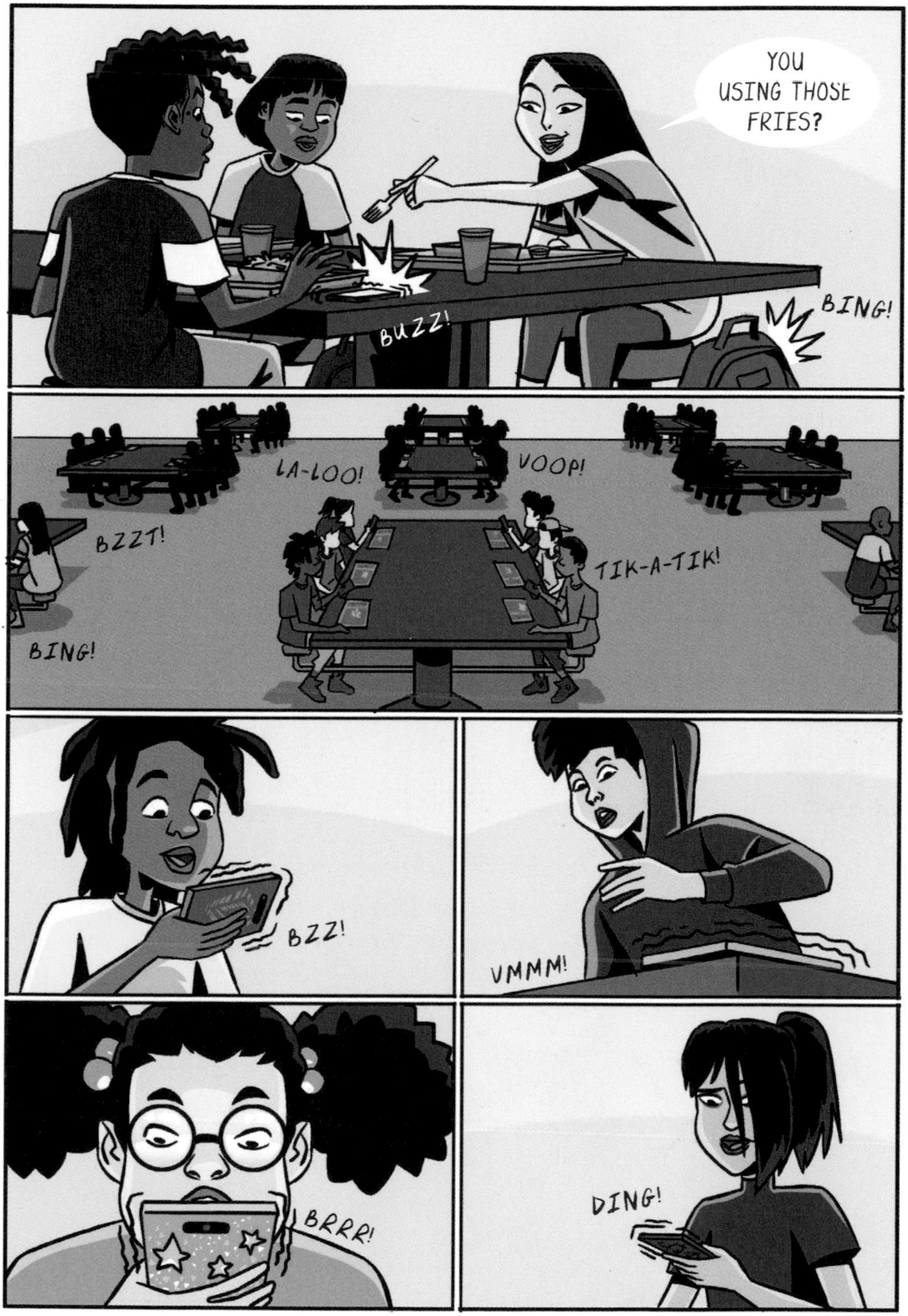
YOU USING THOSE FRIES?
BUZZ!
BING!
LA-LOO!
VOOP!
BZZT!
TIK-A-TIK!
BING!
BZZ!
VMMM!
BRRR!
DING!

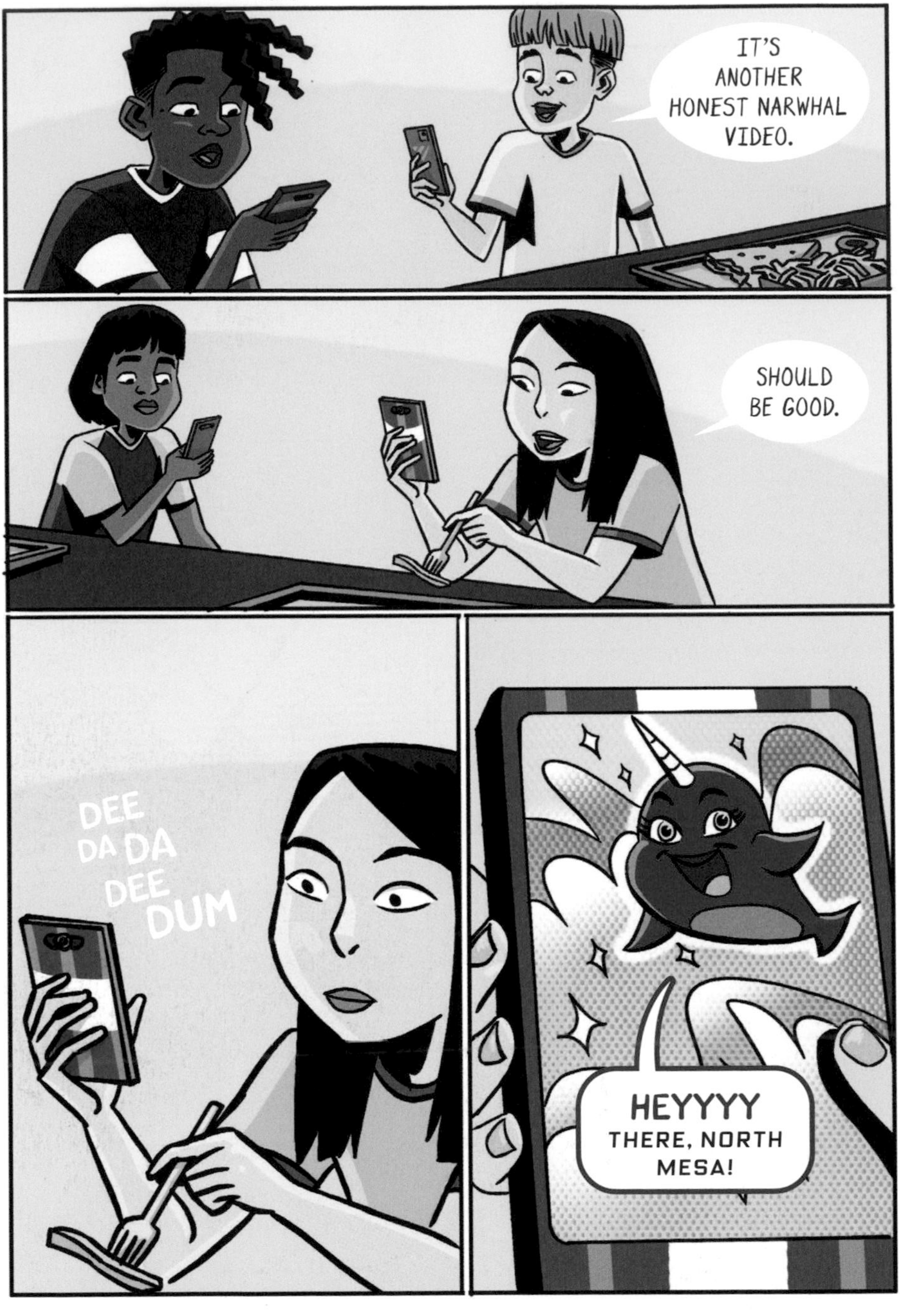
IT'S ANOTHER HONEST NARWHAL VIDEO.
SHOULD BE GOOD.
DEE DA DA DEE DUM
HEYYYY THERE, NORTH MESA!

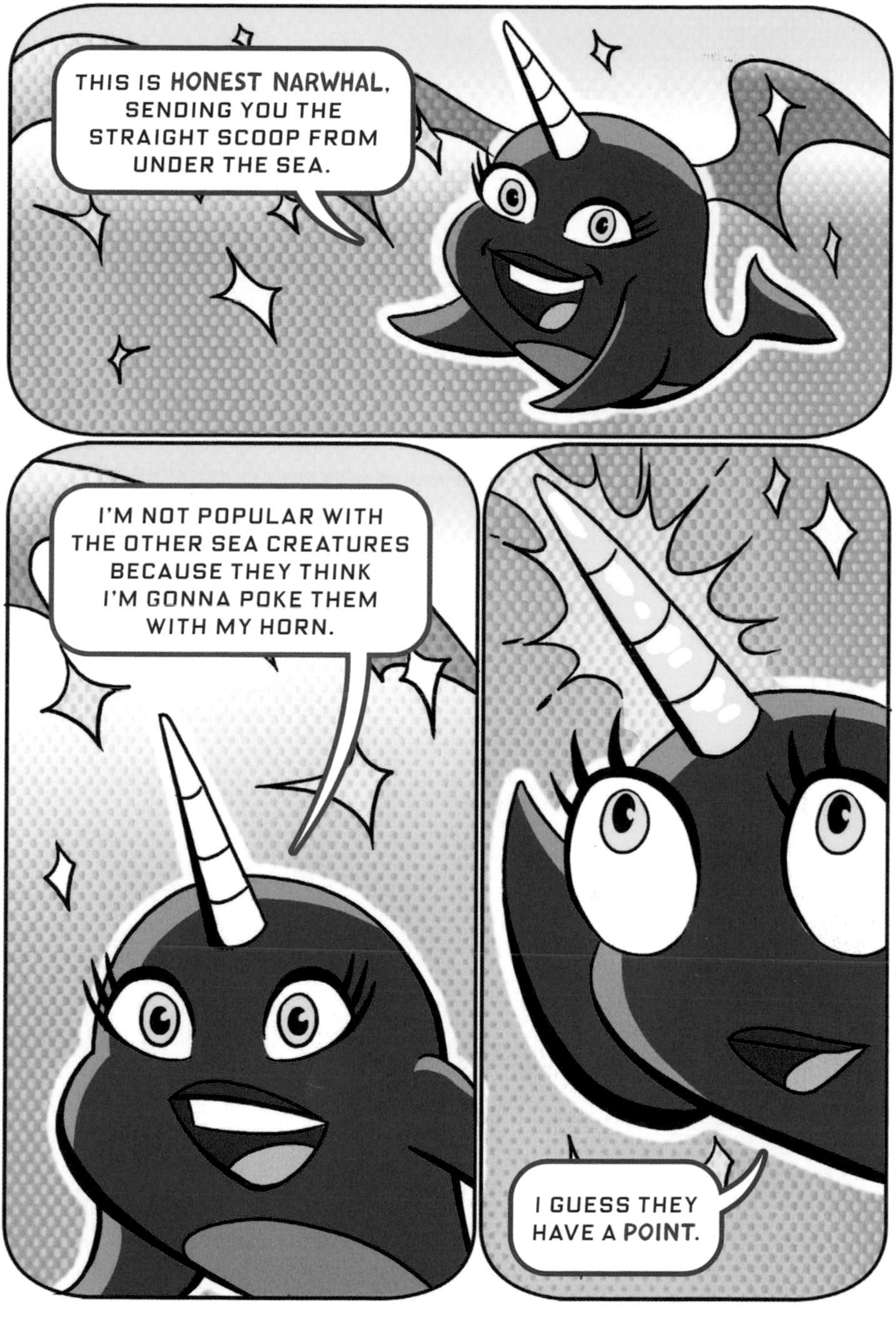
THIS IS HONEST NARWHAL, SENDING YOU THE STRAIGHT SCOOP FROM UNDER THE SEA.
I'M NOT POPULAR WITH THE OTHER SEA CREATURES BECAUSE THEY THINK I'M GONNA POKE THEM WITH MY HORN.
I GUESS THEY HAVE A POINT.

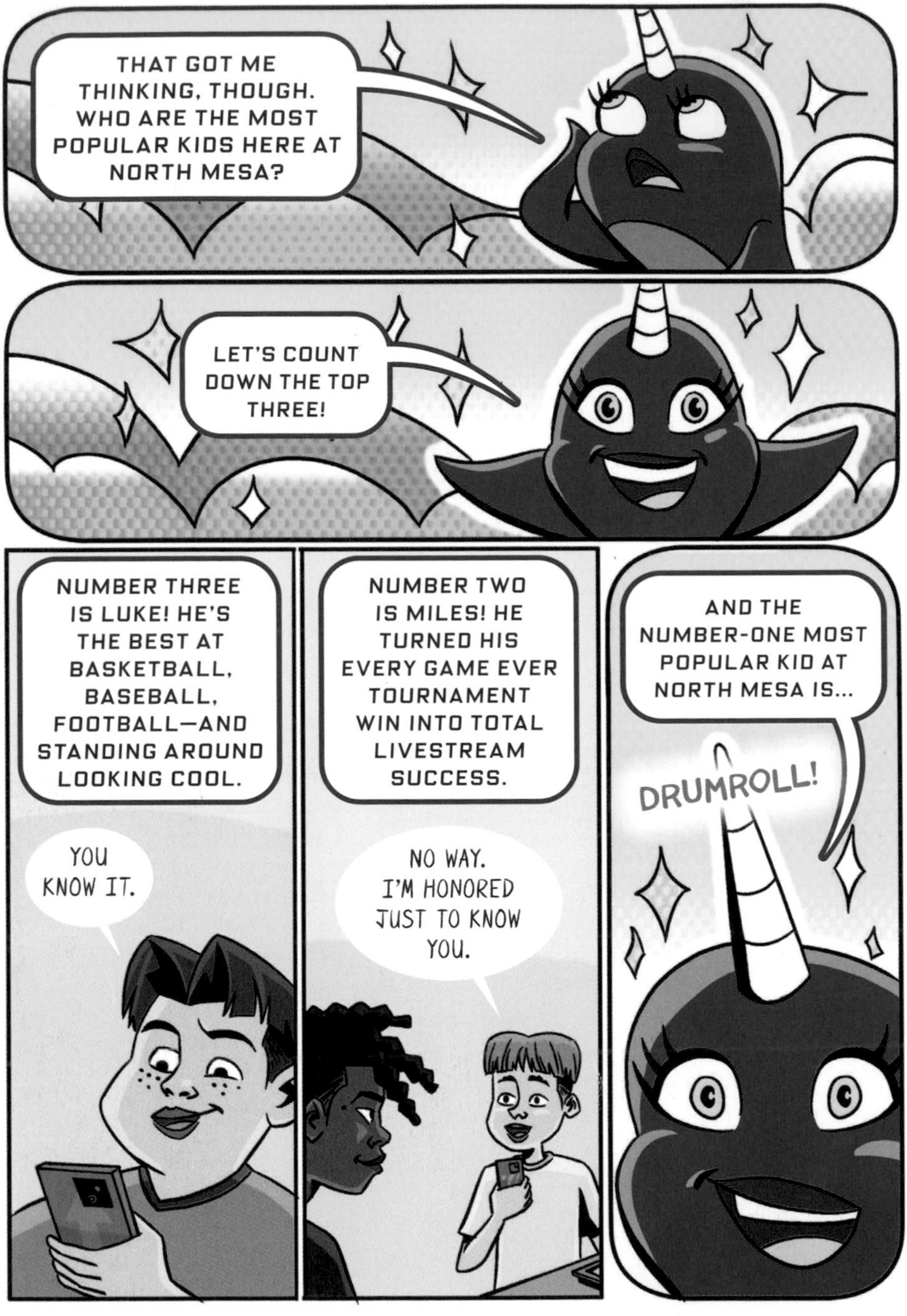
THAT GOT ME THINKING, THOUGH. WHO ARE THE MOST POPULAR KIDS HERE AT NORTH MESA?
LET'S COUNT DOWN THE TOP THREE!
NUMBER THREE IS LUKE! HE'S THE BEST AT BASKETBALL, BASEBALL, FOOTBALL—AND STANDING AROUND LOOKING COOL.
YOU KNOW IT.
NUMBER TWO IS MILES! HE TURNED HIS EVERY GAME EVER TOURNAMENT WIN INTO TOTAL LIVESTREAM SUCCESS.
NO WAY. I'M HONORED JUST TO KNOW YOU.
AND THE NUMBER-ONE MOST POPULAR KID AT NORTH MESA IS...
DRUMROLL!

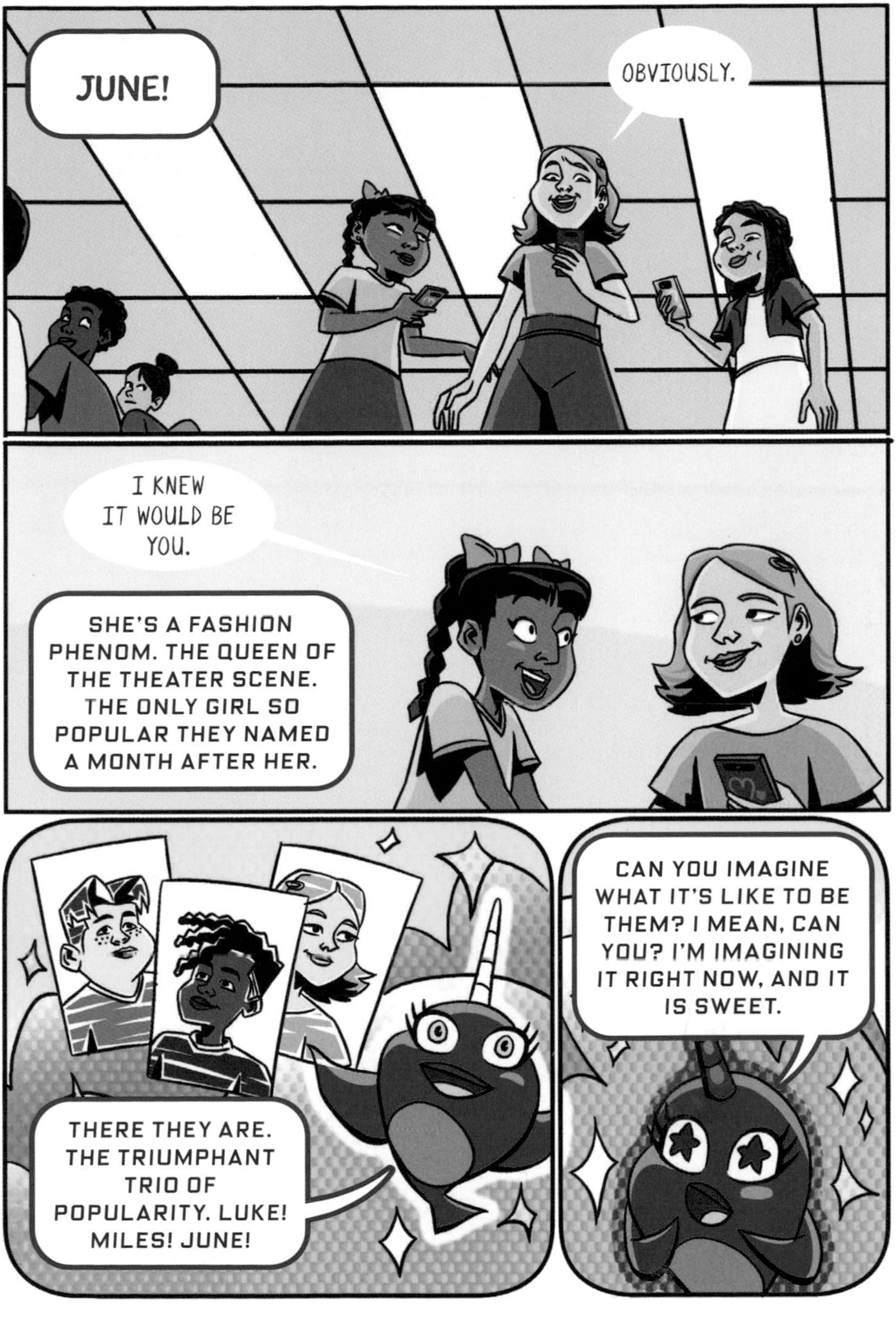
JUNE!
OBVIOUSLY.
I KNEW IT WOULD BE YOU.
SHE'S A FASHION PHENOM. THE QUEEN OF THE THEATER SCENE. THE ONLY GIRL SO POPULAR THEY NAMED A MONTH AFTER HER.
THERE THEY ARE. THE TRIUMPHANT TRIO OF POPULARITY. LUKE! MILES! JUNE!
CAN YOU IMAGINE WHAT IT'S LIKE TO BE THEM? I MEAN, CAN YOU? I'M IMAGINING IT RIGHT NOW, AND IT IS SWEET.

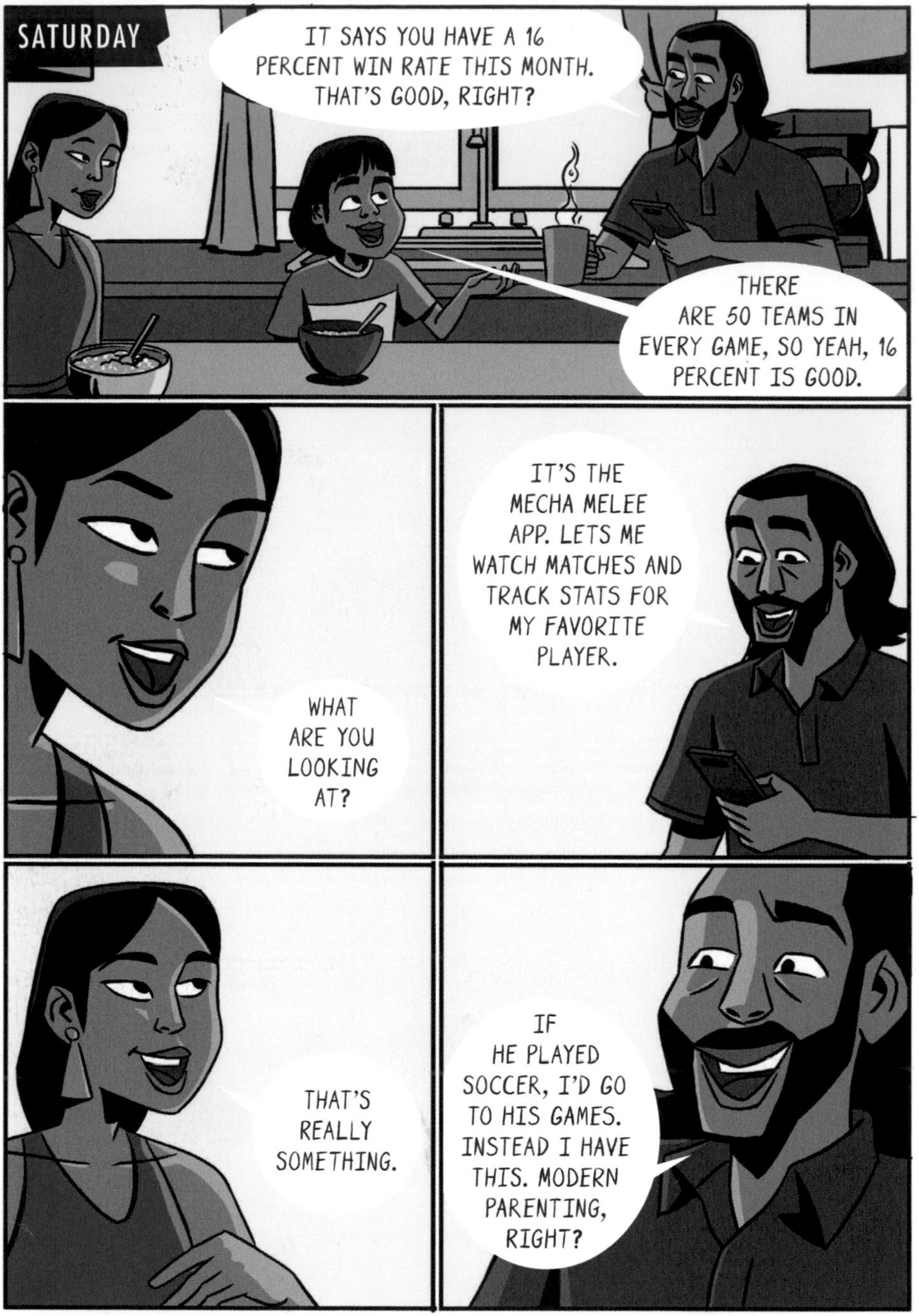
SATURDAY
IT SAYS YOU HAVE A 16 PERCENT WIN RATE THIS MONTH. THAT'S GOOD, RIGHT?
THERE ARE 50 TEAMS IN EVERY GAME, SO YEAH, 16 PERCENT IS GOOD.
WHAT ARE YOU LOOKING AT?
IT'S THE MECHA MELEE APP. LETS ME WATCH MATCHES AND TRACK STATS FOR MY FAVORITE PLAYER.
THAT'S REALLY SOMETHING.
IF HE PLAYED SOCCER, I'D GO TO HIS GAMES. INSTEAD I HAVE THIS. MODERN PARENTING, RIGHT?

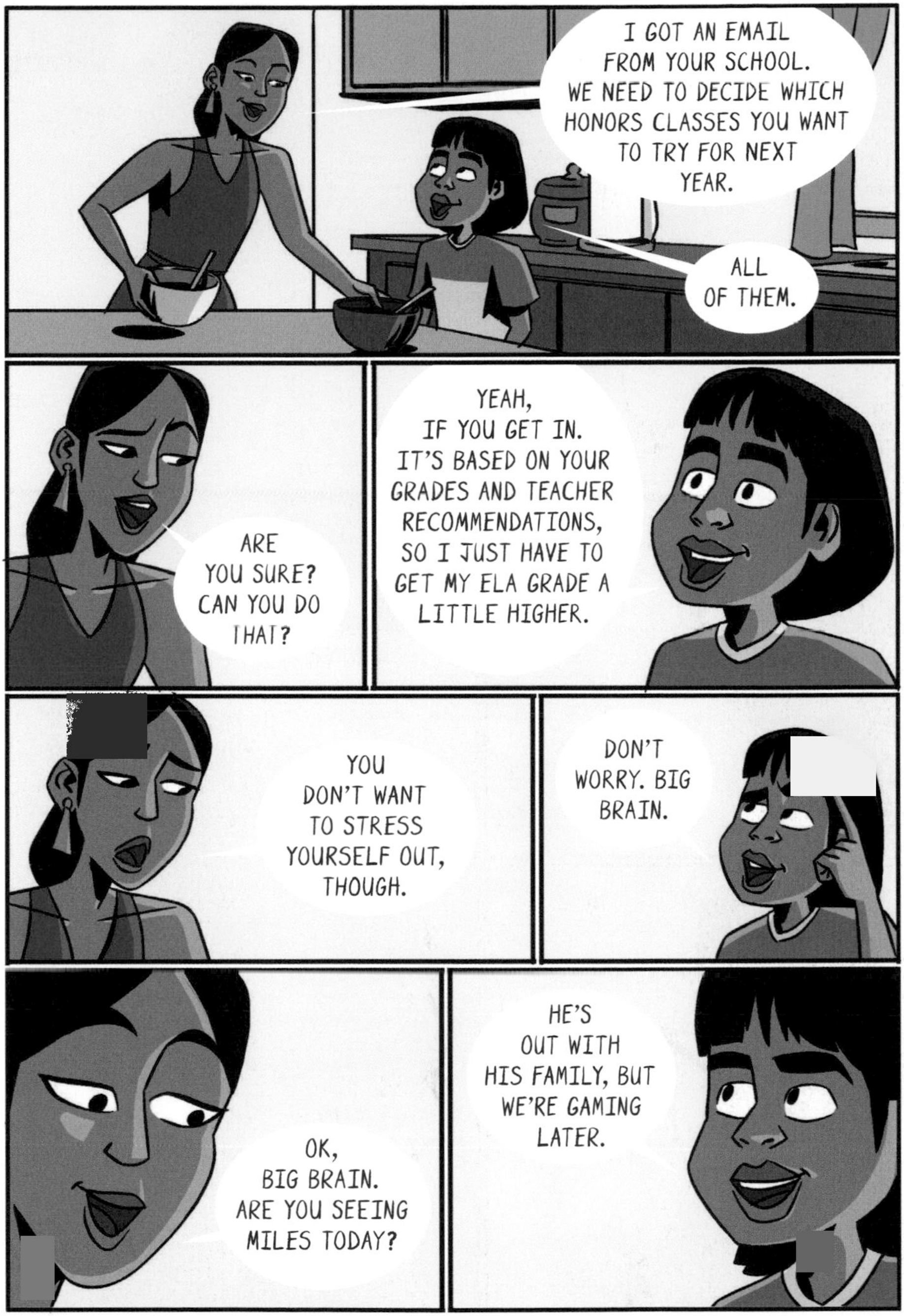
I GOT AN EMAIL FROM YOUR SCHOOL. WE NEED TO DECIDE WHICH HONORS CLASSES YOU WANT TO TRY FOR NEXT YEAR.
ALL OF THEM.
ARE YOU SURE? CAN YOU DO THAT?
YEAH, IF YOU GET IN. IT'S BASED ON YOUR GRADES AND TEACHER RECOMMENDATIONS, SO I JUST HAVE TO GET MY ELA GRADE A LITTLE HIGHER.
YOU DON'T WANT TO STRESS YOURSELF OUT, THOUGH.
DON'T WORRY. BIG BRAIN.
OK, BIG BRAIN. ARE YOU SEEING MILES TODAY?
HE'S OUT WITH HIS FAMILY, BUT WE'RE GAMING LATER.

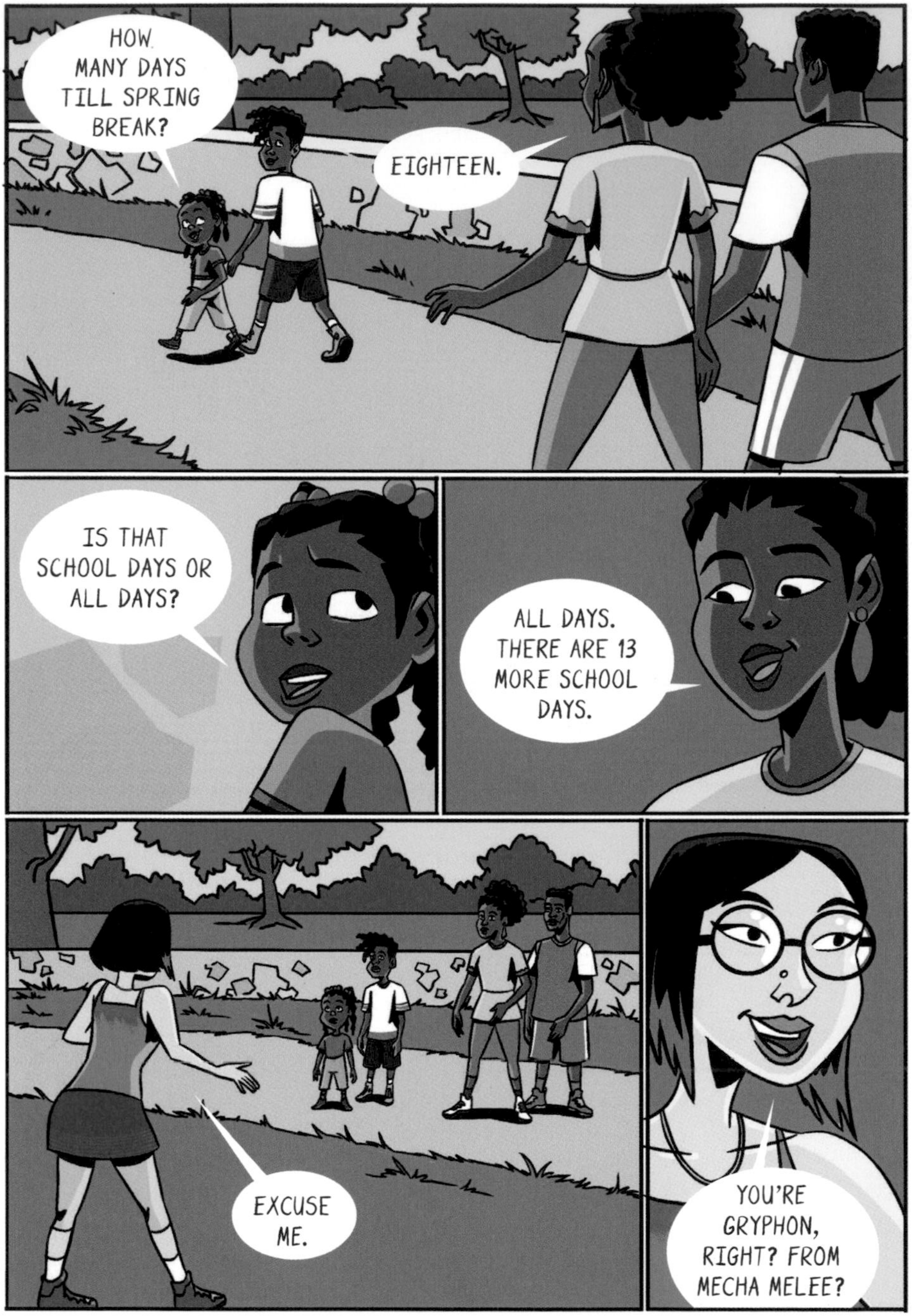
HOW MANY DAYS TILL SPRING BREAK?
EIGHTEEN.
IS THAT SCHOOL DAYS OR ALL DAYS?
ALL DAYS. THERE ARE 13 MORE SCHOOL DAYS.
EXCUSE ME.
YOU'RE GRYPHON, RIGHT? FROM MECHA MELEE?

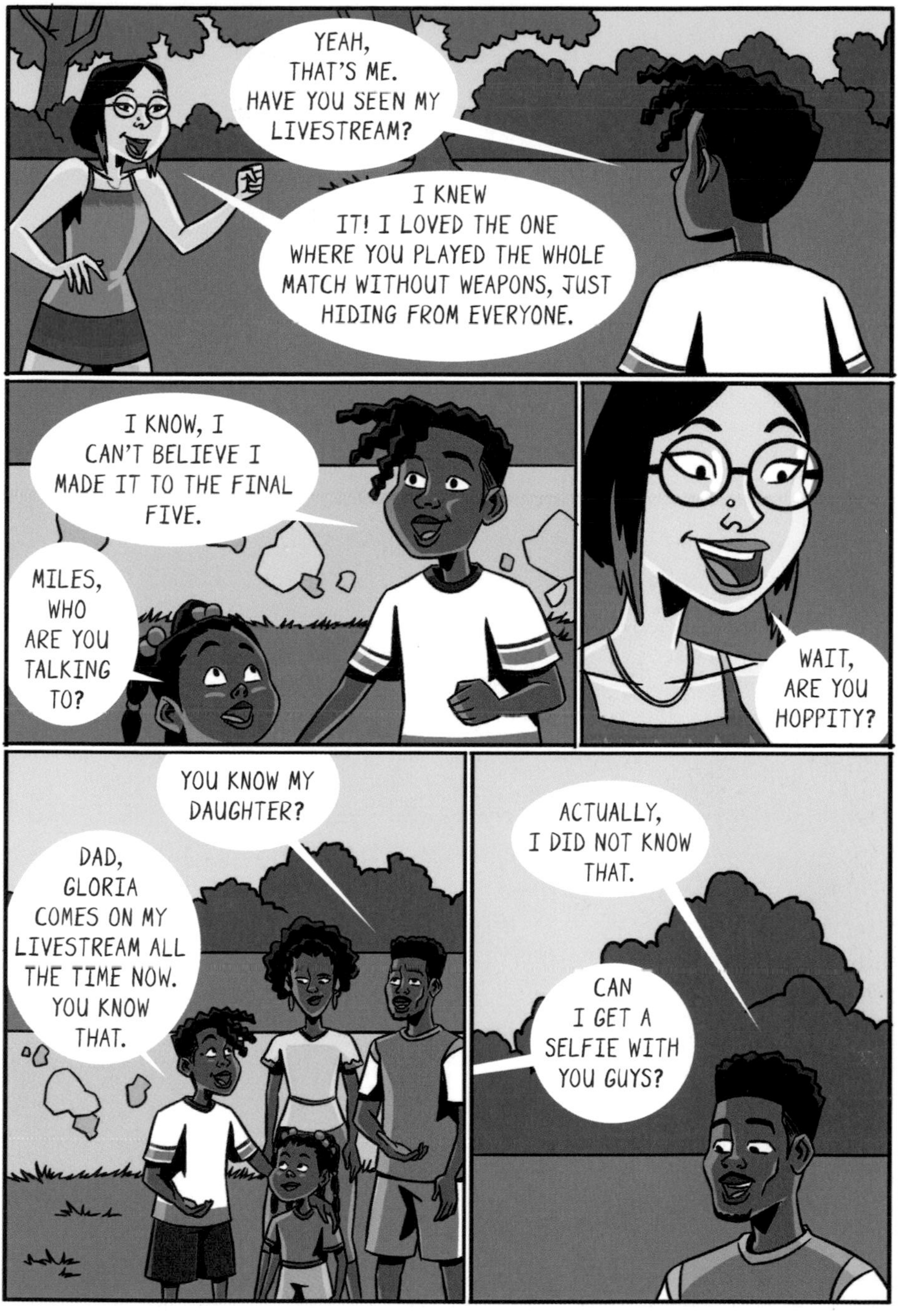
YEAH, THAT'S ME. HAVE YOU SEEN MY LIVESTREAM?
I KNEW IT! I LOVED THE ONE WHERE YOU PLAYED THE WHOLE MATCH WITHOUT WEAPONS, JUST HIDING FROM EVERYONE.
I KNOW, I CAN'T BELIEVE I MADE IT TO THE FINAL FIVE.
MILES, WHO ARE YOU TALKING TO?
WAIT, ARE YOU HOPPITY?
YOU KNOW MY DAUGHTER?
DAD, GLORIA COMES ON MY LIVESTREAM ALL THE TIME NOW. YOU KNOW THAT.
ACTUALLY, I DID NOT KNOW THAT.
CAN I GET A SELFIE WITH YOU GUYS?

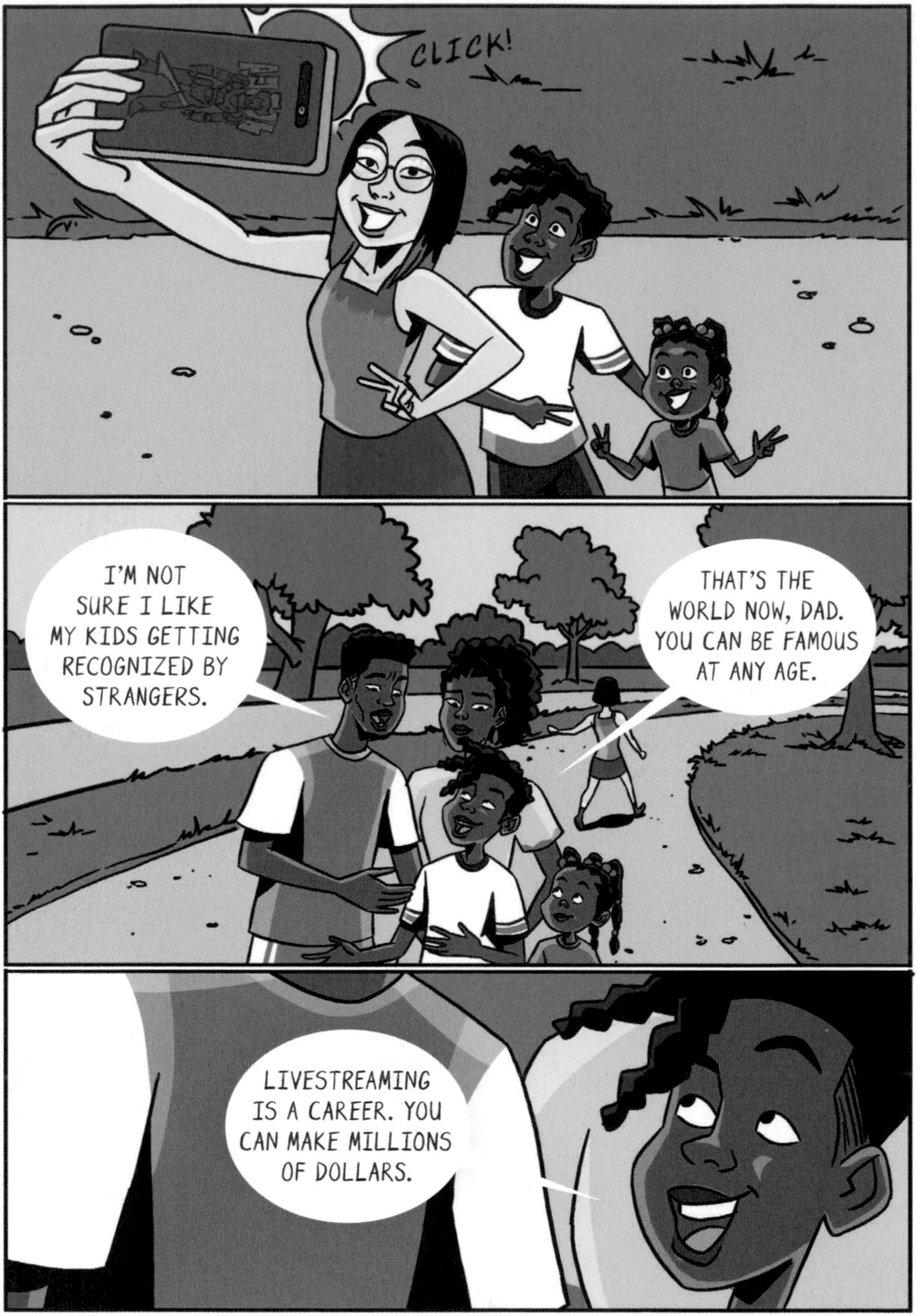
CLICK!
I'M NOT SURE I LIKE MY KIDS GETTING RECOGNIZED BY STRANGERS.
THAT'S THE WORLD NOW, DAD. YOU CAN BE FAMOUS AT ANY AGE.
LIVESTREAMING IS A CAREER. YOU CAN MAKE MILLIONS OF DOLLARS.

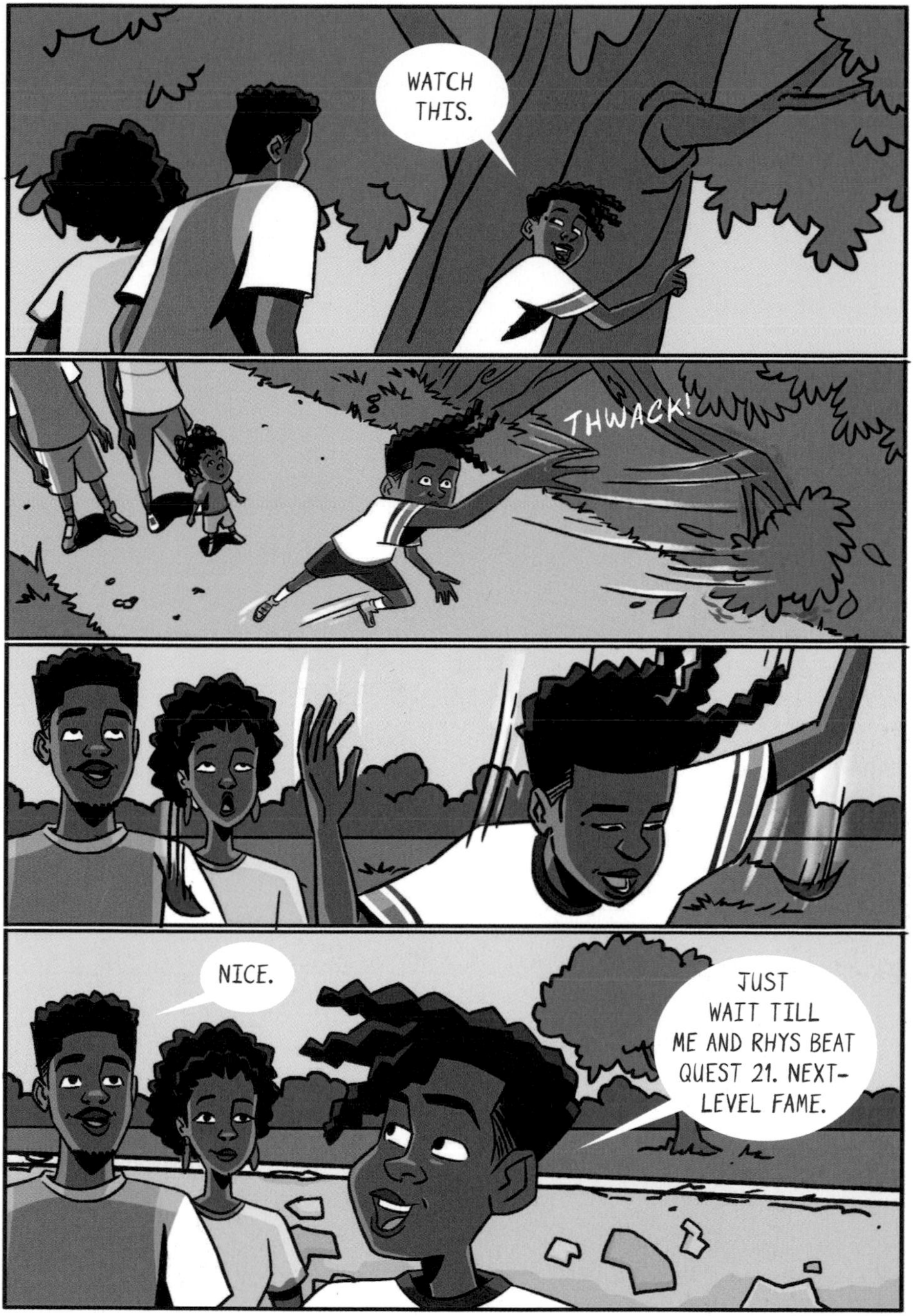
WATCH THIS.
THWACK!
NICE.
JUST WAIT TILL ME AND RHYS BEAT QUEST 21. NEXT-LEVEL FAME.

CHAPTER 3

IMPOSSIBILITIES

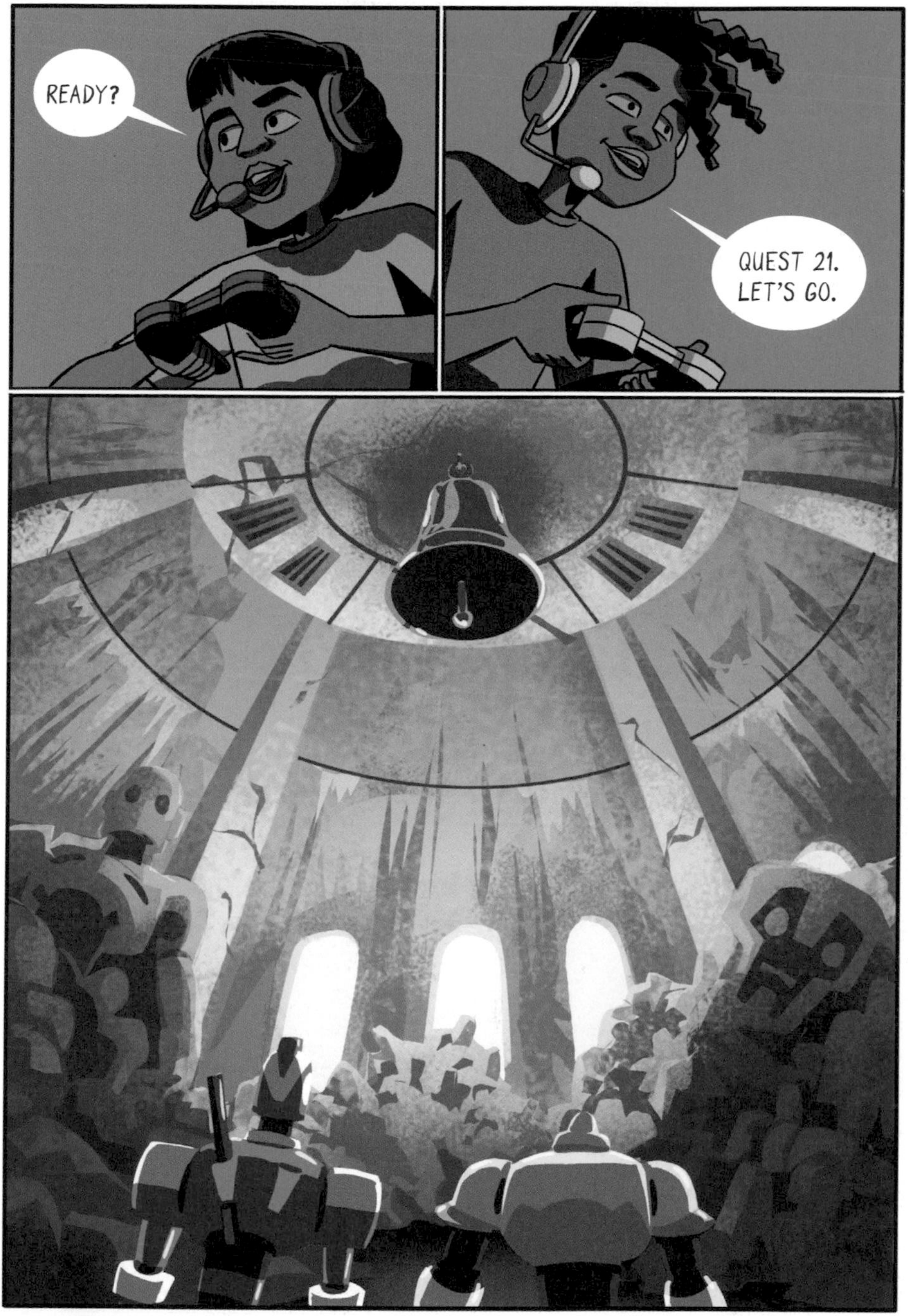
READY?
QUEST 21. LET'S GO.

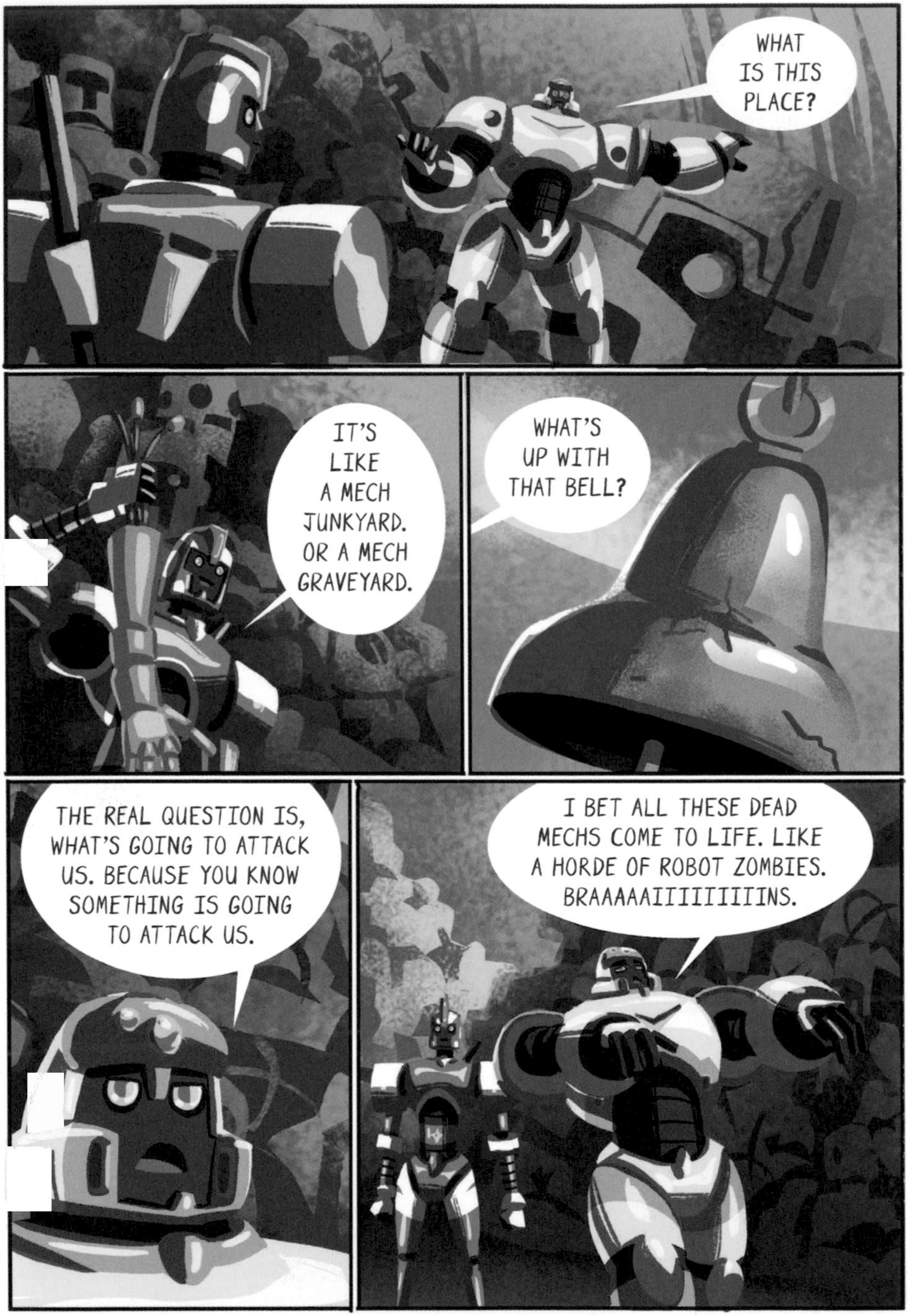
WHAT IS THIS PLACE?
IT'S LIKE A MECH JUNKYARD. OR A MECH GRAVEYARD.
WHAT'S UP WITH THAT BELL?
THE REAL QUESTION IS, WHAT'S GOING TO ATTACK US. BECAUSE YOU KNOW SOMETHING IS GOING TO ATTACK US.
I BET ALL THESE DEAD MECHS COME TO LIFE. LIKE A HORDE OF ROBOT ZOMBIES. BRAAAAAIIIIIIIIINS.

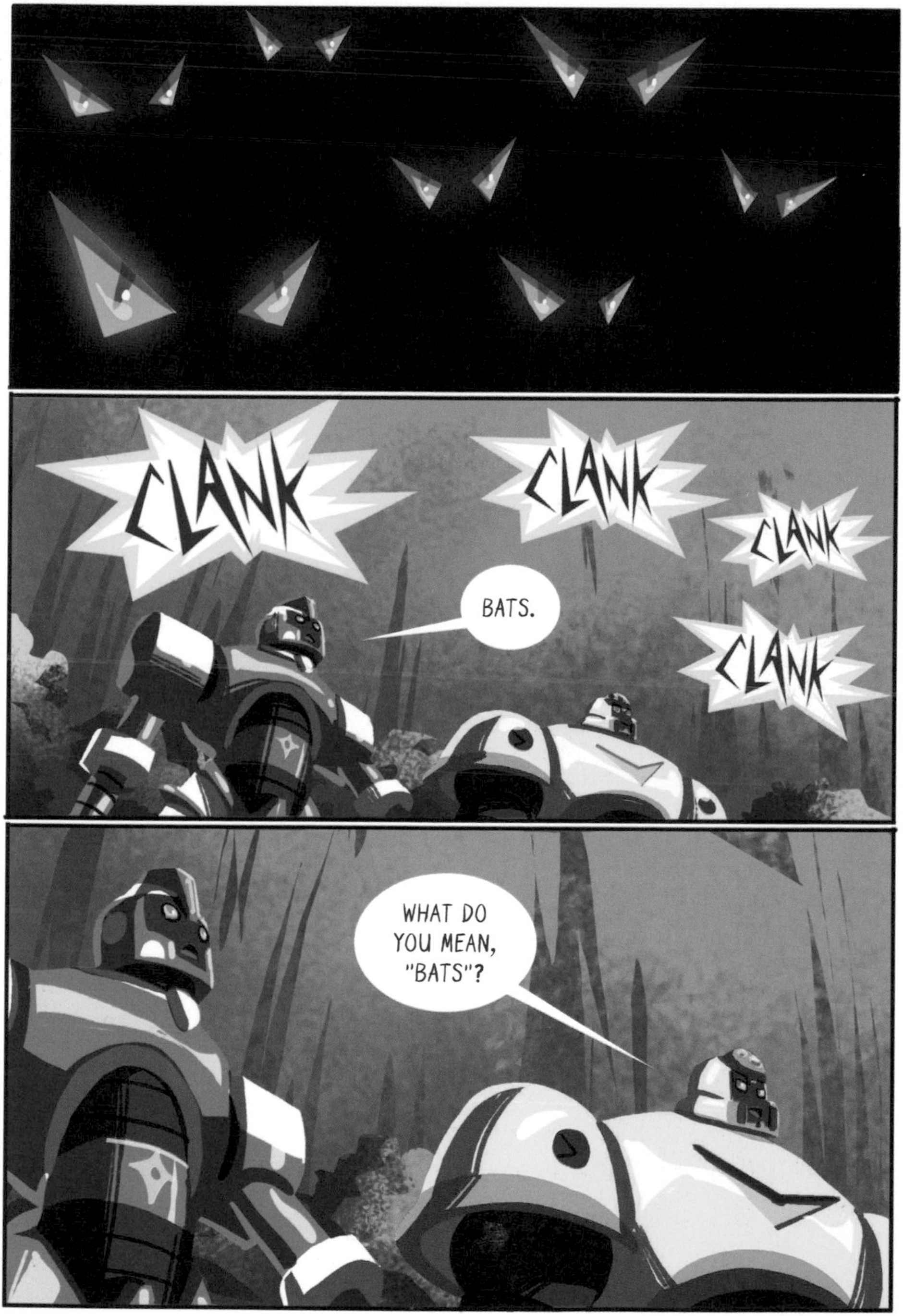
CLANK
CLANK
CLANK
CLANK
BATS.
WHAT DO YOU MEAN, "BATS"?

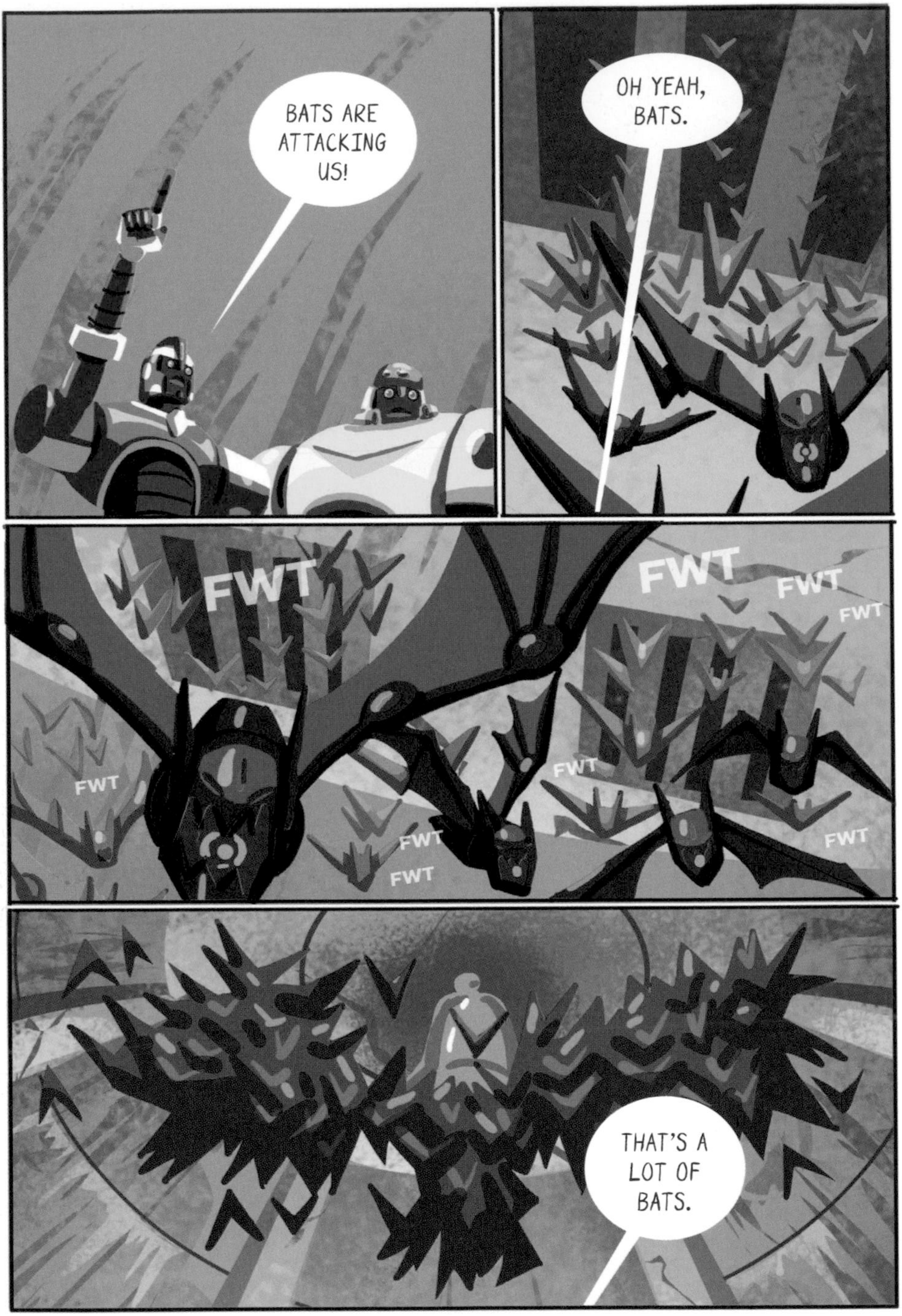
BATS ARE ATTACKING US!
OH YEAH, BATS.
FWT
FWT
FWT
FWT
FWT
FWT
FWT
FWT
FWT
THAT'S A LOT OF BATS.

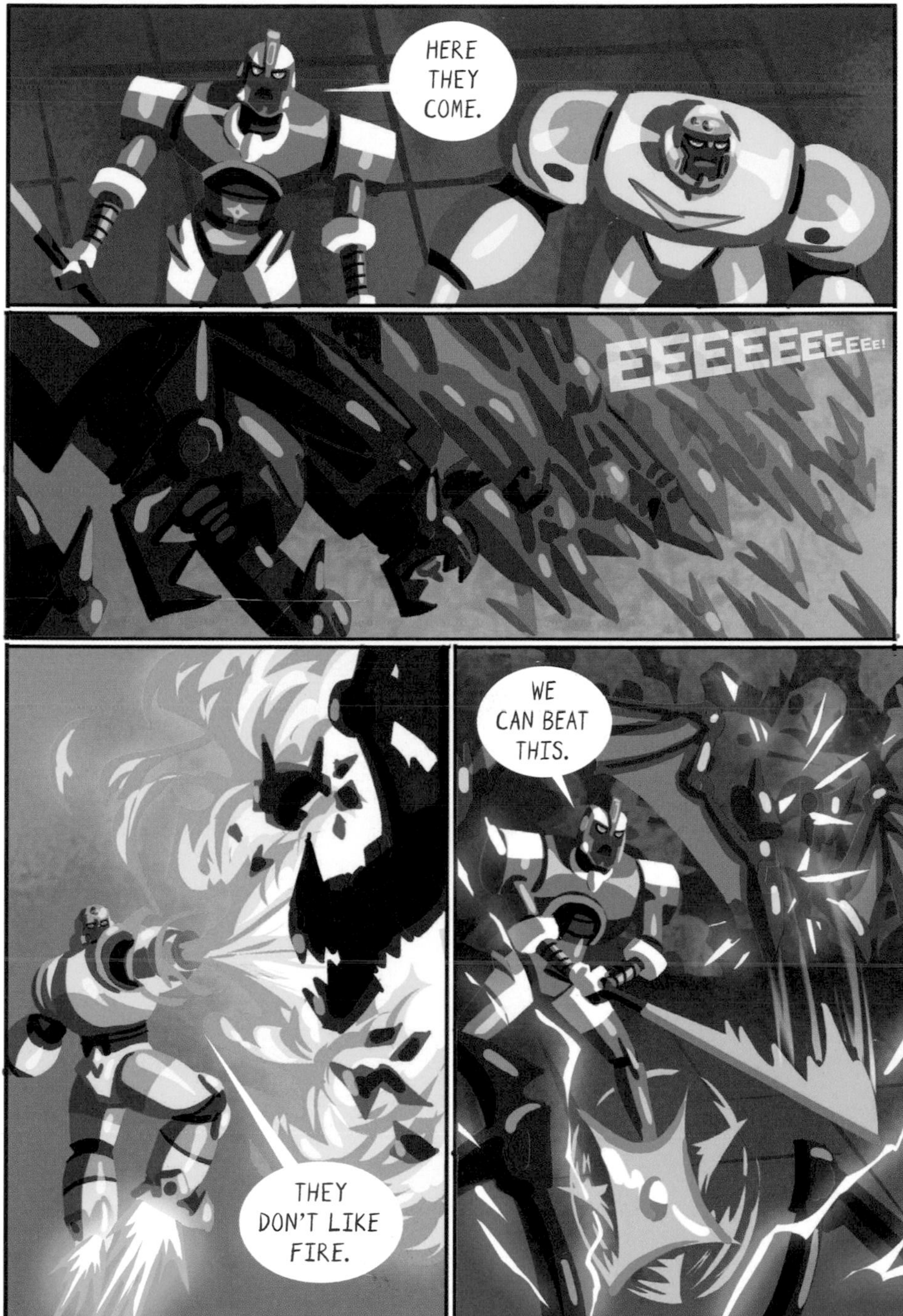
HERE THEY COME.
EEEEEEEEEE!
THEY DON'T LIKE FIRE.
WE CAN BEAT THIS.

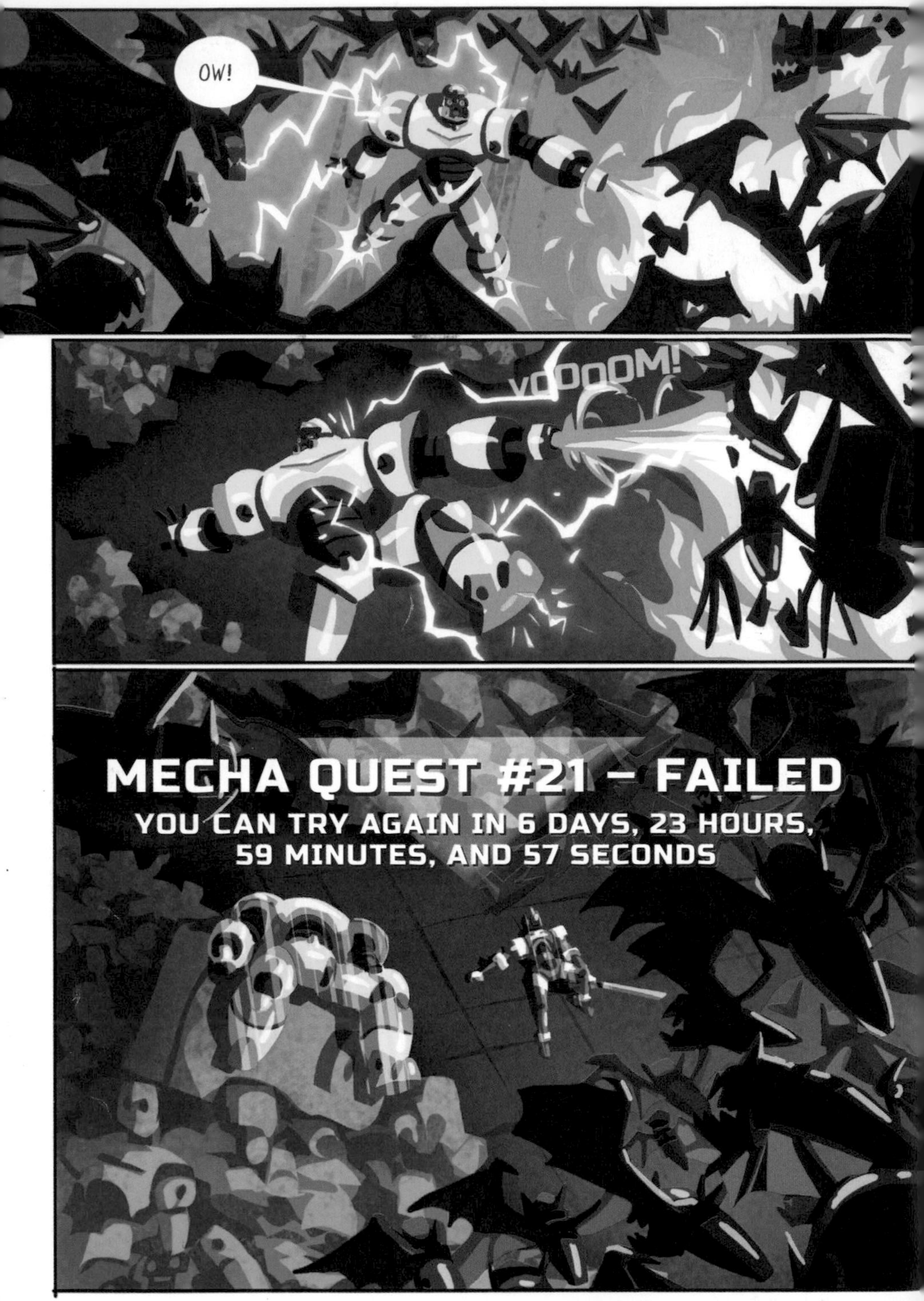
OW!
VOOOOM!
MECHA QUEST #21 – FAILED
YOU CAN TRY AGAIN IN 6 DAYS, 23 HOURS, 59 MINUTES, AND 57 SECONDS

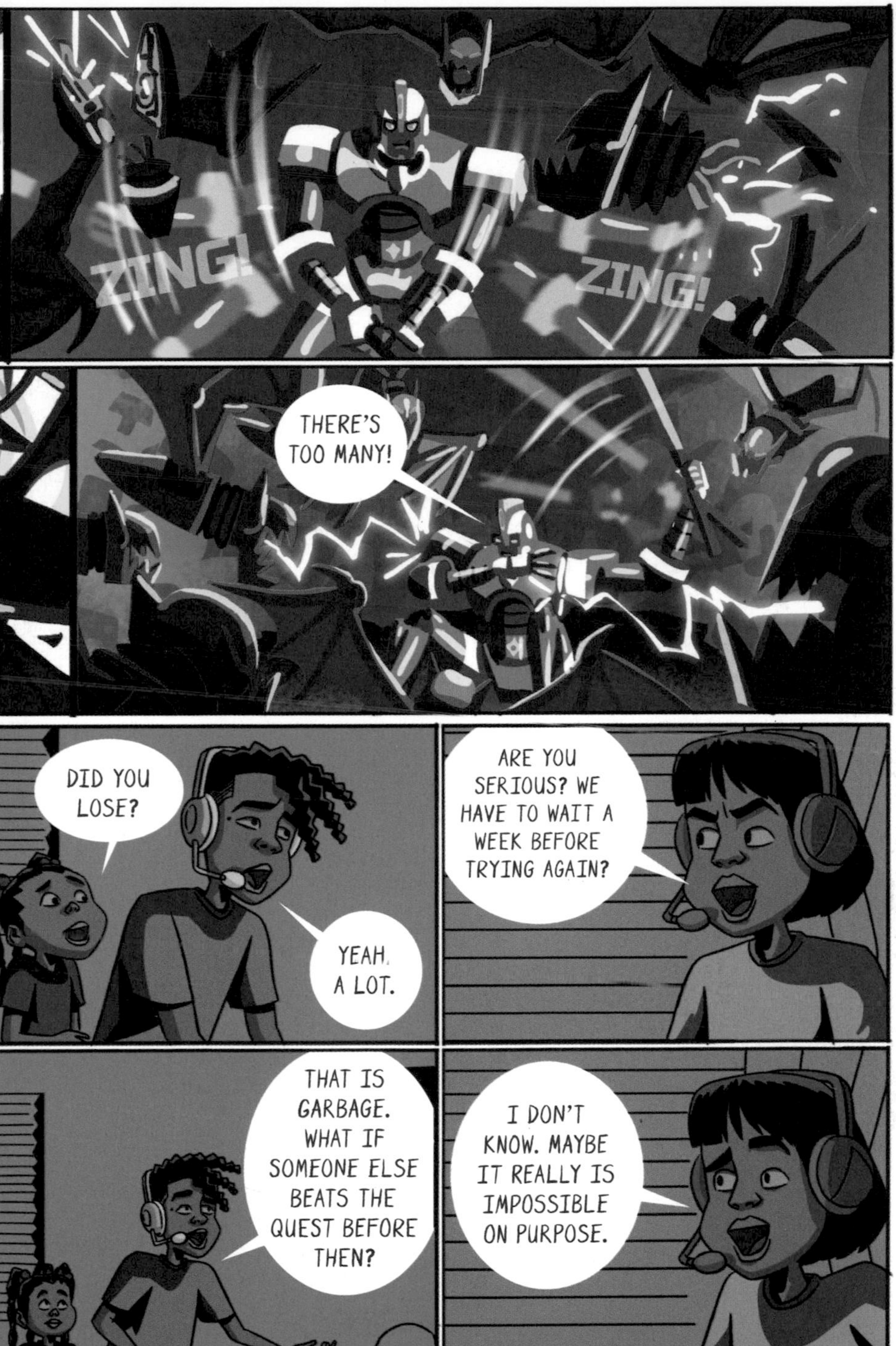
ZING!
ZING!
THERE'S TOO MANY!
DID YOU LOSE?
YEAH. A LOT.
ARE YOU SERIOUS? WE HAVE TO WAIT A WEEK BEFORE TRYING AGAIN?
THAT IS GARBAGE. WHAT IF SOMEONE ELSE BEATS THE QUEST BEFORE THEN?
I DON'T KNOW. MAYBE IT REALLY IS IMPOSSIBLE ON PURPOSE.

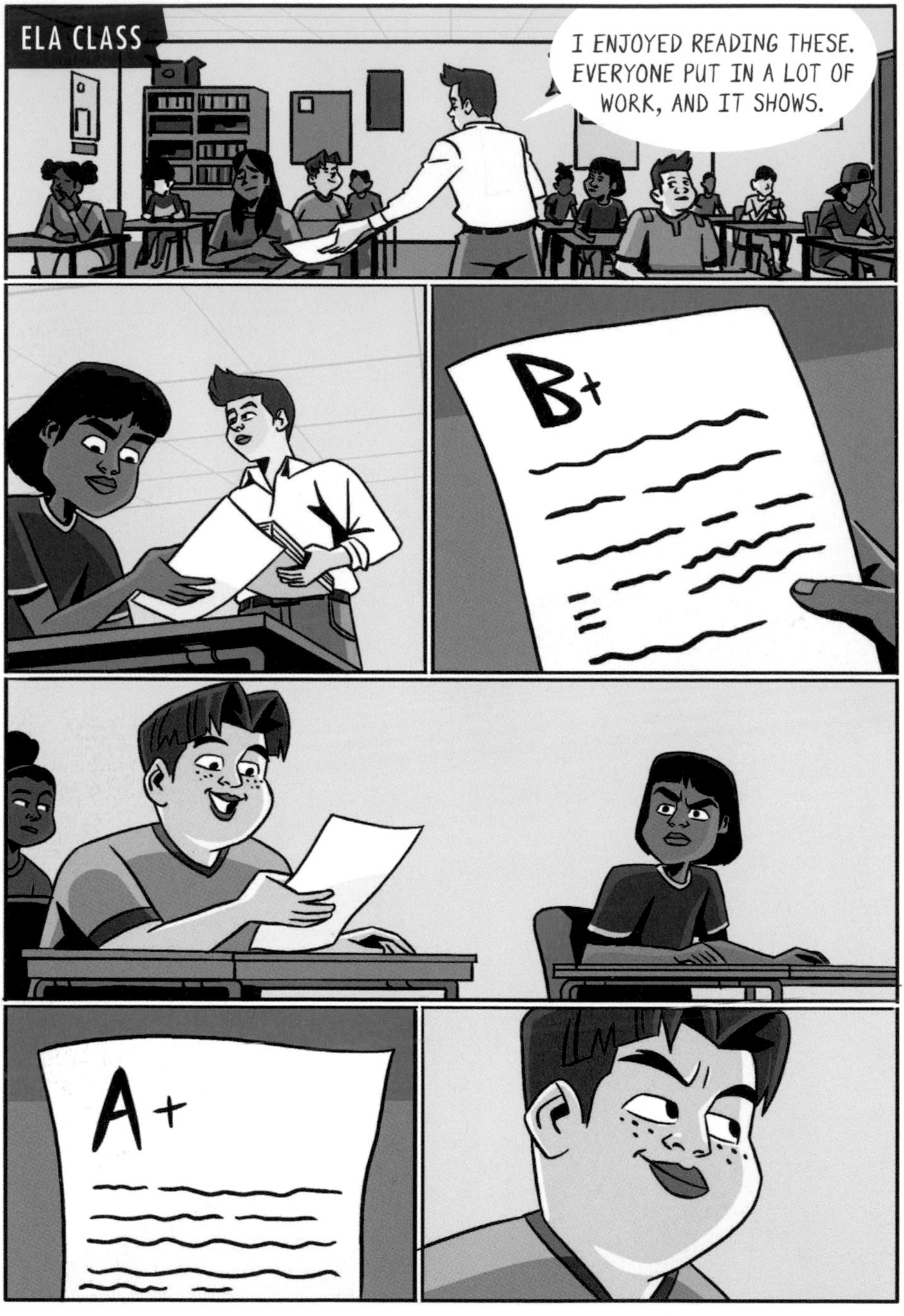
ELA CLASS
I ENJOYED READING THESE. EVERYONE PUT IN A LOT OF WORK, AND IT SHOWS.
B+
A+

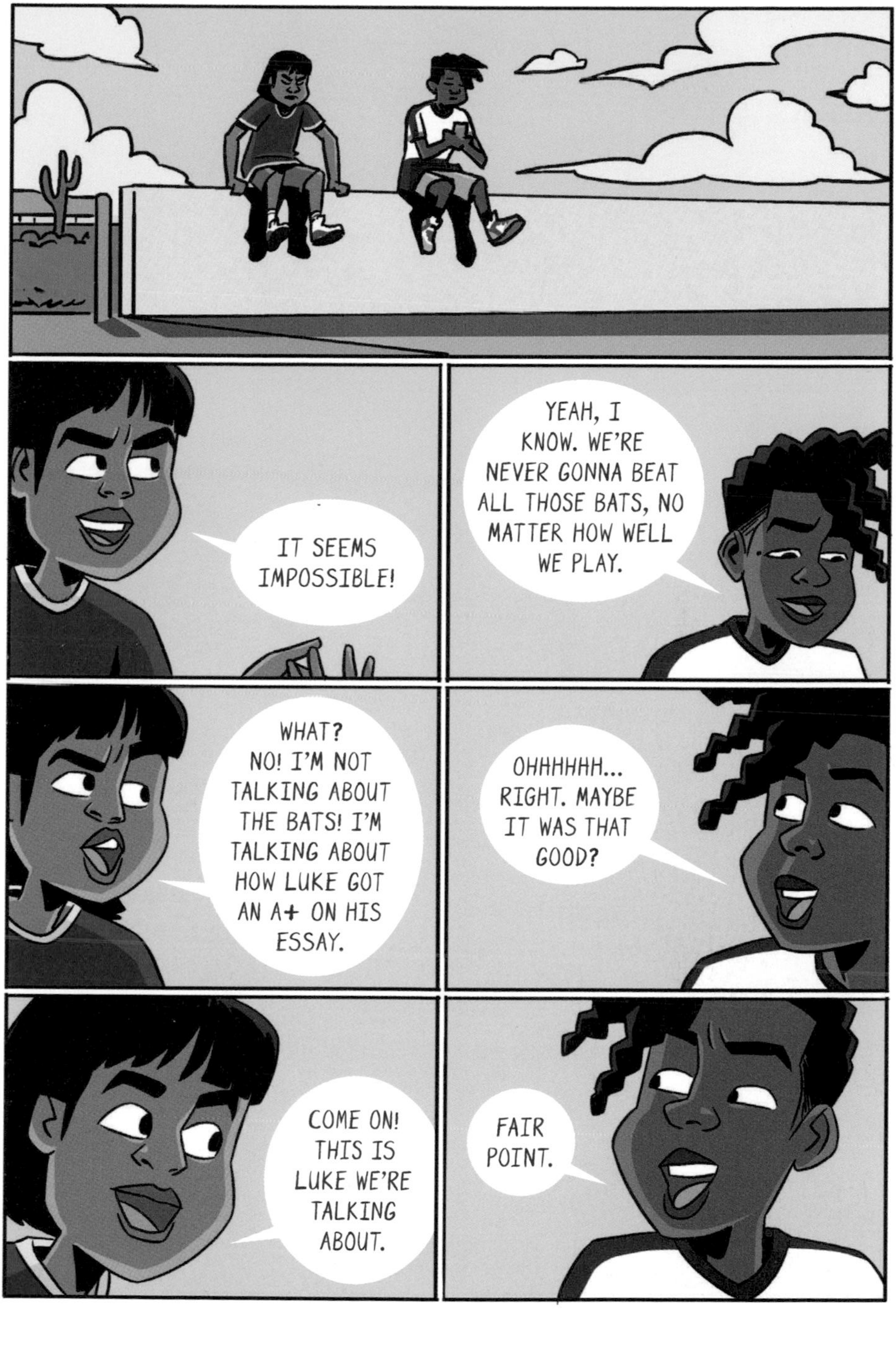
IT SEEMS IMPOSSIBLE!
YEAH, I KNOW. WE'RE NEVER GONNA BEAT ALL THOSE BATS, NO MATTER HOW WELL WE PLAY.
WHAT? NO! I'M NOT TALKING ABOUT THE BATS! I'M TALKING ABOUT HOW LUKE GOT AN A+ ON HIS ESSAY.
OHHHHHH... RIGHT. MAYBE IT WAS THAT GOOD?
COME ON! THIS IS LUKE WE'RE TALKING ABOUT.
FAIR POINT.

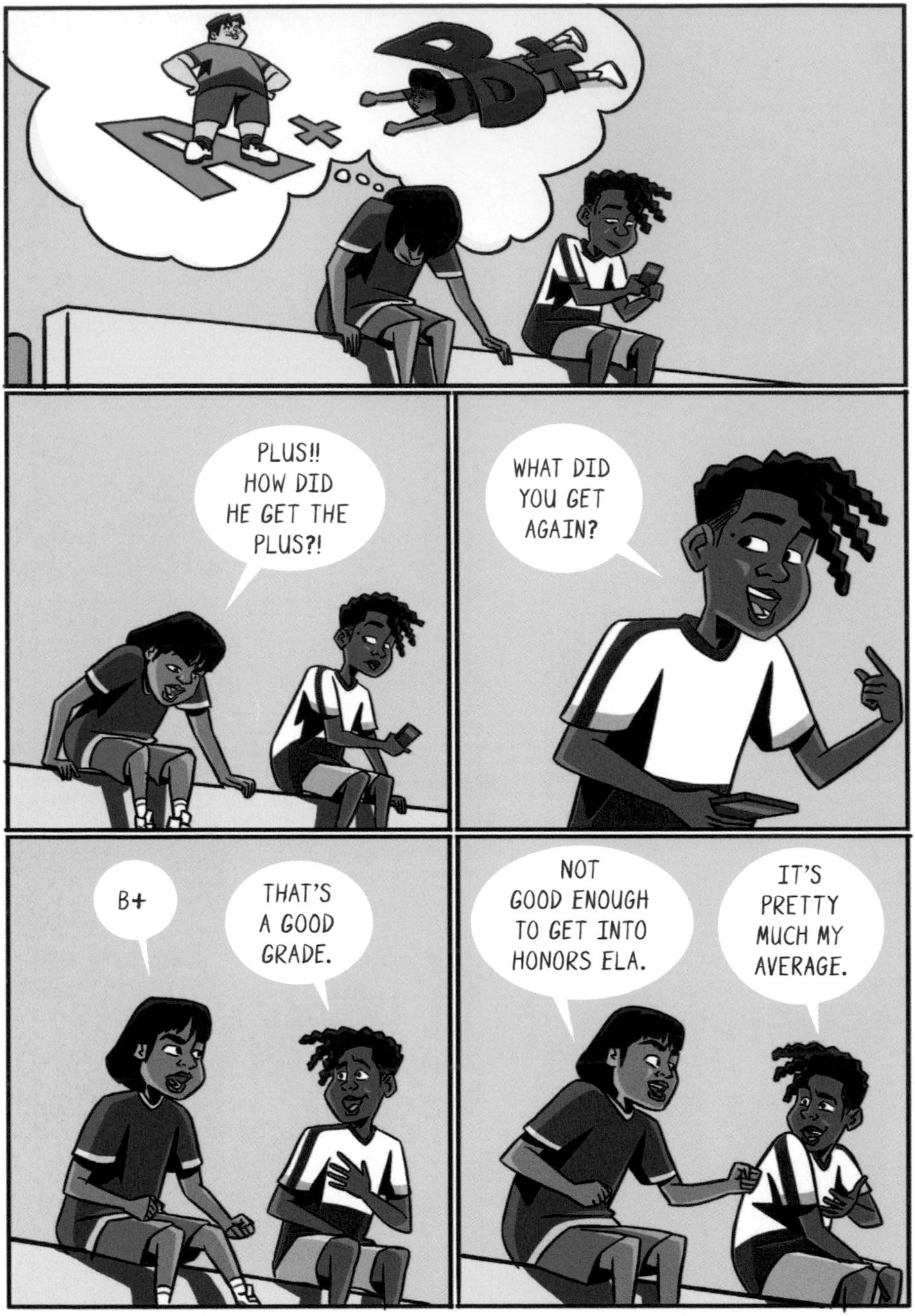
A+
B+
PLUS!! HOW DID HE GET THE PLUS?!
WHAT DID YOU GET AGAIN?
B+
THAT'S A GOOD GRADE.
NOT GOOD ENOUGH TO GET INTO HONORS ELA.
IT'S PRETTY MUCH MY AVERAGE.

CHAPTER 4

A PLACE FOR EVERY PIECE

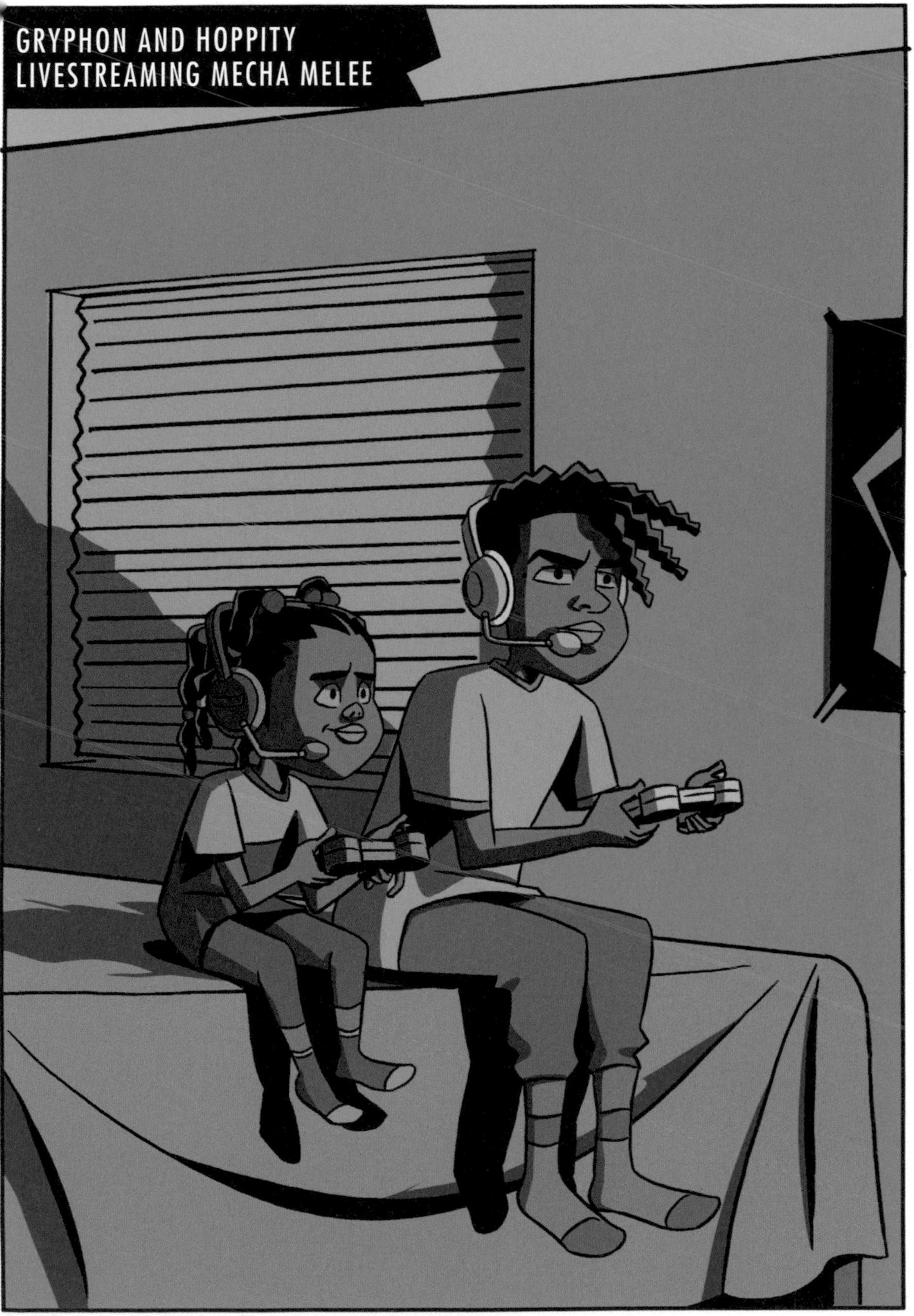
GRYPHON AND HOPPITY
LIVESTREAMING MECHA MELEE

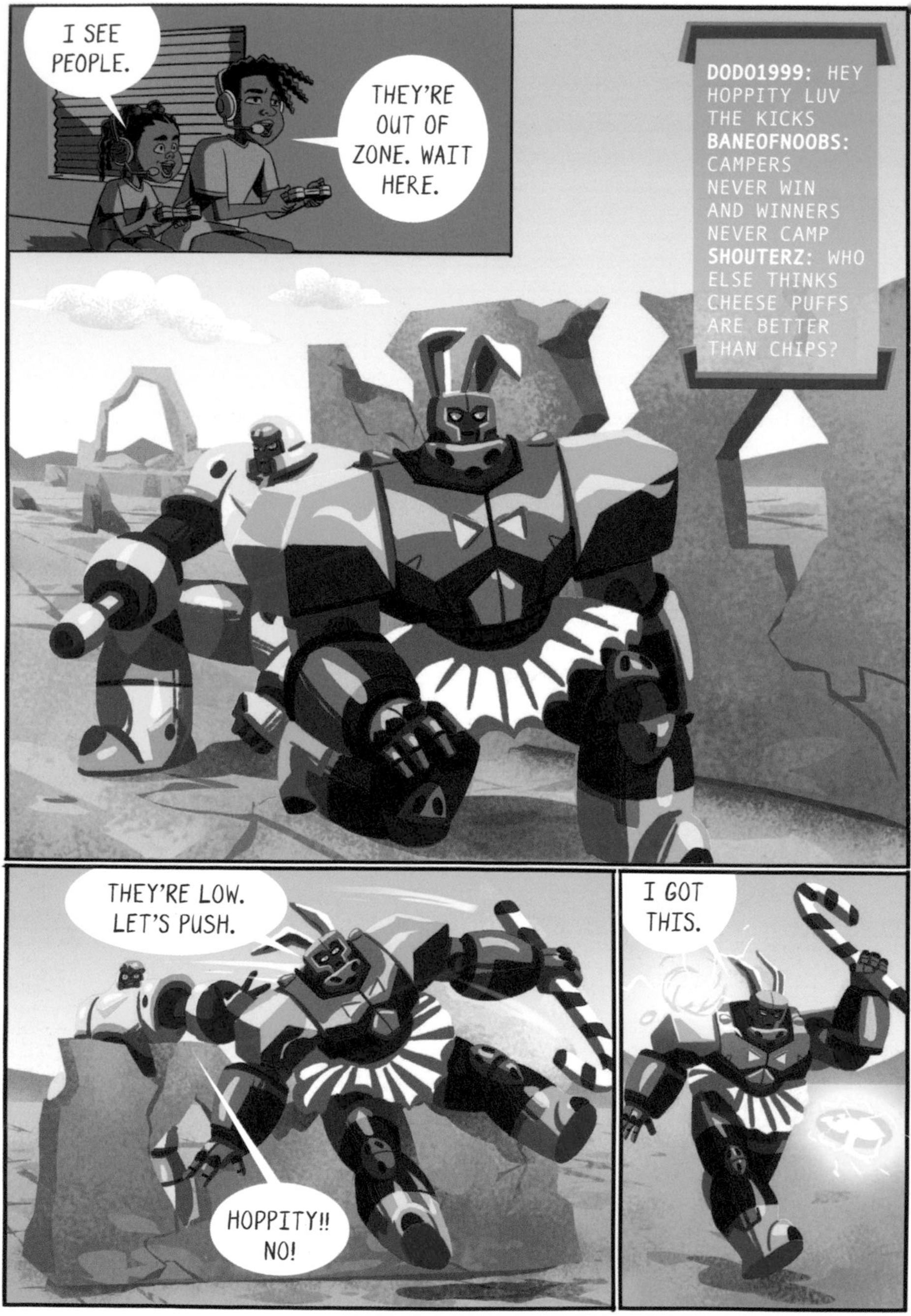
I SEE PEOPLE.
THEY'RE OUT OF ZONE. WAIT HERE.
DODO1999: HEY HOPPITY LUV THE KICKS
BANEOFNOOBS: CAMPERS NEVER WIN AND WINNERS NEVER CAMP
SHOUTERZ: WHO ELSE THINKS CHEESE PUFFS ARE BETTER THAN CHIPS?
THEY'RE LOW. LET'S PUSH.
HOPPITY!! NO!
I GOT THIS.

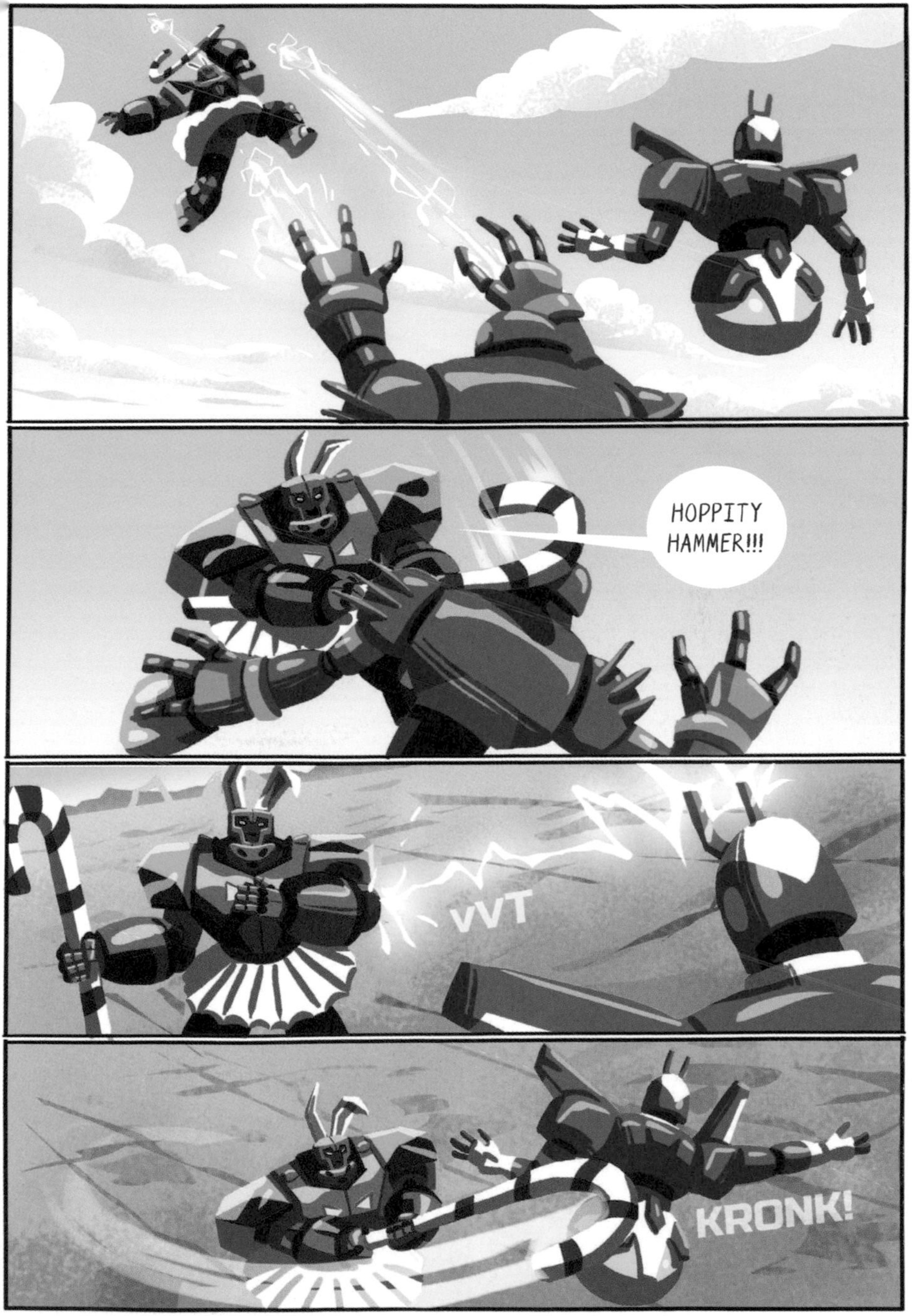
HOPPITY HAMMER!!!
VVT
KRONK!

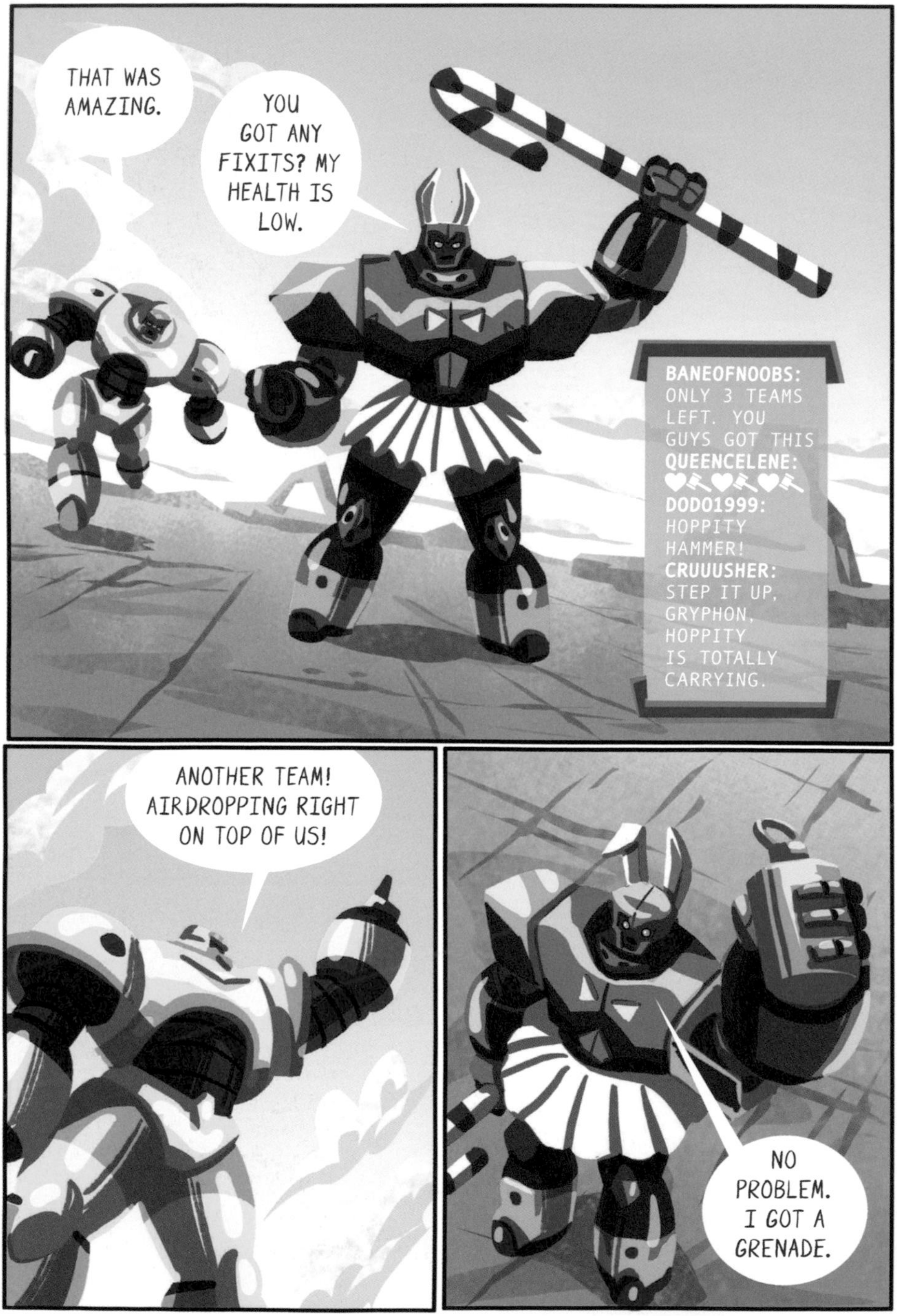
THAT WAS AMAZING.
YOU GOT ANY FIXITS? MY HEALTH IS LOW.
BANEOFNOOBS:
ONLY 3 TEAMS LEFT. YOU GUYS GOT THIS
QUEENCELENE:
DODO1999:
HOPPITY HAMMER!
CRUUUSHER:
STEP IT UP, GRYPHON, HOPPITY IS TOTALLY CARRYING.
ANOTHER TEAM! AIRDROPPING RIGHT ON TOP OF US!
NO PROBLEM. I GOT A GRENADE.

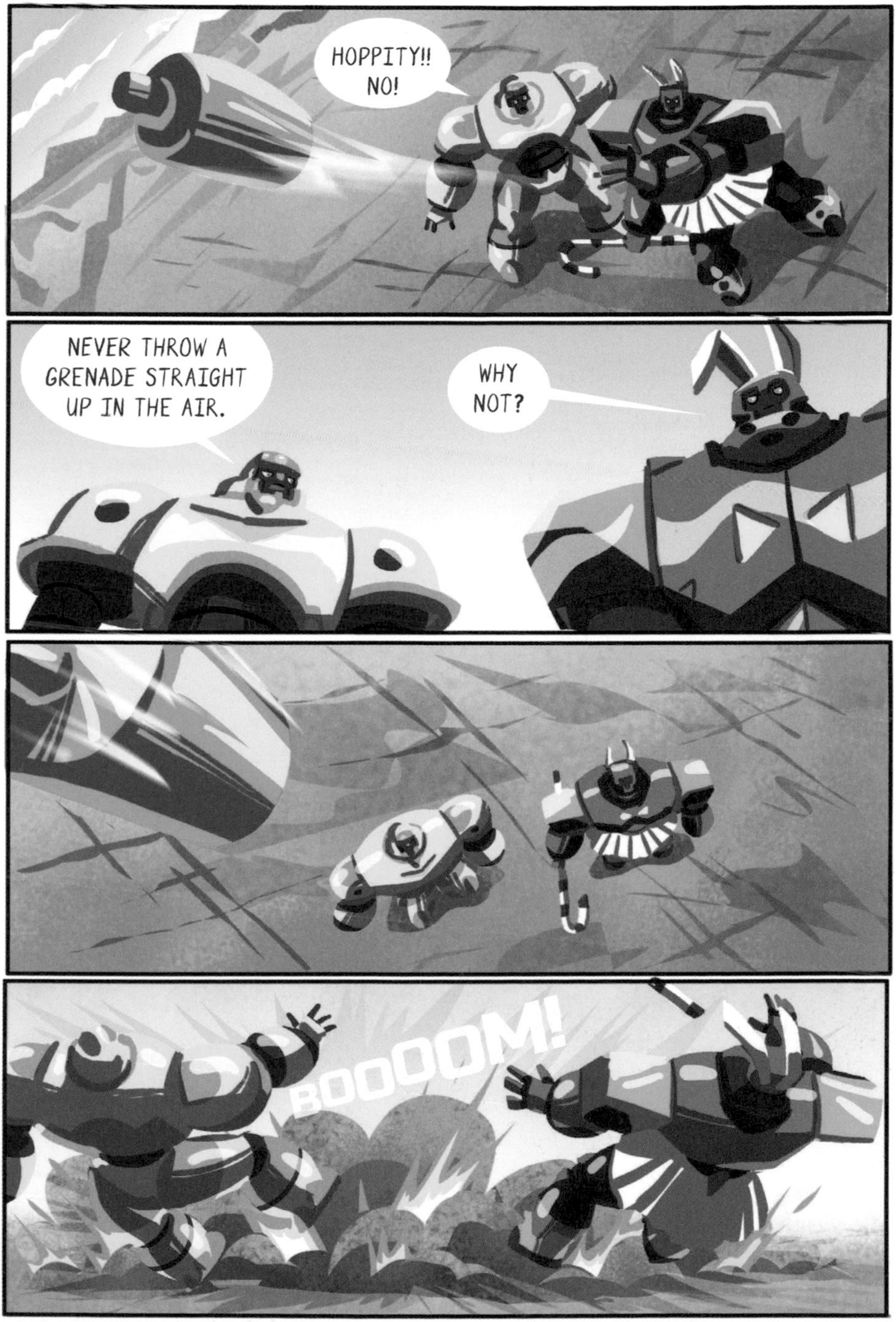
HOPPITY!! NO!
NEVER THROW A GRENADE STRAIGHT UP IN THE AIR.
WHY NOT?
BOOOOOM!

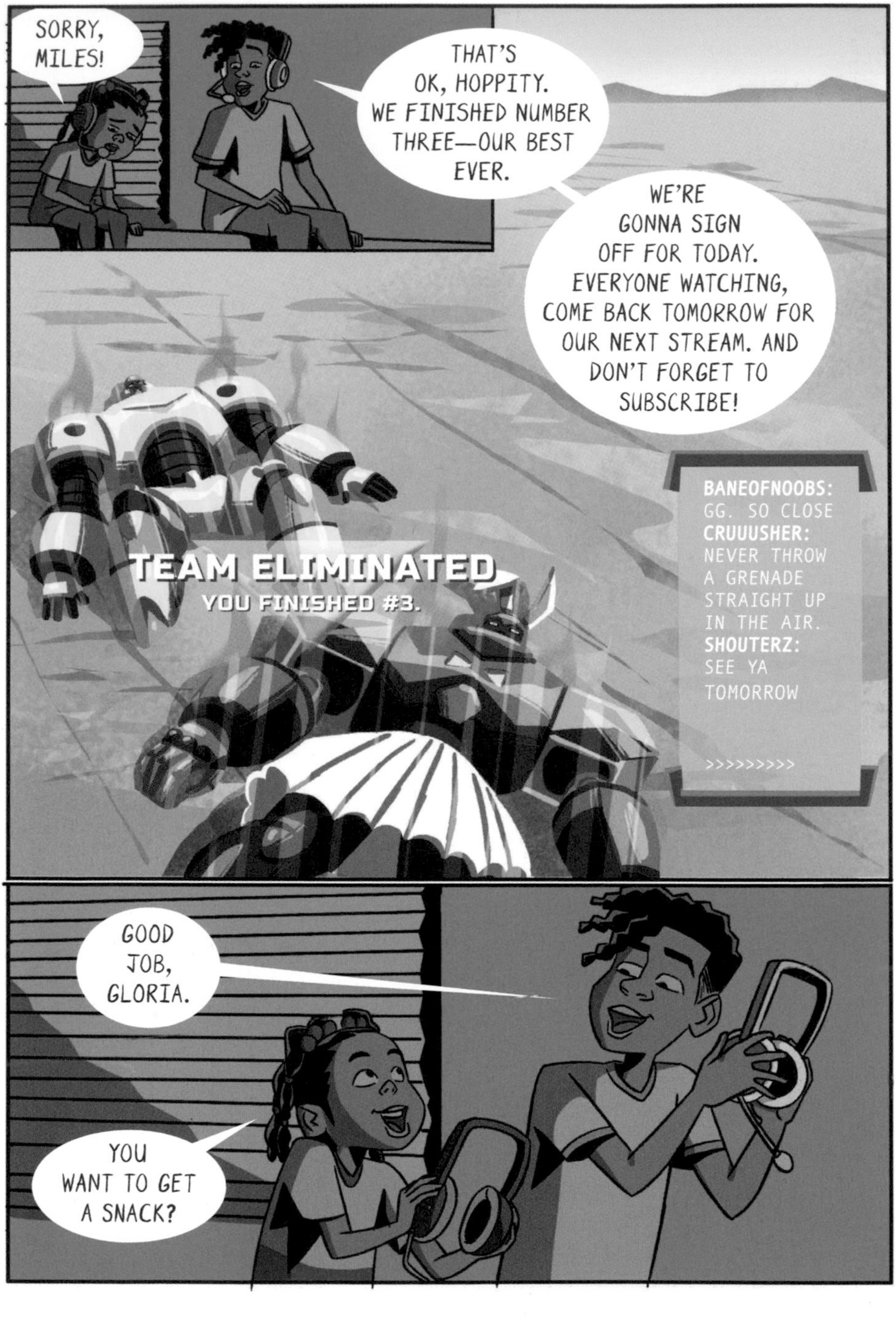
SORRY, MILES!
THAT'S OK, HOPPITY. WE FINISHED NUMBER THREE—OUR BEST EVER.
WE'RE GONNA SIGN OFF FOR TODAY. EVERYONE WATCHING, COME BACK TOMORROW FOR OUR NEXT STREAM. AND DON'T FORGET TO SUBSCRIBE!
TEAM ELIMINATED
YOU FINISHED #3.
BANEOFNOOBS: GG. SO CLOSE
CRUUUSHER: NEVER THROW A GRENADE STRAIGHT UP IN THE AIR.
SHOUTERZ: SEE YA TOMORROW
>>>>>>>>>>
GOOD JOB, GLORIA.
YOU WANT TO GET A SNACK?

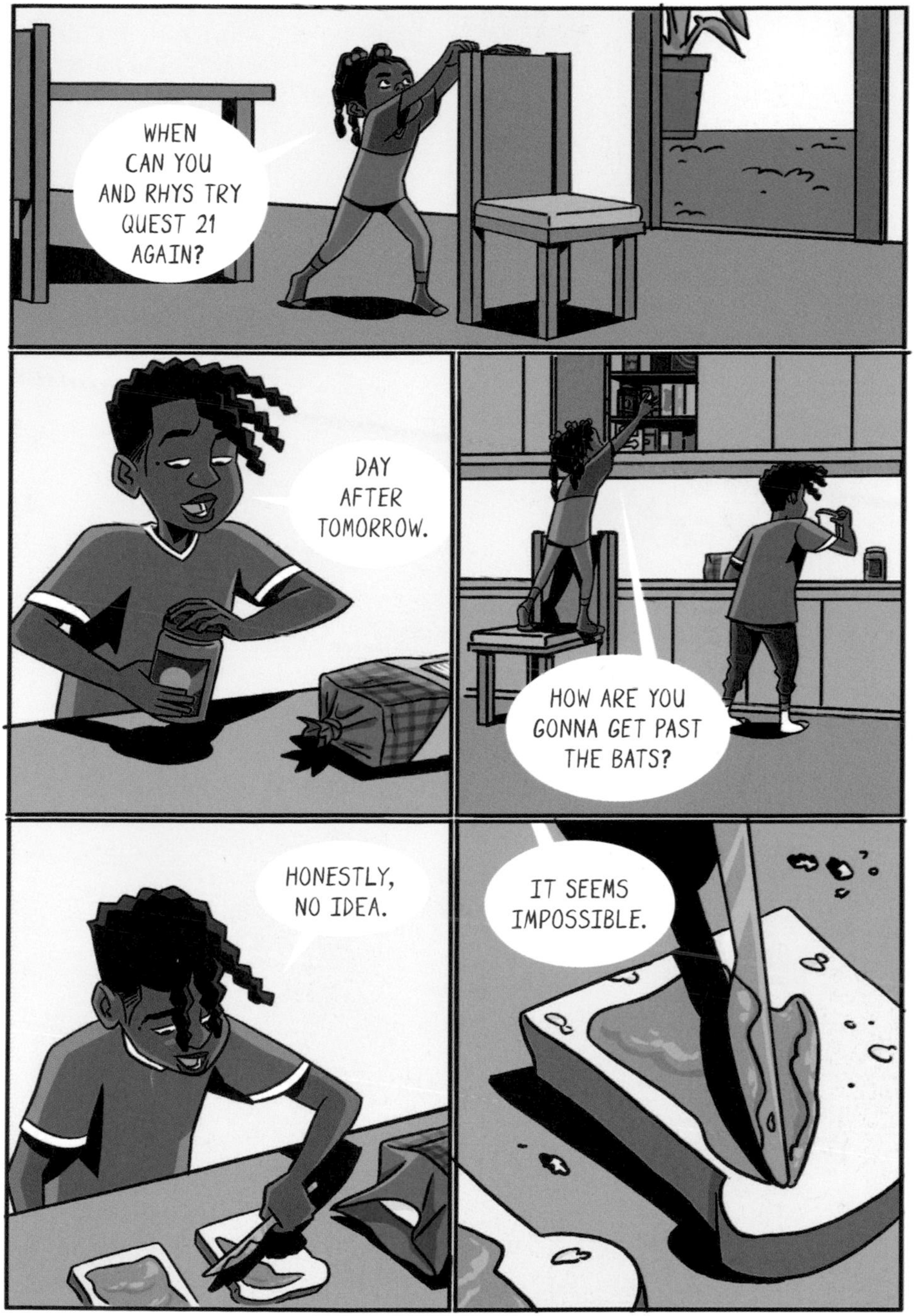
WHEN CAN YOU AND RHYS TRY QUEST 21 AGAIN?
DAY AFTER TOMORROW.
HOW ARE YOU GONNA GET PAST THE BATS?
HONESTLY, NO IDEA.
IT SEEMS IMPOSSIBLE.

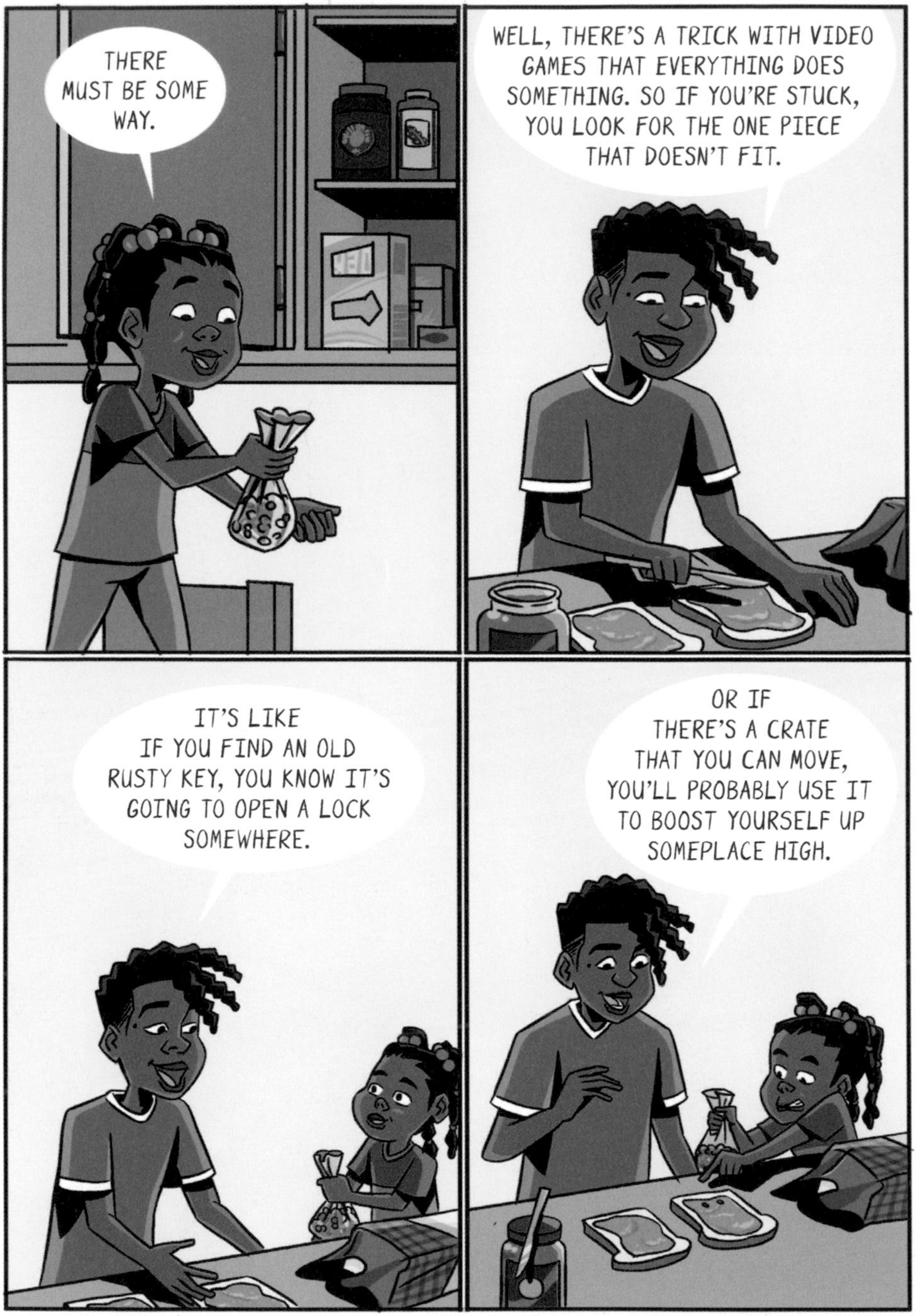
THERE MUST BE SOME WAY.
WELL, THERE'S A TRICK WITH VIDEO GAMES THAT EVERYTHING DOES SOMETHING. SO IF YOU'RE STUCK, YOU LOOK FOR THE ONE PIECE THAT DOESN'T FIT.
IT'S LIKE IF YOU FIND AN OLD RUSTY KEY, YOU KNOW IT'S GOING TO OPEN A LOCK SOMEWHERE.
OR IF THERE'S A CRATE THAT YOU CAN MOVE, YOU'LL PROBABLY USE IT TO BOOST YOURSELF UP SOMEPLACE HIGH.

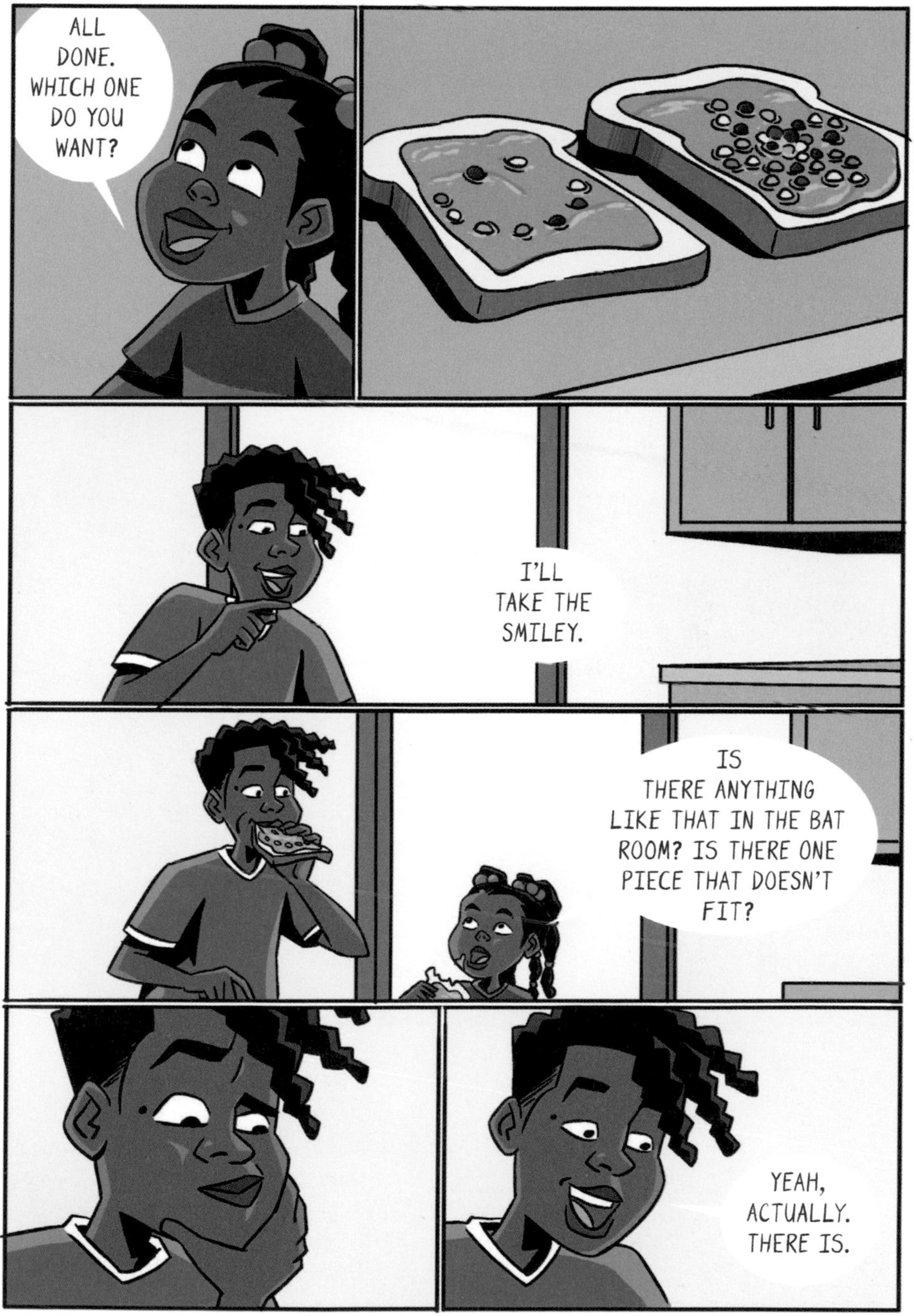
ALL DONE. WHICH ONE DO YOU WANT?
I'LL TAKE THE SMILEY.
IS THERE ANYTHING LIKE THAT IN THE BAT ROOM? IS THERE ONE PIECE THAT DOESN'T FIT?
YEAH, ACTUALLY. THERE IS.

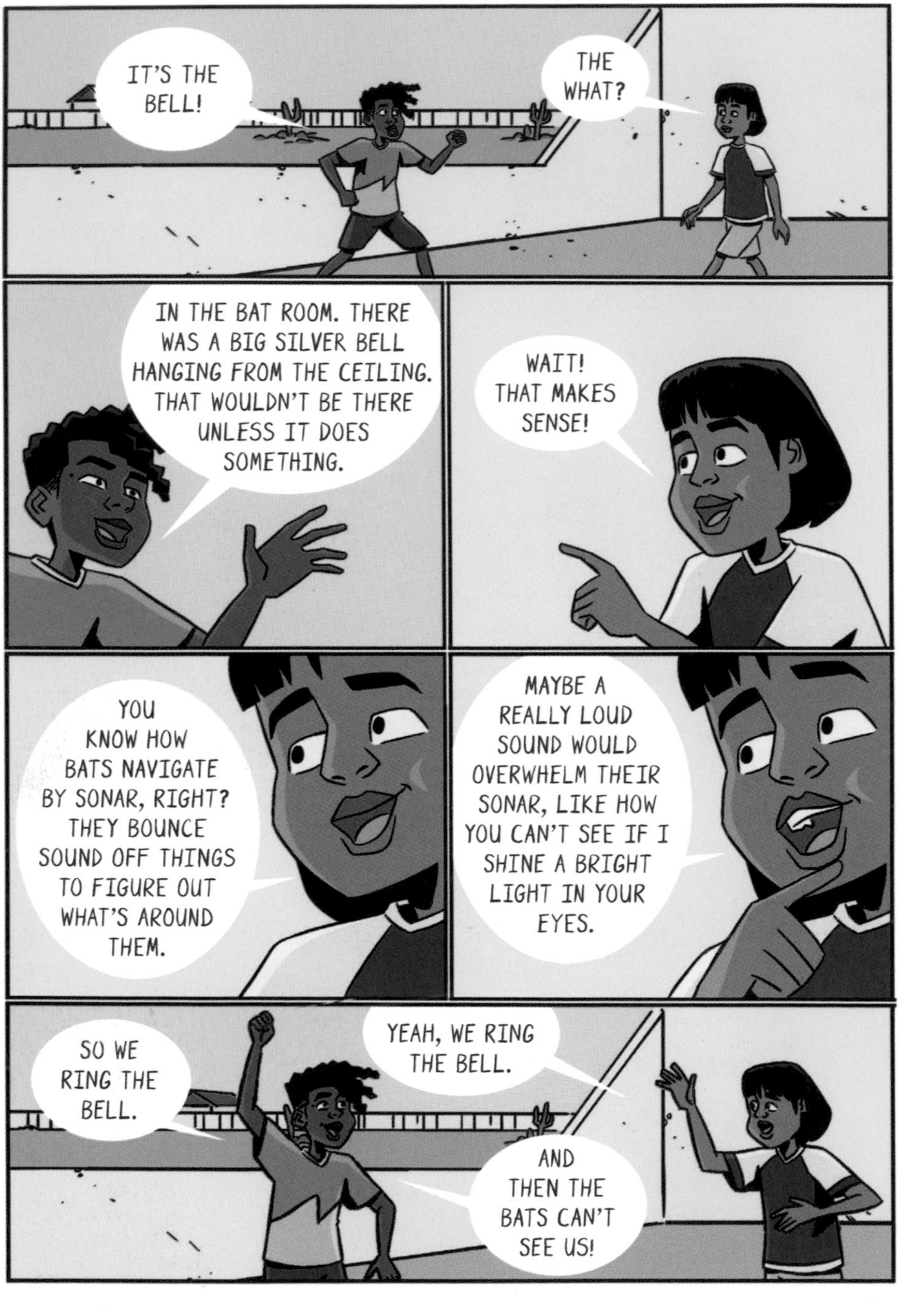
IT'S THE BELL!
THE WHAT?
IN THE BAT ROOM. THERE WAS A BIG SILVER BELL HANGING FROM THE CEILING. THAT WOULDN'T BE THERE UNLESS IT DOES SOMETHING.
WAIT! THAT MAKES SENSE!
YOU KNOW HOW BATS NAVIGATE BY SONAR, RIGHT? THEY BOUNCE SOUND OFF THINGS TO FIGURE OUT WHAT'S AROUND THEM.
MAYBE A REALLY LOUD SOUND WOULD OVERWHELM THEIR SONAR, LIKE HOW YOU CAN'T SEE IF I SHINE A BRIGHT LIGHT IN YOUR EYES.
SO WE RING THE BELL.
YEAH, WE RING THE BELL.
AND THEN THE BATS CAN'T SEE US!

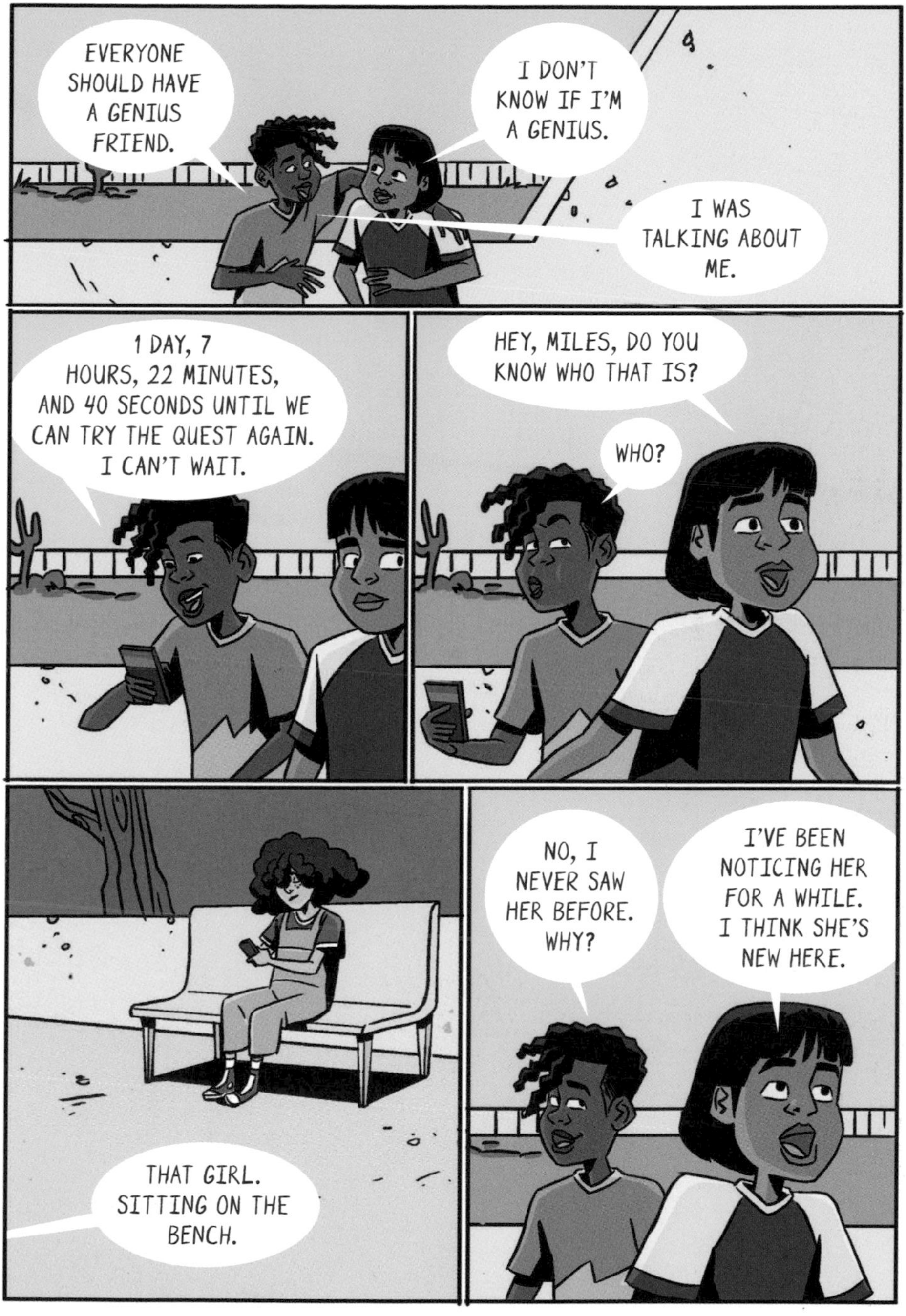
EVERYONE SHOULD HAVE A GENIUS FRIEND.
I DON'T KNOW IF I'M A GENIUS.
I WAS TALKING ABOUT ME.
1 DAY, 7 HOURS, 22 MINUTES, AND 40 SECONDS UNTIL WE CAN TRY THE QUEST AGAIN. I CAN'T WAIT.
HEY, MILES, DO YOU KNOW WHO THAT IS?
WHO?
THAT GIRL. SITTING ON THE BENCH.
NO, I NEVER SAW HER BEFORE. WHY?
I'VE BEEN NOTICING HER FOR A WHILE. I THINK SHE'S NEW HERE.

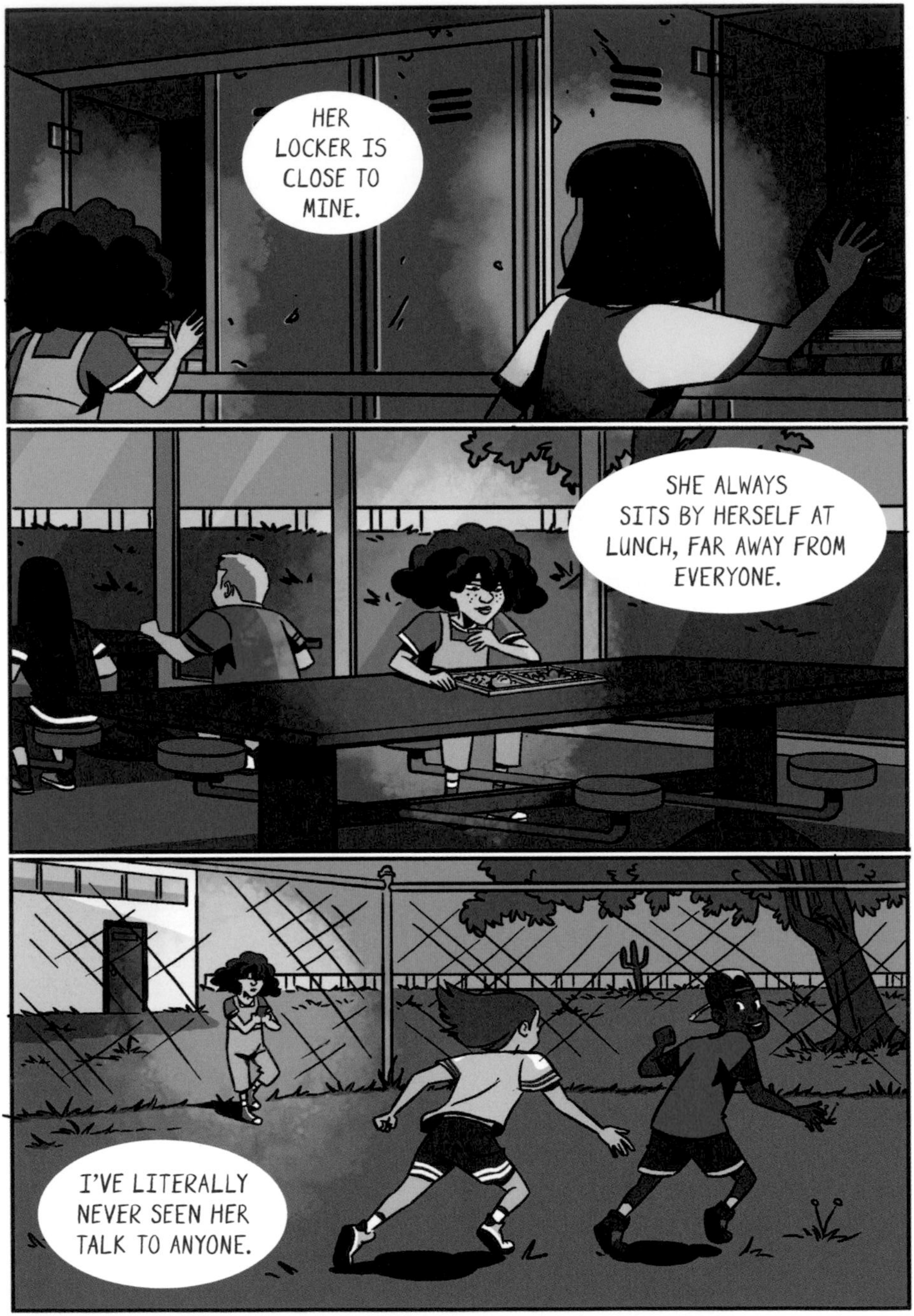
HER LOCKER IS CLOSE TO MINE.
SHE ALWAYS SITS BY HERSELF AT LUNCH, FAR AWAY FROM EVERYONE.
I'VE LITERALLY NEVER SEEN HER TALK TO ANYONE.

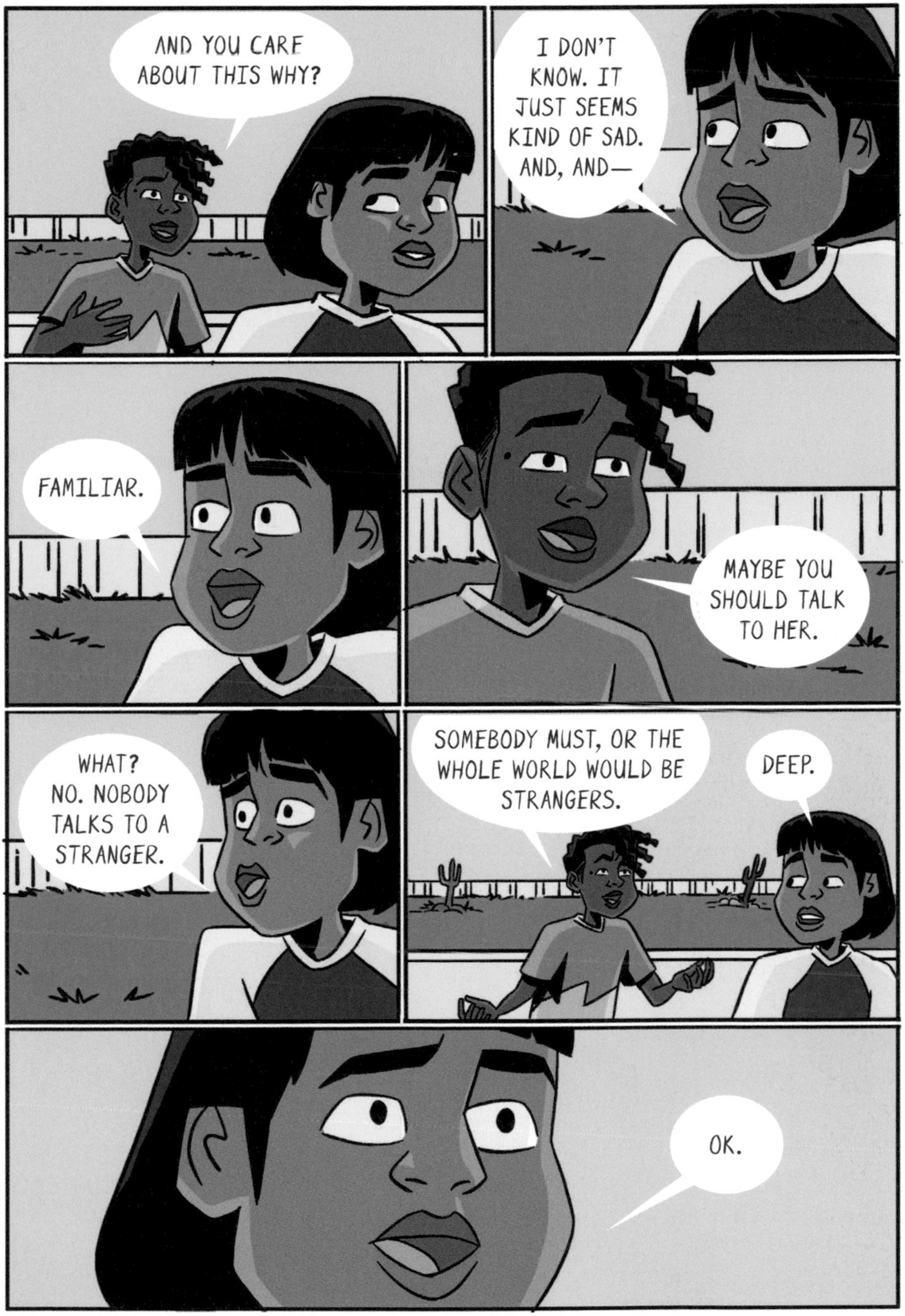
AND YOU CARE ABOUT THIS WHY?
I DON'T KNOW. IT JUST SEEMS KIND OF SAD. AND, AND—
FAMILIAR.
MAYBE YOU SHOULD TALK TO HER.
WHAT? NO. NOBODY TALKS TO A STRANGER.
SOMEBODY MUST, OR THE WHOLE WORLD WOULD BE STRANGERS.
DEEP.
OK.

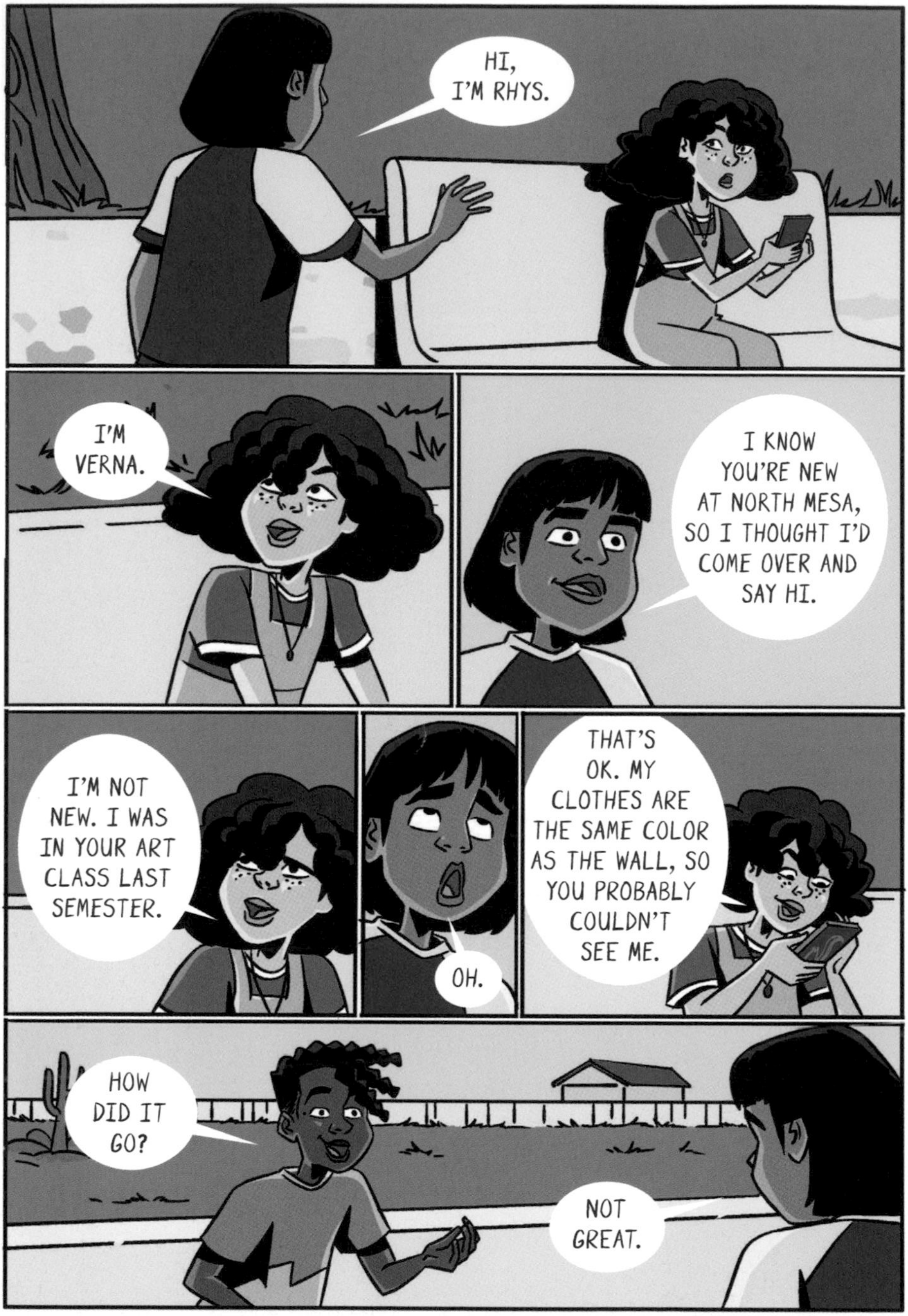
HI, I'M RHYS.
I'M VERNA.
I KNOW YOU'RE NEW AT NORTH MESA, SO I THOUGHT I'D COME OVER AND SAY HI.
I'M NOT NEW. I WAS IN YOUR ART CLASS LAST SEMESTER.
OH.
THAT'S OK. MY CLOTHES ARE THE SAME COLOR AS THE WALL, SO YOU PROBABLY COULDN'T SEE ME.
HOW DID IT GO?
NOT GREAT.

CHAPTER 5

THE NEXT ROOM

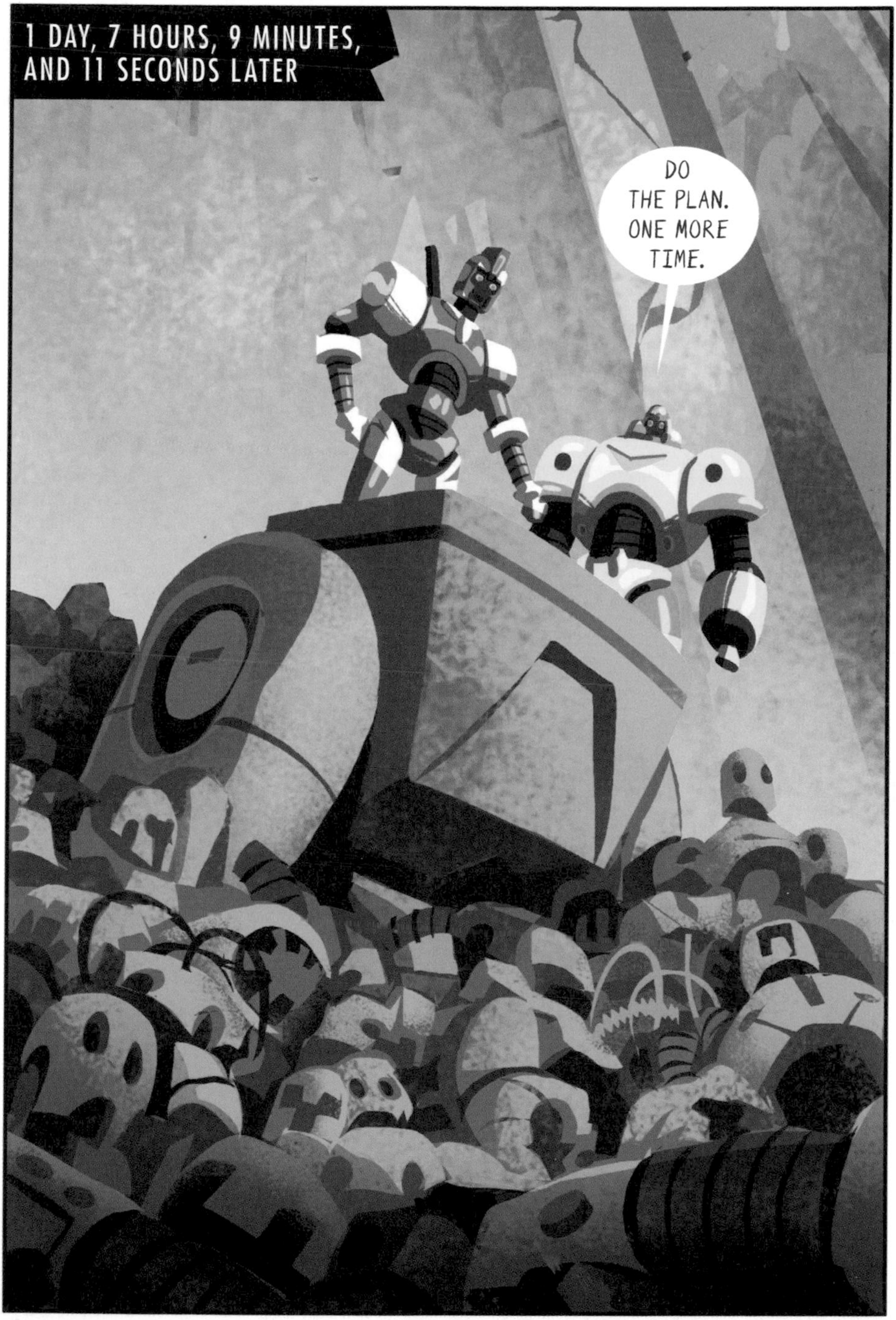
1 DAY, 7 HOURS, 9 MINUTES, AND 11 SECONDS LATER
DO THE PLAN. ONE MORE TIME.

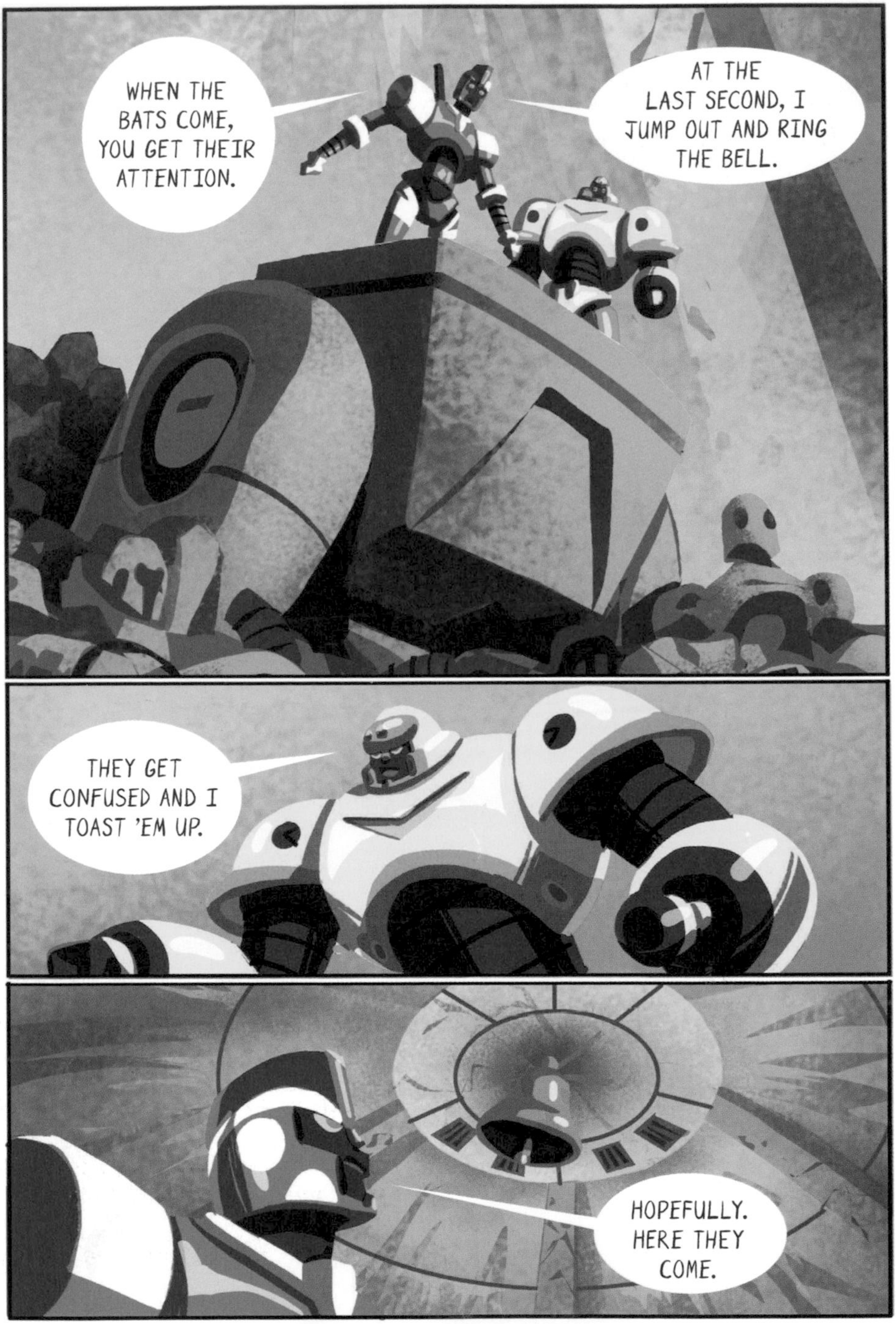
WHEN THE BATS COME, YOU GET THEIR ATTENTION.
AT THE LAST SECOND, I JUMP OUT AND RING THE BELL.
THEY GET CONFUSED AND I TOAST 'EM UP.
HOPEFULLY. HERE THEY COME.

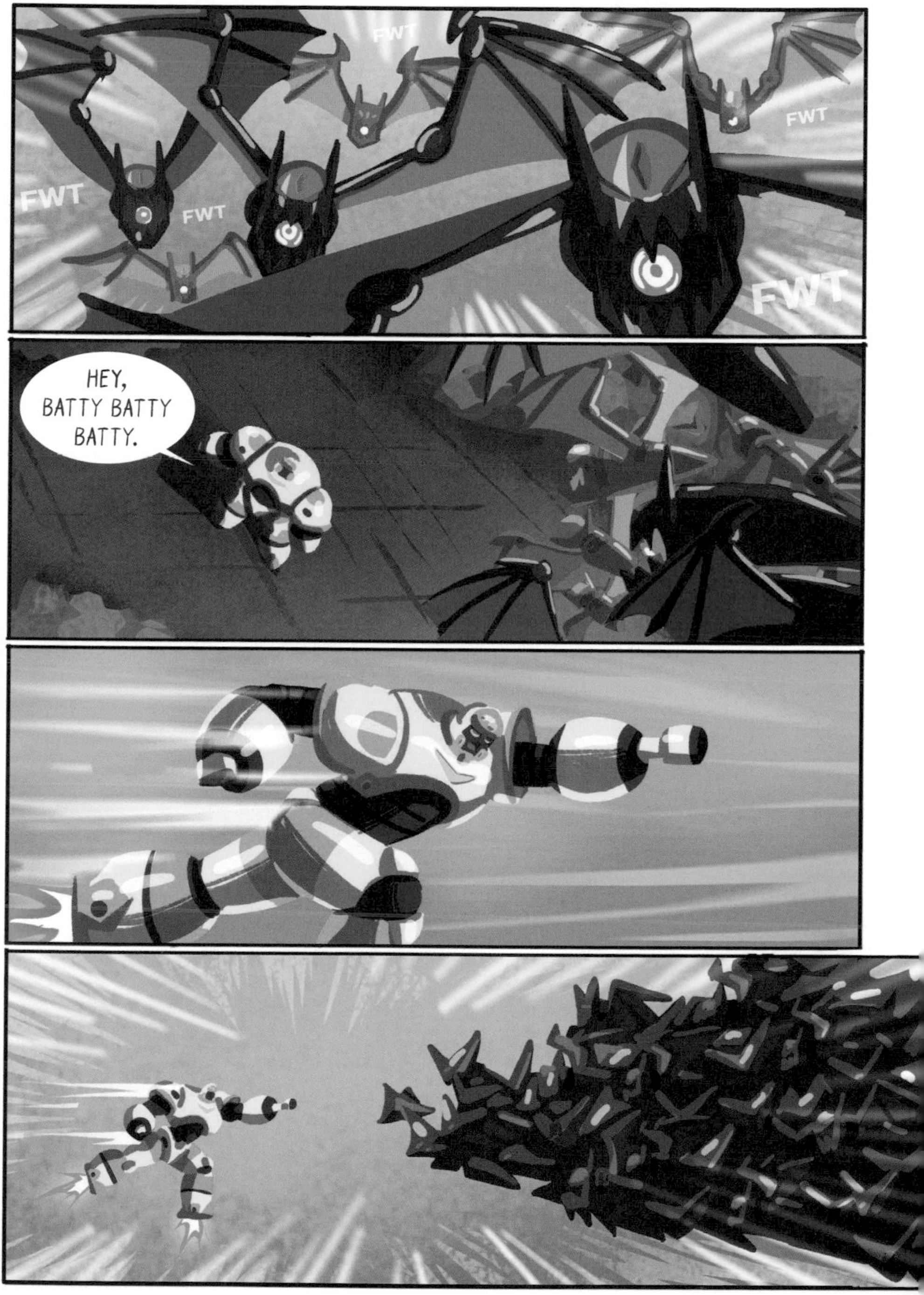
FWT
FWT
FWT
FWT
FWT
FWT
HEY, BATTY BATTY BATTY.

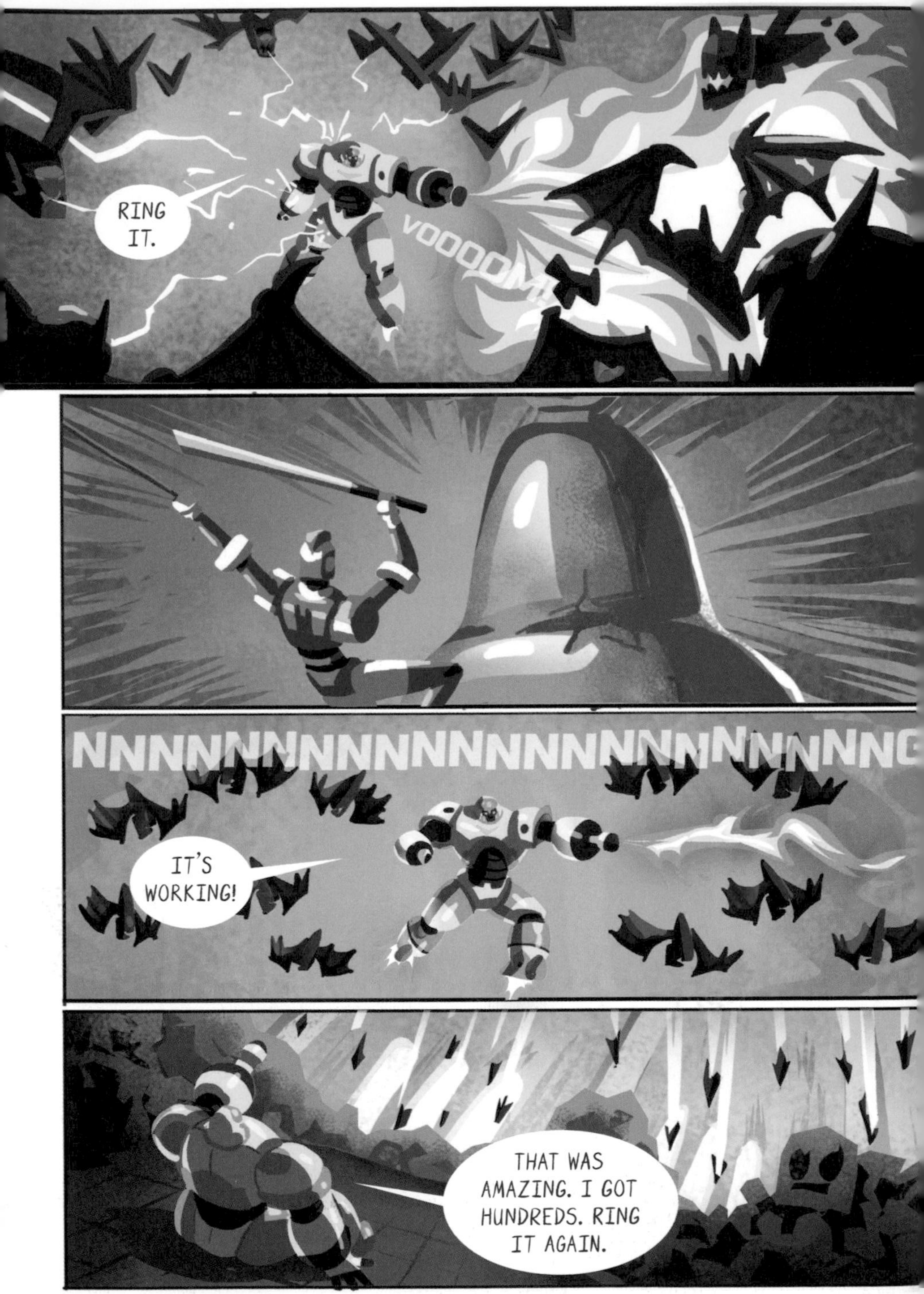
RING IT.
VOOOOOM!
NNNNNNNNNNNNNNNNNNNNNNNNNNNG
IT'S WORKING!
THAT WAS AMAZING. I GOT HUNDREDS. RING IT AGAIN.

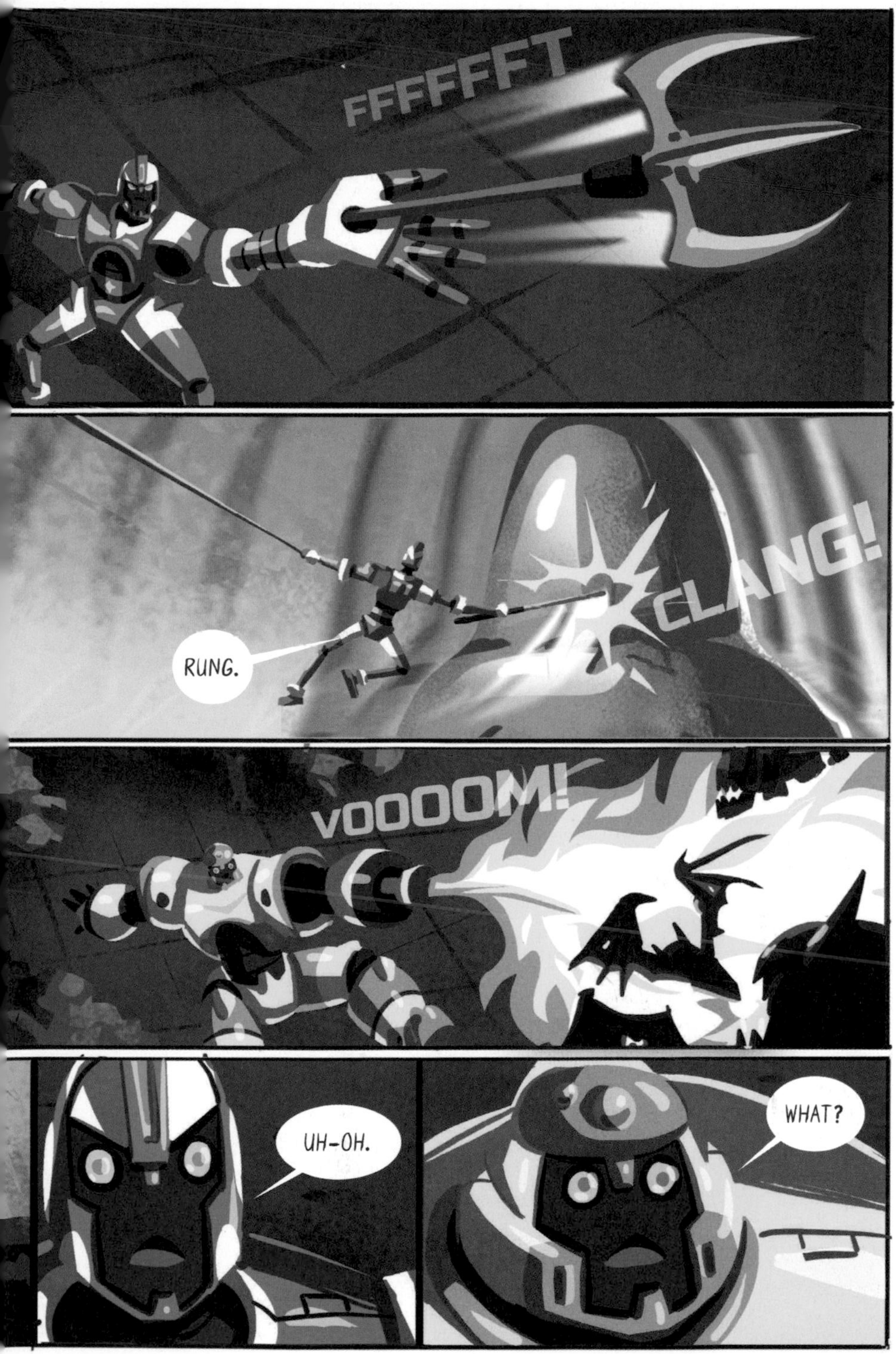
FFFFFFT
RUNG.
CLANG!
VOOOOM!
UH-OH.
WHAT?

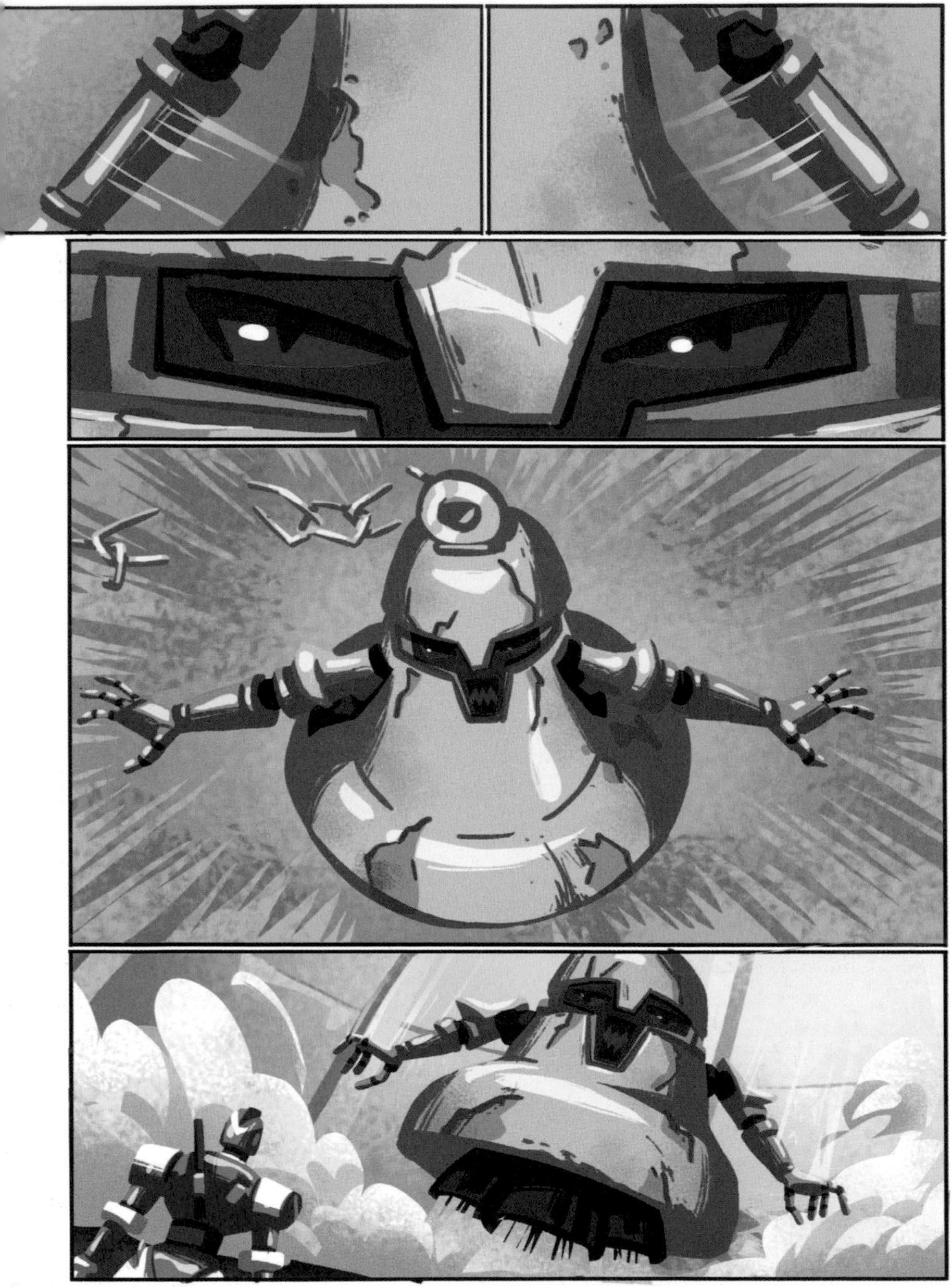

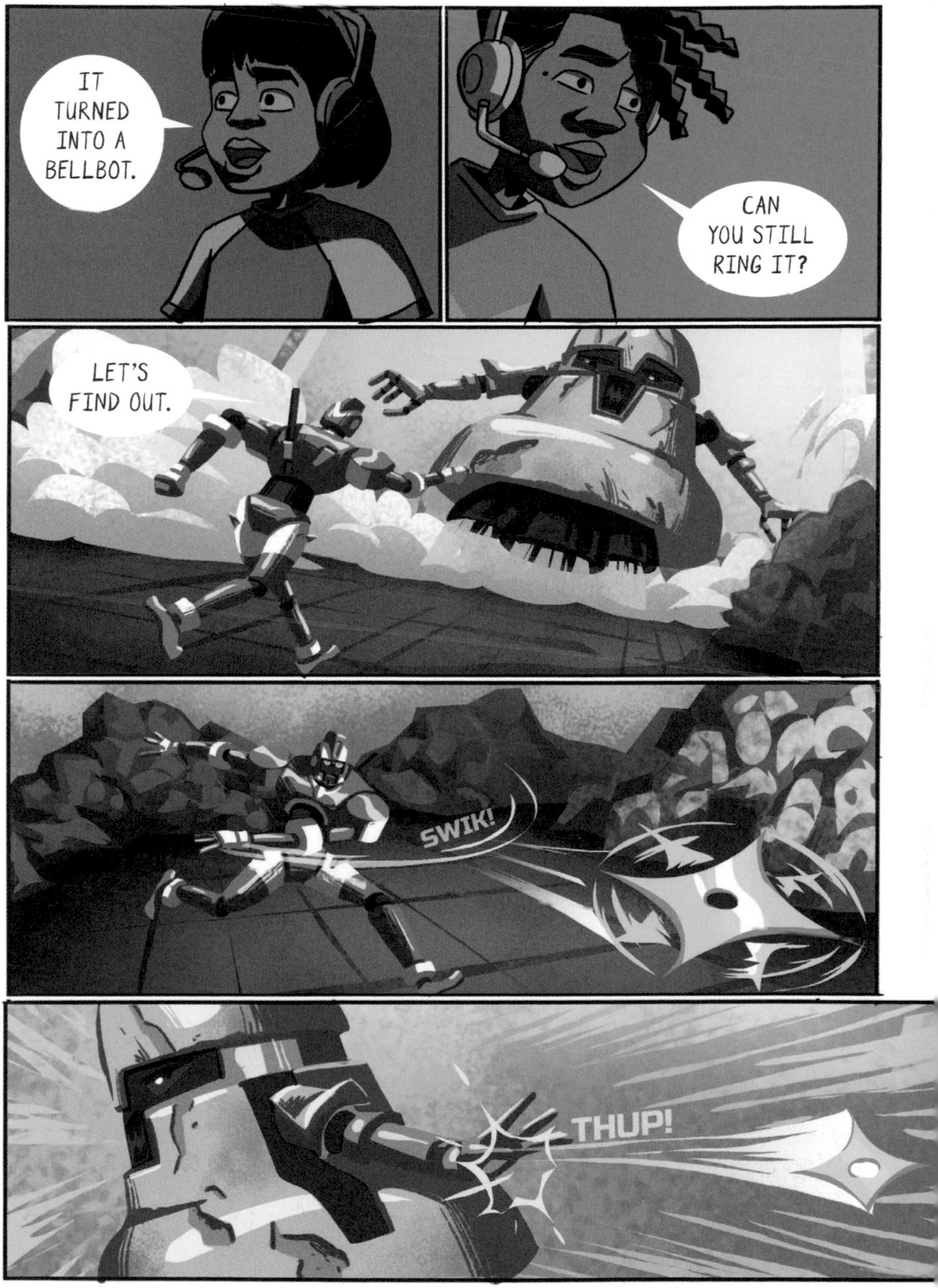
IT TURNED INTO A BELLBOT.
CAN YOU STILL RING IT?
LET'S FIND OUT.
SWIK!
THUP!

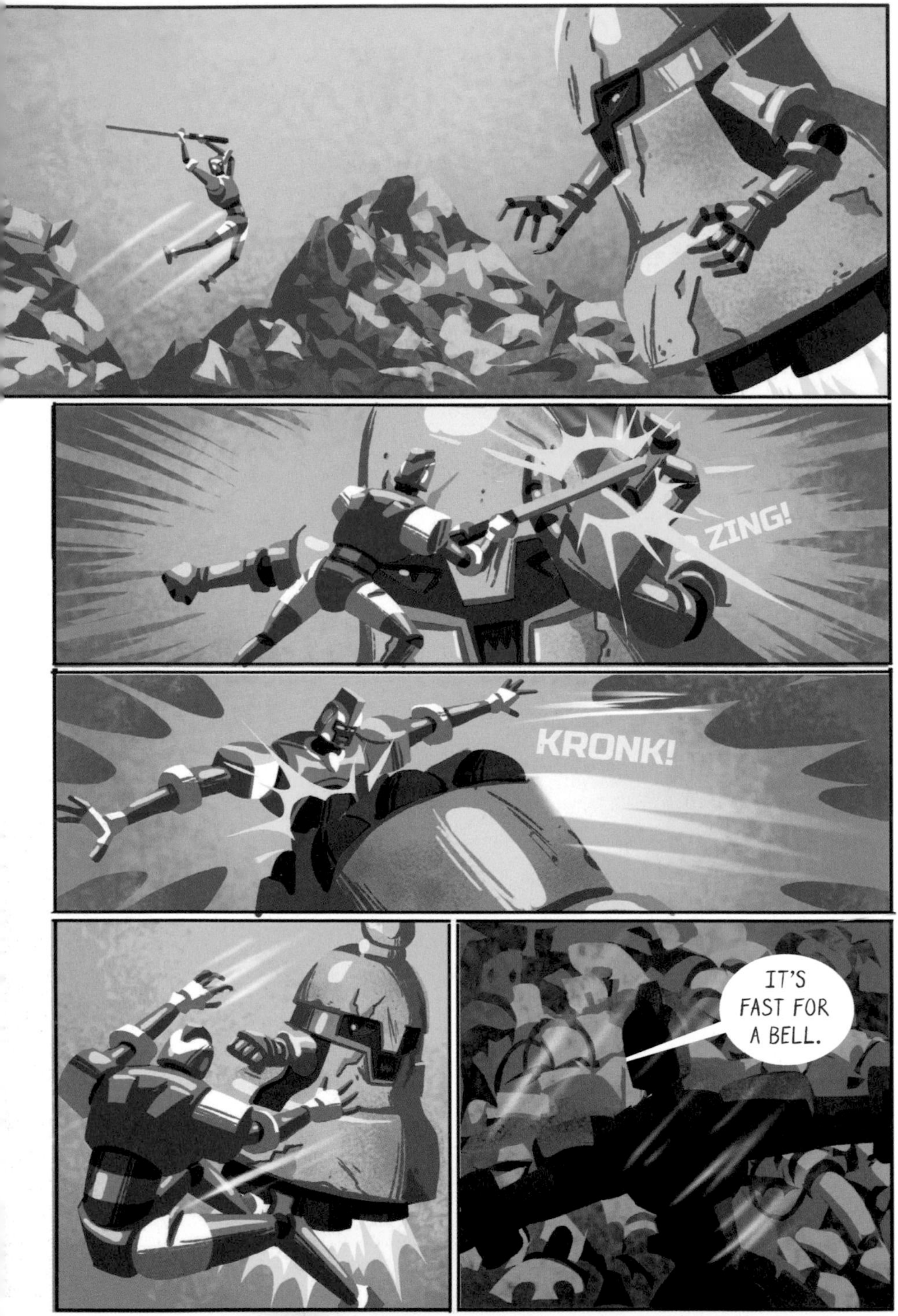
ZING!
KRONK!
IT'S FAST FOR A BELL.

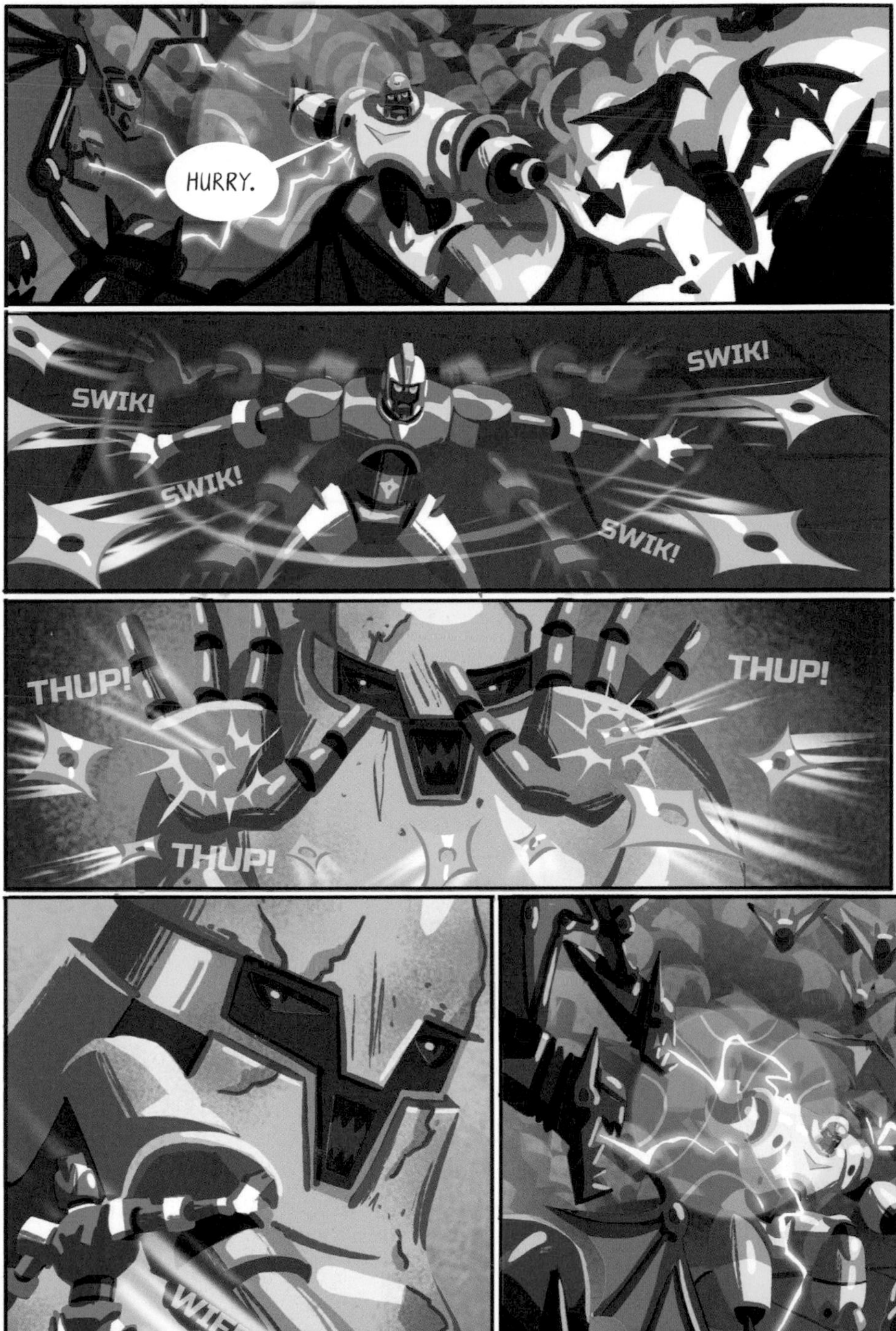
HURRY.
SWIK!
SWIK!
SWIK!
SWIK!
THUP!
THUP!
THUP!
WIFF!

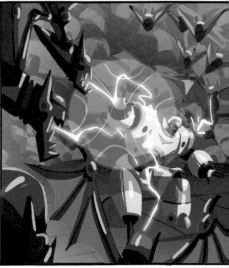

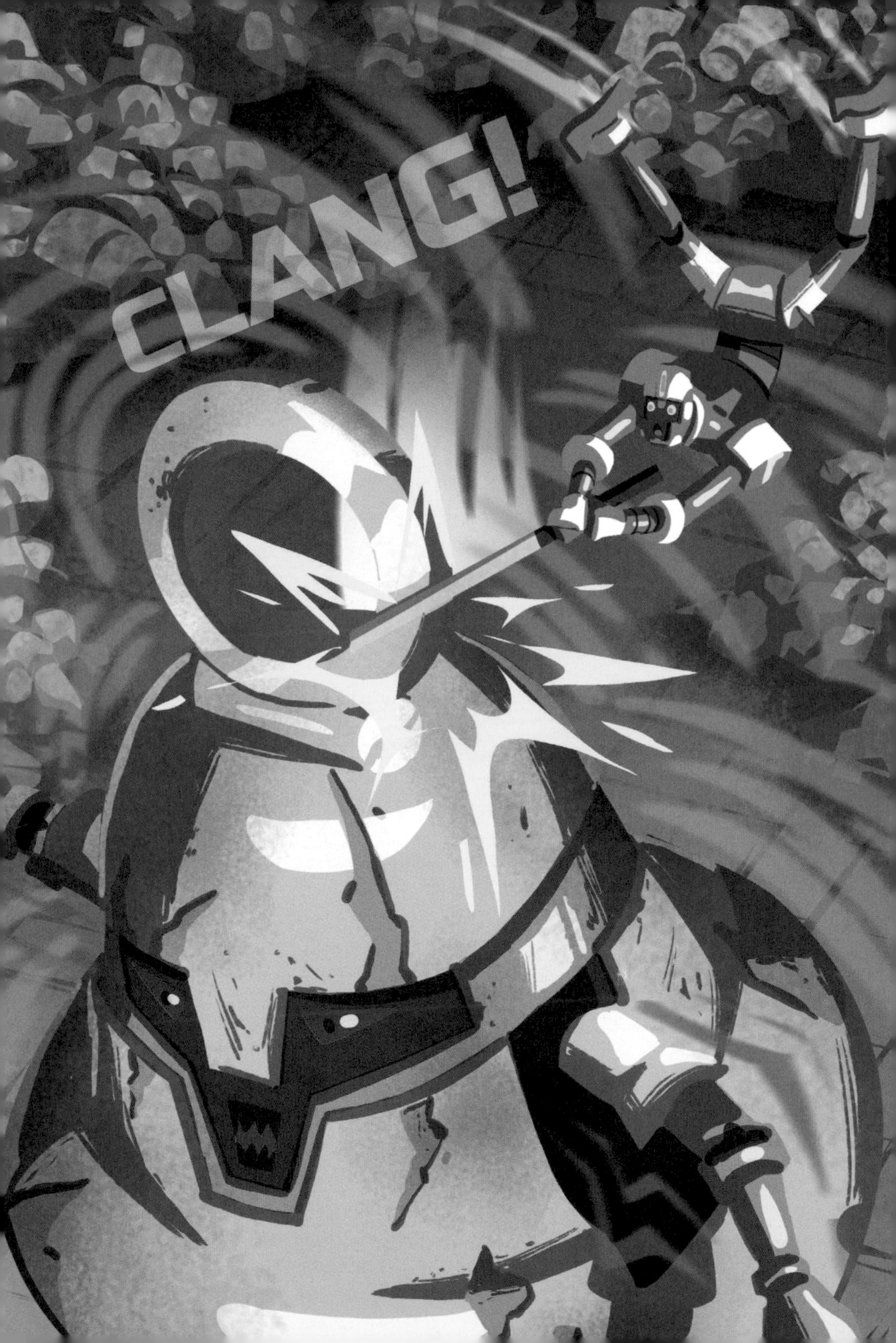
CLANG!

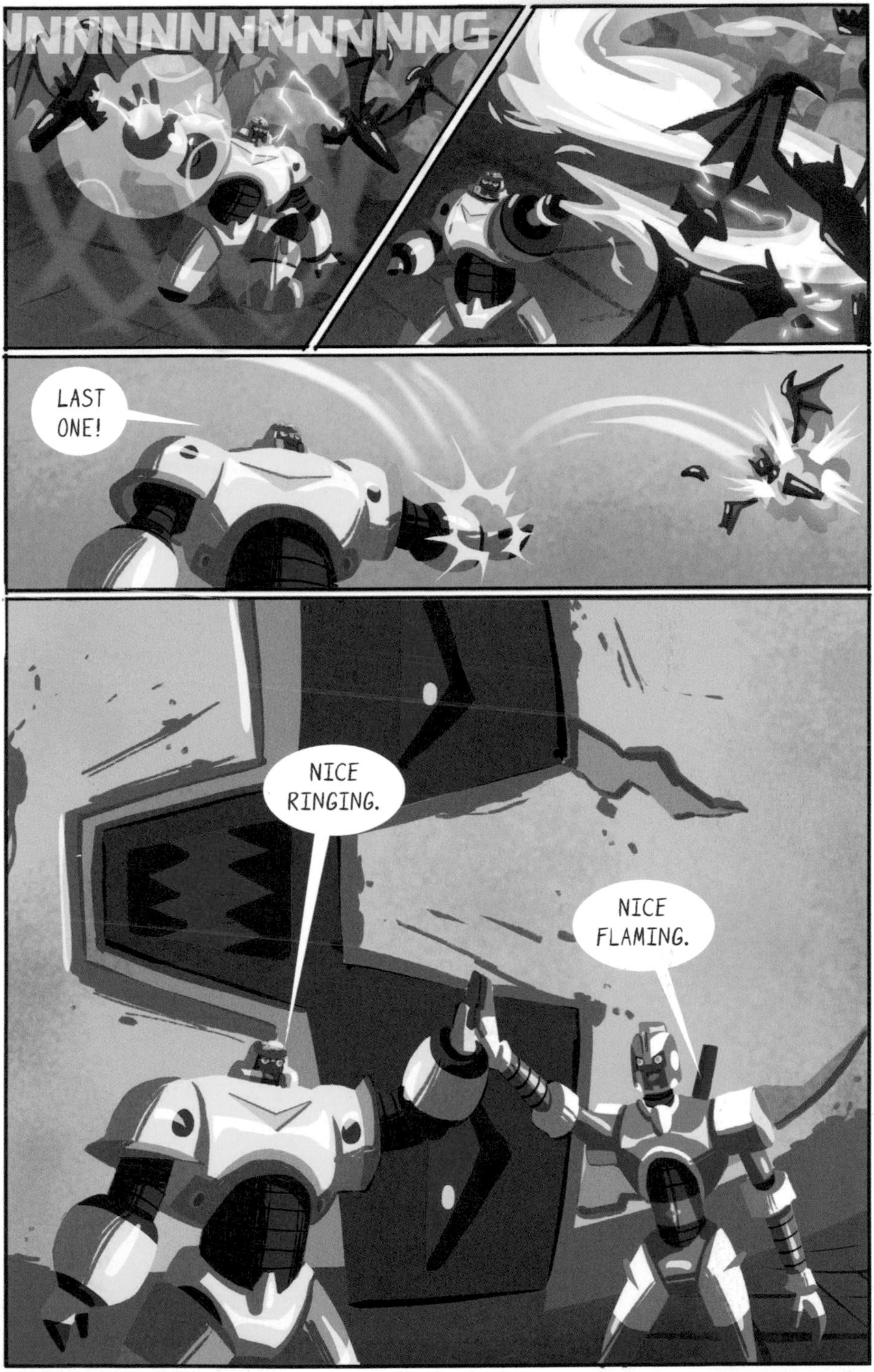
NNNNNNNNNNNNNG
LAST ONE!
NICE RINGING.
NICE FLAMING.

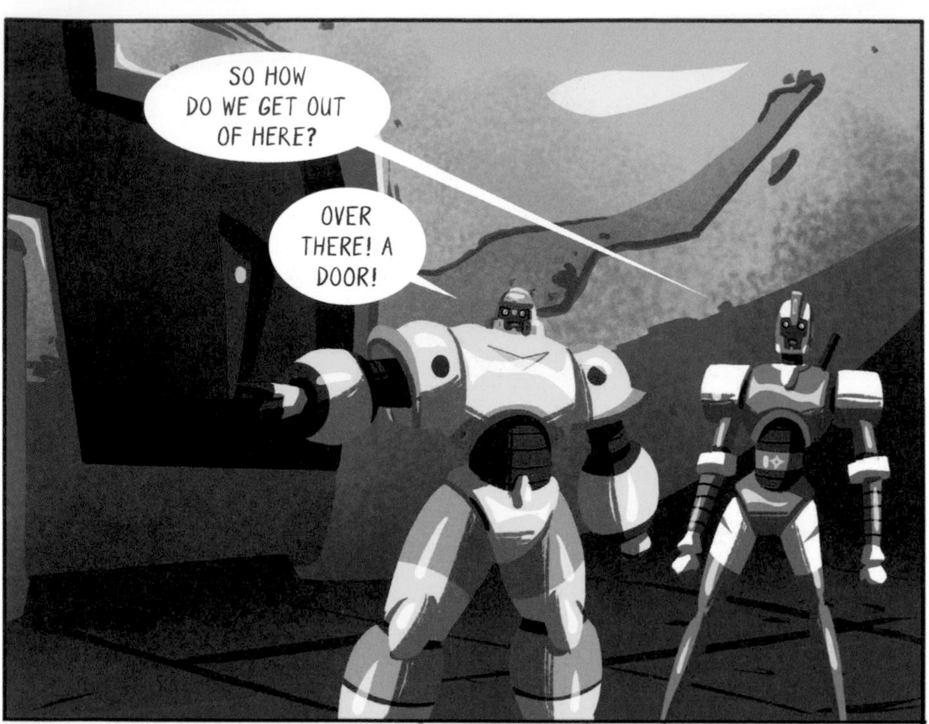
SO HOW DO WE GET OUT OF HERE?
OVER THERE! A DOOR!

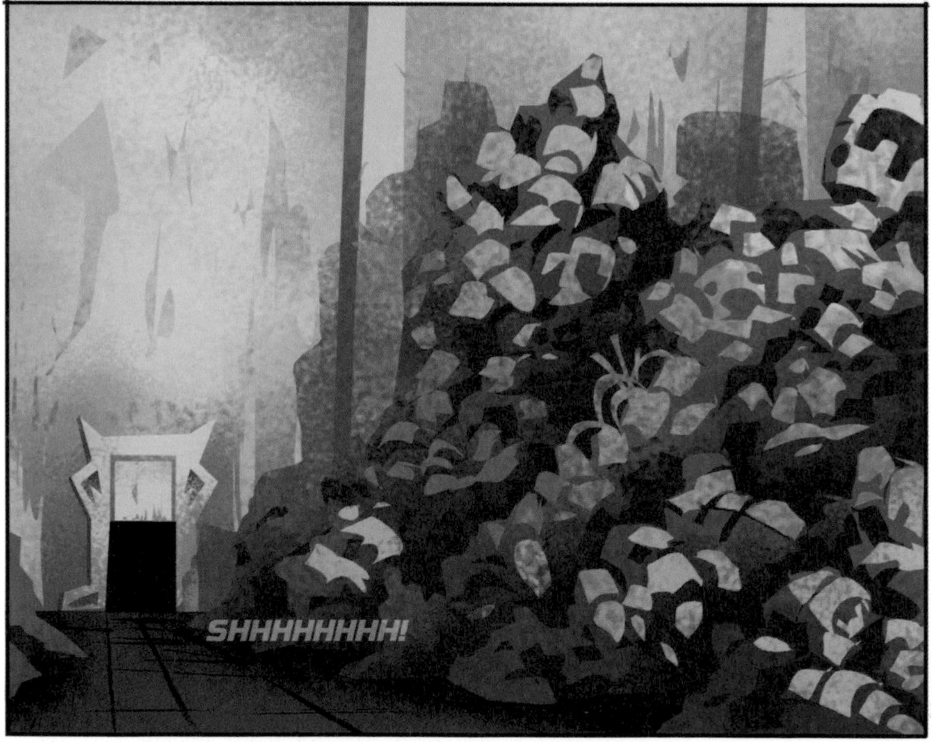
SHHHHHHHH!

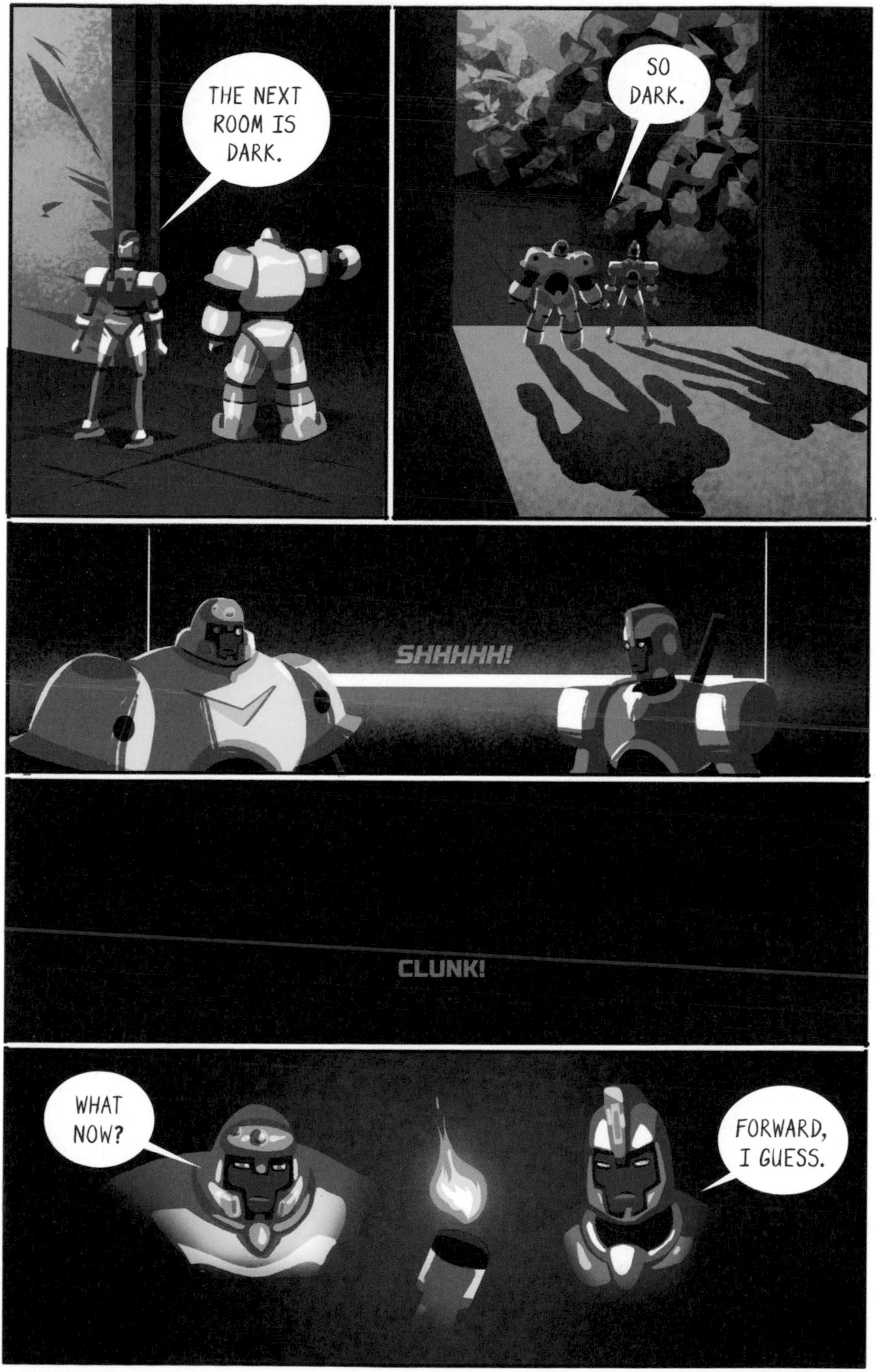
THE NEXT ROOM IS DARK.
SO DARK.
SHHHHH!
CLUNK!
WHAT NOW?
FORWARD, I GUESS.

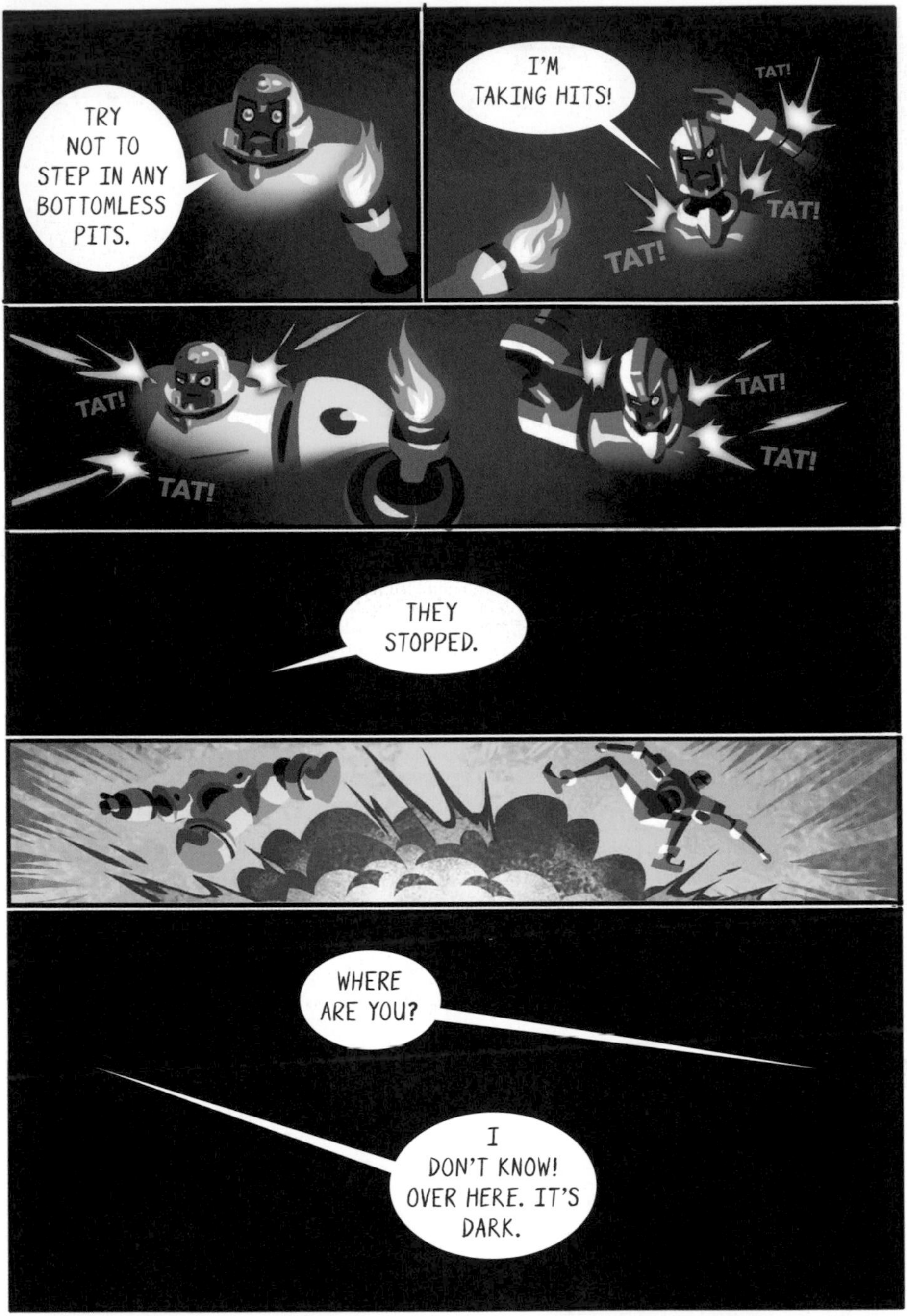
TRY NOT TO STEP IN ANY BOTTOMLESS PITS.
I'M TAKING HITS!
TAT!
TAT!
TAT!
TAT!
TAT!
TAT!
TAT!
THEY STOPPED.
WHERE ARE YOU?
I DON'T KNOW! OVER HERE. IT'S DARK.

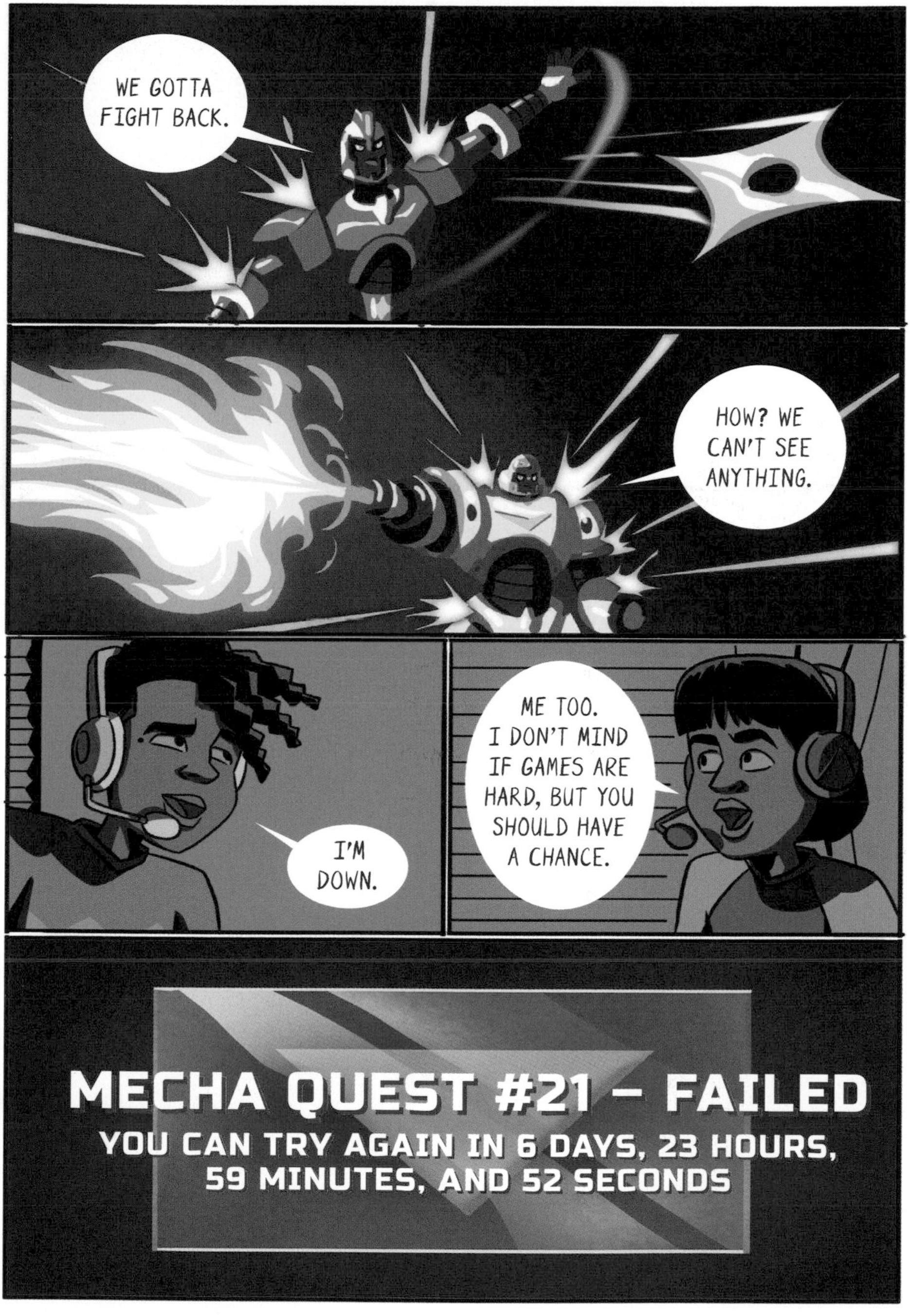
WE GOTTA FIGHT BACK.
HOW? WE CAN'T SEE ANYTHING.
I'M DOWN.
ME TOO. I DON'T MIND IF GAMES ARE HARD, BUT YOU SHOULD HAVE A CHANCE.
MECHA QUEST #21 – FAILED
YOU CAN TRY AGAIN IN 6 DAYS, 23 HOURS, 59 MINUTES, AND 52 SECONDS

CHAPTER 6
DOWN

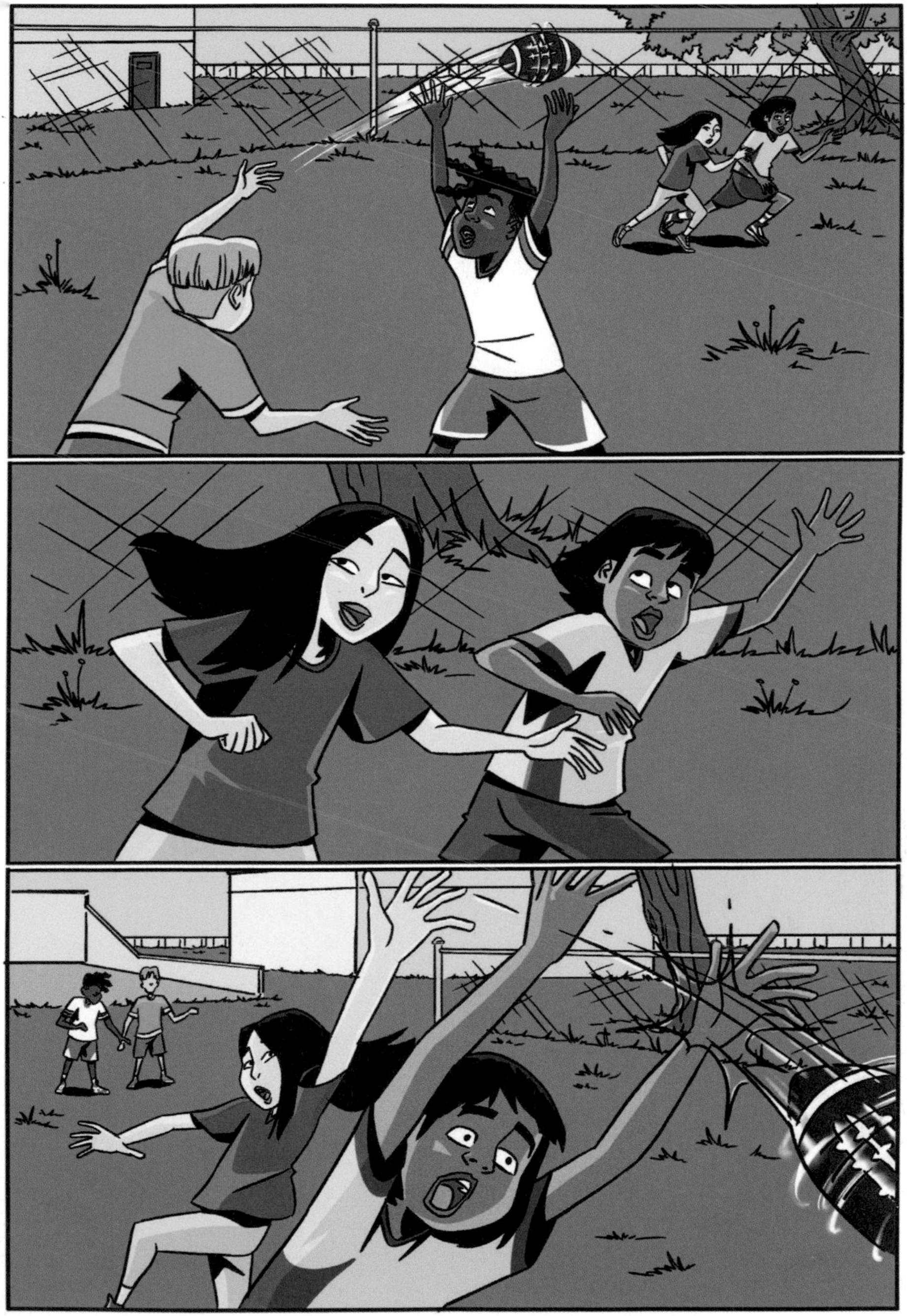

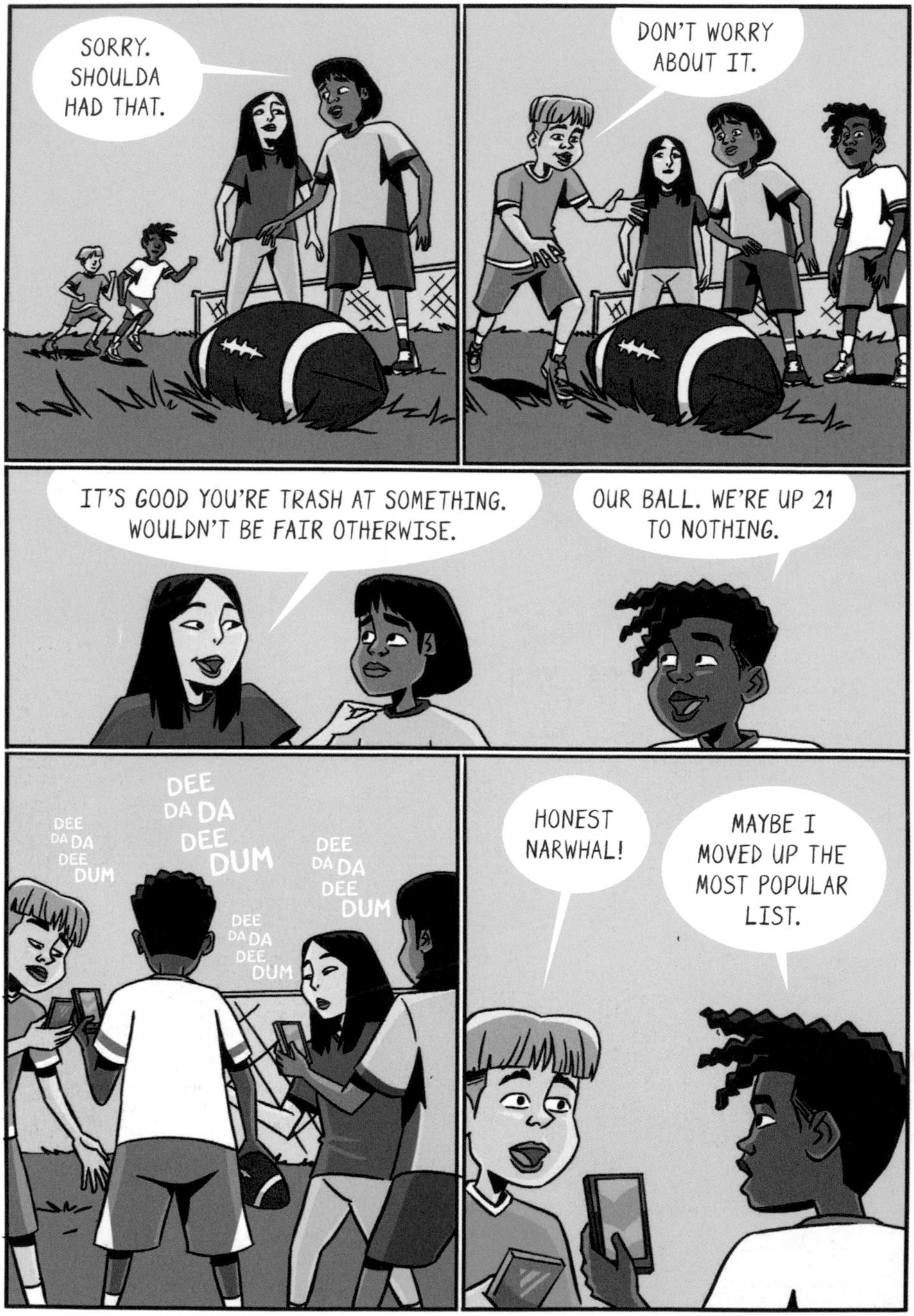
SORRY. SHOULDA HAD THAT.
DON'T WORRY ABOUT IT.
IT'S GOOD YOU'RE TRASH AT SOMETHING. WOULDN'T BE FAIR OTHERWISE.
OUR BALL. WE'RE UP 21 TO NOTHING.
DEE DA DA DEE DUM
DEE DA DA DEE DUM
DEE DA DA DEE DUM
DEE DA DA DEE DUM
HONEST NARWHAL!
MAYBE I MOVED UP THE MOST POPULAR LIST.

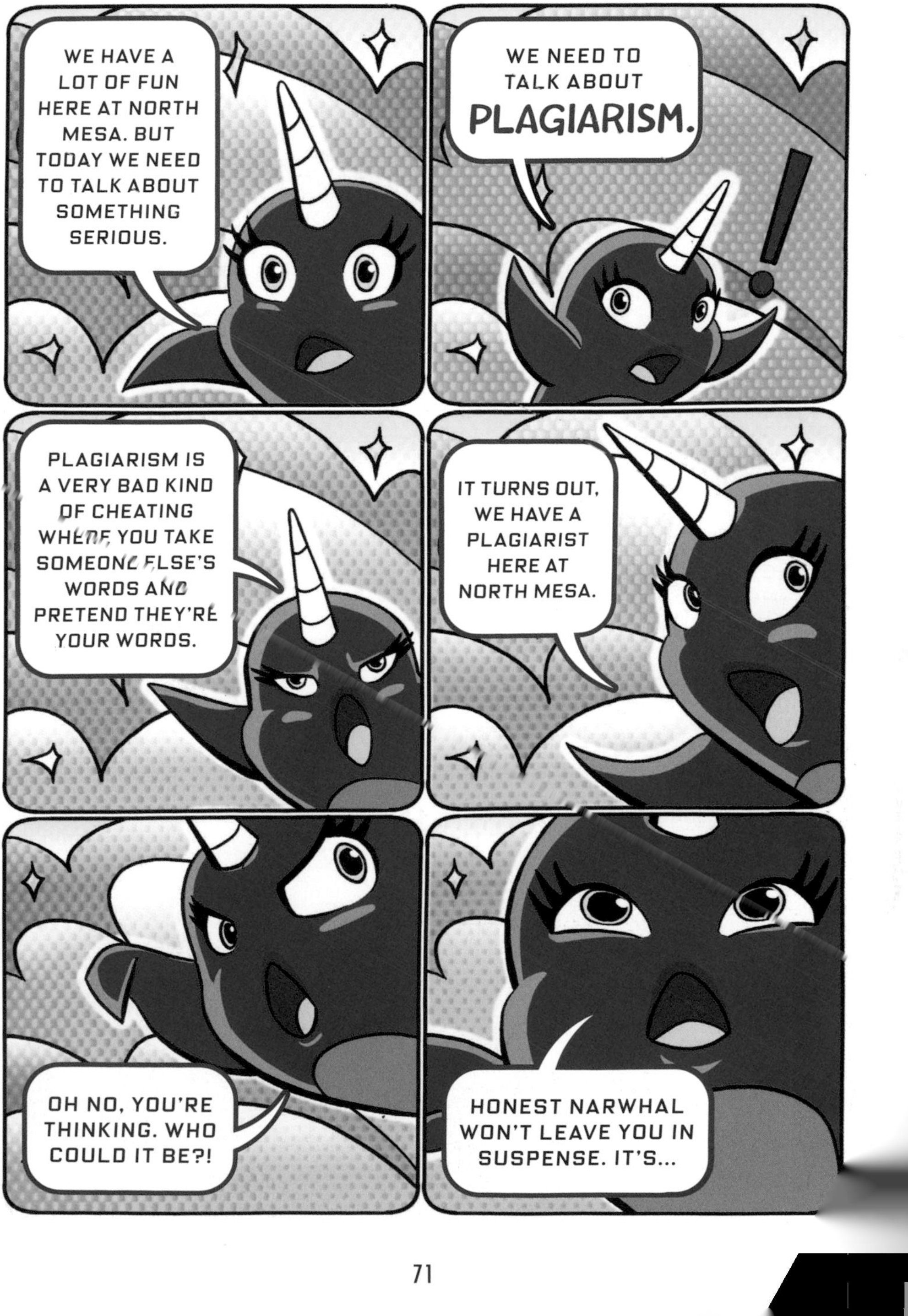

WE HAVE A LOT OF FUN HERE AT NORTH MESA. BUT TODAY WE NEED TO TALK ABOUT SOMETHING SERIOUS.
WE NEED TO TALK ABOUT PLAGIARISM.
!
PLAGIARISM IS A VERY BAD KIND OF CHEATING WHERE YOU TAKE SOMEONE ELSE'S WORDS AND PRETEND THEY'RE YOUR WORDS.
IT TURNS OUT, WE HAVE A PLAGIARIST HERE AT NORTH MESA.
OH NO, YOU'RE THINKING. WHO COULD IT BE?!
HONEST NARWHAL WON'T LEAVE YOU IN SUSPENSE. IT'S...

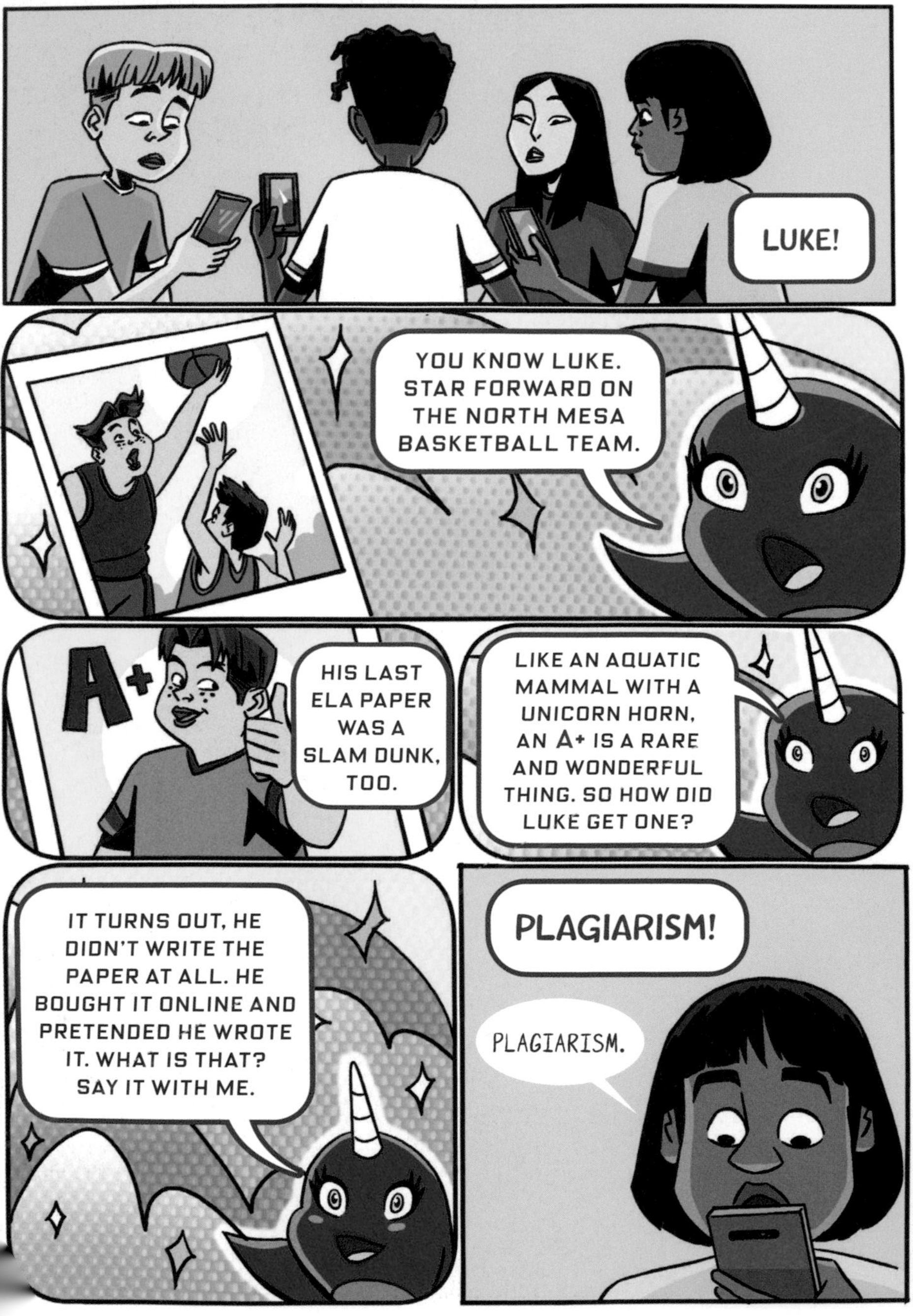
LUKE!
YOU KNOW LUKE. STAR FORWARD ON THE NORTH MESA BASKETBALL TEAM.
A+
HIS LAST ELA PAPER WAS A SLAM DUNK, TOO.
LIKE AN AQUATIC MAMMAL WITH A UNICORN HORN, AN A+ IS A RARE AND WONDERFUL THING. SO HOW DID LUKE GET ONE?
IT TURNS OUT, HE DIDN'T WRITE THE PAPER AT ALL. HE BOUGHT IT ONLINE AND PRETENDED HE WROTE IT. WHAT IS THAT? SAY IT WITH ME.
PLAGIARISM!
PLAGIARISM.

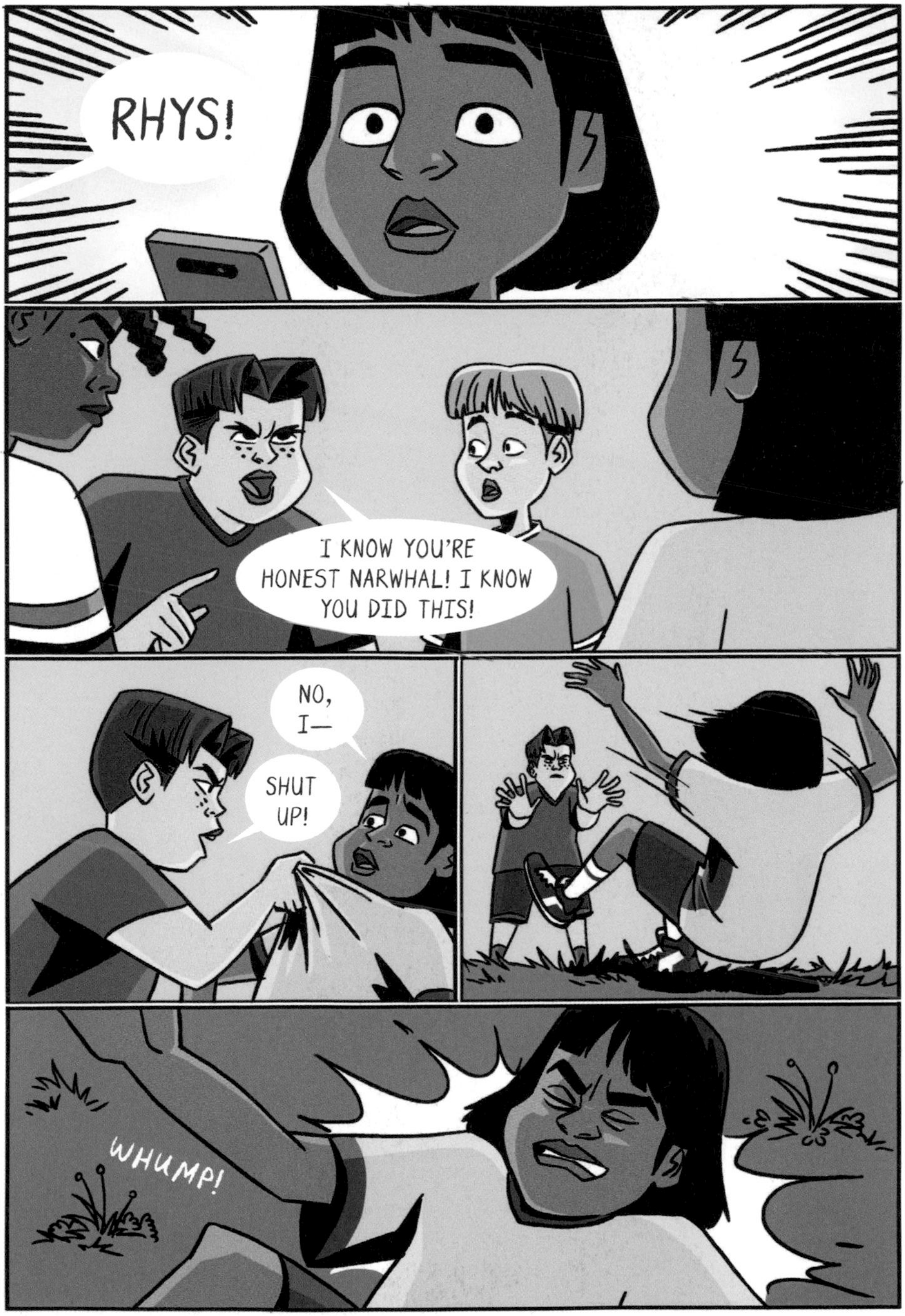
RHYS!
I KNOW YOU'RE HONEST NARWHAL! I KNOW YOU DID THIS!
NO, I—
SHUT UP!
WHUMP!

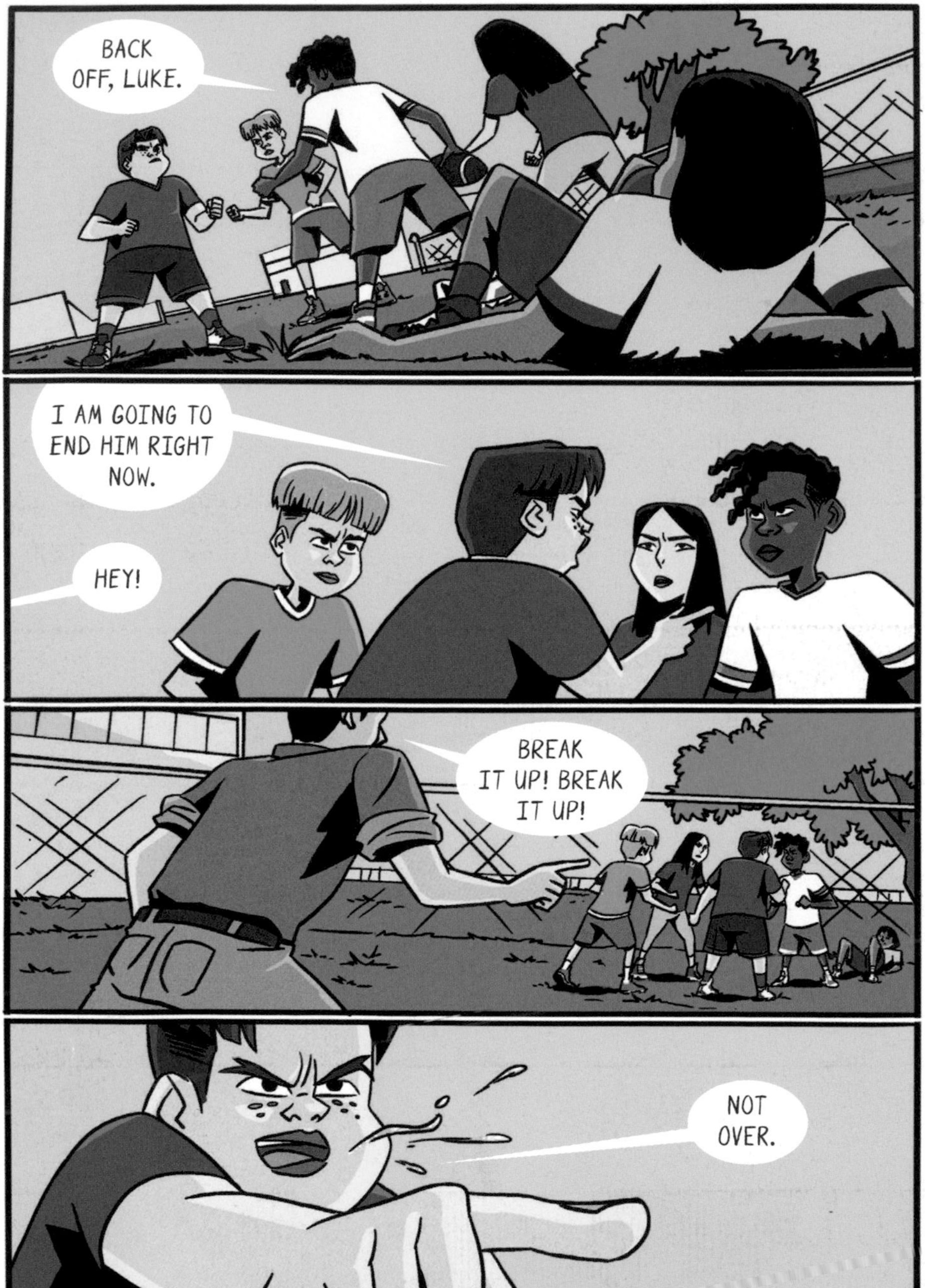
BACK OFF, LUKE.
I AM GOING TO END HIM RIGHT NOW.
HEY!
BREAK IT UP! BREAK IT UP!
NOT OVER.

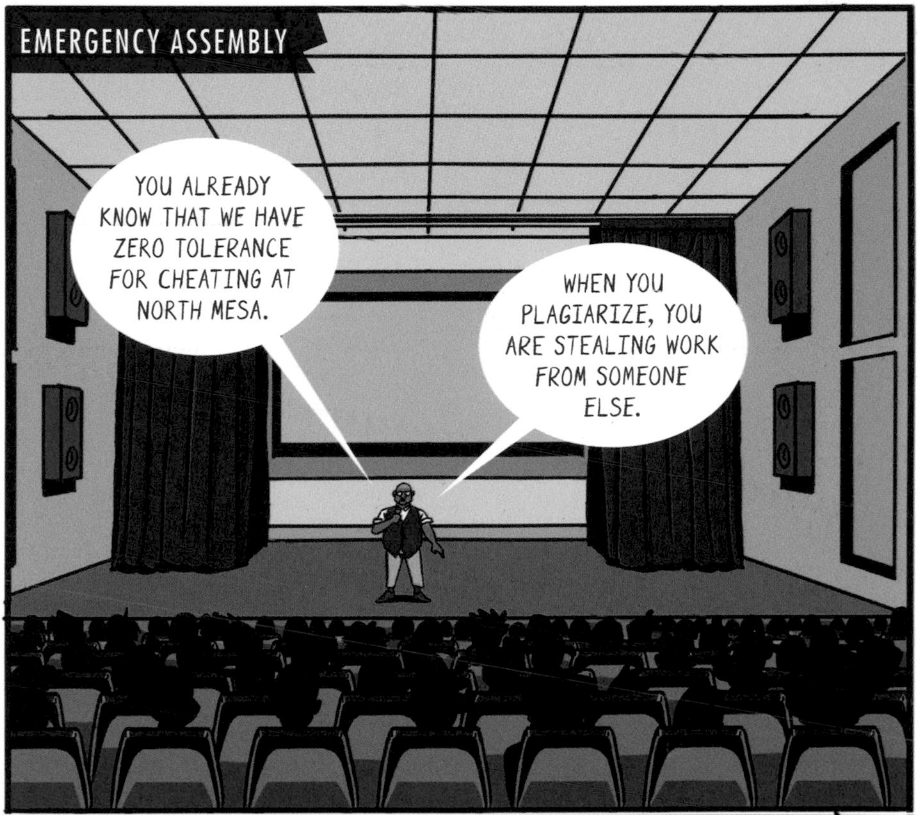
EMERGENCY ASSEMBLY
YOU ALREADY KNOW THAT WE HAVE ZERO TOLERANCE FOR CHEATING AT NORTH MESA.
WHEN YOU PLAGIARIZE, YOU ARE STEALING WORK FROM SOMEONE ELSE.

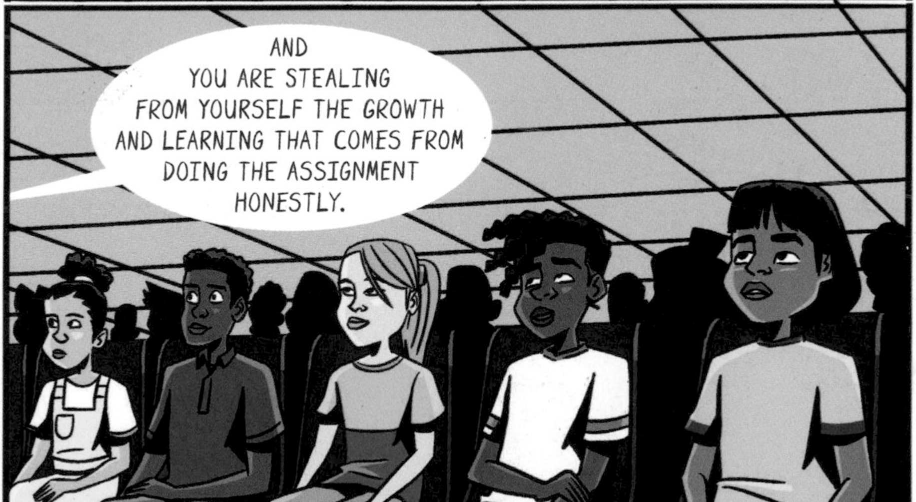
AND YOU ARE STEALING FROM YOURSELF THE GROWTH AND LEARNING THAT COMES FROM DOING THE ASSIGNMENT HONESTLY.

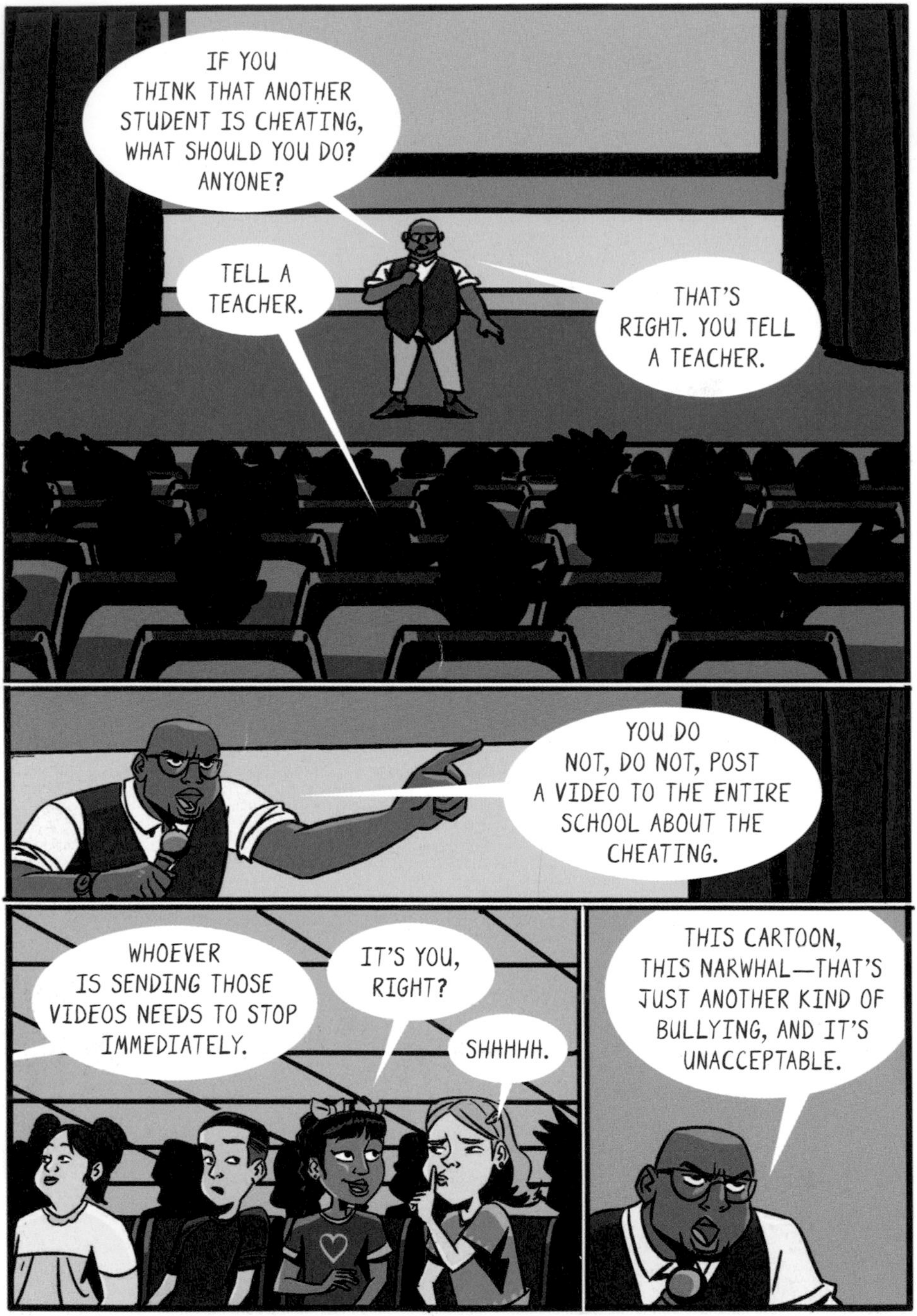
IF YOU THINK THAT ANOTHER STUDENT IS CHEATING, WHAT SHOULD YOU DO? ANYONE?
TELL A TEACHER.
THAT'S RIGHT. YOU TELL A TEACHER.
YOU DO NOT, DO NOT, POST A VIDEO TO THE ENTIRE SCHOOL ABOUT THE CHEATING.
WHOEVER IS SENDING THOSE VIDEOS NEEDS TO STOP IMMEDIATELY.
IT'S YOU, RIGHT?
SHHHHH.
THIS CARTOON, THIS NARWHAL—THAT'S JUST ANOTHER KIND OF BULLYING, AND IT'S UNACCEPTABLE.

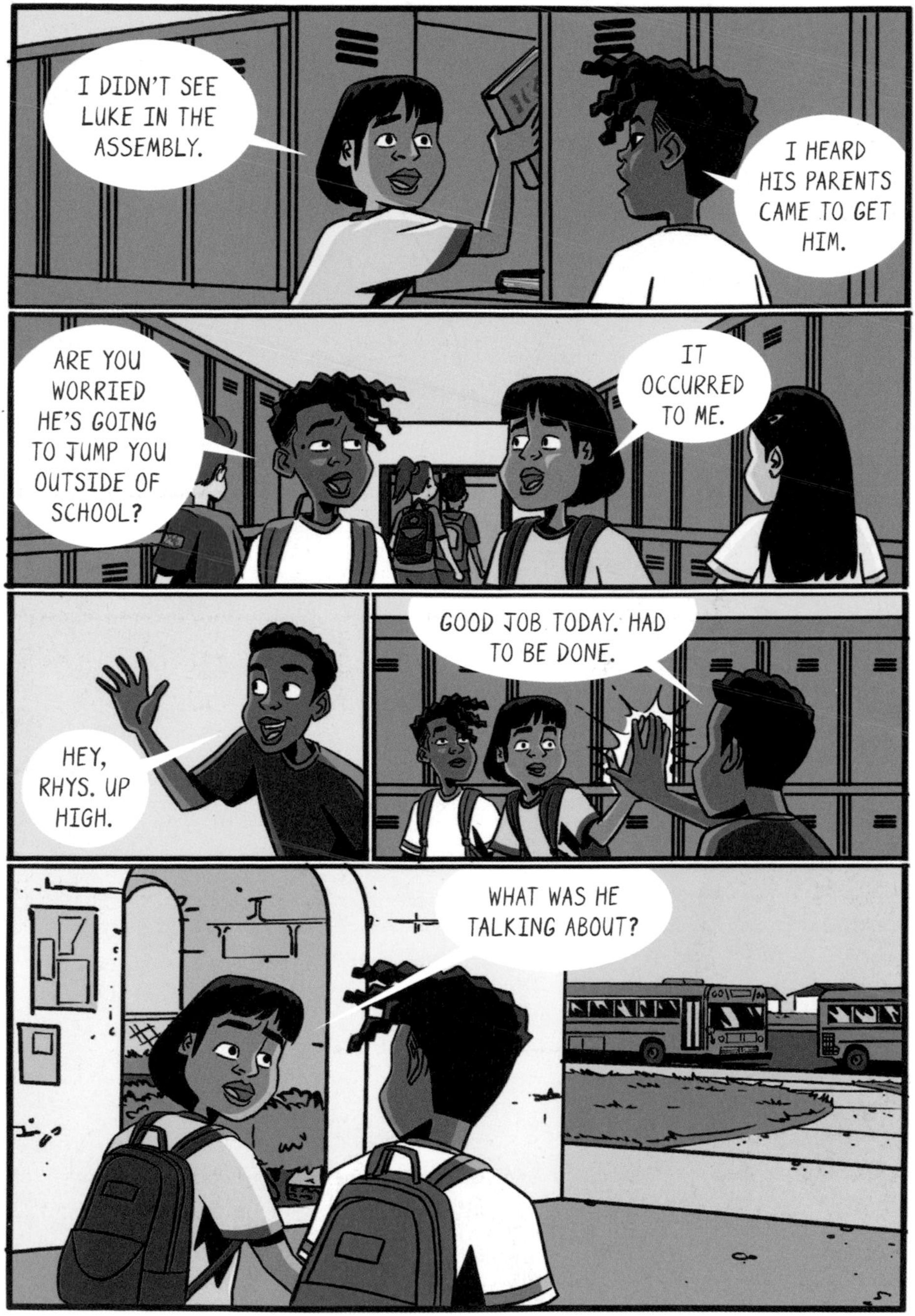
I DIDN'T SEE LUKE IN THE ASSEMBLY.
I HEARD HIS PARENTS CAME TO GET HIM.
ARE YOU WORRIED HE'S GOING TO JUMP YOU OUTSIDE OF SCHOOL?
IT OCCURRED TO ME.
HEY, RHYS. UP HIGH.
GOOD JOB TODAY. HAD TO BE DONE.
WHAT WAS HE TALKING ABOUT?

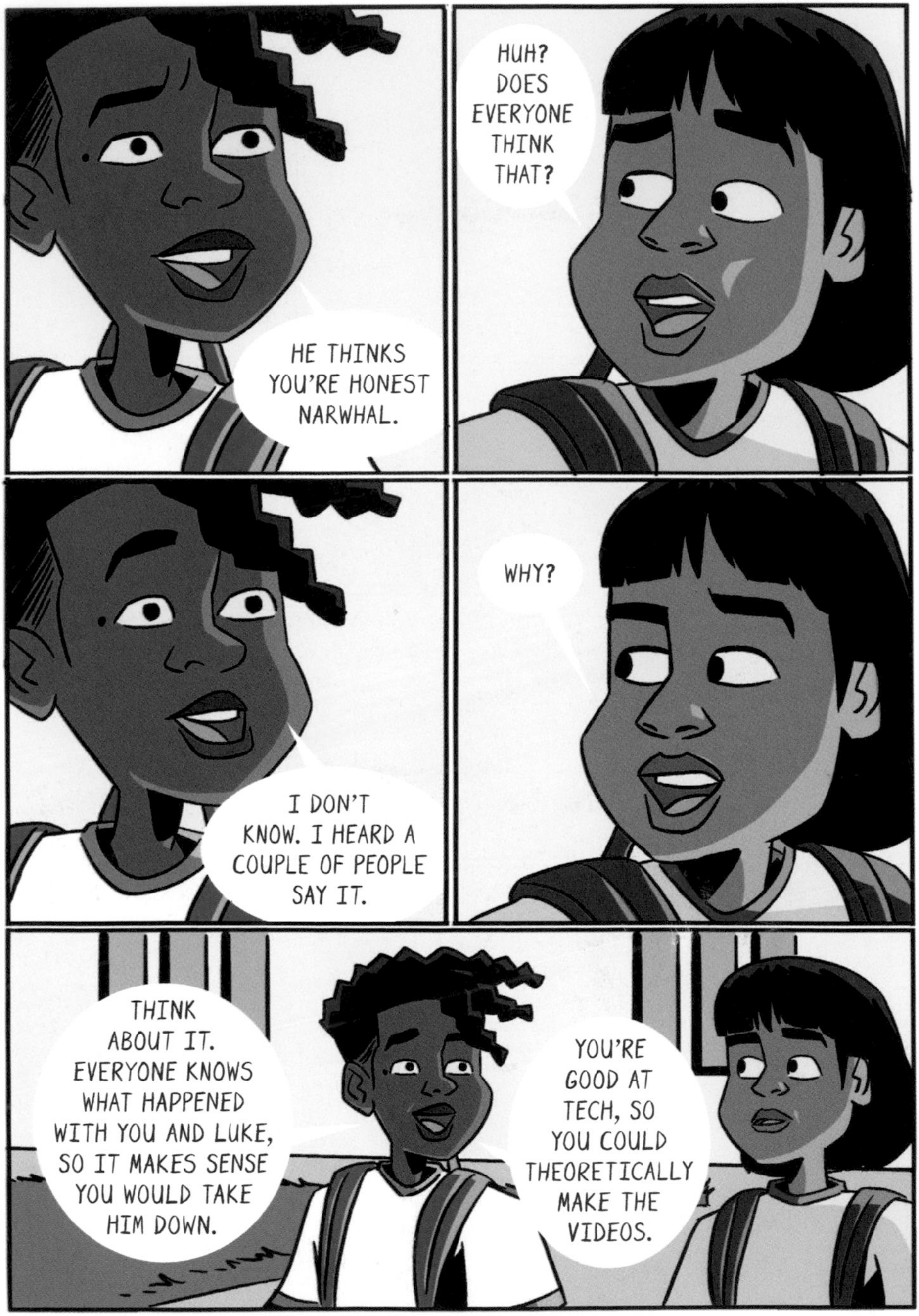
HE THINKS YOU'RE HONEST NARWHAL.
HUH? DOES EVERYONE THINK THAT?
I DON'T KNOW. I HEARD A COUPLE OF PEOPLE SAY IT.
WHY?
THINK ABOUT IT. EVERYONE KNOWS WHAT HAPPENED WITH YOU AND LUKE, SO IT MAKES SENSE YOU WOULD TAKE HIM DOWN.
YOU'RE GOOD AT TECH, SO YOU COULD THEORETICALLY MAKE THE VIDEOS.

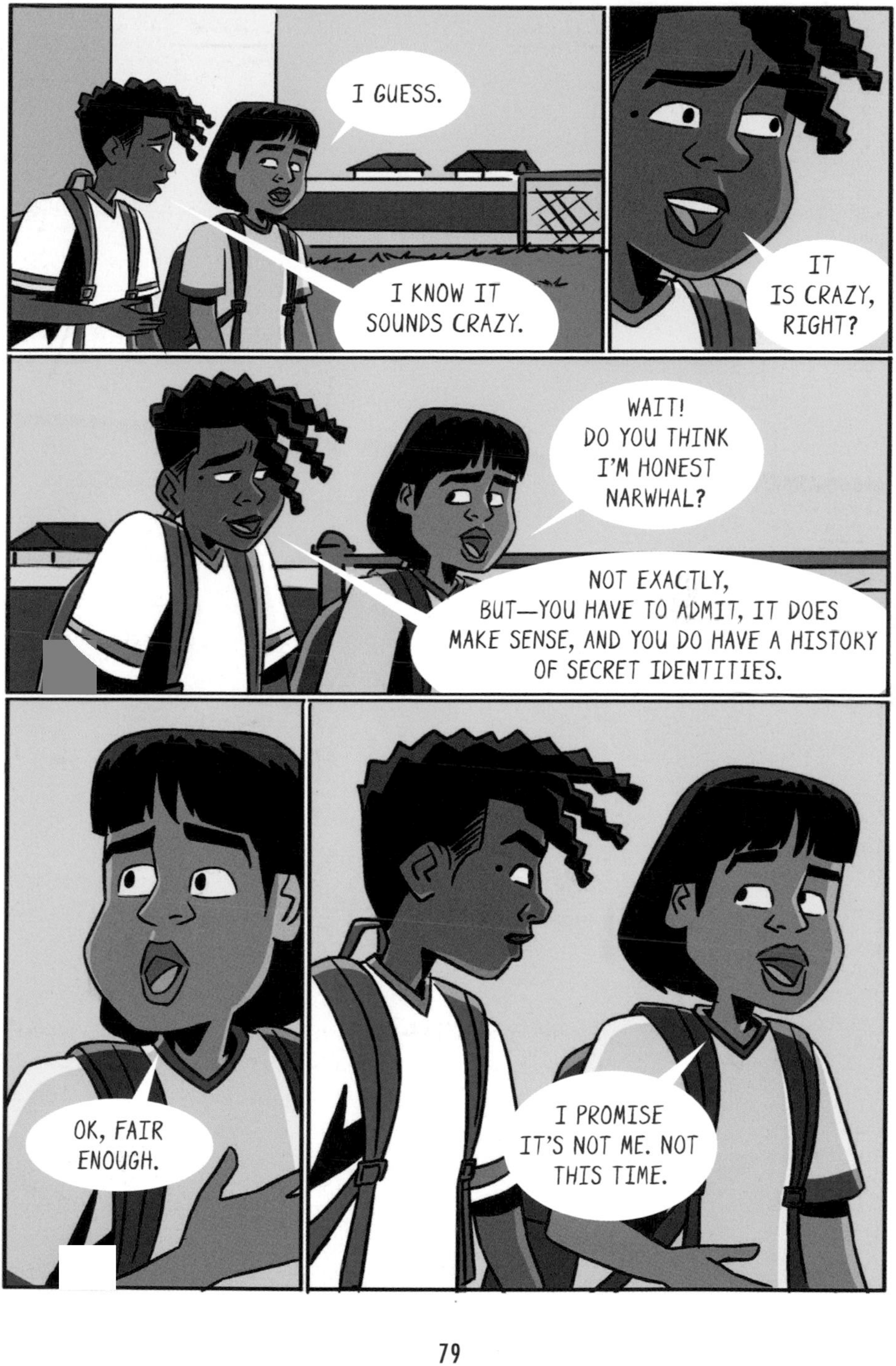
I GUESS.
I KNOW IT SOUNDS CRAZY.
IT IS CRAZY, RIGHT?
WAIT! DO YOU THINK I'M HONEST NARWHAL?
NOT EXACTLY, BUT—YOU HAVE TO ADMIT, IT DOES MAKE SENSE, AND YOU DO HAVE A HISTORY OF SECRET IDENTITIES.
OK, FAIR ENOUGH.
I PROMISE IT'S NOT ME. NOT THIS TIME.

CHAPTER 7
WARRIOR KINGS

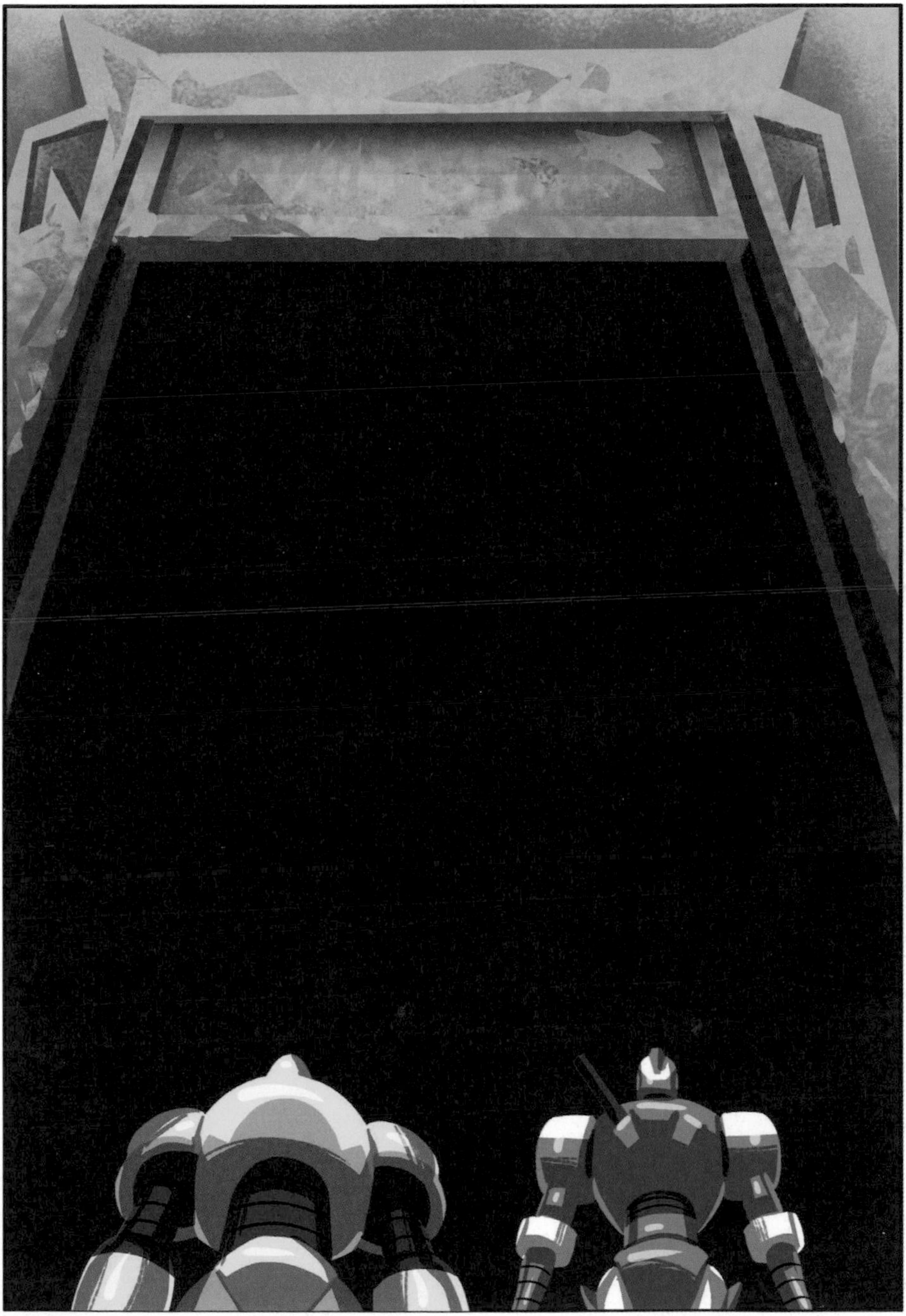

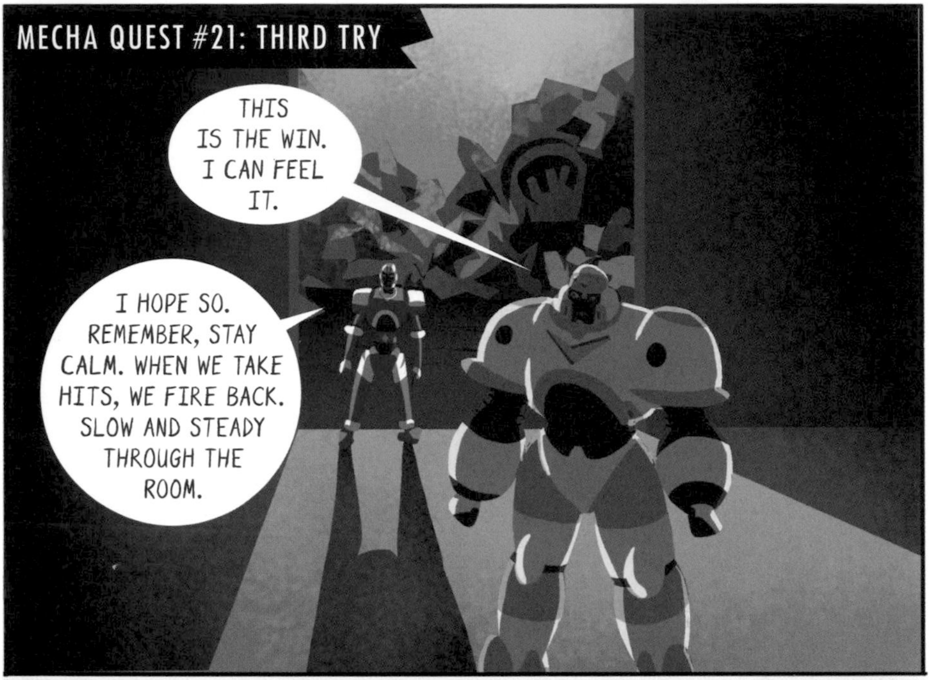
MECHA QUEST #21: THIRD TRY
THIS IS THE WIN. I CAN FEEL IT.
I HOPE SO. REMEMBER, STAY CALM. WHEN WE TAKE HITS, WE FIRE BACK. SLOW AND STEADY THROUGH THE ROOM.

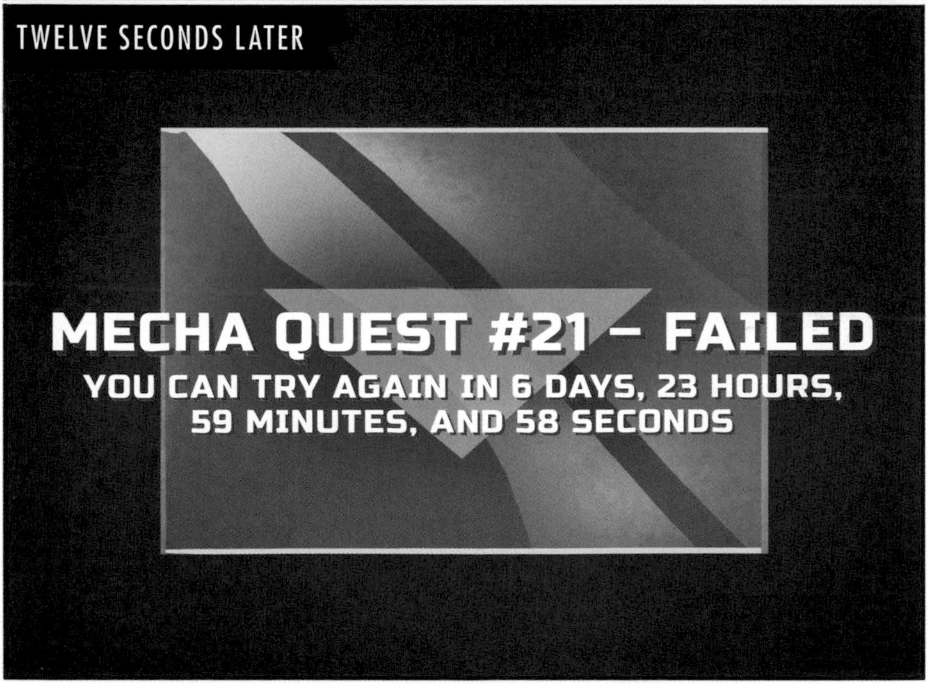
TWELVE SECONDS LATER
MECHA QUEST #21 – FAILED
YOU CAN TRY AGAIN IN 6 DAYS, 23 HOURS, 59 MINUTES, AND 58 SECONDS

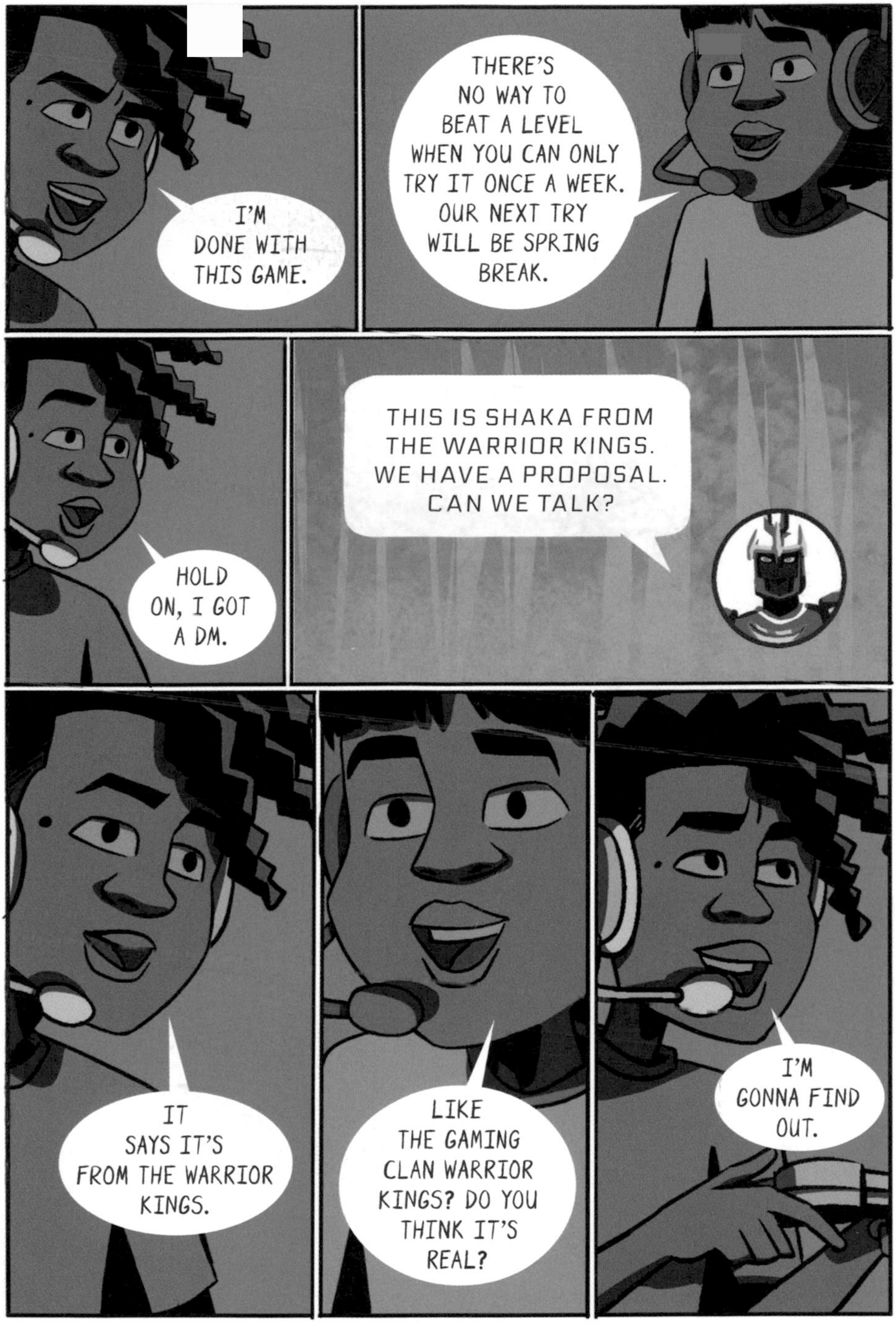
I'M DONE WITH THIS GAME.
THERE'S NO WAY TO BEAT A LEVEL WHEN YOU CAN ONLY TRY IT ONCE A WEEK. OUR NEXT TRY WILL BE SPRING BREAK.
HOLD ON, I GOT A DM.
THIS IS SHAKA FROM THE WARRIOR KINGS. WE HAVE A PROPOSAL. CAN WE TALK?
IT SAYS IT'S FROM THE WARRIOR KINGS.
LIKE THE GAMING CLAN WARRIOR KINGS? DO YOU THINK IT'S REAL?
I'M GONNA FIND OUT.

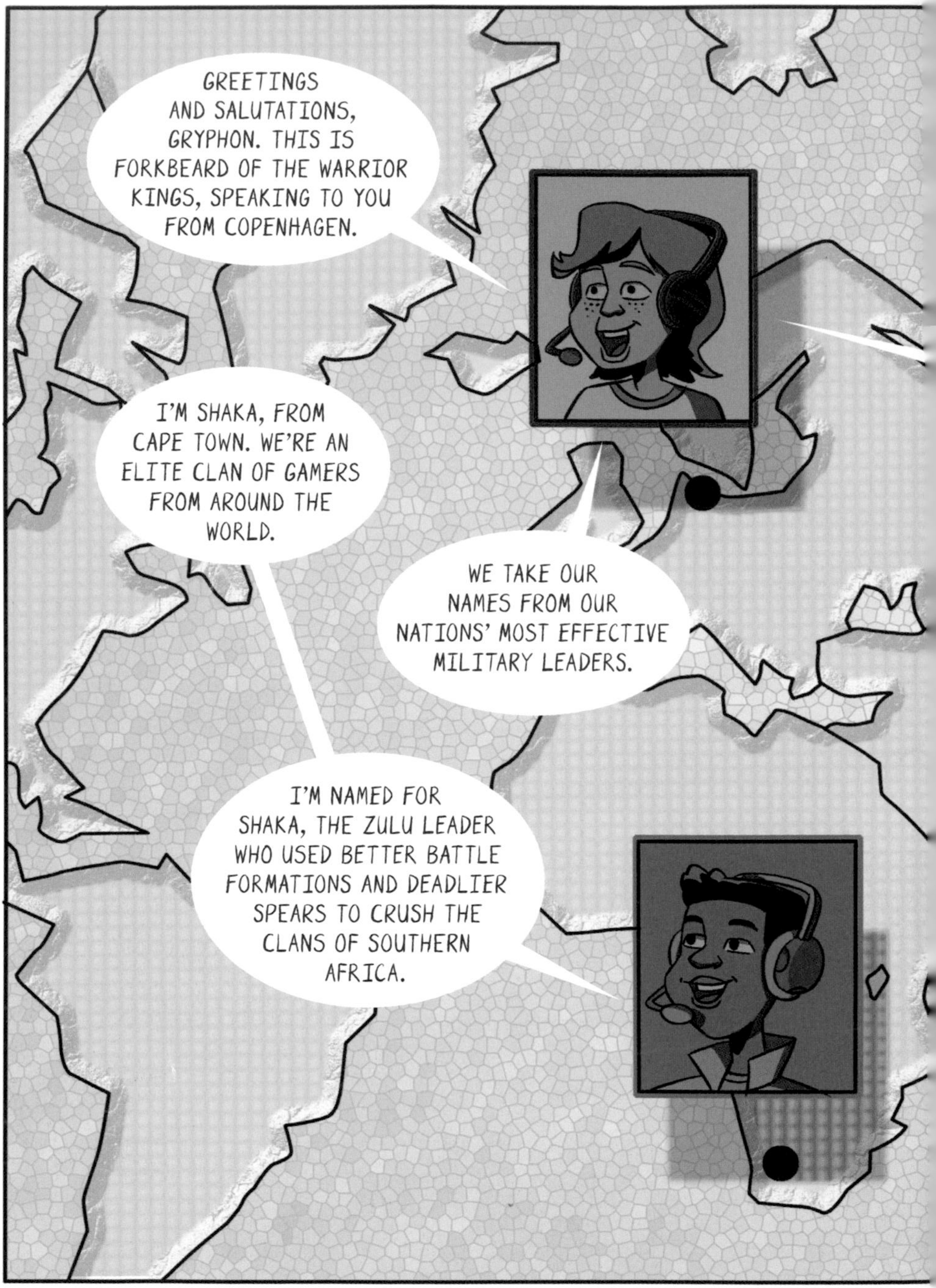
GREETINGS AND SALUTATIONS, GRYPHON. THIS IS FORKBEARD OF THE WARRIOR KINGS, SPEAKING TO YOU FROM COPENHAGEN.
I'M SHAKA, FROM CAPE TOWN. WE'RE AN ELITE CLAN OF GAMERS FROM AROUND THE WORLD.
WE TAKE OUR NAMES FROM OUR NATIONS' MOST EFFECTIVE MILITARY LEADERS.
I'M NAMED FOR SHAKA, THE ZULU LEADER WHO USED BETTER BATTLE FORMATIONS AND DEADLIER SPEARS TO CRUSH THE CLANS OF SOUTHERN AFRICA.

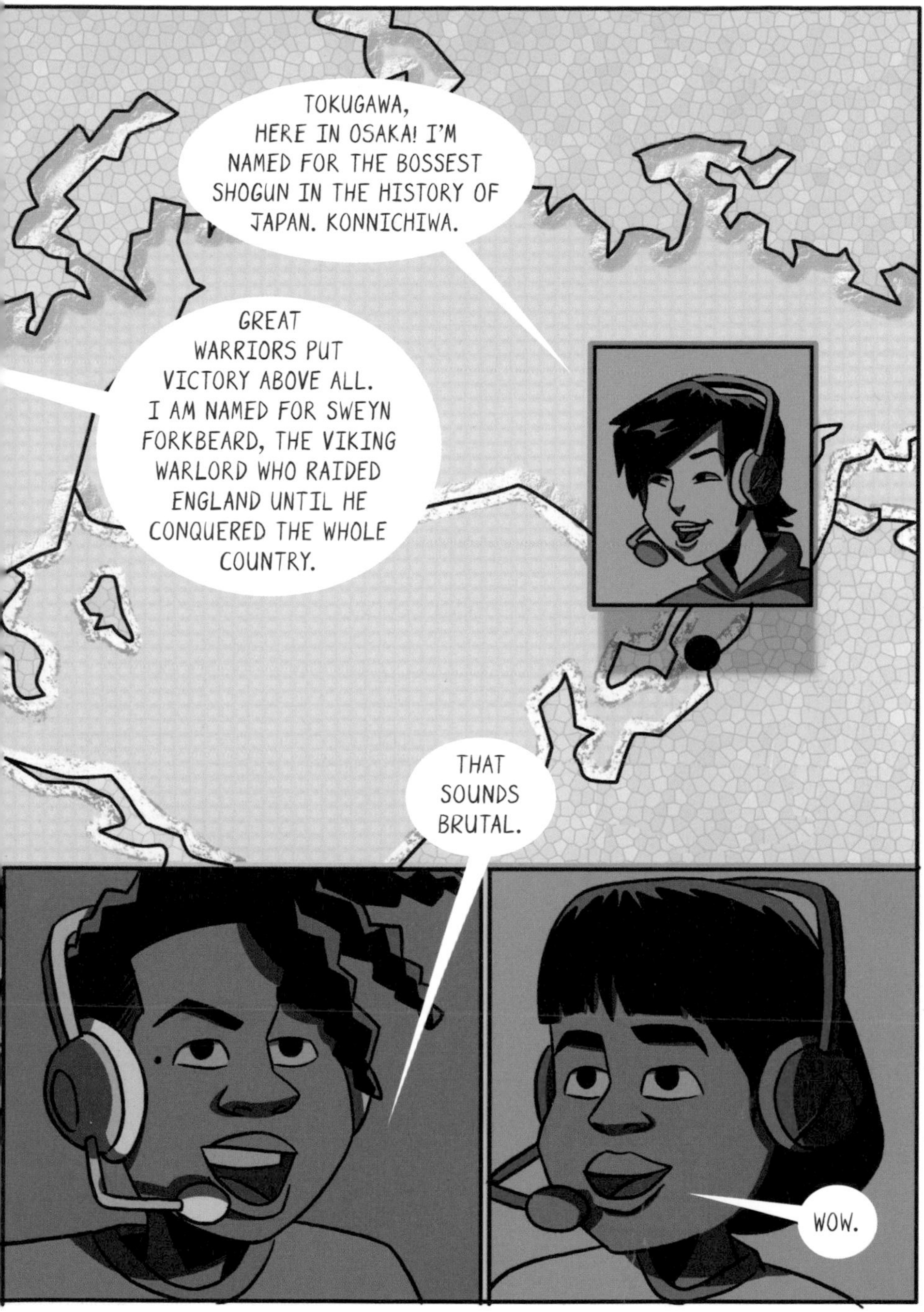
TOKUGAWA, HERE IN OSAKA! I'M NAMED FOR THE BOSSEST SHOGUN IN THE HISTORY OF JAPAN. KONNICHIWA.
GREAT WARRIORS PUT VICTORY ABOVE ALL. I AM NAMED FOR SWEYN FORKBEARD, THE VIKING WARLORD WHO RAIDED ENGLAND UNTIL HE CONQUERED THE WHOLE COUNTRY.
THAT SOUNDS BRUTAL.
WOW.

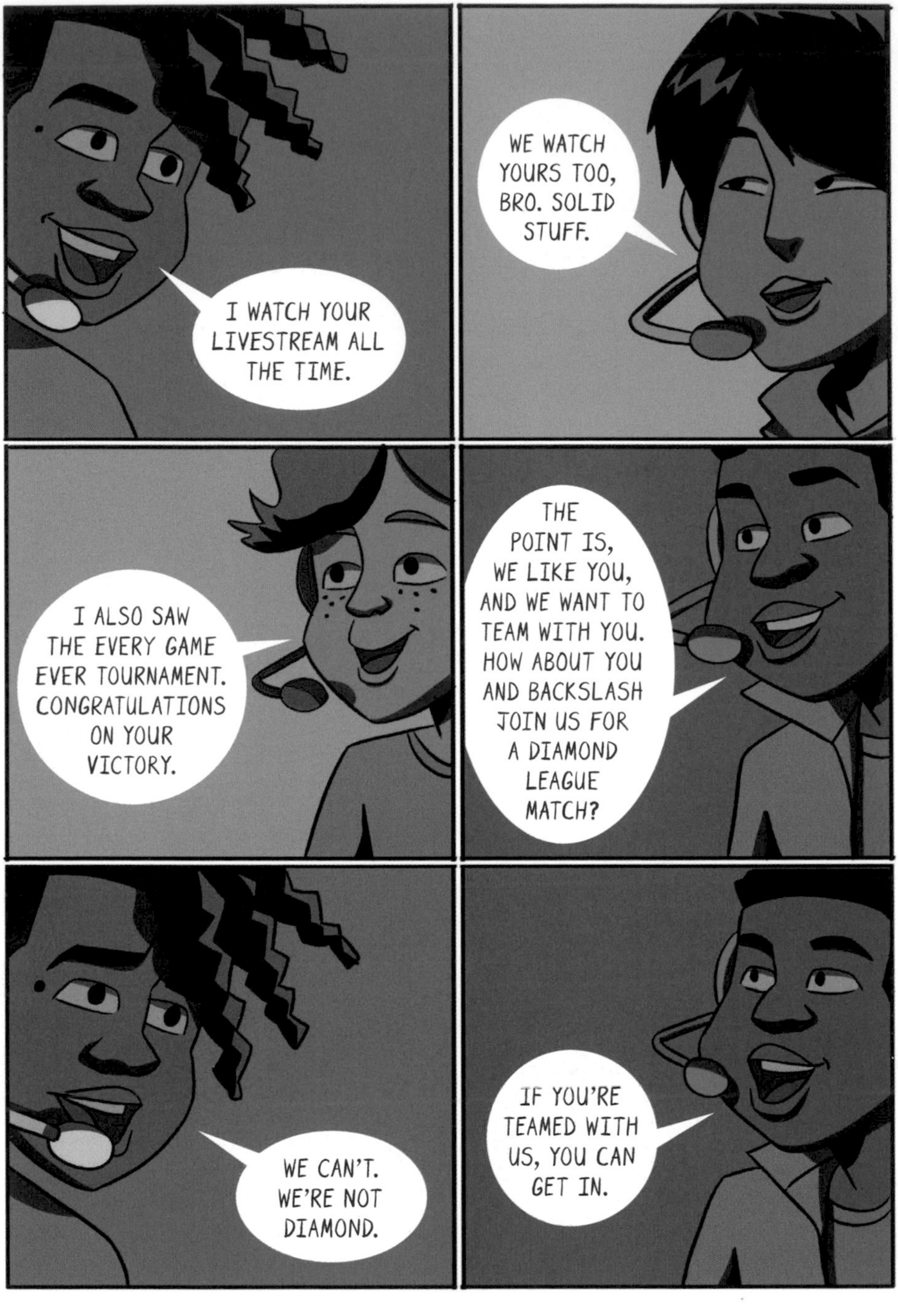
I WATCH YOUR LIVESTREAM ALL THE TIME.
WE WATCH YOURS TOO, BRO. SOLID STUFF.
I ALSO SAW THE EVERY GAME EVER TOURNAMENT. CONGRATULATIONS ON YOUR VICTORY.
THE POINT IS, WE LIKE YOU, AND WE WANT TO TEAM WITH YOU. HOW ABOUT YOU AND BACKSLASH JOIN US FOR A DIAMOND LEAGUE MATCH?
WE CAN'T. WE'RE NOT DIAMOND.
IF YOU'RE TEAMED WITH US, YOU CAN GET IN.

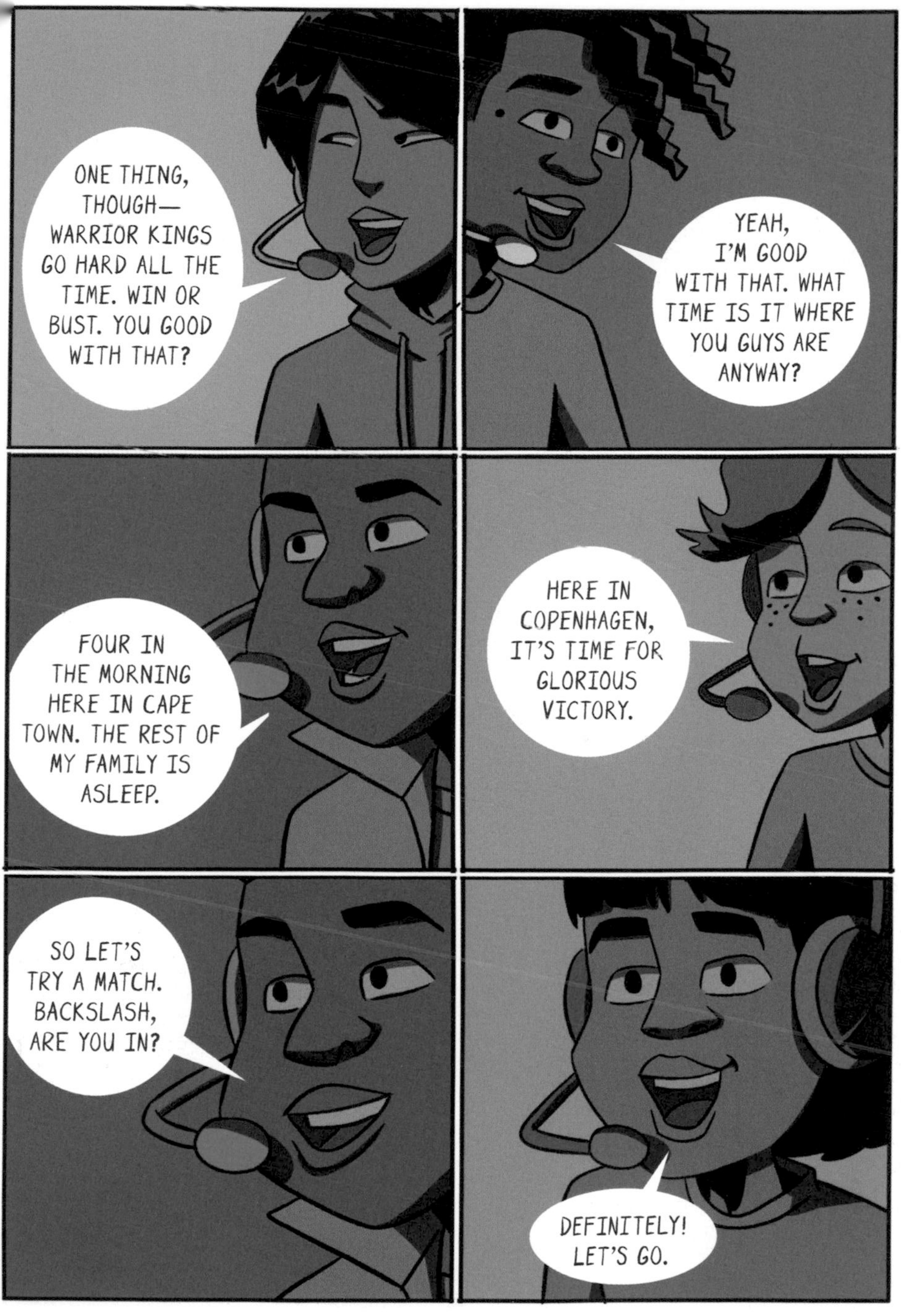
ONE THING, THOUGH— WARRIOR KINGS GO HARD ALL THE TIME. WIN OR BUST. YOU GOOD WITH THAT?
YEAH, I'M GOOD WITH THAT. WHAT TIME IS IT WHERE YOU GUYS ARE ANYWAY?
FOUR IN THE MORNING HERE IN CAPE TOWN. THE REST OF MY FAMILY IS ASLEEP.
HERE IN COPENHAGEN, IT'S TIME FOR GLORIOUS VICTORY.
SO LET'S TRY A MATCH. BACKSLASH, ARE YOU IN?
DEFINITELY! LET'S GO.

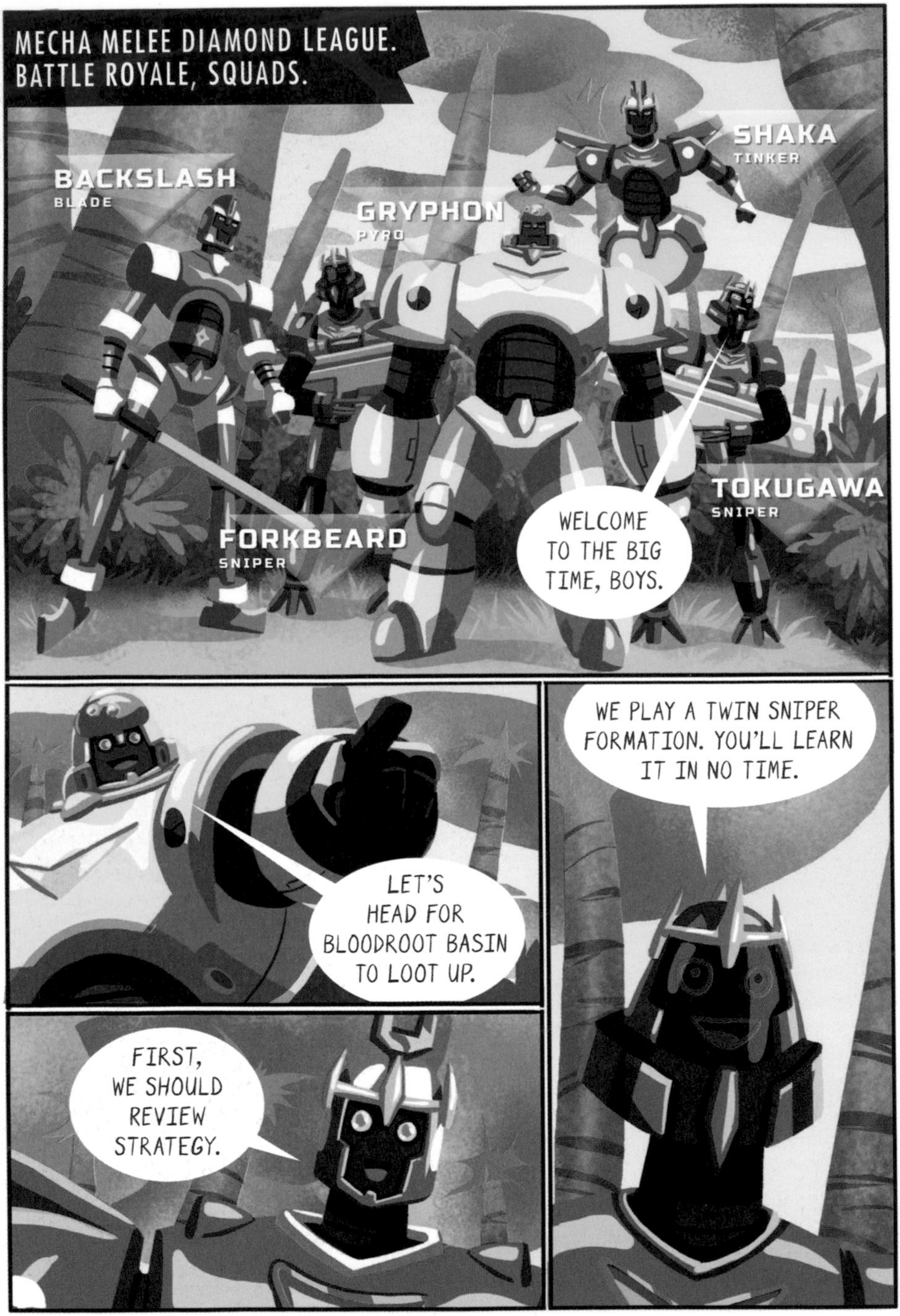
MECHA MELEE DIAMOND LEAGUE.
BATTLE ROYALE, SQUADS.
BACKSLASH
BLADE
GRYPHON
PYRO
SHAKA
TINKER
FORKBEARD
SNIPER
TOKUGAWA
SNIPER
WELCOME TO THE BIG TIME, BOYS.
LET'S HEAD FOR BLOODROOT BASIN TO LOOT UP.
WE PLAY A TWIN SNIPER FORMATION. YOU'LL LEARN IT IN NO TIME.
FIRST, WE SHOULD REVIEW STRATEGY.

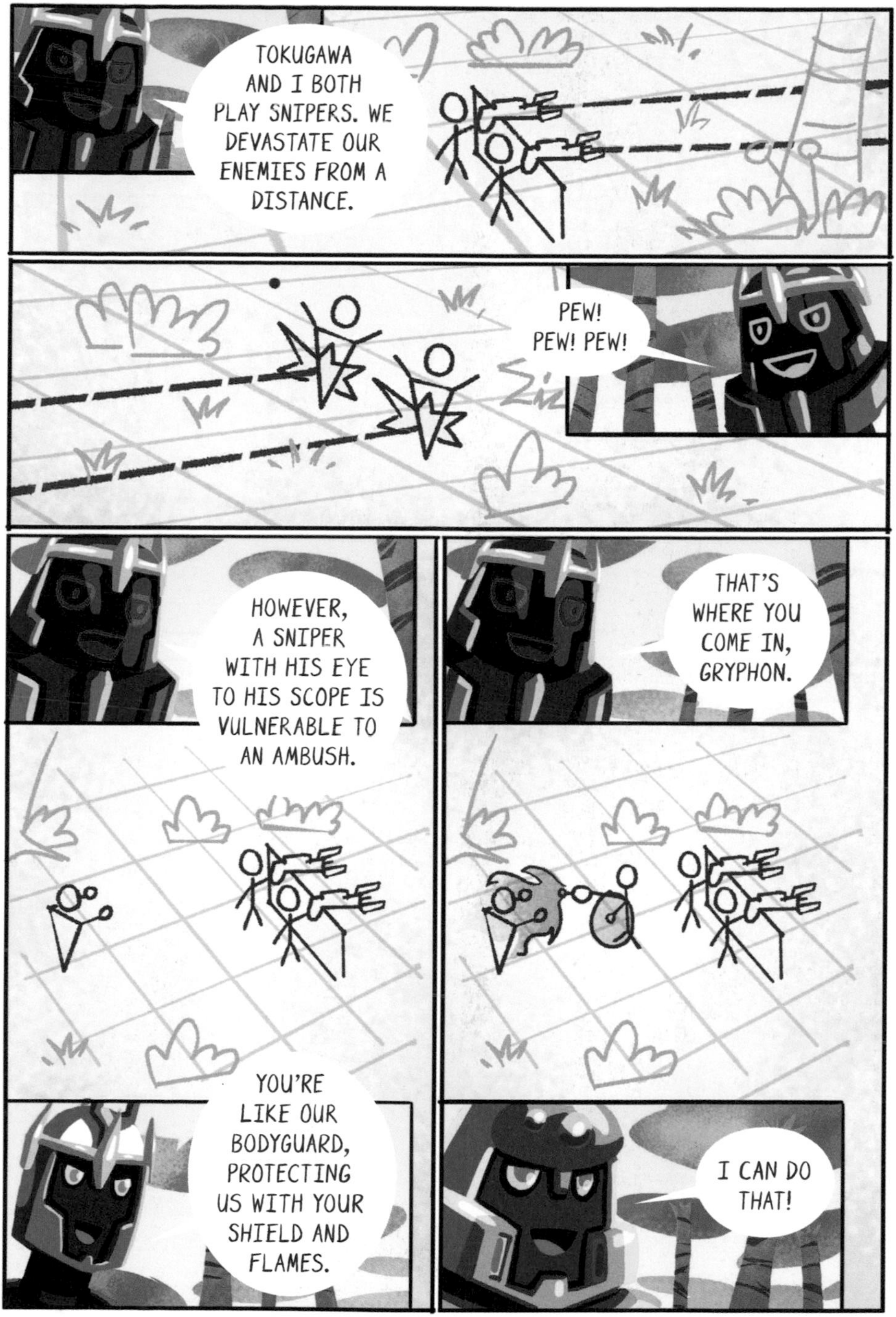
TOKUGAWA AND I BOTH PLAY SNIPERS. WE DEVASTATE OUR ENEMIES FROM A DISTANCE.
PEW! PEW! PEW!
HOWEVER, A SNIPER WITH HIS EYE TO HIS SCOPE IS VULNERABLE TO AN AMBUSH.
THAT'S WHERE YOU COME IN, GRYPHON.
YOU'RE LIKE OUR BODYGUARD, PROTECTING US WITH YOUR SHIELD AND FLAMES.
I CAN DO THAT!

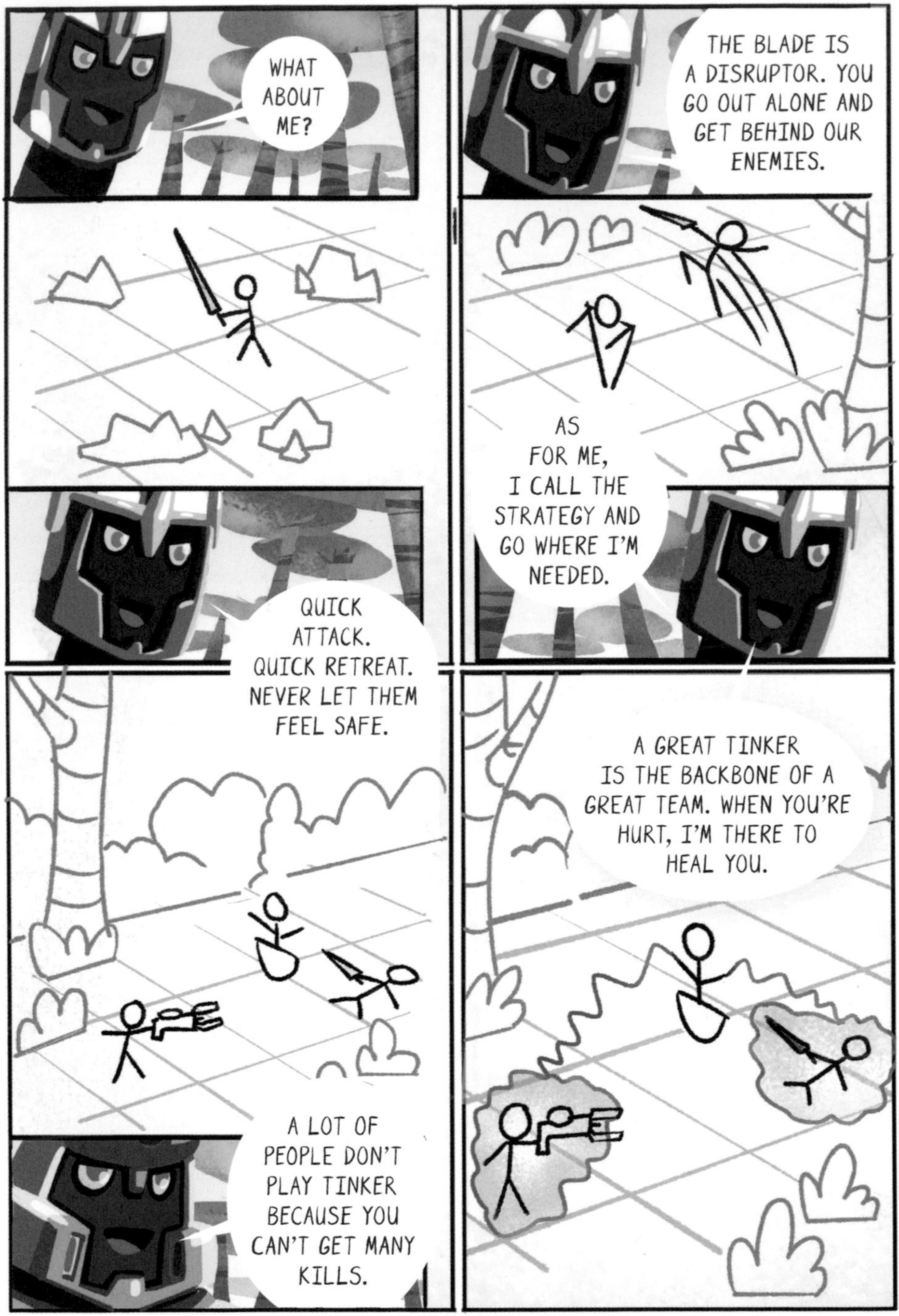
WHAT ABOUT ME?
THE BLADE IS A DISRUPTOR. YOU GO OUT ALONE AND GET BEHIND OUR ENEMIES.
QUICK ATTACK. QUICK RETREAT. NEVER LET THEM FEEL SAFE.
AS FOR ME, I CALL THE STRATEGY AND GO WHERE I'M NEEDED.
A LOT OF PEOPLE DON'T PLAY TINKER BECAUSE YOU CAN'T GET MANY KILLS.
A GREAT TINKER IS THE BACKBONE OF A GREAT TEAM. WHEN YOU'RE HURT, I'M THERE TO HEAL YOU.

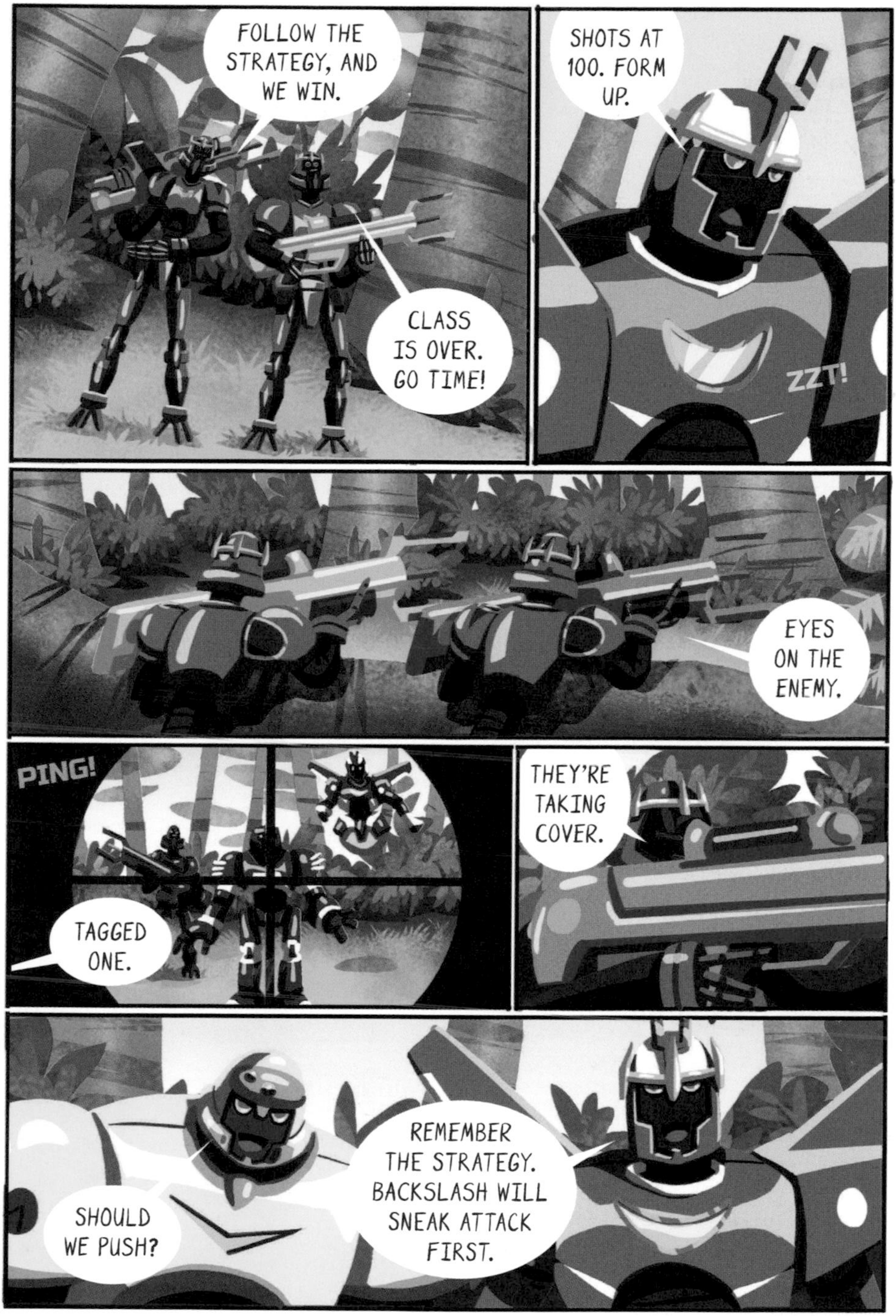
FOLLOW THE STRATEGY, AND WE WIN.
CLASS IS OVER. GO TIME!
SHOTS AT 100. FORM UP.
ZZT!
EYES ON THE ENEMY.
PING!
TAGGED ONE.
THEY'RE TAKING COVER.
SHOULD WE PUSH?
REMEMBER THE STRATEGY. BACKSLASH WILL SNEAK ATTACK FIRST.

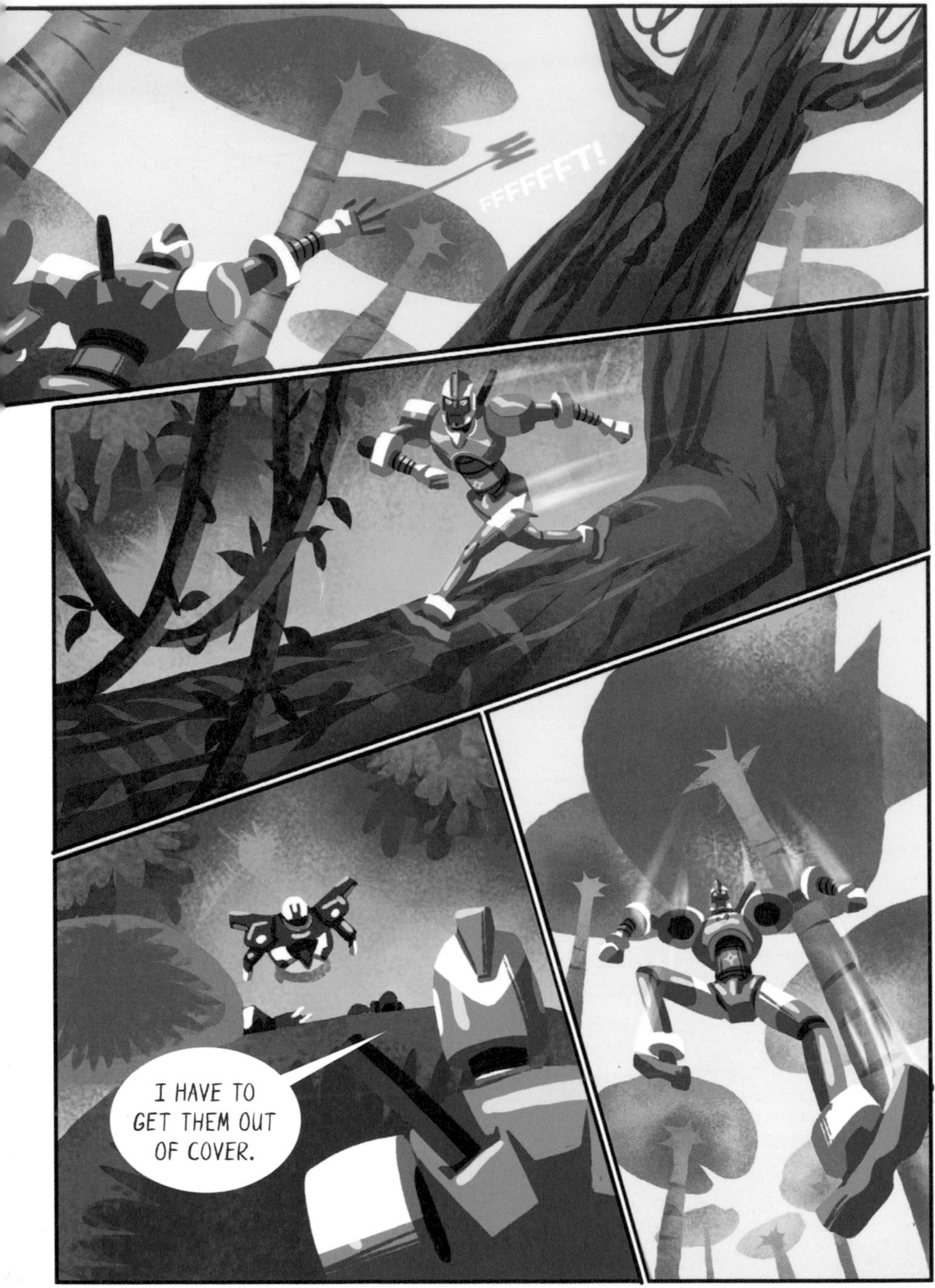
FFFFFFT!
I HAVE TO GET THEM OUT OF COVER.

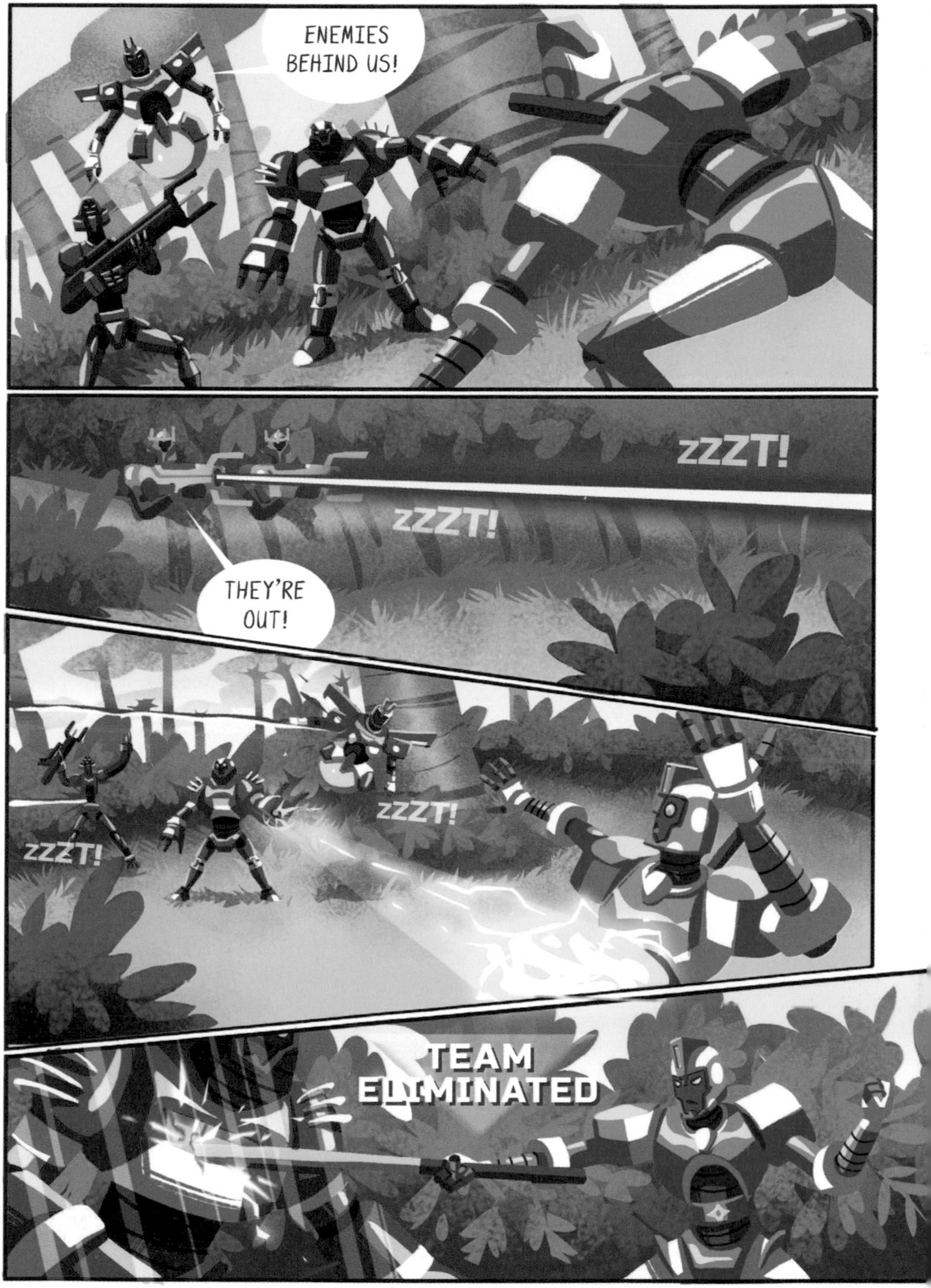
ENEMIES BEHIND US!
ZZZT!
ZZZT!
THEY'RE OUT!
ZZZT!
ZZZT!
TEAM ELIMINATED

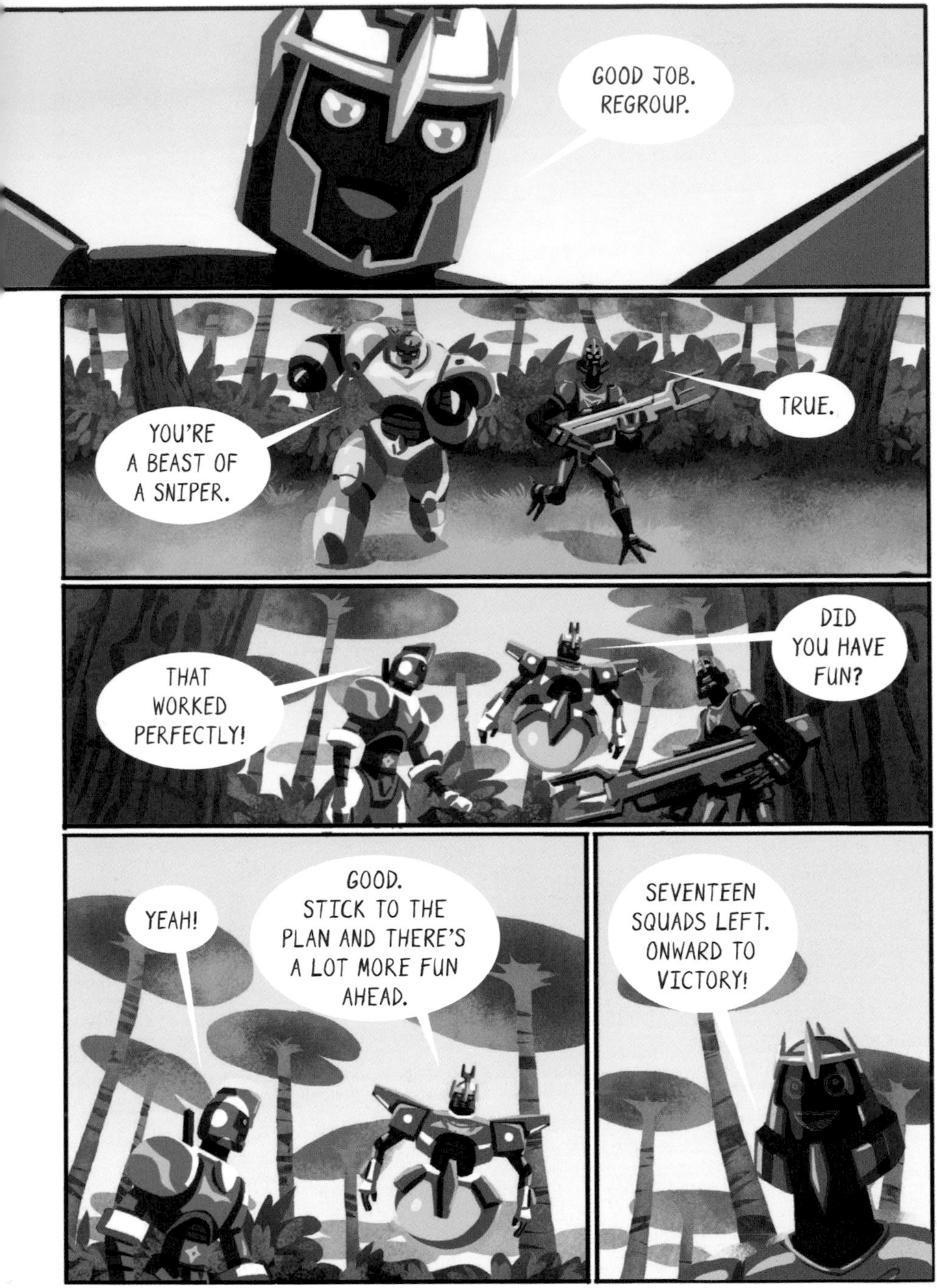
GOOD JOB. REGROUP.
YOU'RE A BEAST OF A SNIPER.
TRUE.
THAT WORKED PERFECTLY!
DID YOU HAVE FUN?
YEAH!
GOOD. STICK TO THE PLAN AND THERE'S A LOT MORE FUN AHEAD.
SEVENTEEN SQUADS LEFT. ONWARD TO VICTORY!

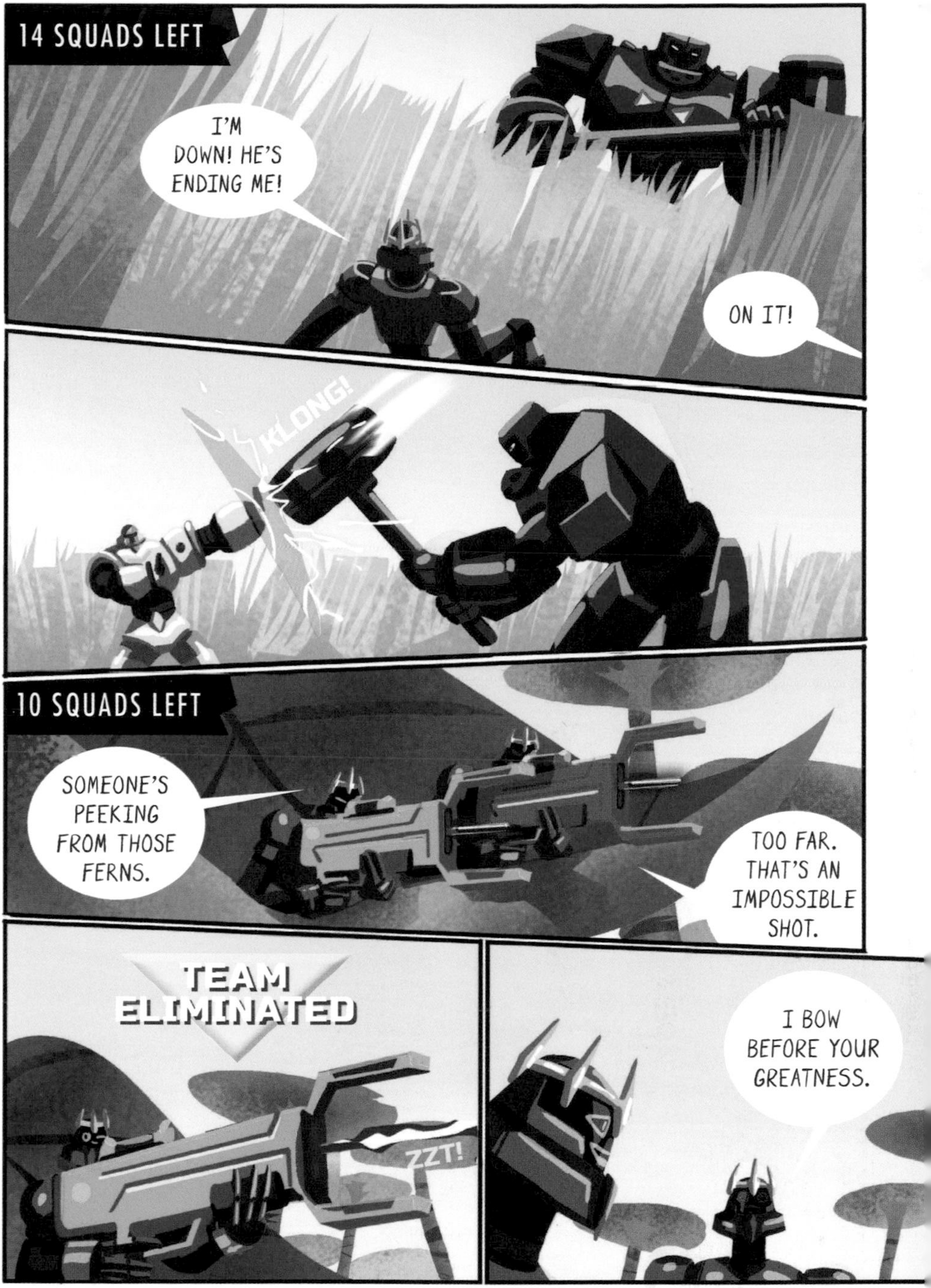
14 SQUADS LEFT
I'M DOWN! HE'S ENDING ME!
ON IT!
KLONG!
10 SQUADS LEFT
SOMEONE'S PEEKING FROM THOSE FERNS.
TOO FAR. THAT'S AN IMPOSSIBLE SHOT.
TEAM ELIMINATED
ZZT!
I BOW BEFORE YOUR GREATNESS.

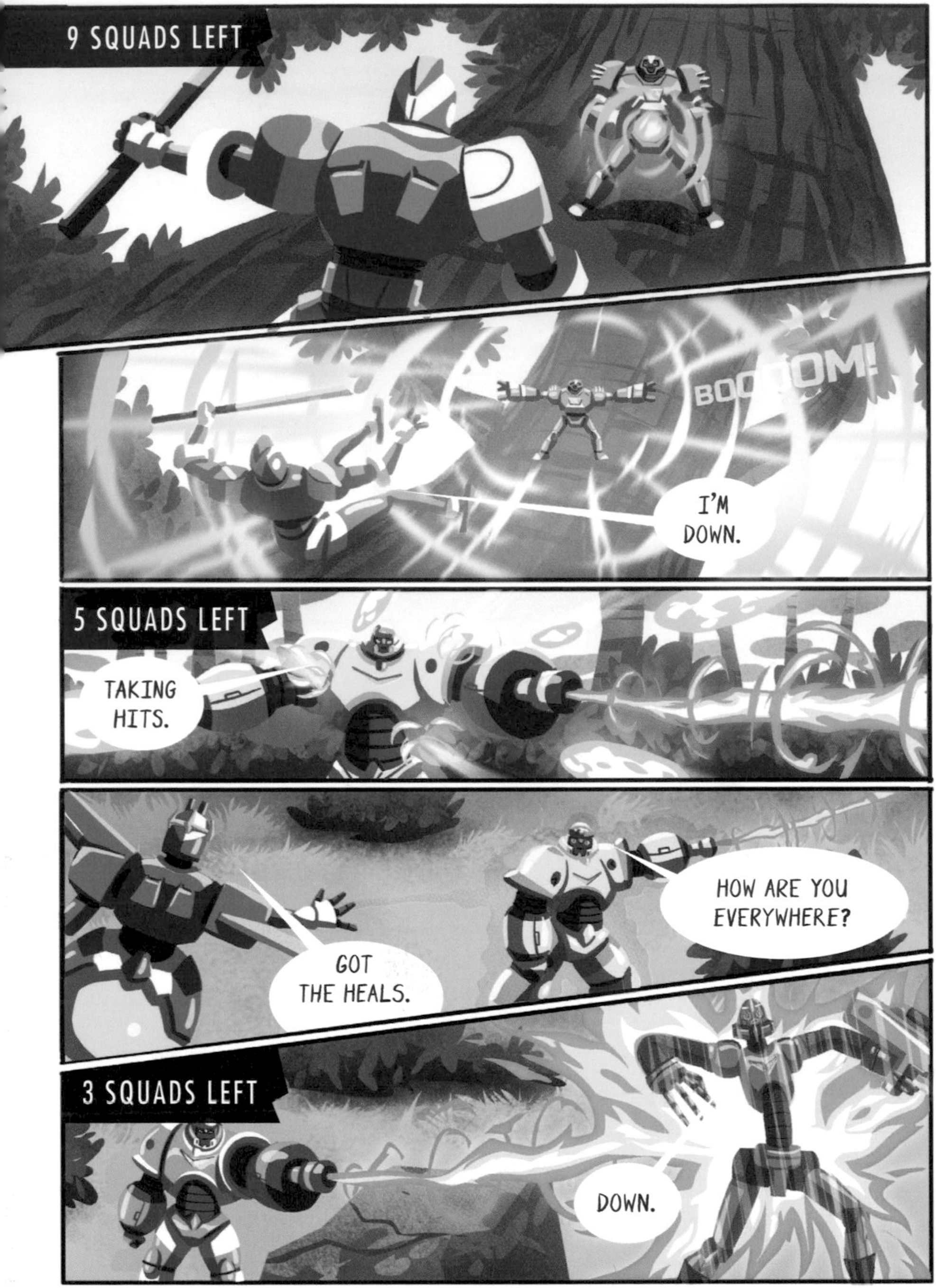
9 SQUADS LEFT
BOOOOM!
I'M DOWN.
5 SQUADS LEFT
TAKING HITS.
HOW ARE YOU EVERYWHERE?
GOT THE HEALS.
3 SQUADS LEFT
DOWN.

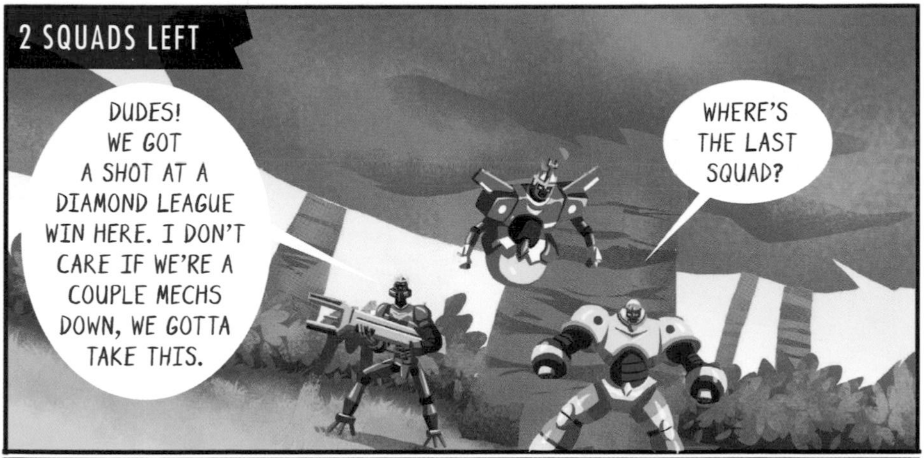
2 SQUADS LEFT
DUDES! WE GOT A SHOT AT A DIAMOND LEAGUE WIN HERE. I DON'T CARE IF WE'RE A COUPLE MECHS DOWN, WE GOTTA TAKE THIS.
WHERE'S THE LAST SQUAD?

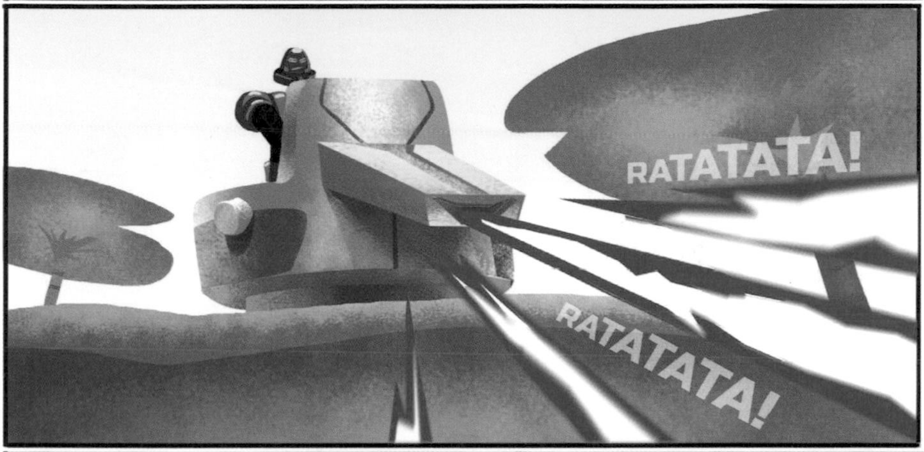
RATATATA!
RATATATA!

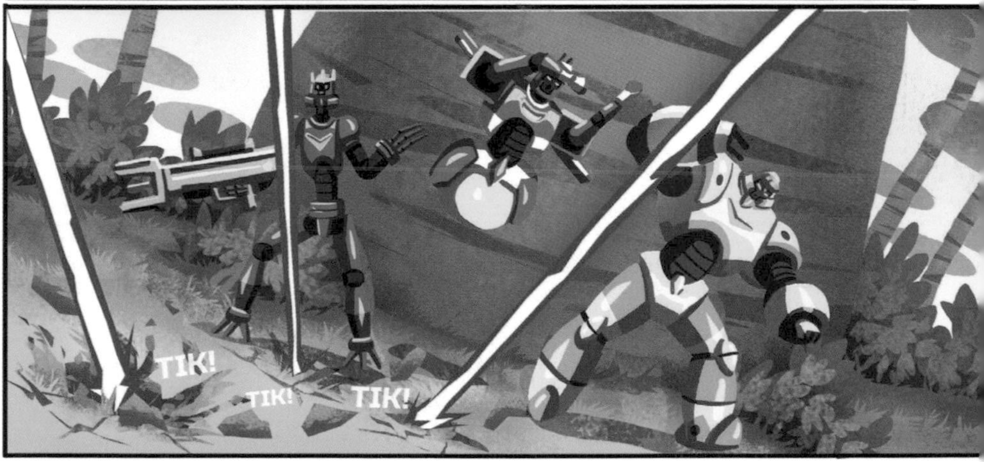
TIK!
TIK!
TIK!

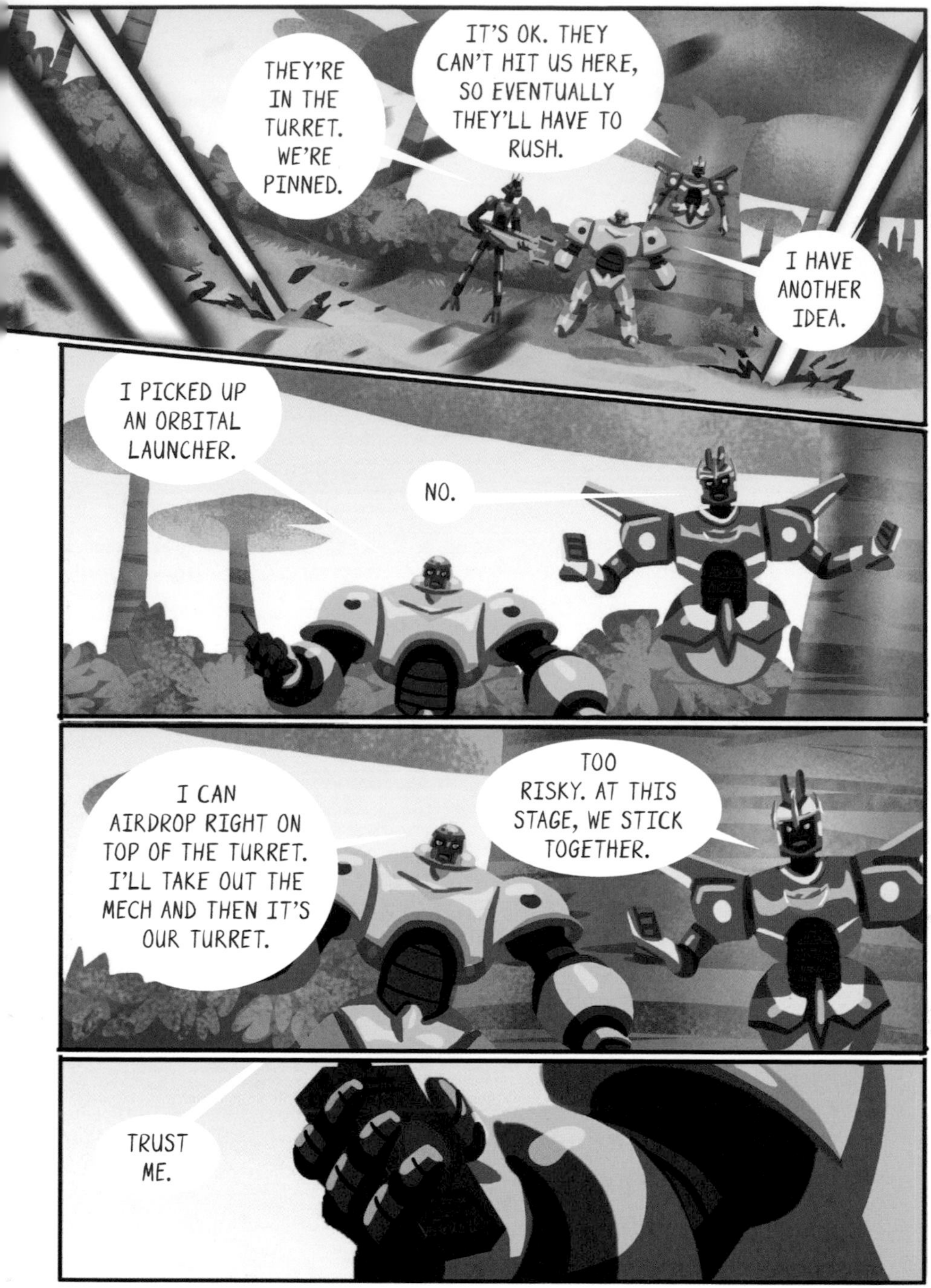
THEY'RE IN THE TURRET. WE'RE PINNED.
IT'S OK. THEY CAN'T HIT US HERE, SO EVENTUALLY THEY'LL HAVE TO RUSH.
I HAVE ANOTHER IDEA.
I PICKED UP AN ORBITAL LAUNCHER.
NO.
I CAN AIRDROP RIGHT ON TOP OF THE TURRET. I'LL TAKE OUT THE MECH AND THEN IT'S OUR TURRET.
TOO RISKY. AT THIS STAGE, WE STICK TOGETHER.
TRUST ME.

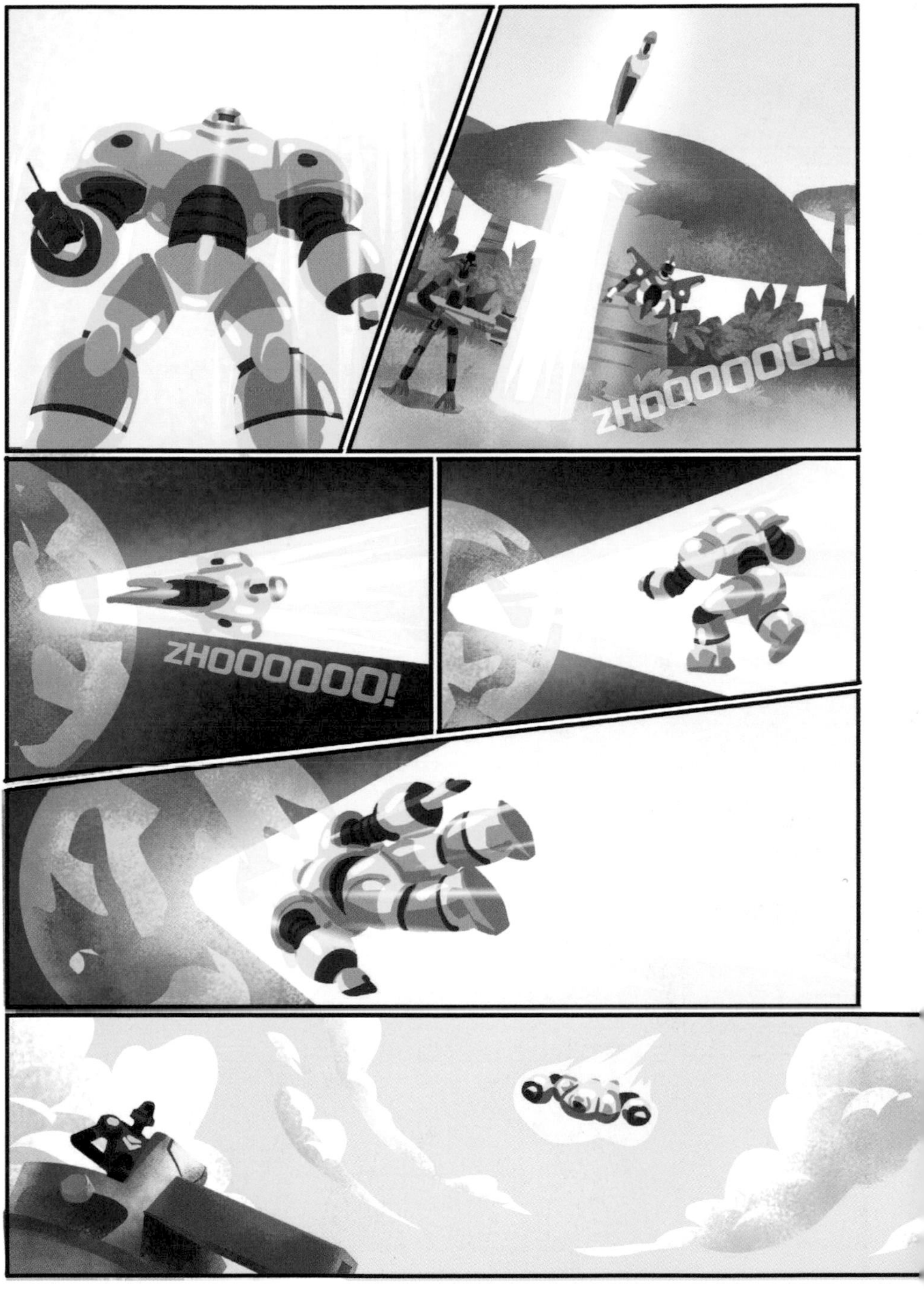

ZHOOOOOO!
ZHOOOOOO!

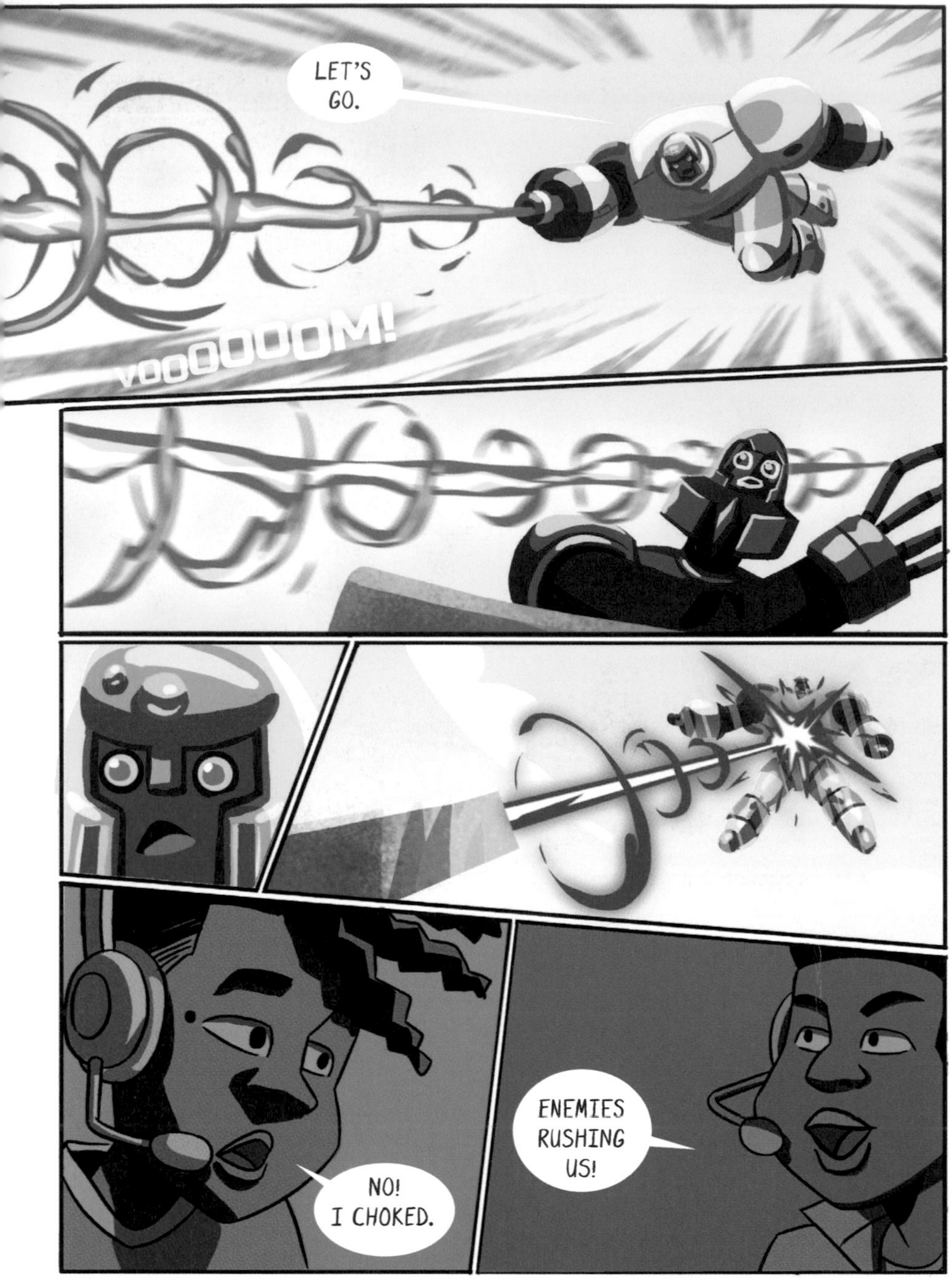
LET'S GO.
VOOOOOOM!
NO! I CHOKED.
ENEMIES RUSHING US!

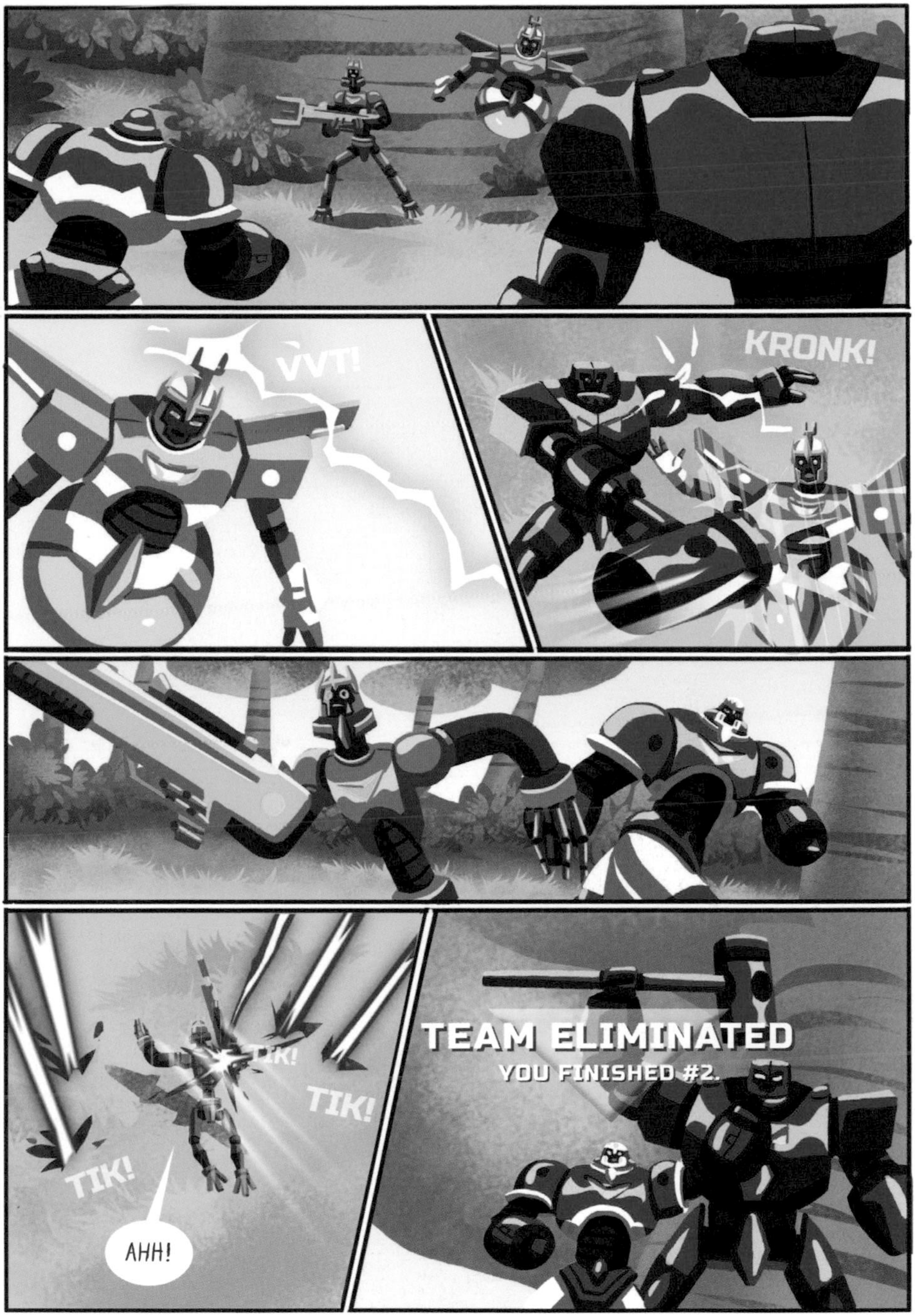
VVT!
KRONK!
TIK!
TIK!
TIK!
AHH!
TEAM ELIMINATED
YOU FINISHED #2.

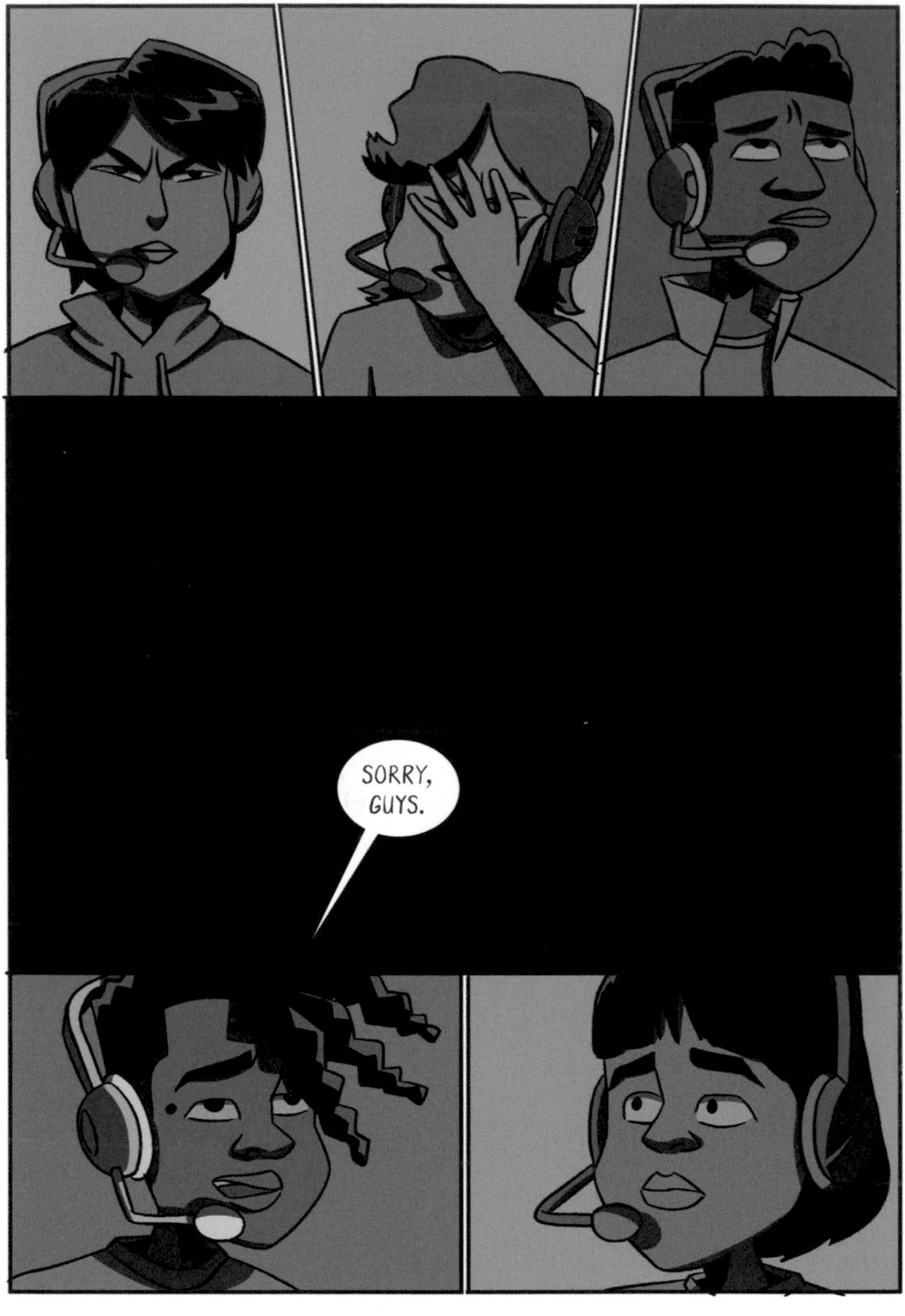
SORRY, GUYS.

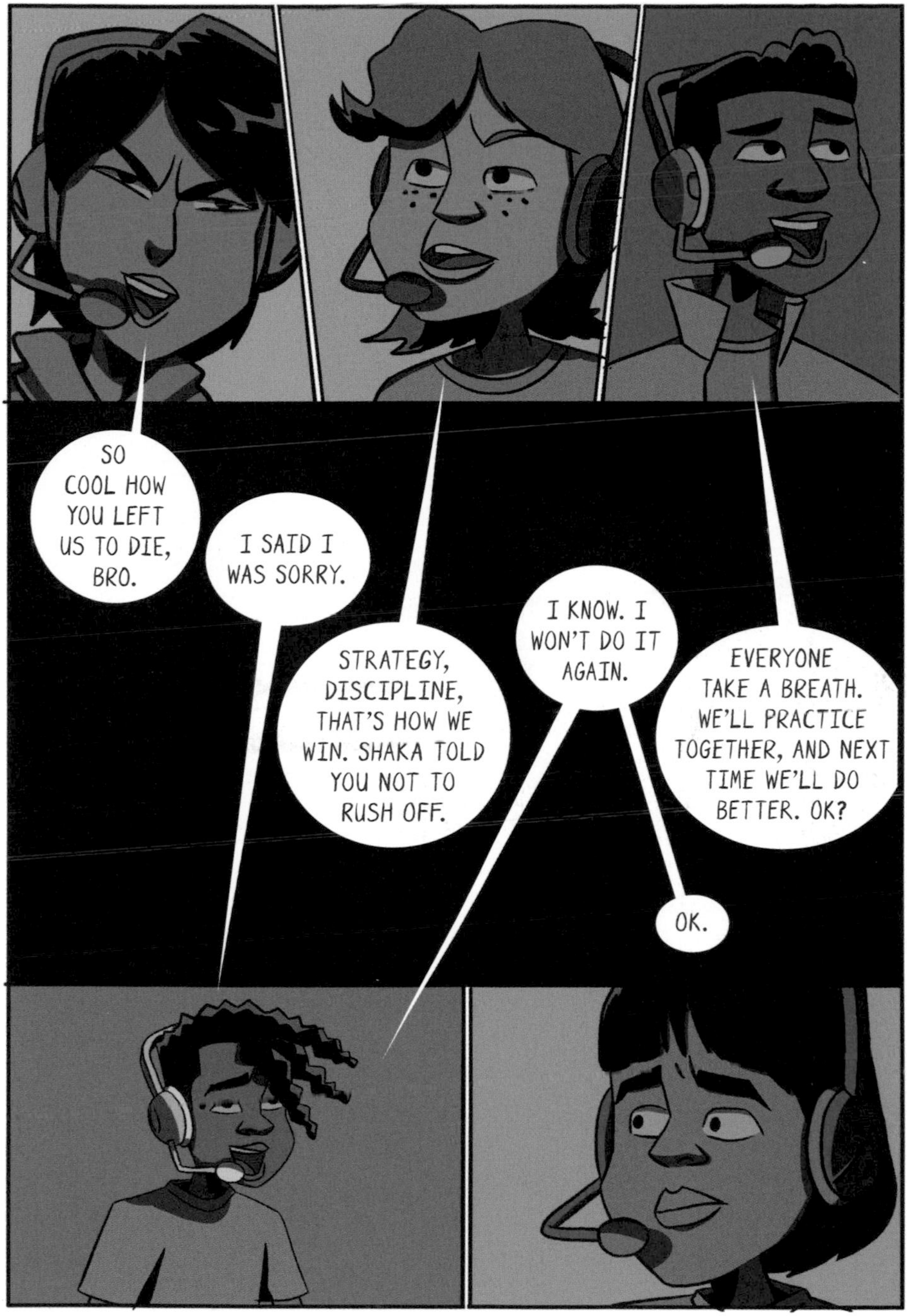
SO COOL HOW YOU LEFT US TO DIE, BRO.
I SAID I WAS SORRY.
STRATEGY, DISCIPLINE, THAT'S HOW WE WIN. SHAKA TOLD YOU NOT TO RUSH OFF.
I KNOW. I WON'T DO IT AGAIN.
EVERYONE TAKE A BREATH. WE'LL PRACTICE TOGETHER, AND NEXT TIME WE'LL DO BETTER. OK?
OK.

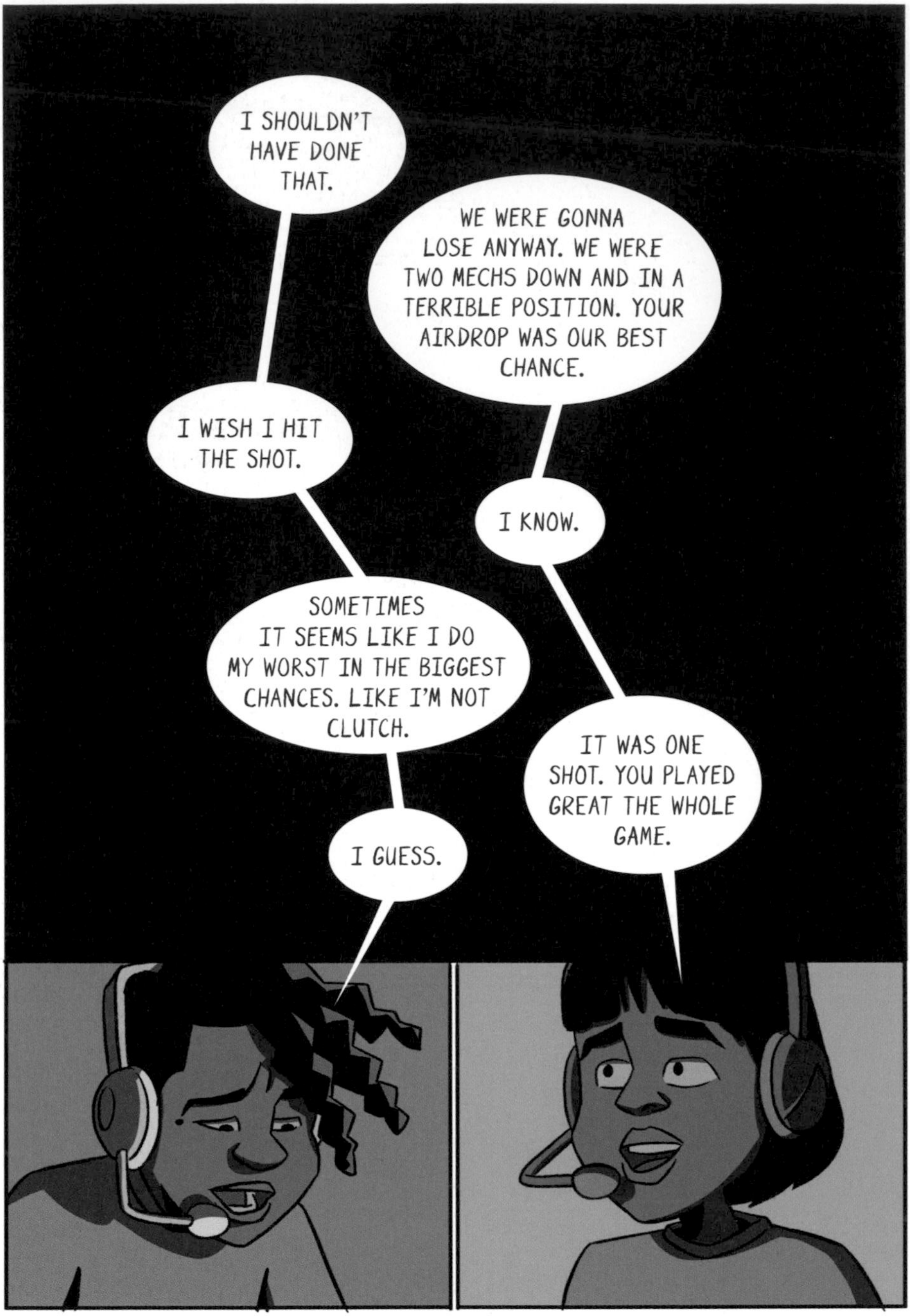
I SHOULDN'T HAVE DONE THAT.
WE WERE GONNA LOSE ANYWAY. WE WERE TWO MECHS DOWN AND IN A TERRIBLE POSITION. YOUR AIRDROP WAS OUR BEST CHANCE.
I WISH I HIT THE SHOT.
I KNOW.
SOMETIMES IT SEEMS LIKE I DO MY WORST IN THE BIGGEST CHANCES. LIKE I'M NOT CLUTCH.
IT WAS ONE SHOT. YOU PLAYED GREAT THE WHOLE GAME.
I GUESS.

CHAPTER 8

INFINITE REIGN

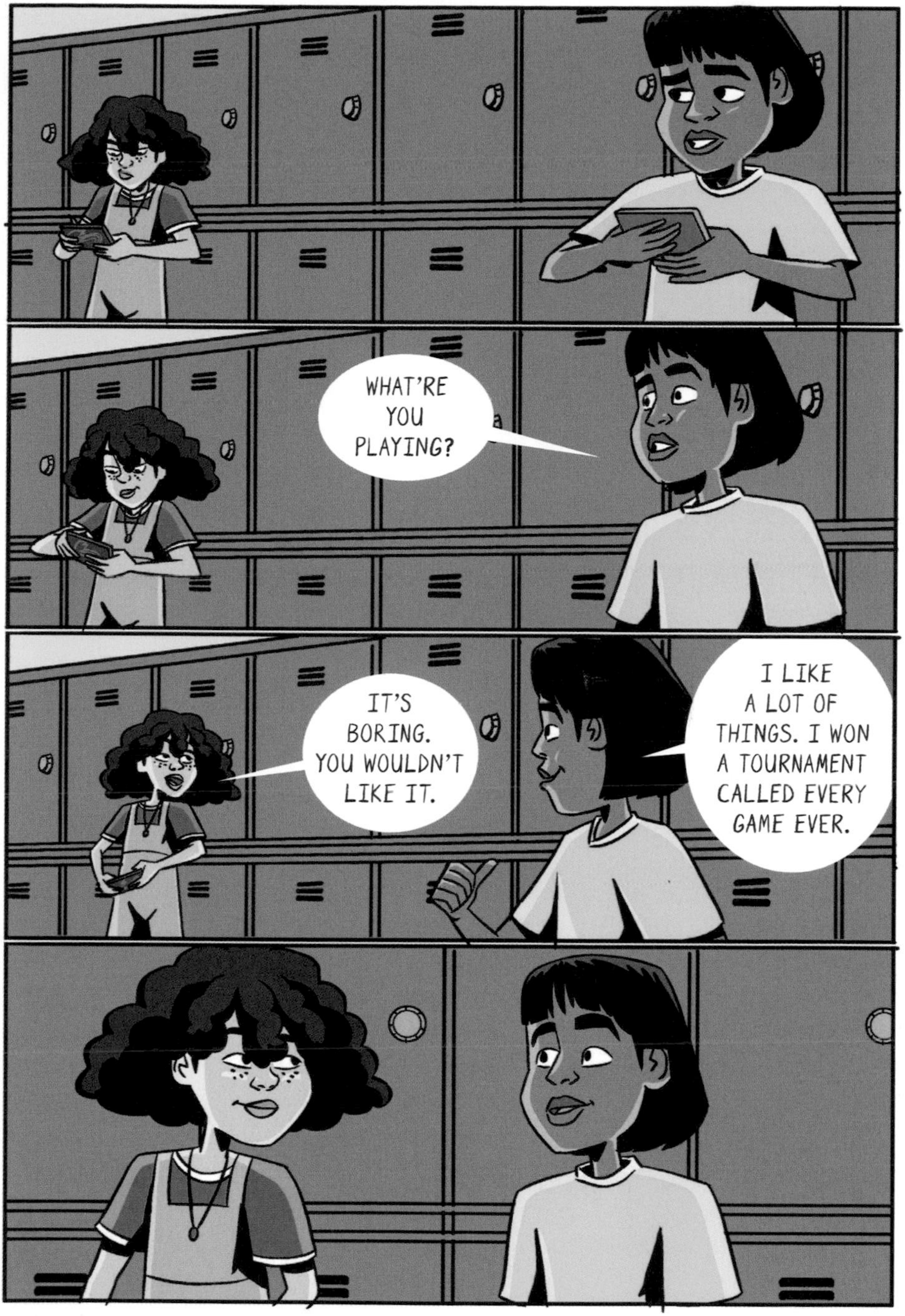
WHAT'RE YOU PLAYING?
IT'S BORING. YOU WOULDN'T LIKE IT.
I LIKE A LOT OF THINGS. I WON A TOURNAMENT CALLED EVERY GAME EVER.

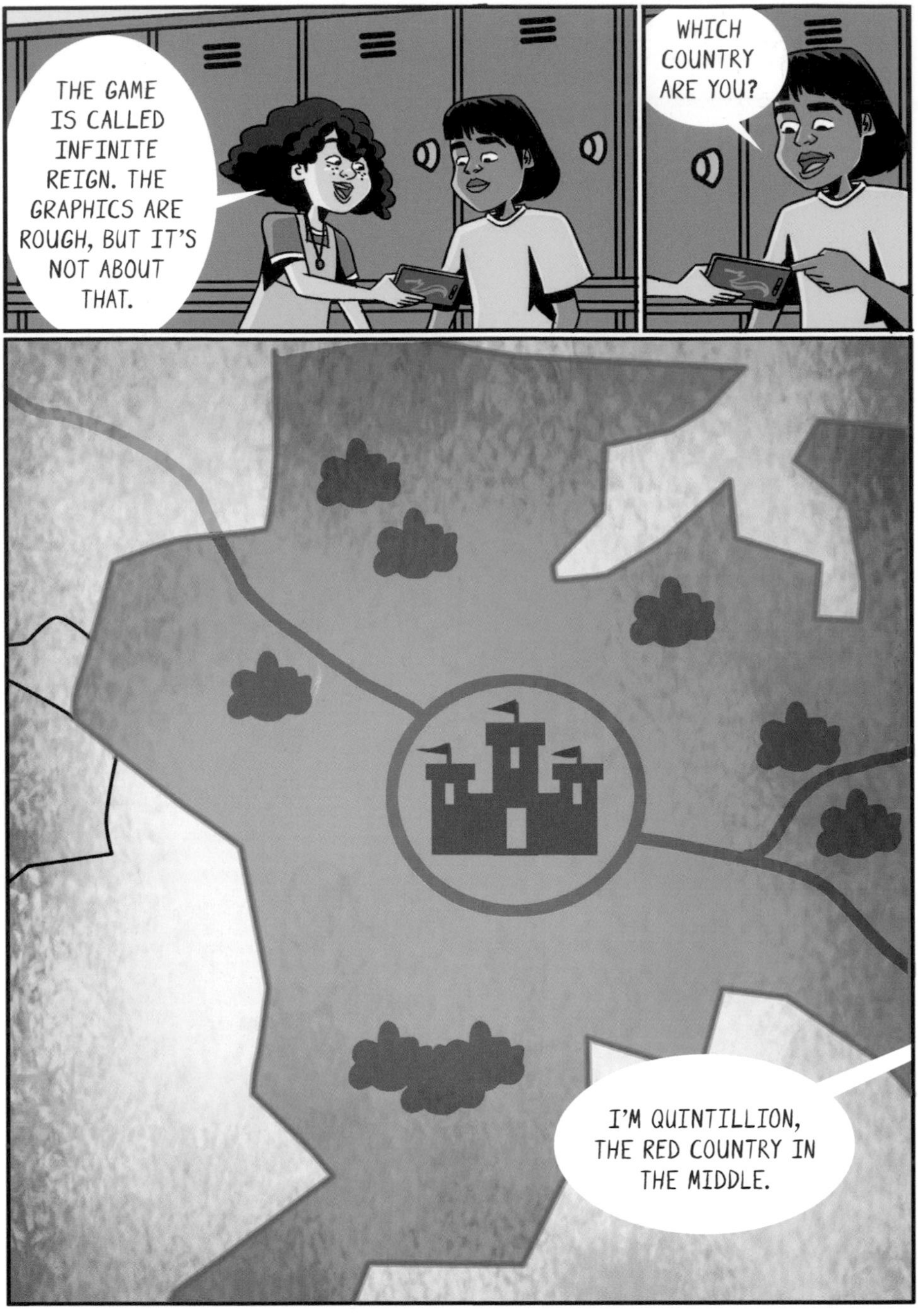
THE GAME IS CALLED INFINITE REIGN. THE GRAPHICS ARE ROUGH, BUT IT'S NOT ABOUT THAT.
WHICH COUNTRY ARE YOU?
I'M QUINTILLION, THE RED COUNTRY IN THE MIDDLE.

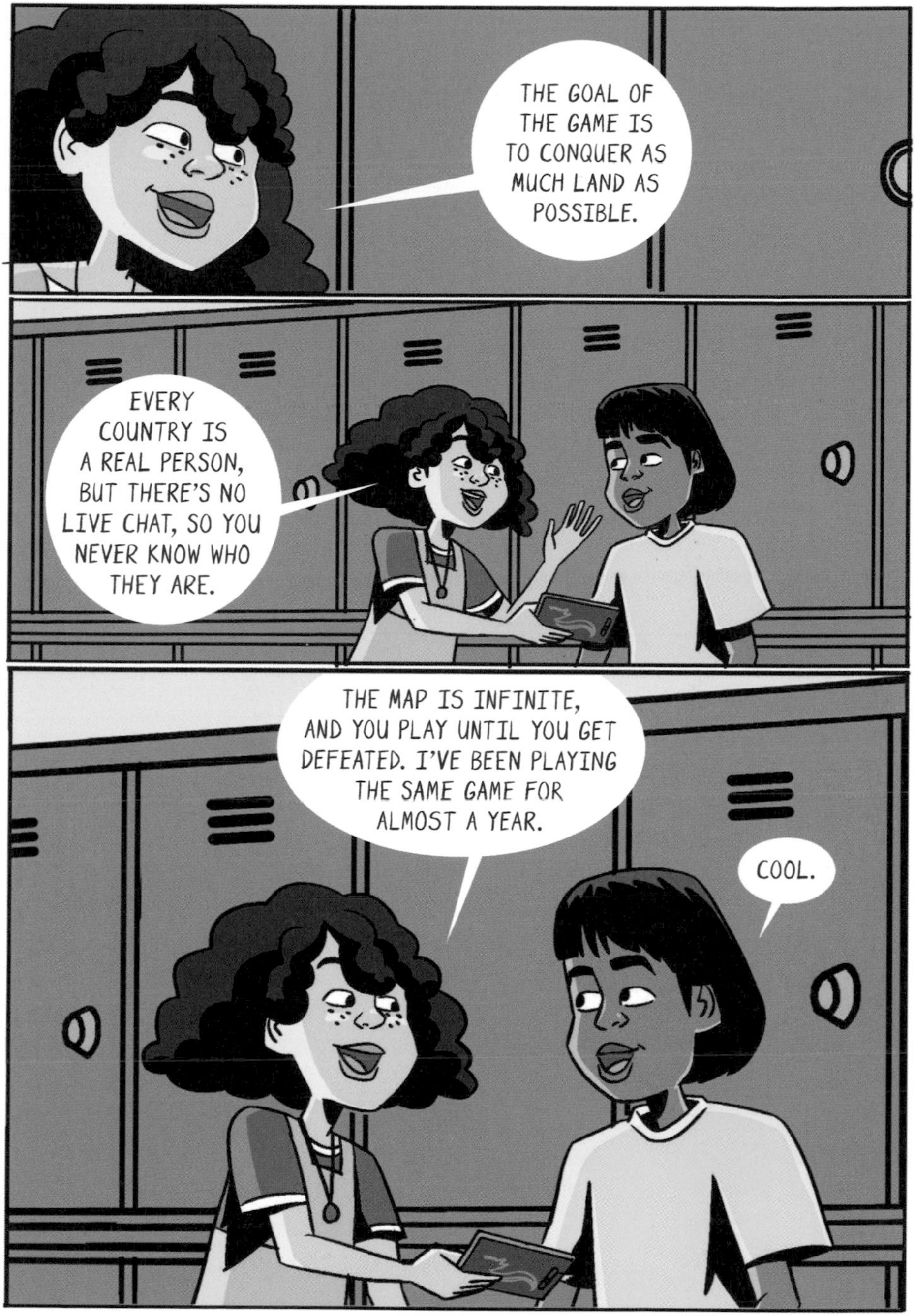
THE GOAL OF THE GAME IS TO CONQUER AS MUCH LAND AS POSSIBLE.
EVERY COUNTRY IS A REAL PERSON, BUT THERE'S NO LIVE CHAT, SO YOU NEVER KNOW WHO THEY ARE.
THE MAP IS INFINITE, AND YOU PLAY UNTIL YOU GET DEFEATED. I'VE BEEN PLAYING THE SAME GAME FOR ALMOST A YEAR.
COOL.

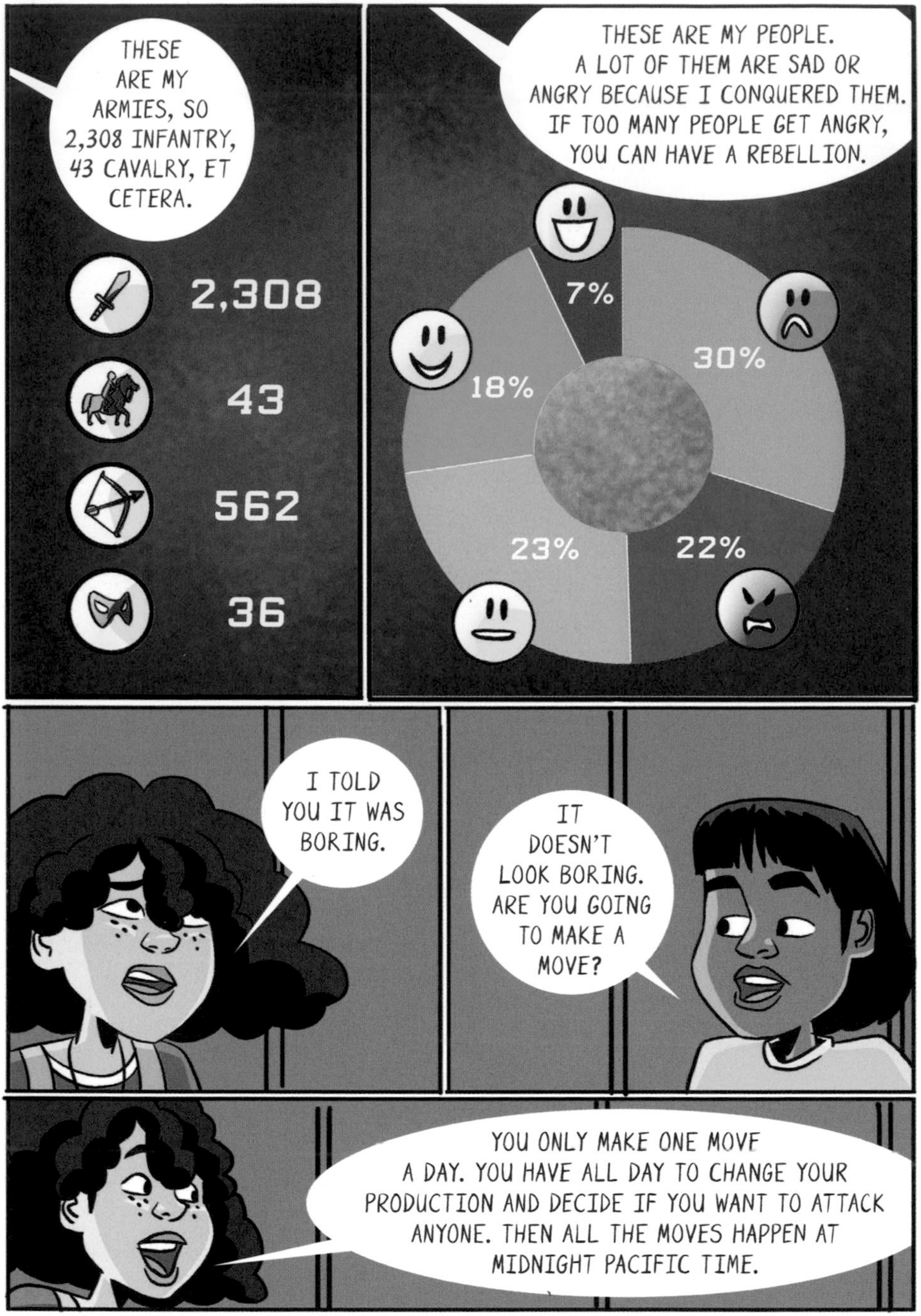
THESE ARE MY ARMIES, SO 2,308 INFANTRY, 43 CAVALRY, ET CETERA.
2,308
43
562
36
THESE ARE MY PEOPLE. A LOT OF THEM ARE SAD OR ANGRY BECAUSE I CONQUERED THEM. IF TOO MANY PEOPLE GET ANGRY, YOU CAN HAVE A REBELLION.
7%
30%
18%
23%
22%
I TOLD YOU IT WAS BORING.
IT DOESN'T LOOK BORING. ARE YOU GOING TO MAKE A MOVE?
YOU ONLY MAKE ONE MOVE A DAY. YOU HAVE ALL DAY TO CHANGE YOUR PRODUCTION AND DECIDE IF YOU WANT TO ATTACK ANYONE. THEN ALL THE MOVES HAPPEN AT MIDNIGHT PACIFIC TIME.

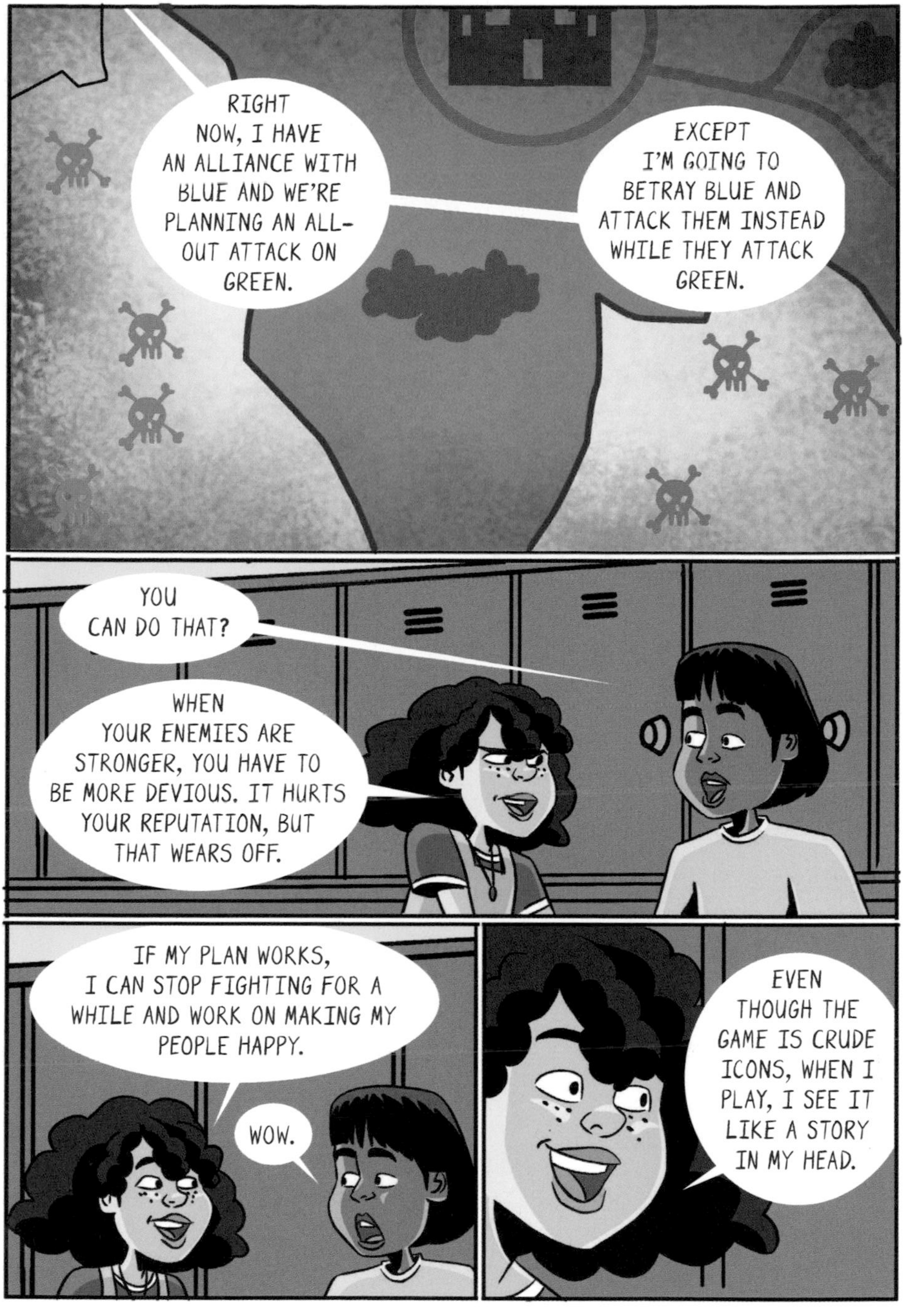
RIGHT NOW, I HAVE AN ALLIANCE WITH BLUE AND WE'RE PLANNING AN ALL-OUT ATTACK ON GREEN.
EXCEPT I'M GOING TO BETRAY BLUE AND ATTACK THEM INSTEAD WHILE THEY ATTACK GREEN.
YOU CAN DO THAT?
WHEN YOUR ENEMIES ARE STRONGER, YOU HAVE TO BE MORE DEVIOUS. IT HURTS YOUR REPUTATION, BUT THAT WEARS OFF.
IF MY PLAN WORKS, I CAN STOP FIGHTING FOR A WHILE AND WORK ON MAKING MY PEOPLE HAPPY.
WOW.
EVEN THOUGH THE GAME IS CRUDE ICONS, WHEN I PLAY, I SEE IT LIKE A STORY IN MY HEAD.

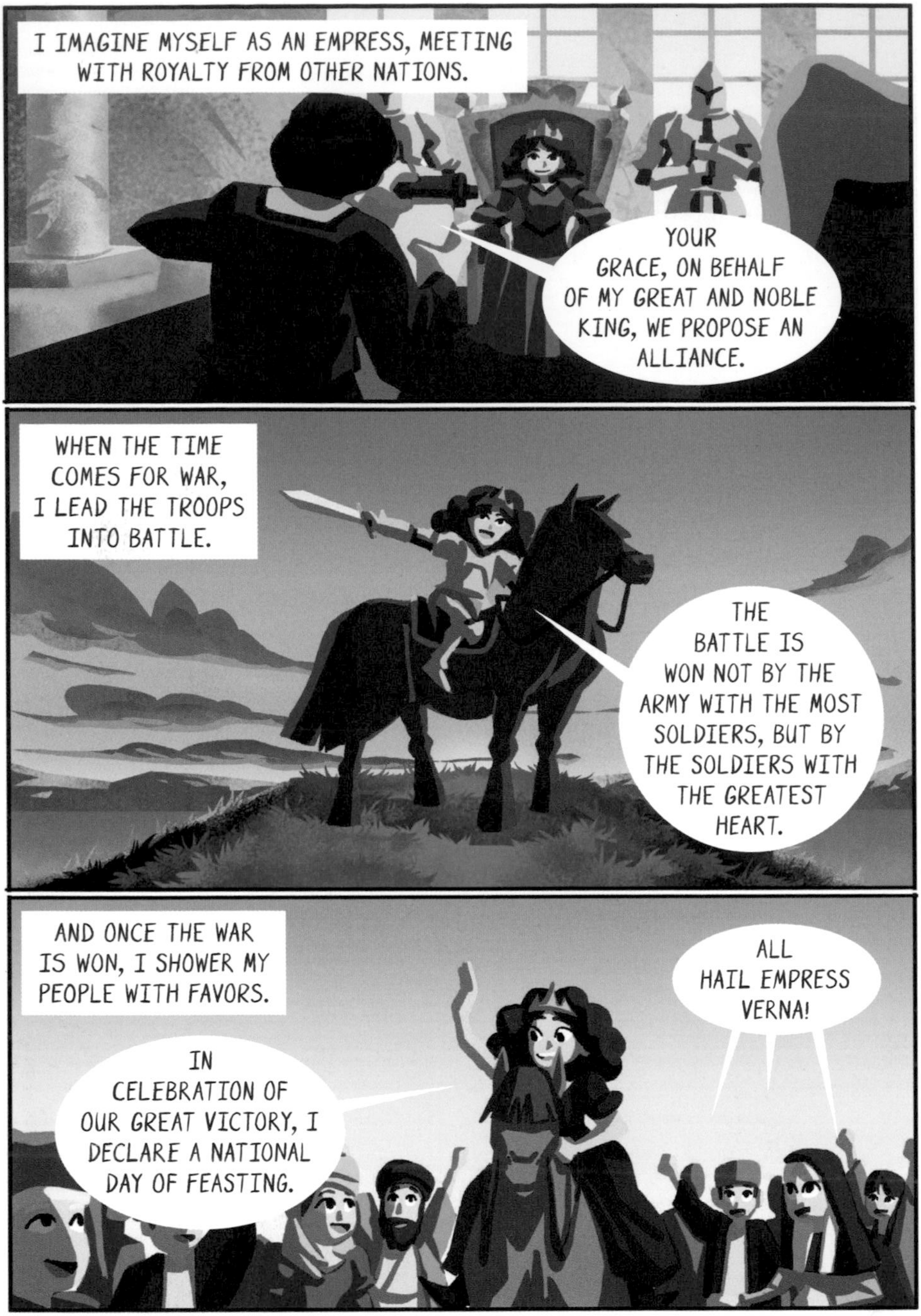
I IMAGINE MYSELF AS AN EMPRESS, MEETING WITH ROYALTY FROM OTHER NATIONS.
YOUR GRACE, ON BEHALF OF MY GREAT AND NOBLE KING, WE PROPOSE AN ALLIANCE.
WHEN THE TIME COMES FOR WAR, I LEAD THE TROOPS INTO BATTLE.
THE BATTLE IS WON NOT BY THE ARMY WITH THE MOST SOLDIERS, BUT BY THE SOLDIERS WITH THE GREATEST HEART.
AND ONCE THE WAR IS WON, I SHOWER MY PEOPLE WITH FAVORS.
ALL HAIL EMPRESS VERNA!
IN CELEBRATION OF OUR GREAT VICTORY, I DECLARE A NATIONAL DAY OF FEASTING.

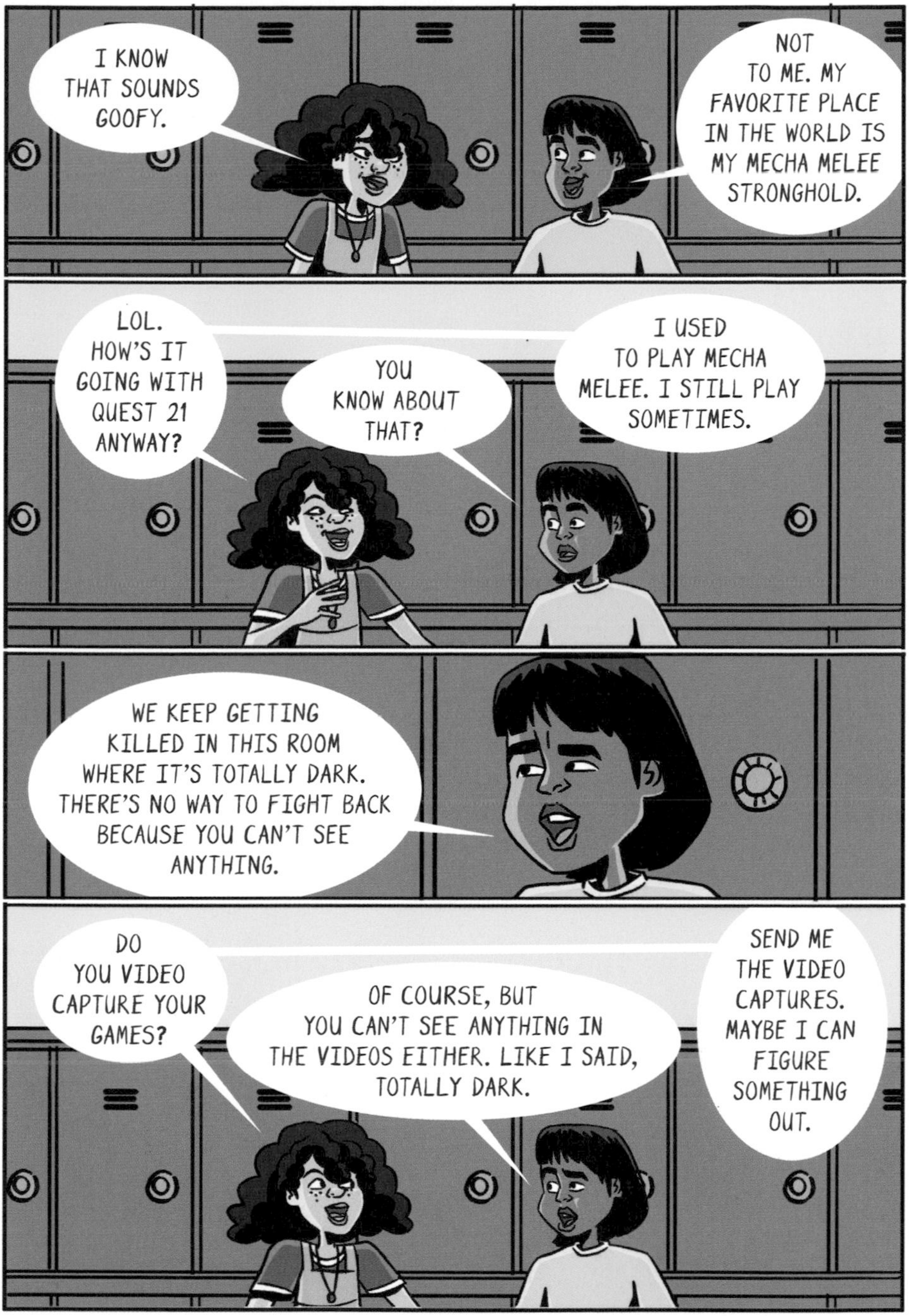
I KNOW THAT SOUNDS GOOFY.
NOT TO ME. MY FAVORITE PLACE IN THE WORLD IS MY MECHA MELEE STRONGHOLD.
LOL. HOW'S IT GOING WITH QUEST 21 ANYWAY?
YOU KNOW ABOUT THAT?
I USED TO PLAY MECHA MELEE. I STILL PLAY SOMETIMES.
WE KEEP GETTING KILLED IN THIS ROOM WHERE IT'S TOTALLY DARK. THERE'S NO WAY TO FIGHT BACK BECAUSE YOU CAN'T SEE ANYTHING.
DO YOU VIDEO CAPTURE YOUR GAMES?
OF COURSE, BUT YOU CAN'T SEE ANYTHING IN THE VIDEOS EITHER. LIKE I SAID, TOTALLY DARK.
SEND ME THE VIDEO CAPTURES. MAYBE I CAN FIGURE SOMETHING OUT.

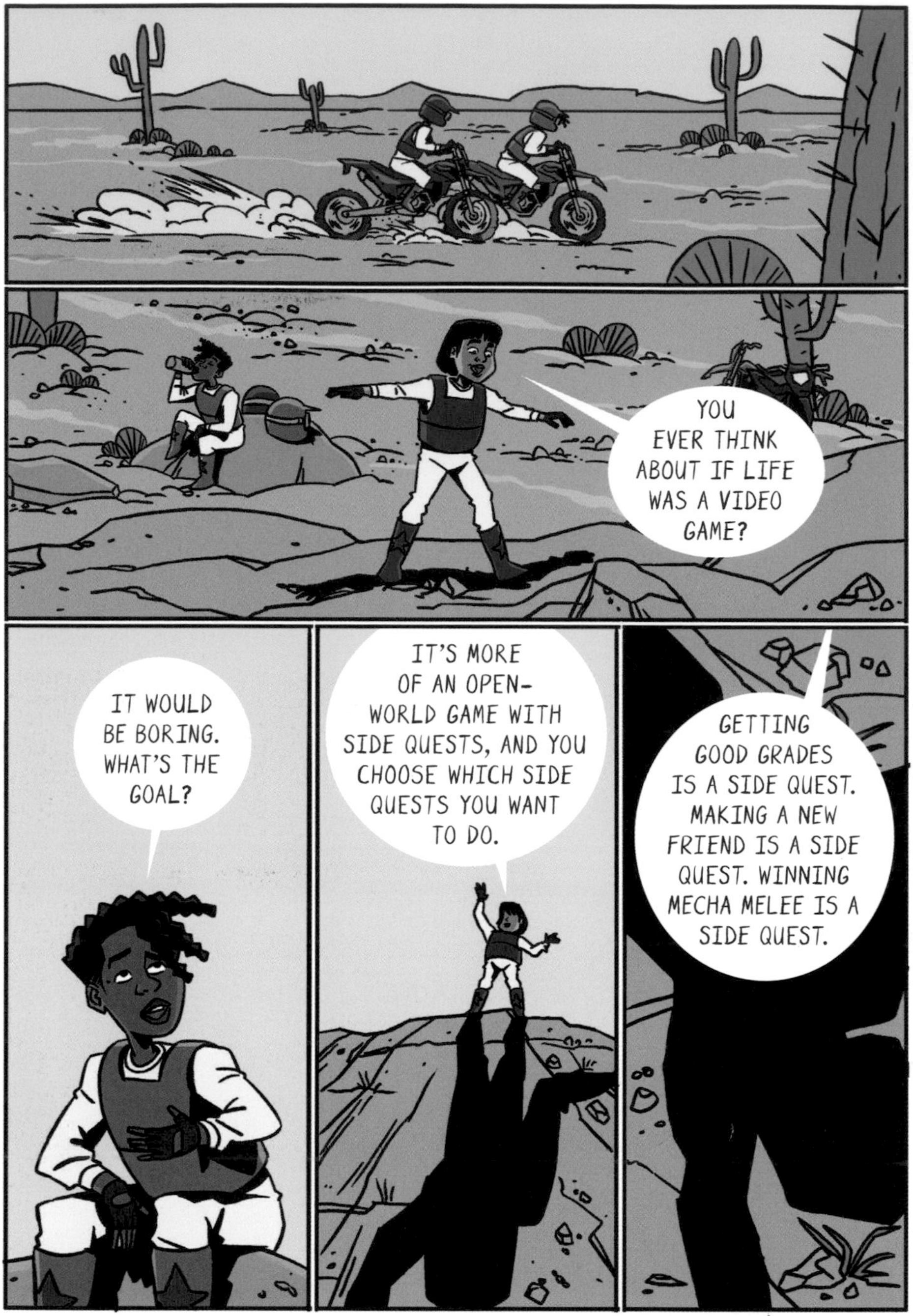
YOU EVER THINK ABOUT IF LIFE WAS A VIDEO GAME?
IT WOULD BE BORING. WHAT'S THE GOAL?
IT'S MORE OF AN OPEN-WORLD GAME WITH SIDE QUESTS, AND YOU CHOOSE WHICH SIDE QUESTS YOU WANT TO DO.
GETTING GOOD GRADES IS A SIDE QUEST. MAKING A NEW FRIEND IS A SIDE QUEST. WINNING MECHA MELEE IS A SIDE QUEST.

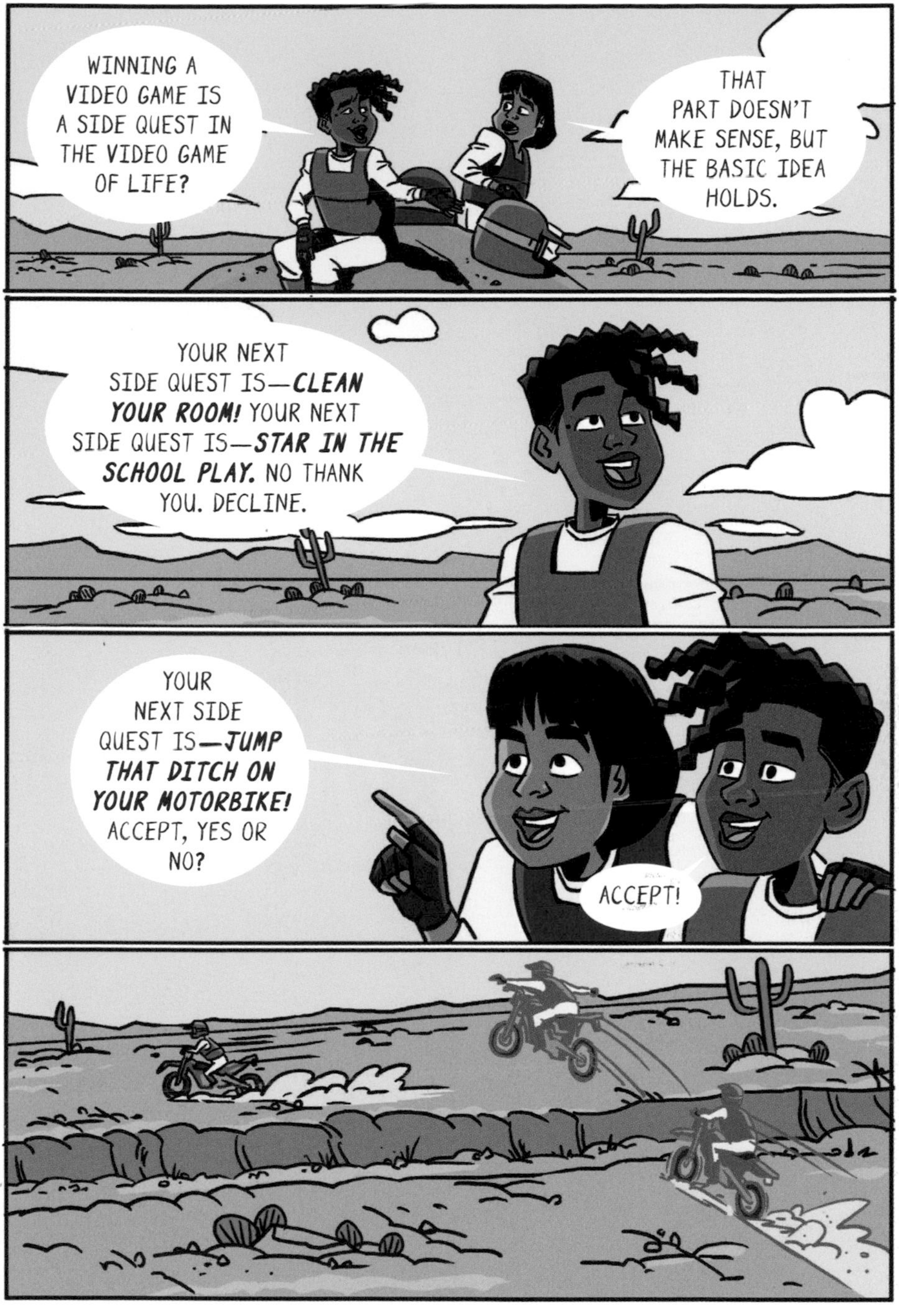
WINNING A VIDEO GAME IS A SIDE QUEST IN THE VIDEO GAME OF LIFE?
THAT PART DOESN'T MAKE SENSE, BUT THE BASIC IDEA HOLDS.
YOUR NEXT SIDE QUEST IS—**CLEAN YOUR ROOM!** YOUR NEXT SIDE QUEST IS—**STAR IN THE SCHOOL PLAY.** NO THANK YOU. DECLINE.
YOUR NEXT SIDE QUEST IS—**JUMP THAT DITCH ON YOUR MOTORBIKE!** ACCEPT, YES OR NO?
ACCEPT!

CHAPTER 9

BULLY VIGILANTE

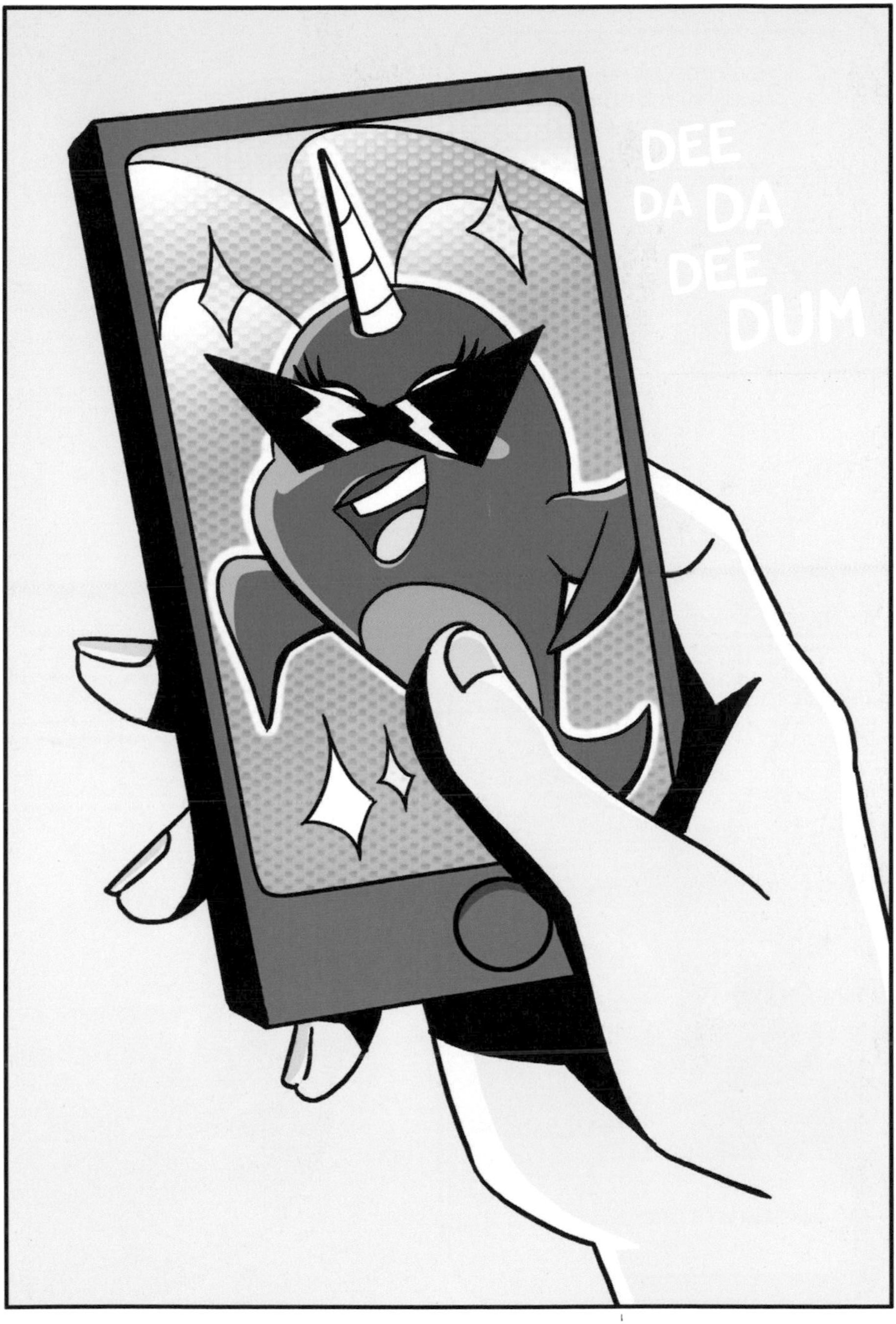
DEE
DA DA
DEE
DUM

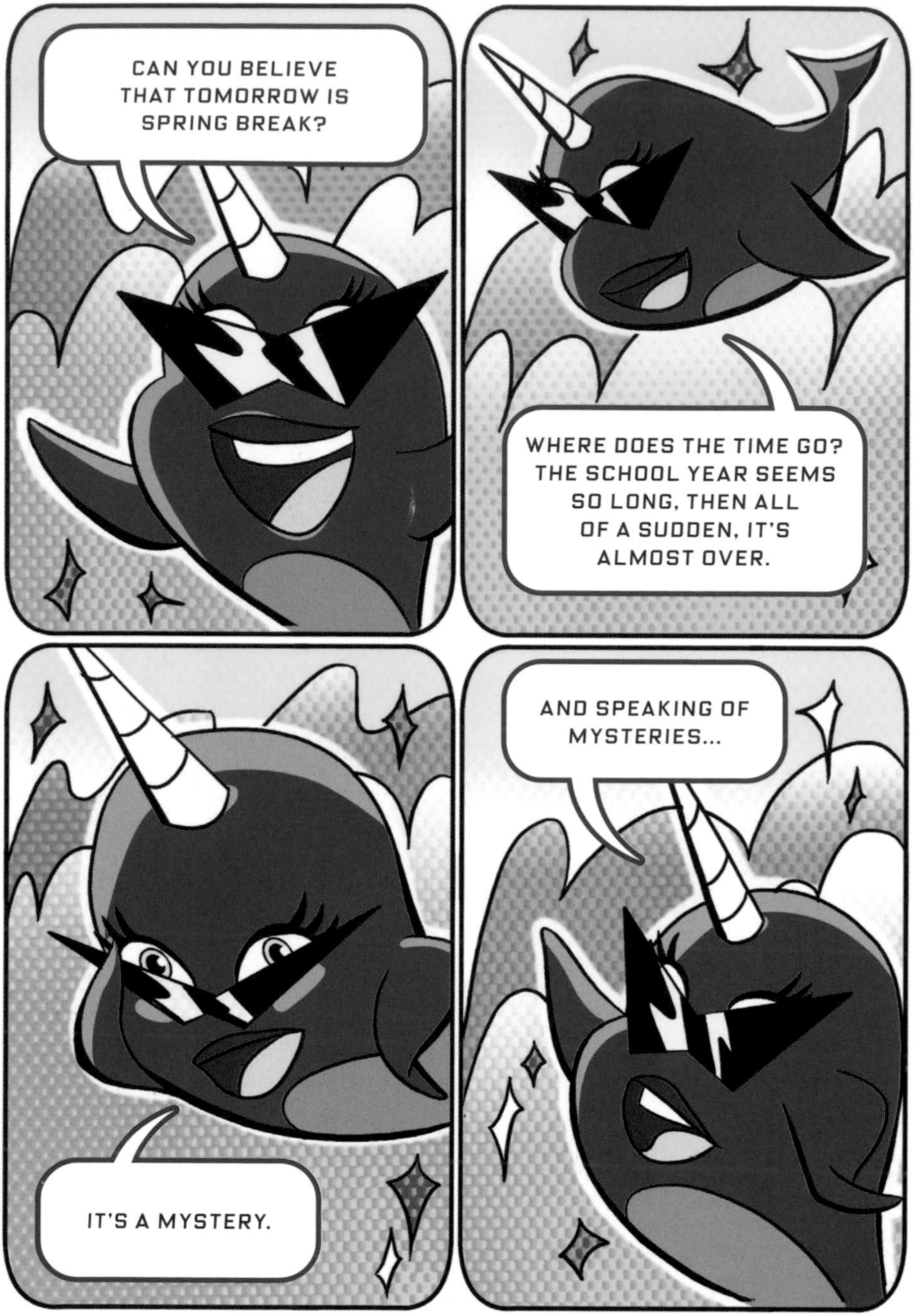
CAN YOU BELIEVE THAT TOMORROW IS SPRING BREAK?
WHERE DOES THE TIME GO? THE SCHOOL YEAR SEEMS SO LONG, THEN ALL OF A SUDDEN, IT'S ALMOST OVER.
IT'S A MYSTERY.
AND SPEAKING OF MYSTERIES...

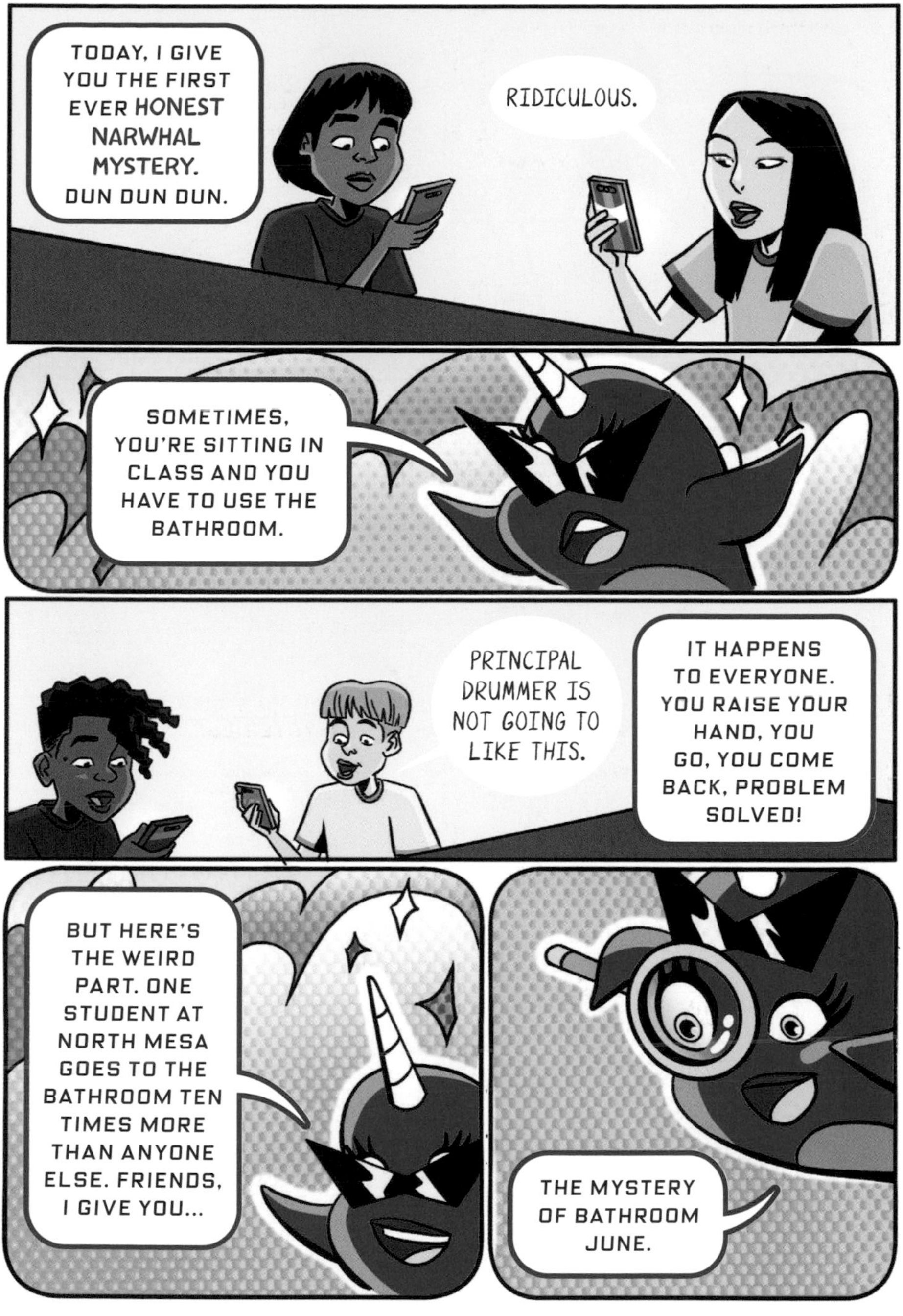

TODAY, I GIVE YOU THE FIRST EVER HONEST NARWHAL MYSTERY. DUN DUN DUN.
RIDICULOUS.
SOMETIMES, YOU'RE SITTING IN CLASS AND YOU HAVE TO USE THE BATHROOM.
PRINCIPAL DRUMMER IS NOT GOING TO LIKE THIS.
IT HAPPENS TO EVERYONE. YOU RAISE YOUR HAND, YOU GO, YOU COME BACK, PROBLEM SOLVED!
BUT HERE'S THE WEIRD PART. ONE STUDENT AT NORTH MESA GOES TO THE BATHROOM TEN TIMES MORE THAN ANYONE ELSE. FRIENDS, I GIVE YOU...
THE MYSTERY OF BATHROOM JUNE.

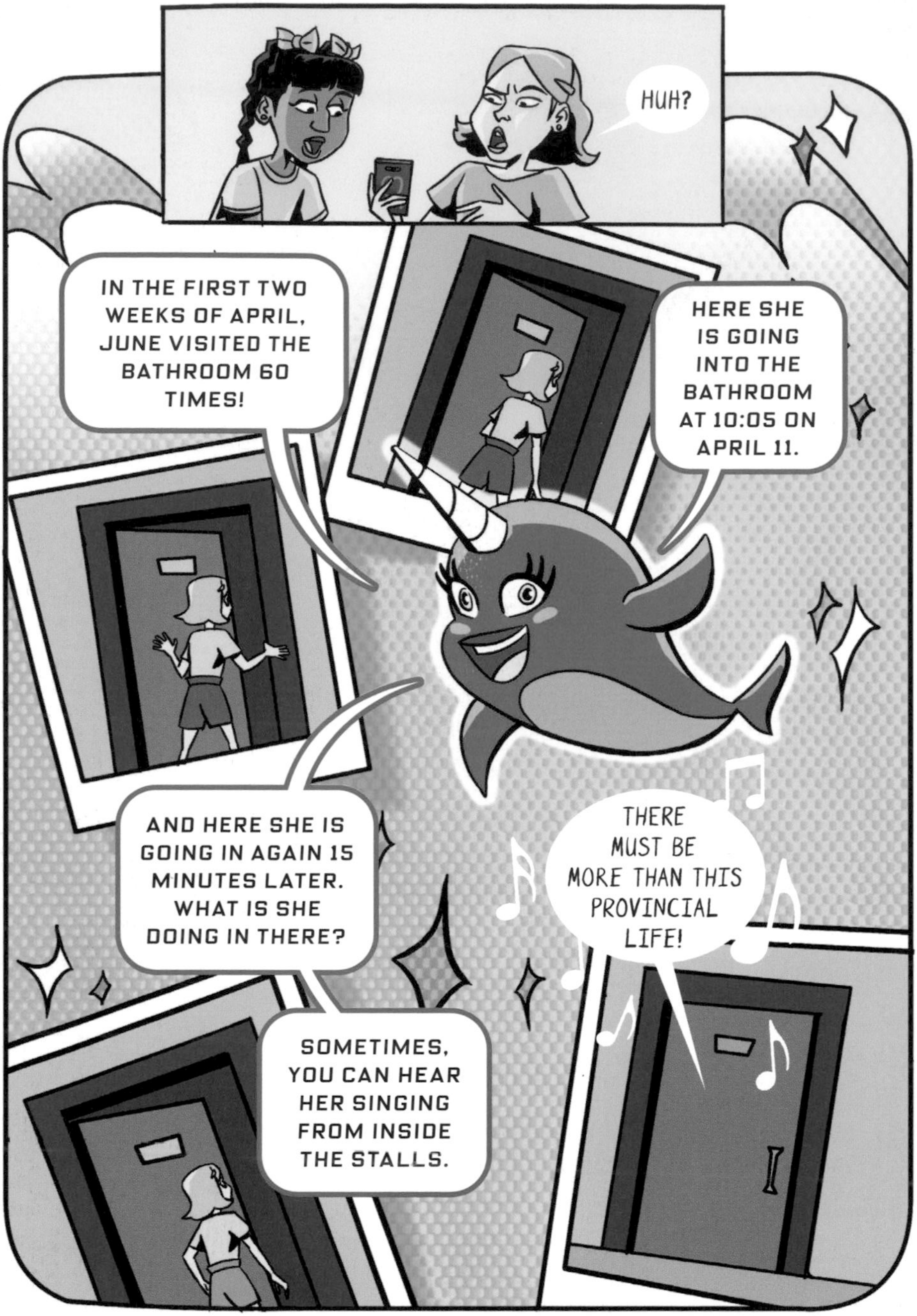
HUH?
IN THE FIRST TWO WEEKS OF APRIL, JUNE VISITED THE BATHROOM 60 TIMES!
HERE SHE IS GOING INTO THE BATHROOM AT 10:05 ON APRIL 11.
AND HERE SHE IS GOING IN AGAIN 15 MINUTES LATER. WHAT IS SHE DOING IN THERE?
THERE MUST BE MORE THAN THIS PROVINCIAL LIFE!
SOMETIMES, YOU CAN HEAR HER SINGING FROM INSIDE THE STALLS.

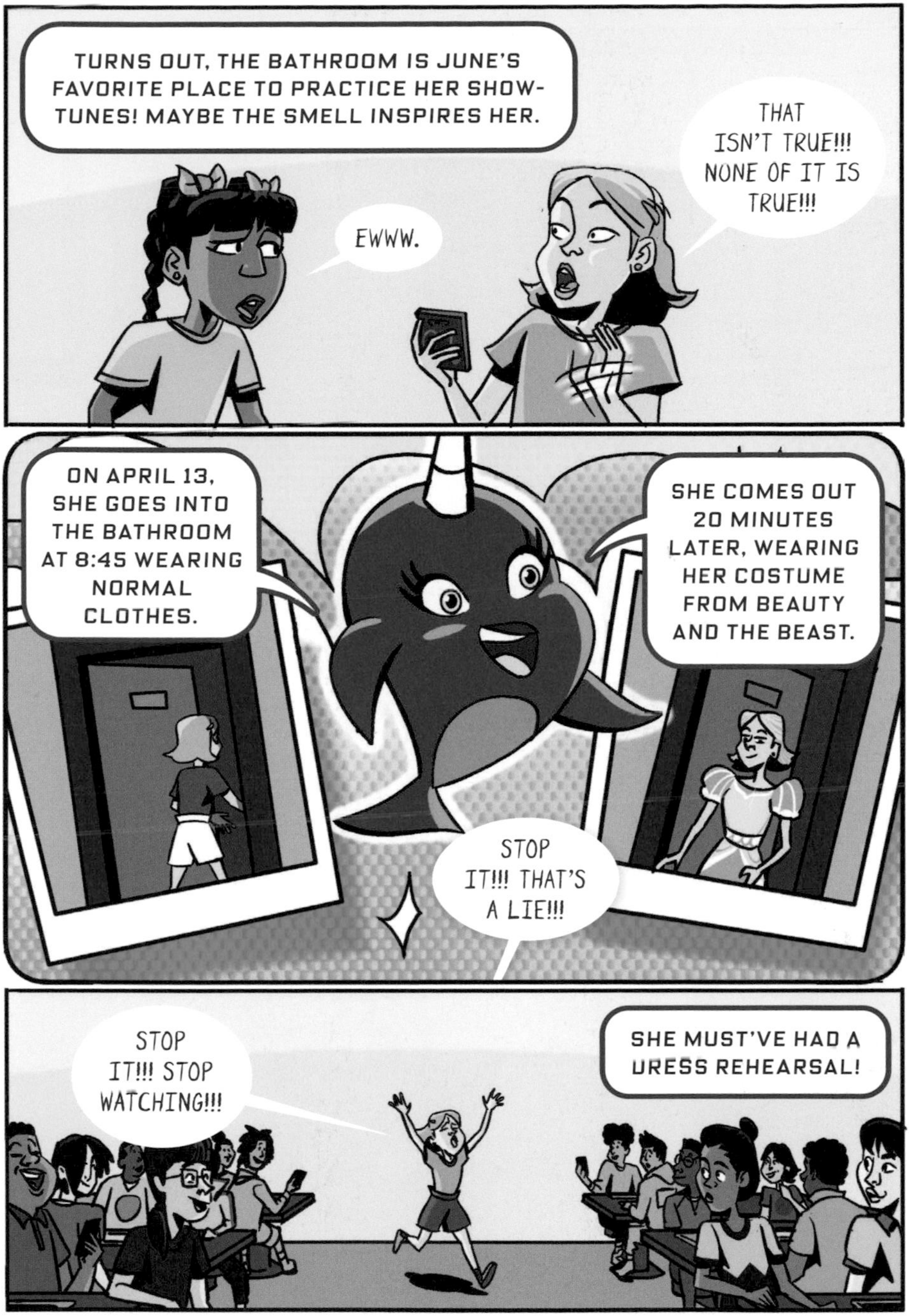
TURNS OUT, THE BATHROOM IS JUNE'S FAVORITE PLACE TO PRACTICE HER SHOW-TUNES! MAYBE THE SMELL INSPIRES HER.
EWWW.
THAT ISN'T TRUE!!! NONE OF IT IS TRUE!!!
ON APRIL 13, SHE GOES INTO THE BATHROOM AT 8:45 WEARING NORMAL CLOTHES.
SHE COMES OUT 20 MINUTES LATER, WEARING HER COSTUME FROM BEAUTY AND THE BEAST.
STOP IT!!! THAT'S A LIE!!!
STOP IT!!! STOP WATCHING!!!
SHE MUST'VE HAD A DRESS REHEARSAL!

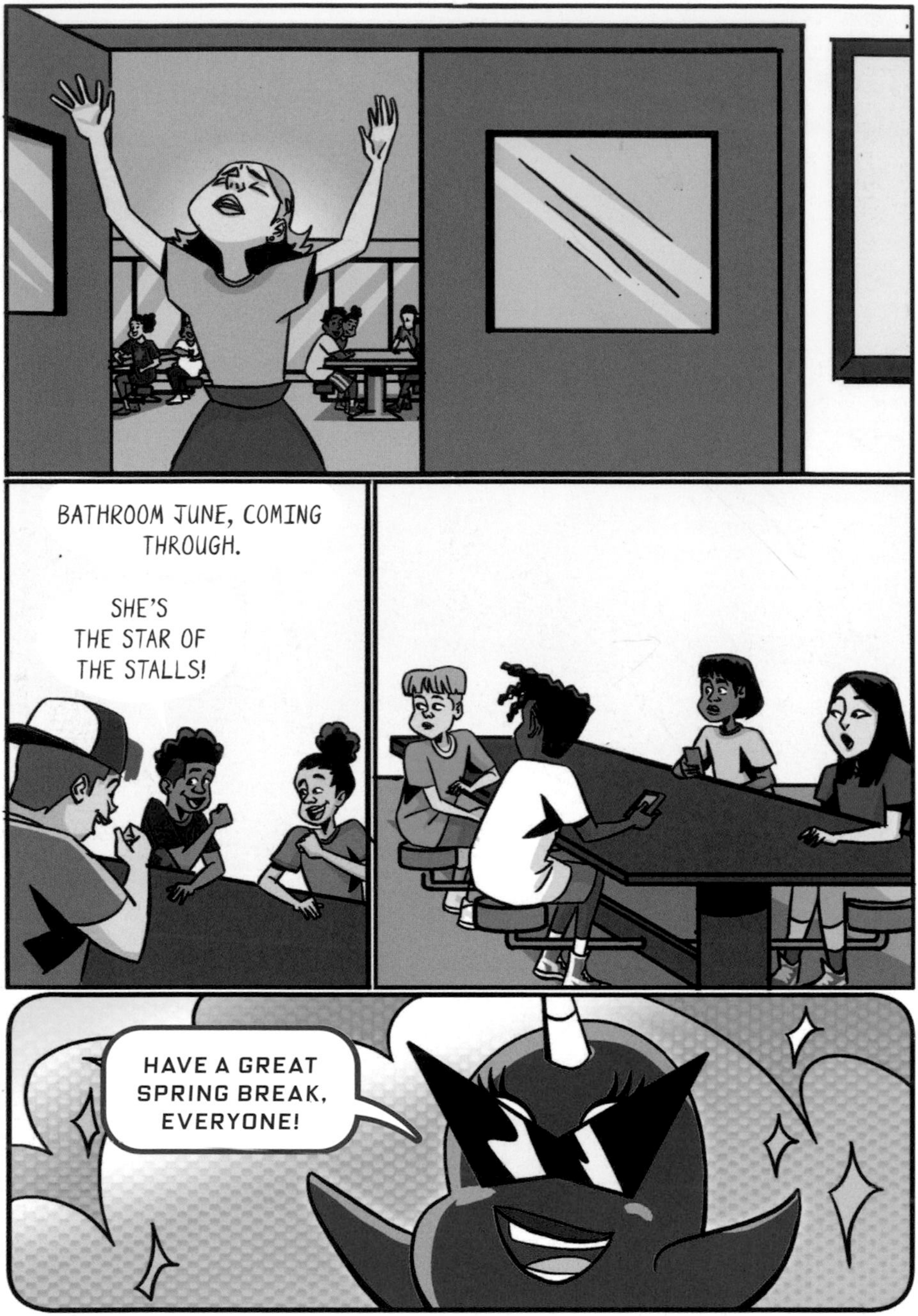
BATHROOM JUNE, COMING THROUGH.
SHE'S THE STAR OF THE STALLS!
HAVE A GREAT SPRING BREAK, EVERYONE!

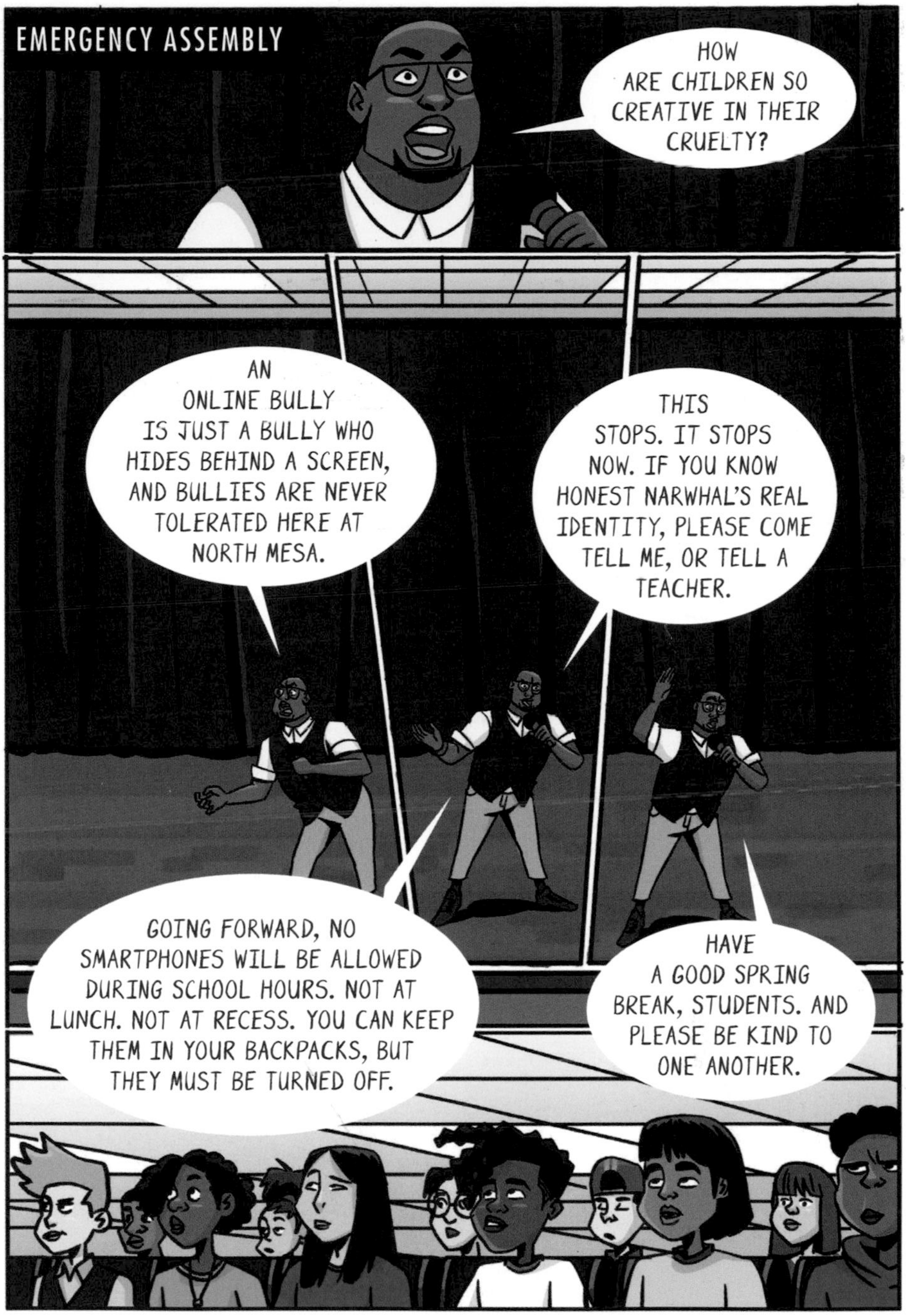
EMERGENCY ASSEMBLY
HOW ARE CHILDREN SO CREATIVE IN THEIR CRUELTY?
AN ONLINE BULLY IS JUST A BULLY WHO HIDES BEHIND A SCREEN, AND BULLIES ARE NEVER TOLERATED HERE AT NORTH MESA.
THIS STOPS. IT STOPS NOW. IF YOU KNOW HONEST NARWHAL'S REAL IDENTITY, PLEASE COME TELL ME, OR TELL A TEACHER.
GOING FORWARD, NO SMARTPHONES WILL BE ALLOWED DURING SCHOOL HOURS. NOT AT LUNCH. NOT AT RECESS. YOU CAN KEEP THEM IN YOUR BACKPACKS, BUT THEY MUST BE TURNED OFF.
HAVE A GOOD SPRING BREAK, STUDENTS. AND PLEASE BE KIND TO ONE ANOTHER.

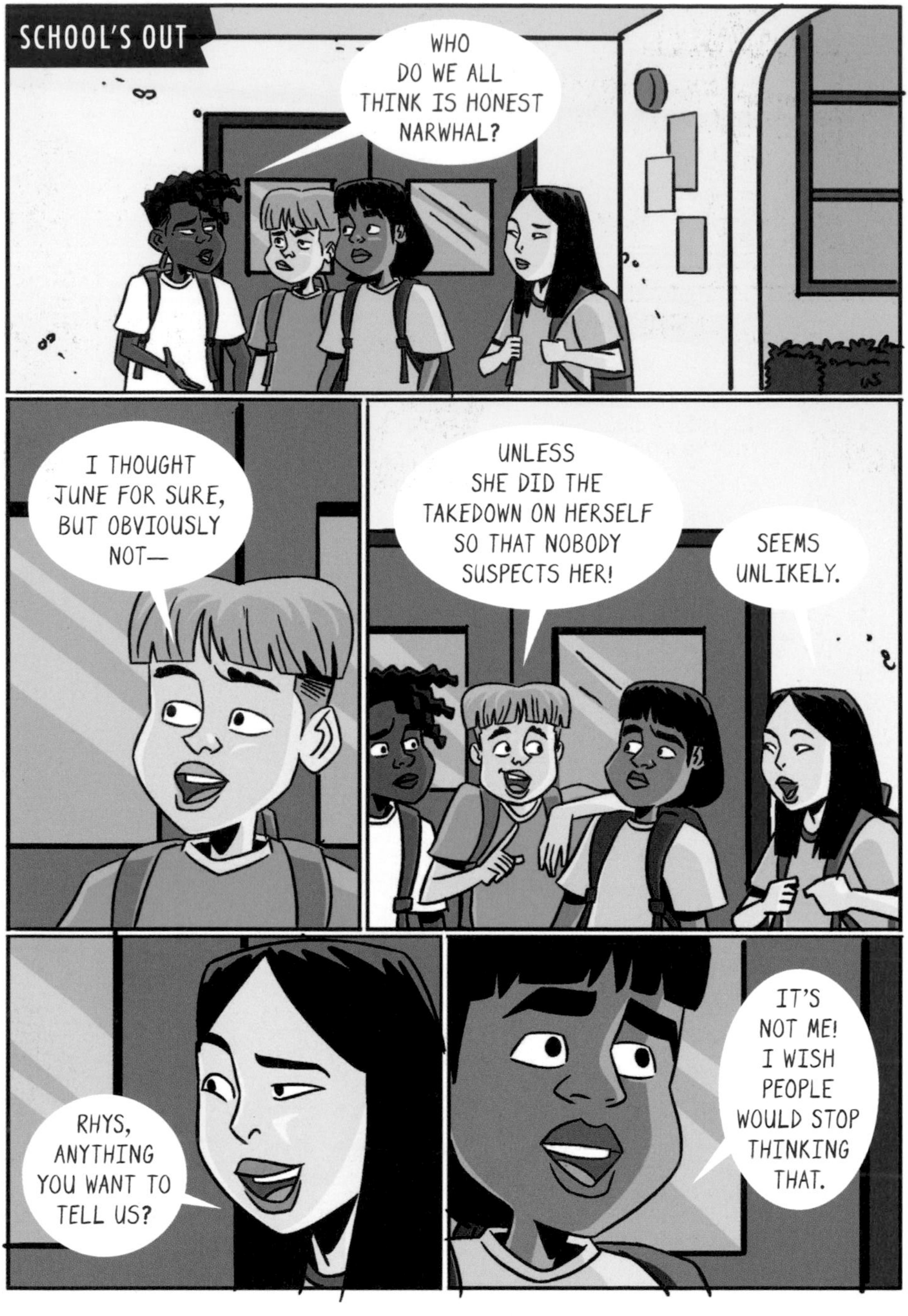
SCHOOL'S OUT
WHO DO WE ALL THINK IS HONEST NARWHAL?
I THOUGHT JUNE FOR SURE, BUT OBVIOUSLY NOT—
UNLESS SHE DID THE TAKEDOWN ON HERSELF SO THAT NOBODY SUSPECTS HER!
SEEMS UNLIKELY.
RHYS, ANYTHING YOU WANT TO TELL US?
IT'S NOT ME! I WISH PEOPLE WOULD STOP THINKING THAT.

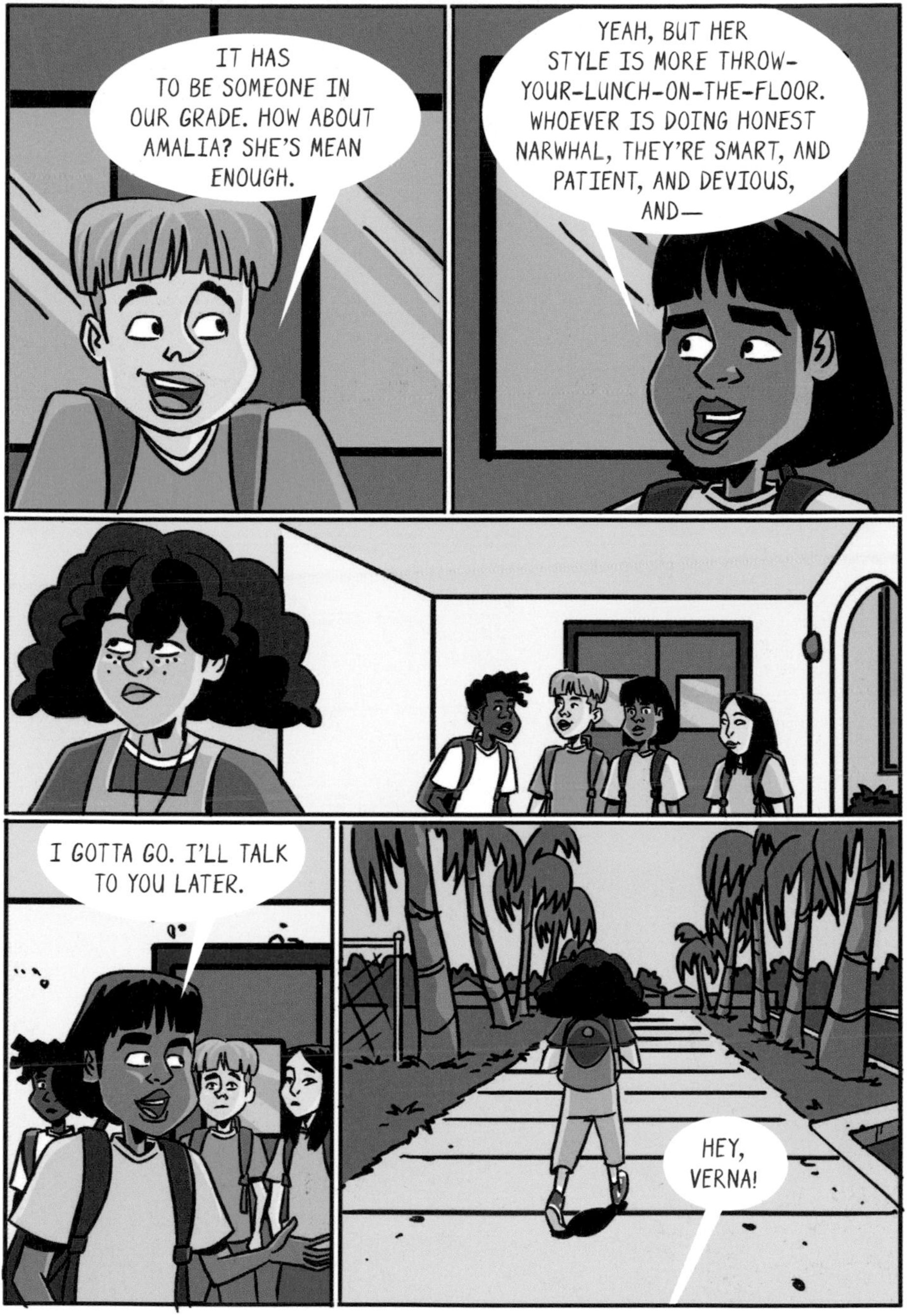
IT HAS TO BE SOMEONE IN OUR GRADE. HOW ABOUT AMALIA? SHE'S MEAN ENOUGH.
YEAH, BUT HER STYLE IS MORE THROW-YOUR-LUNCH-ON-THE-FLOOR. WHOEVER IS DOING HONEST NARWHAL, THEY'RE SMART, AND PATIENT, AND DEVIOUS, AND—
I GOTTA GO. I'LL TALK TO YOU LATER.
HEY, VERNA!

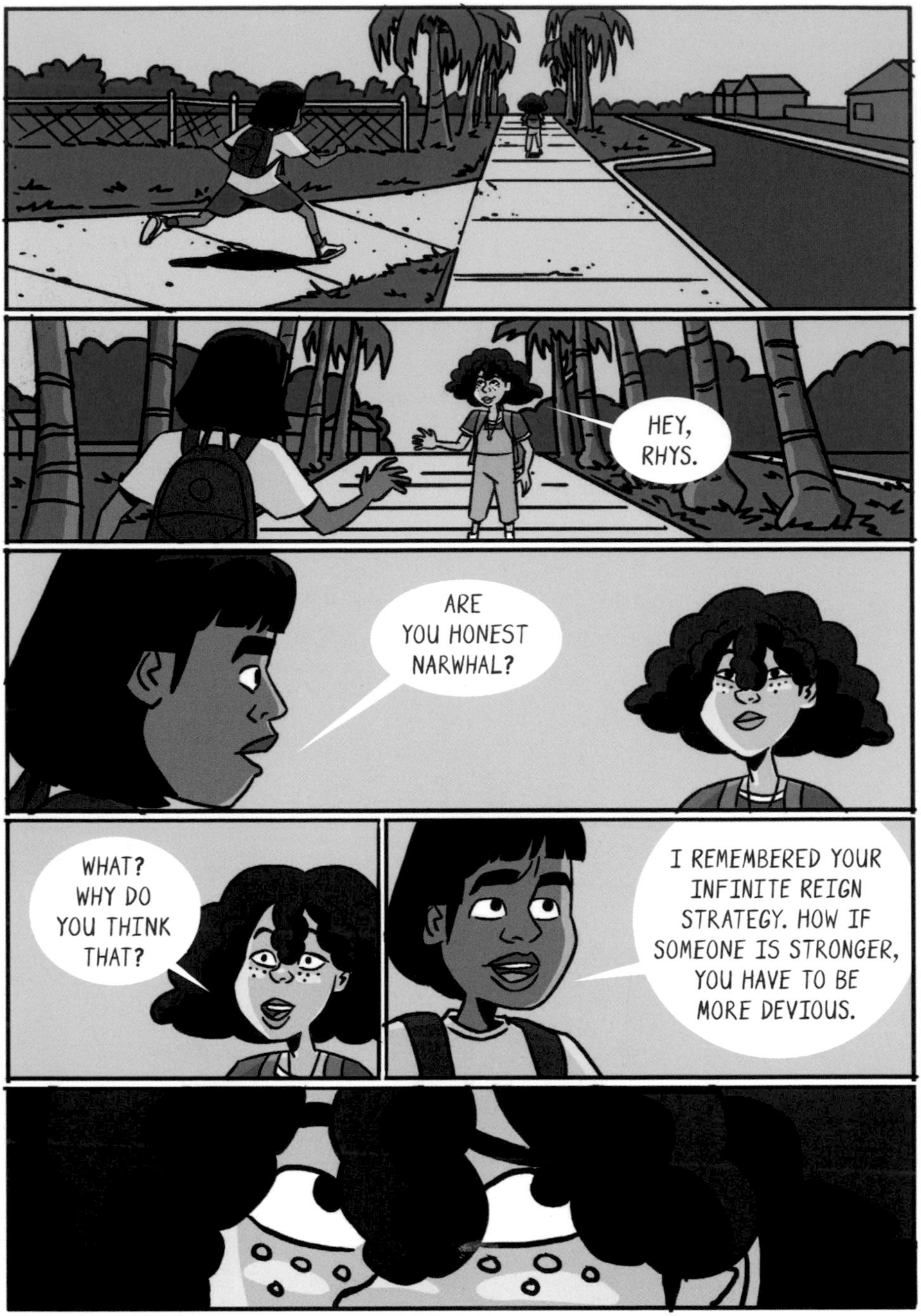
HEY,
RHYS.
ARE
YOU HONEST
NARWHAL?
WHAT?
WHY DO
YOU THINK
THAT?
I REMEMBERED YOUR
INFINITE REIGN
STRATEGY. HOW IF
SOMEONE IS STRONGER,
YOU HAVE TO BE
MORE DEVIOUS.

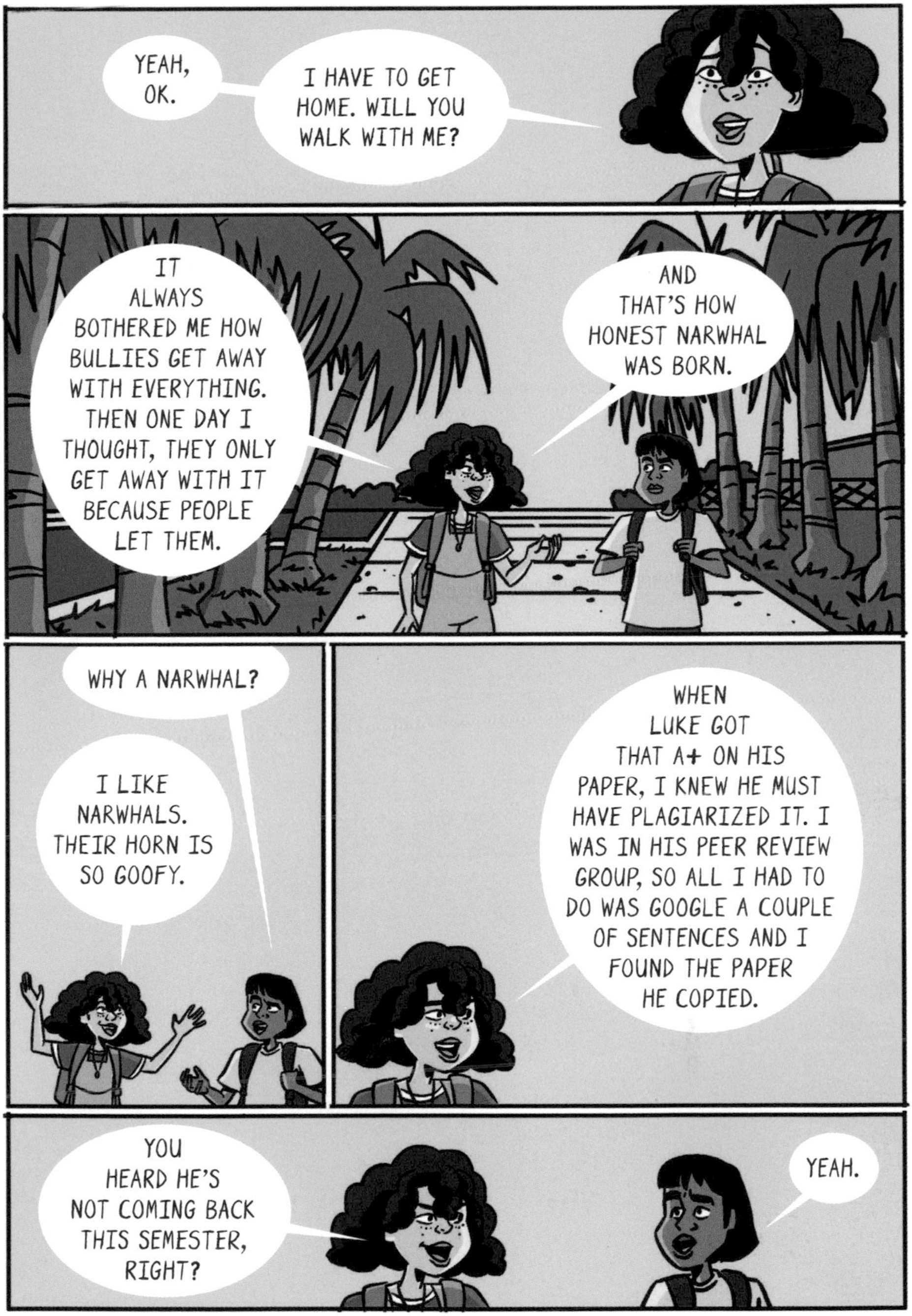
YEAH, OK.
I HAVE TO GET HOME. WILL YOU WALK WITH ME?
IT ALWAYS BOTHERED ME HOW BULLIES GET AWAY WITH EVERYTHING. THEN ONE DAY I THOUGHT, THEY ONLY GET AWAY WITH IT BECAUSE PEOPLE LET THEM.
AND THAT'S HOW HONEST NARWHAL WAS BORN.
WHY A NARWHAL?
I LIKE NARWHALS. THEIR HORN IS SO GOOFY.
WHEN LUKE GOT THAT A+ ON HIS PAPER, I KNEW HE MUST HAVE PLAGIARIZED IT. I WAS IN HIS PEER REVIEW GROUP, SO ALL I HAD TO DO WAS GOOGLE A COUPLE OF SENTENCES AND I FOUND THE PAPER HE COPIED.
YOU HEARD HE'S NOT COMING BACK THIS SEMESTER, RIGHT?
YEAH.

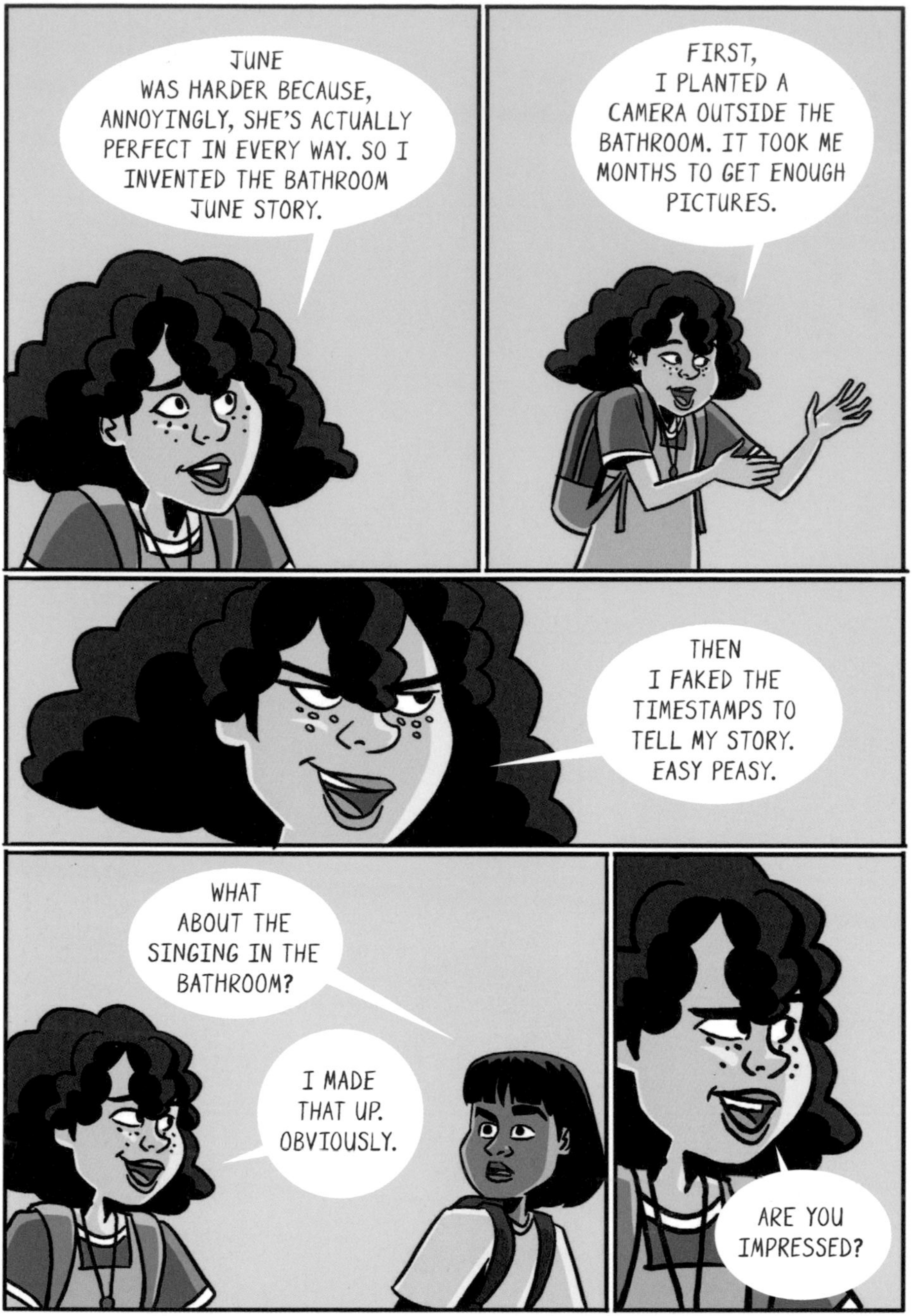
JUNE WAS HARDER BECAUSE, ANNOYINGLY, SHE'S ACTUALLY PERFECT IN EVERY WAY. SO I INVENTED THE BATHROOM JUNE STORY.
FIRST, I PLANTED A CAMERA OUTSIDE THE BATHROOM. IT TOOK ME MONTHS TO GET ENOUGH PICTURES.
THEN I FAKED THE TIMESTAMPS TO TELL MY STORY. EASY PEASY.
WHAT ABOUT THE SINGING IN THE BATHROOM?
I MADE THAT UP. OBVIOUSLY.
ARE YOU IMPRESSED?

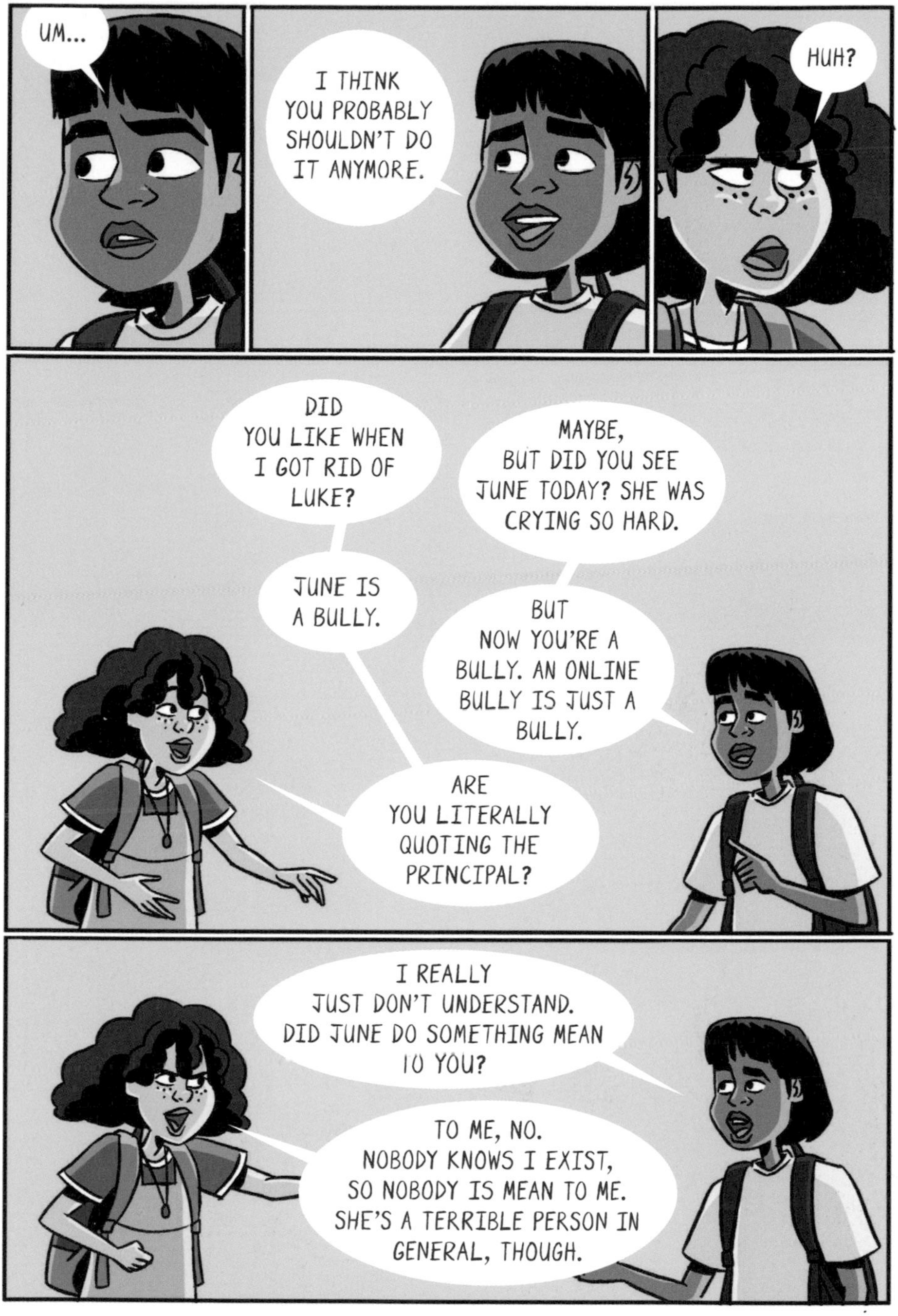
UM...
I THINK YOU PROBABLY SHOULDN'T DO IT ANYMORE.
HUH?
DID YOU LIKE WHEN I GOT RID OF LUKE?
MAYBE, BUT DID YOU SEE JUNE TODAY? SHE WAS CRYING SO HARD.
JUNE IS A BULLY.
BUT NOW YOU'RE A BULLY. AN ONLINE BULLY IS JUST A BULLY.
ARE YOU LITERALLY QUOTING THE PRINCIPAL?
I REALLY JUST DON'T UNDERSTAND. DID JUNE DO SOMETHING MEAN TO YOU?
TO ME, NO. NOBODY KNOWS I EXIST, SO NOBODY IS MEAN TO ME. SHE'S A TERRIBLE PERSON IN GENERAL, THOUGH.

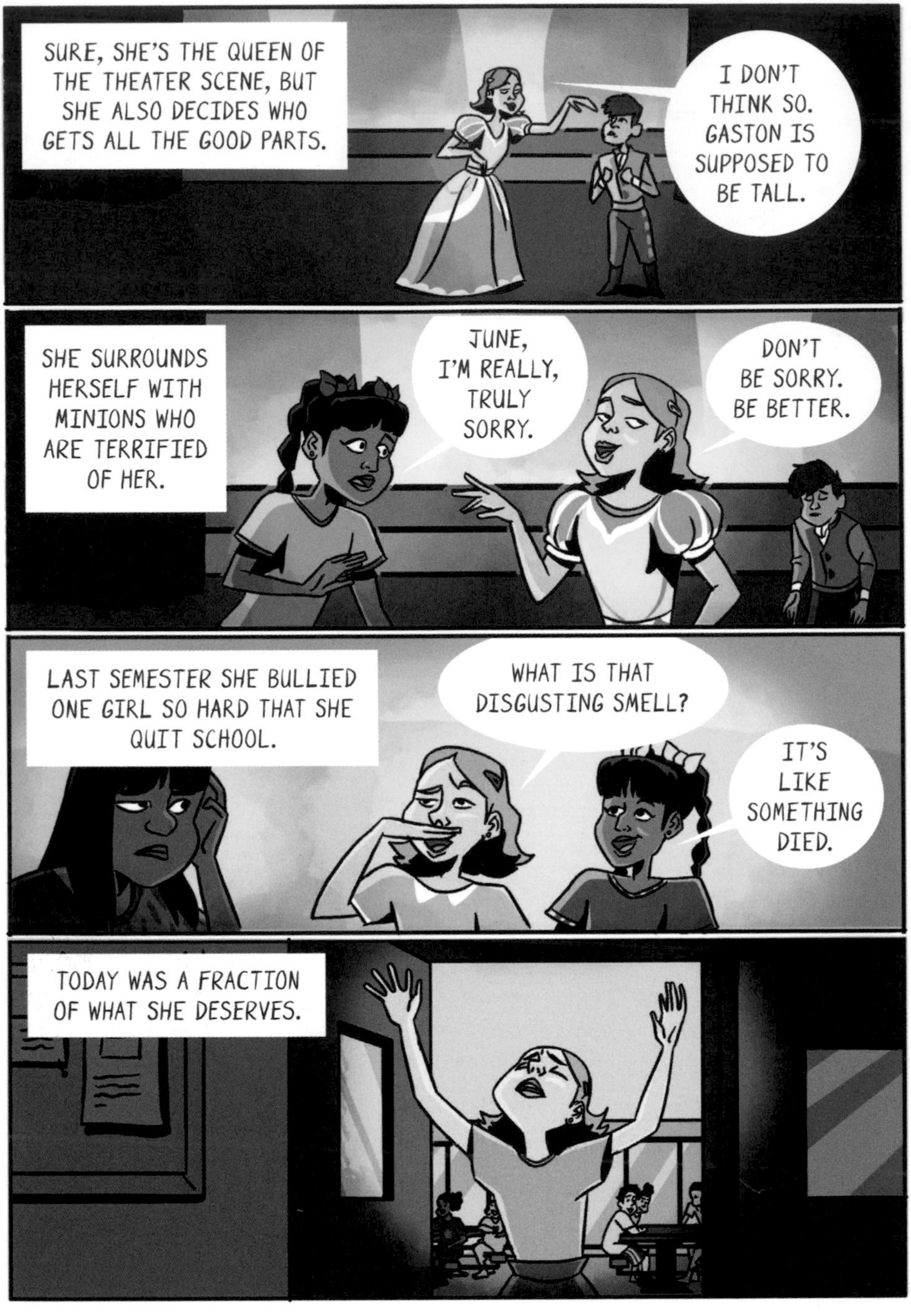
SURE, SHE'S THE QUEEN OF THE THEATER SCENE, BUT SHE ALSO DECIDES WHO GETS ALL THE GOOD PARTS.
I DON'T THINK SO. GASTON IS SUPPOSED TO BE TALL.
SHE SURROUNDS HERSELF WITH MINIONS WHO ARE TERRIFIED OF HER.
JUNE, I'M REALLY, TRULY SORRY.
DON'T BE SORRY. BE BETTER.
LAST SEMESTER SHE BULLIED ONE GIRL SO HARD THAT SHE QUIT SCHOOL.
WHAT IS THAT DISGUSTING SMELL?
IT'S LIKE SOMETHING DIED.
TODAY WAS A FRACTION OF WHAT SHE DESERVES.

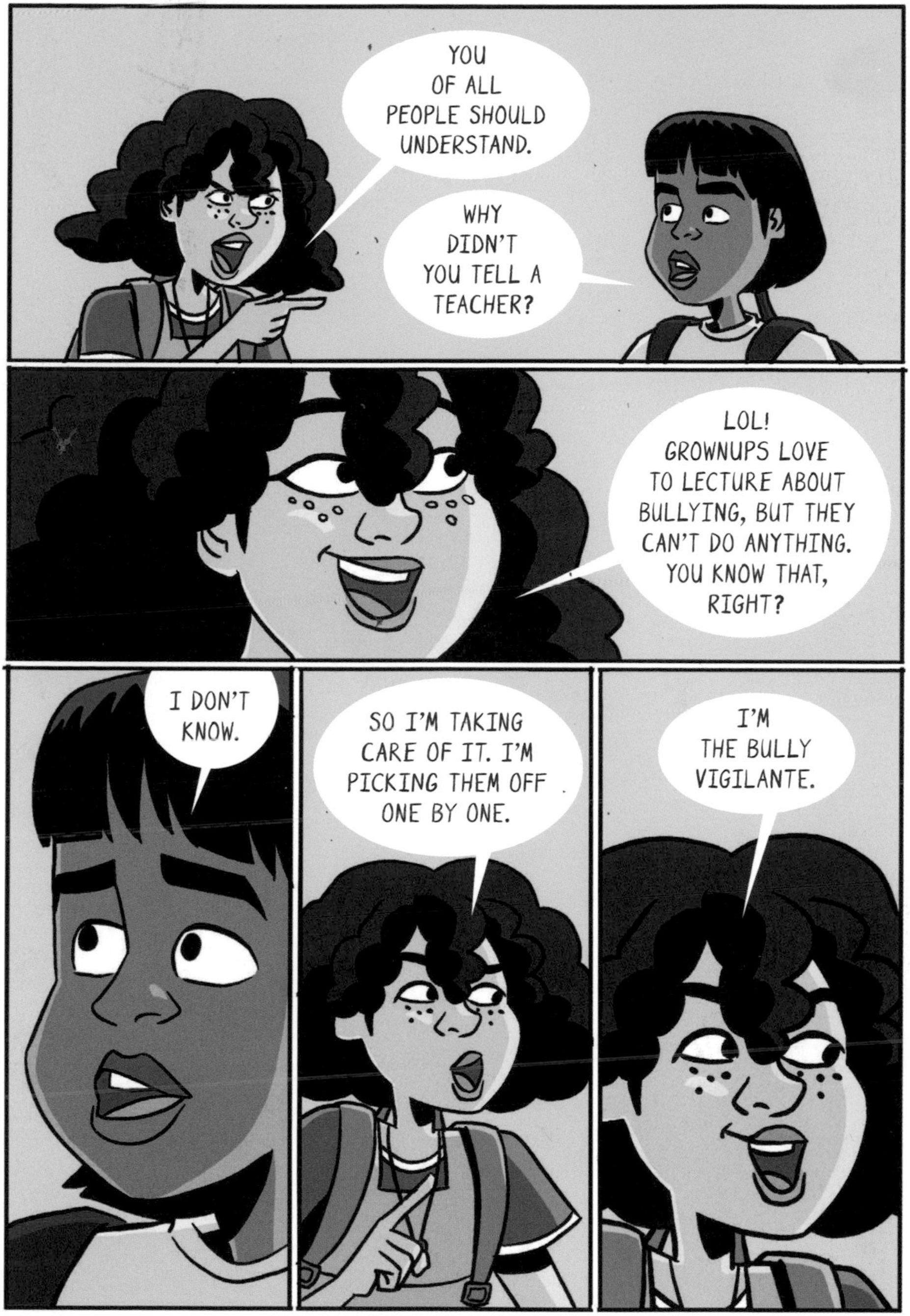
YOU OF ALL PEOPLE SHOULD UNDERSTAND.
WHY DIDN'T YOU TELL A TEACHER?
LOL! GROWNUPS LOVE TO LECTURE ABOUT BULLYING, BUT THEY CAN'T DO ANYTHING. YOU KNOW THAT, RIGHT?
I DON'T KNOW.
SO I'M TAKING CARE OF IT. I'M PICKING THEM OFF ONE BY ONE.
I'M THE BULLY VIGILANTE.

CHAPTER 10

BREAK

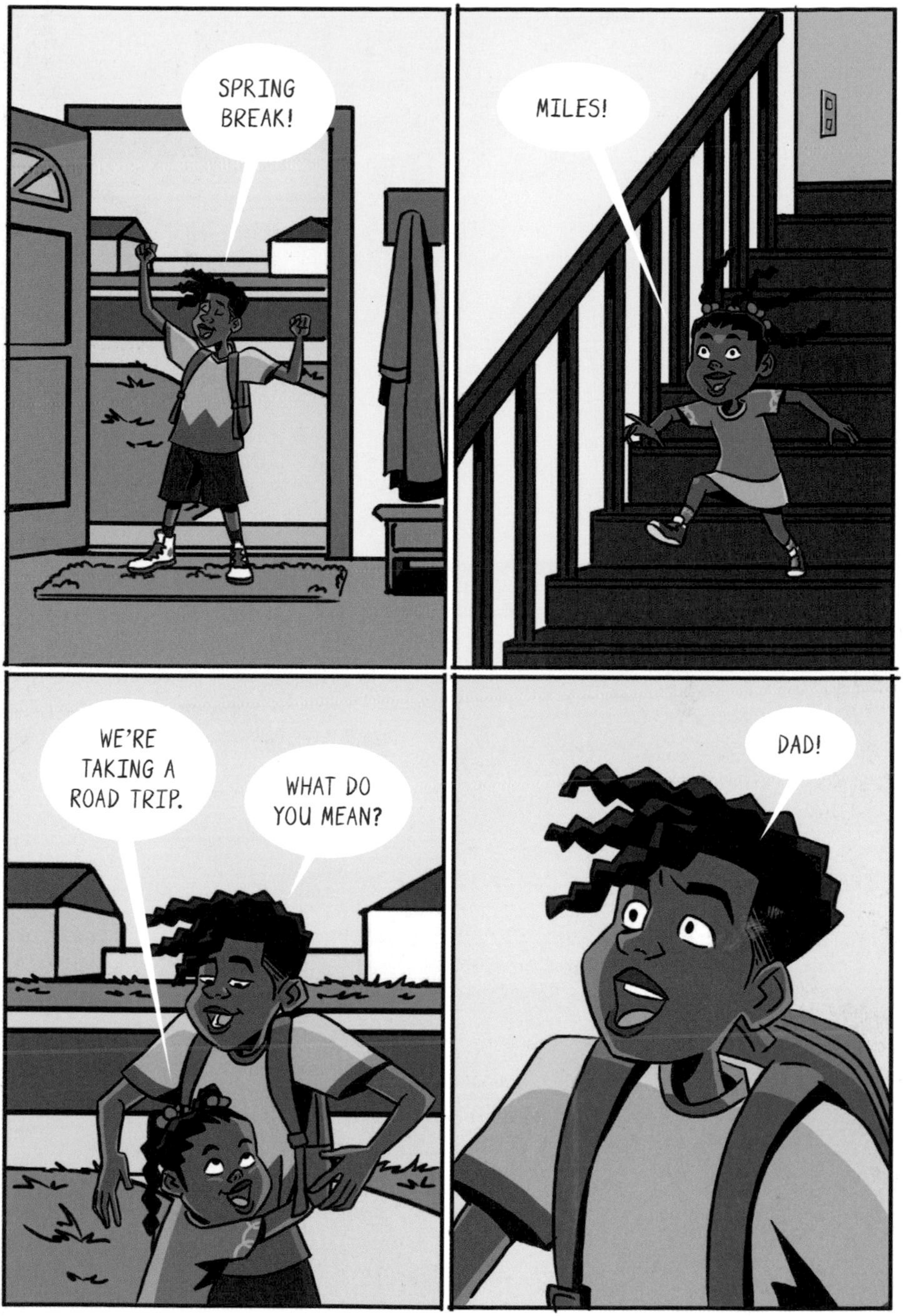
SPRING BREAK!
MILES!
WE'RE TAKING A ROAD TRIP.
WHAT DO YOU MEAN?
DAD!

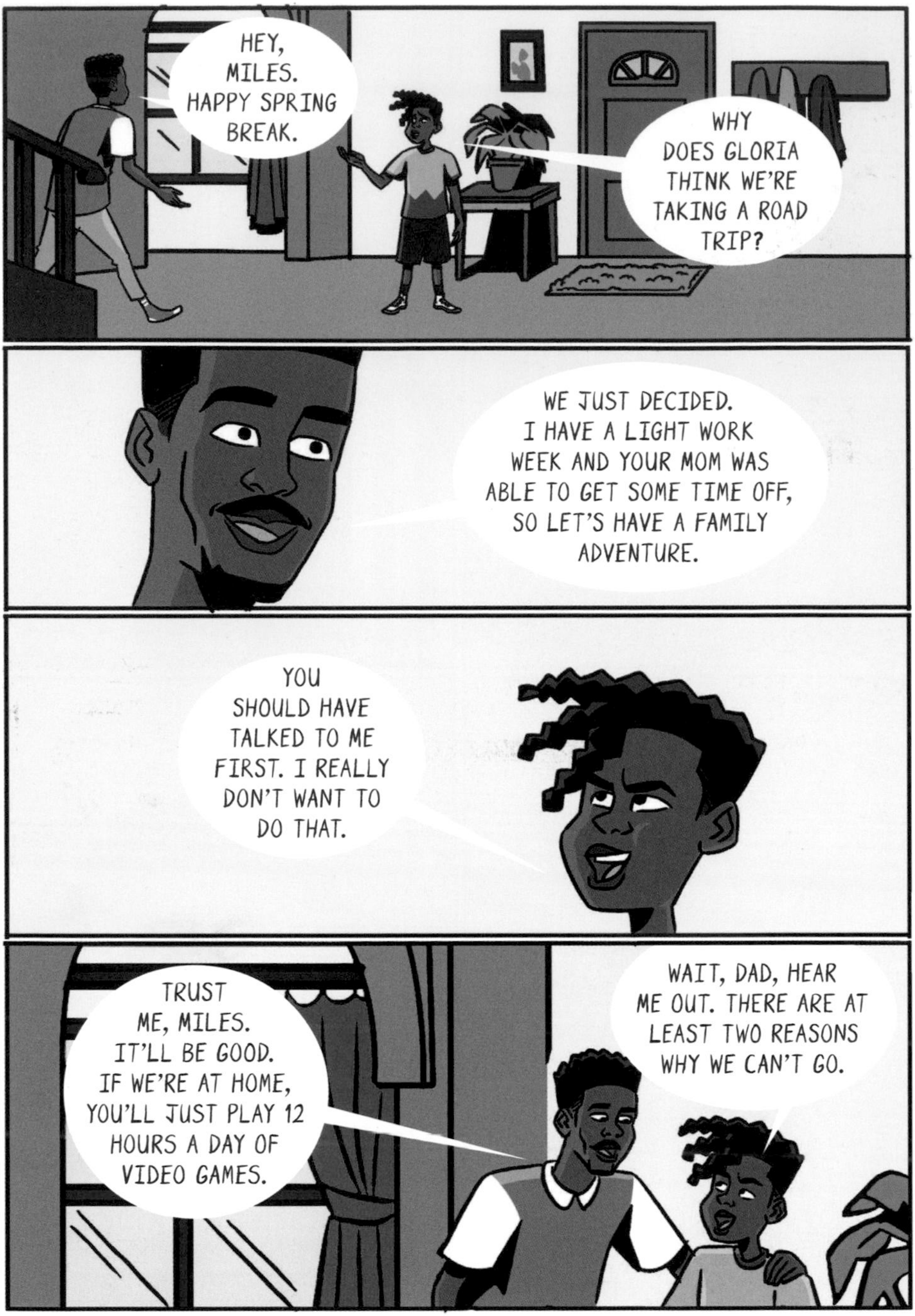
HEY, MILES. HAPPY SPRING BREAK.
WHY DOES GLORIA THINK WE'RE TAKING A ROAD TRIP?
WE JUST DECIDED. I HAVE A LIGHT WORK WEEK AND YOUR MOM WAS ABLE TO GET SOME TIME OFF, SO LET'S HAVE A FAMILY ADVENTURE.
YOU SHOULD HAVE TALKED TO ME FIRST. I REALLY DON'T WANT TO DO THAT.
TRUST ME, MILES. IT'LL BE GOOD. IF WE'RE AT HOME, YOU'LL JUST PLAY 12 HOURS A DAY OF VIDEO GAMES.
WAIT, DAD, HEAR ME OUT. THERE ARE AT LEAST TWO REASONS WHY WE CAN'T GO.

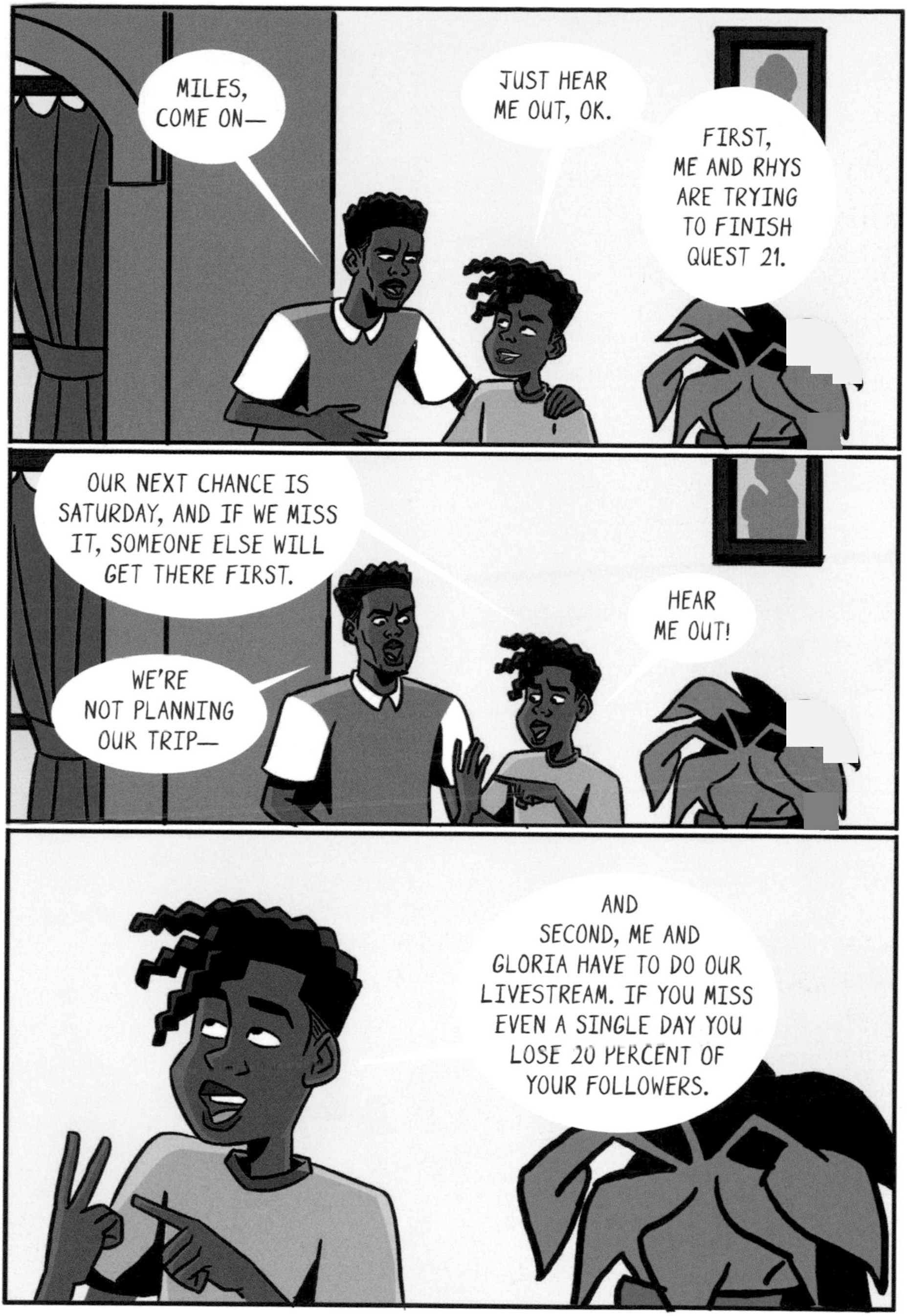
MILES, COME ON—
JUST HEAR ME OUT, OK.
FIRST, ME AND RHYS ARE TRYING TO FINISH QUEST 21.
OUR NEXT CHANCE IS SATURDAY, AND IF WE MISS IT, SOMEONE ELSE WILL GET THERE FIRST.
WE'RE NOT PLANNING OUR TRIP—
HEAR ME OUT!
AND SECOND, ME AND GLORIA HAVE TO DO OUR LIVESTREAM. IF YOU MISS EVEN A SINGLE DAY YOU LOSE 20 PERCENT OF YOUR FOLLOWERS.

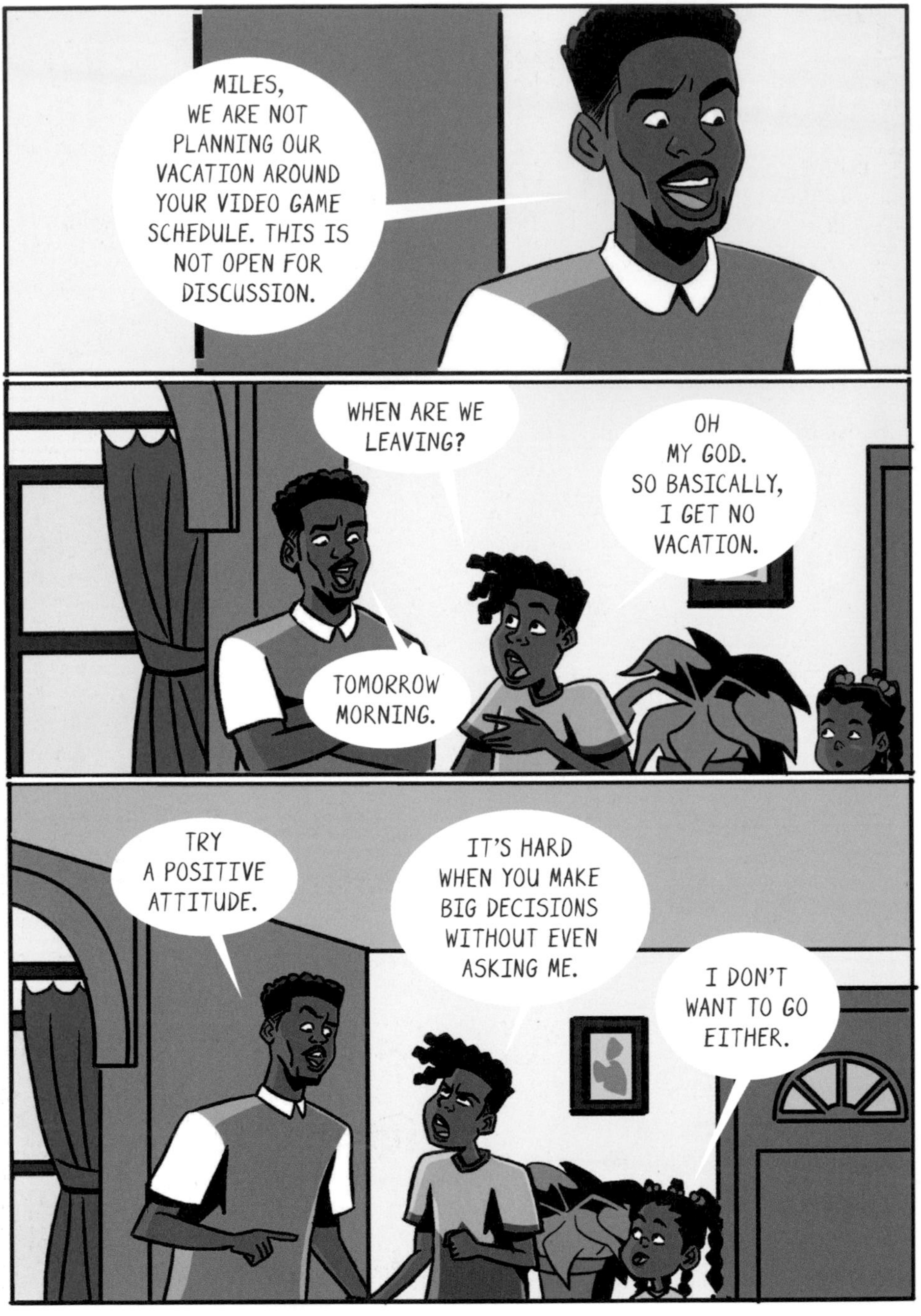
MILES, WE ARE NOT PLANNING OUR VACATION AROUND YOUR VIDEO GAME SCHEDULE. THIS IS NOT OPEN FOR DISCUSSION.
WHEN ARE WE LEAVING?
TOMORROW MORNING.
OH MY GOD. SO BASICALLY, I GET NO VACATION.
TRY A POSITIVE ATTITUDE.
IT'S HARD WHEN YOU MAKE BIG DECISIONS WITHOUT EVEN ASKING ME.
I DON'T WANT TO GO EITHER.

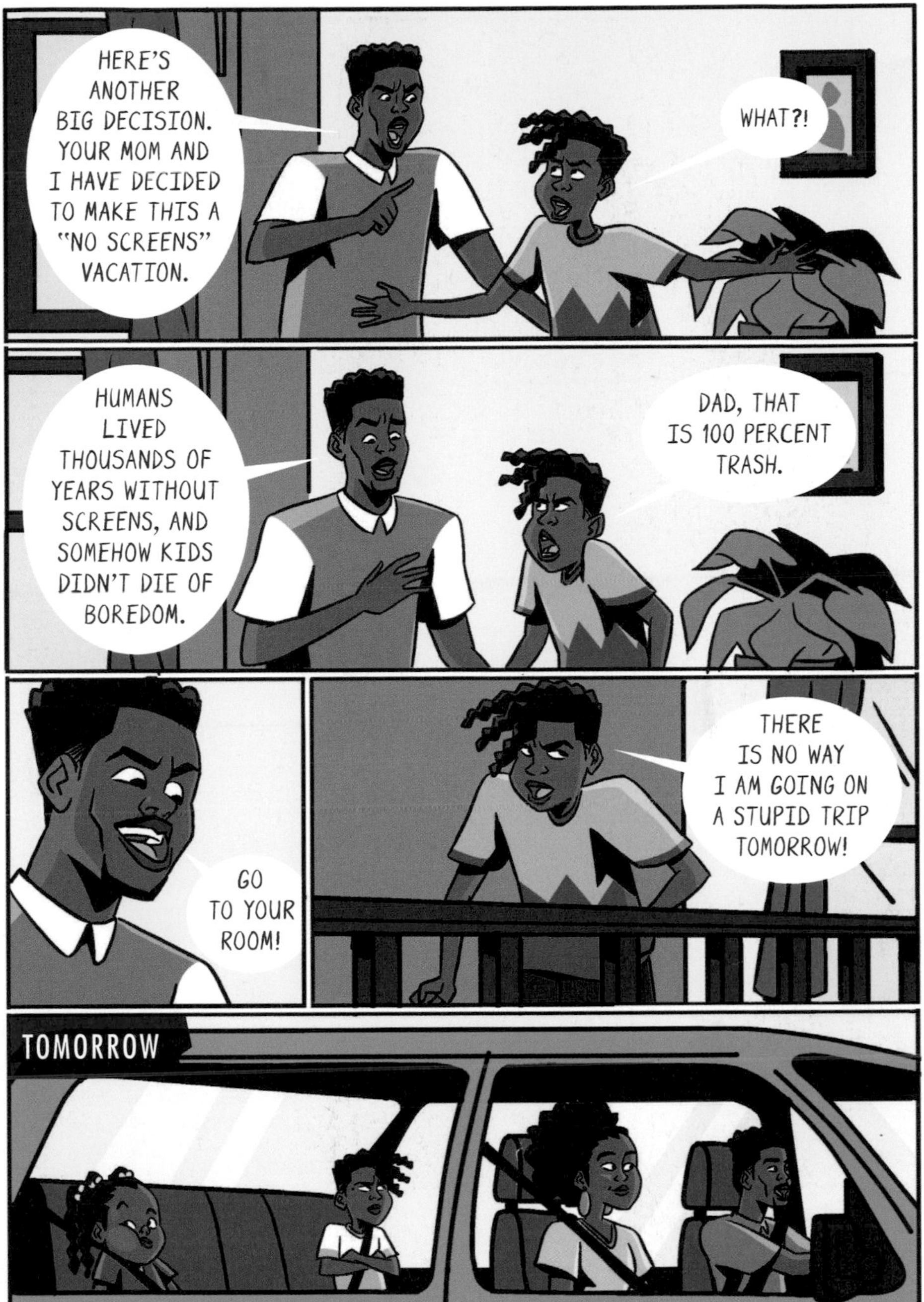
HERE'S ANOTHER BIG DECISION. YOUR MOM AND I HAVE DECIDED TO MAKE THIS A "NO SCREENS" VACATION.
WHAT?!
HUMANS LIVED THOUSANDS OF YEARS WITHOUT SCREENS, AND SOMEHOW KIDS DIDN'T DIE OF BOREDOM.
DAD, THAT IS 100 PERCENT TRASH.
THERE IS NO WAY I AM GOING ON A STUPID TRIP TOMORROW!
GO TO YOUR ROOM!
TOMORROW

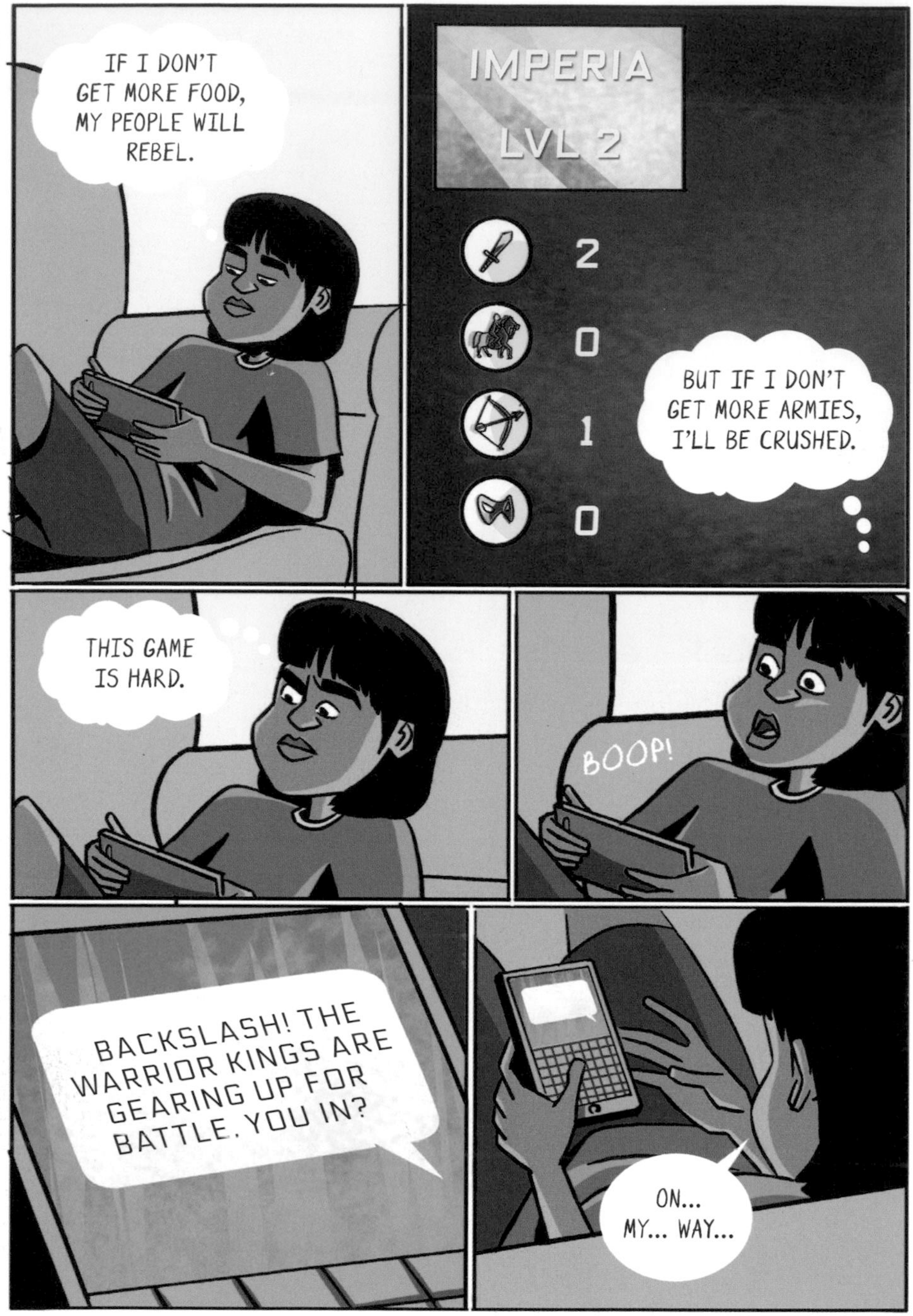
IF I DON'T GET MORE FOOD, MY PEOPLE WILL REBEL.
IMPERIA
LVL 2
2
0
1
0
BUT IF I DON'T GET MORE ARMIES, I'LL BE CRUSHED.
THIS GAME IS HARD.
BOOP!
BACKSLASH! THE WARRIOR KINGS ARE GEARING UP FOR BATTLE. YOU IN?
ON... MY... WAY...

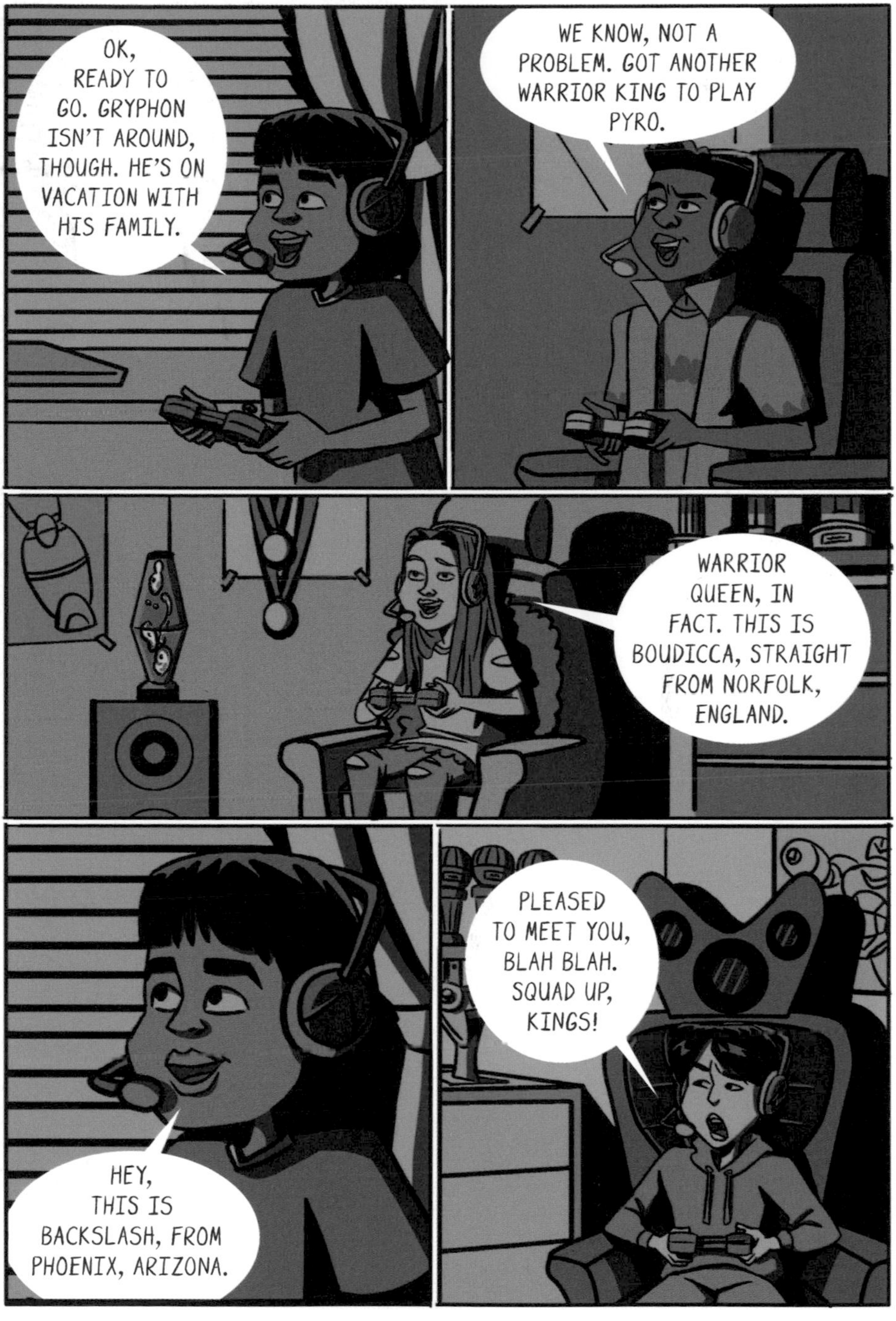
OK, READY TO GO. GRYPHON ISN'T AROUND, THOUGH. HE'S ON VACATION WITH HIS FAMILY.
WE KNOW, NOT A PROBLEM. GOT ANOTHER WARRIOR KING TO PLAY PYRO.
WARRIOR QUEEN, IN FACT. THIS IS BOUDICCA, STRAIGHT FROM NORFOLK, ENGLAND.
HEY, THIS IS BACKSLASH, FROM PHOENIX, ARIZONA.
PLEASED TO MEET YOU, BLAH BLAH. SQUAD UP, KINGS!

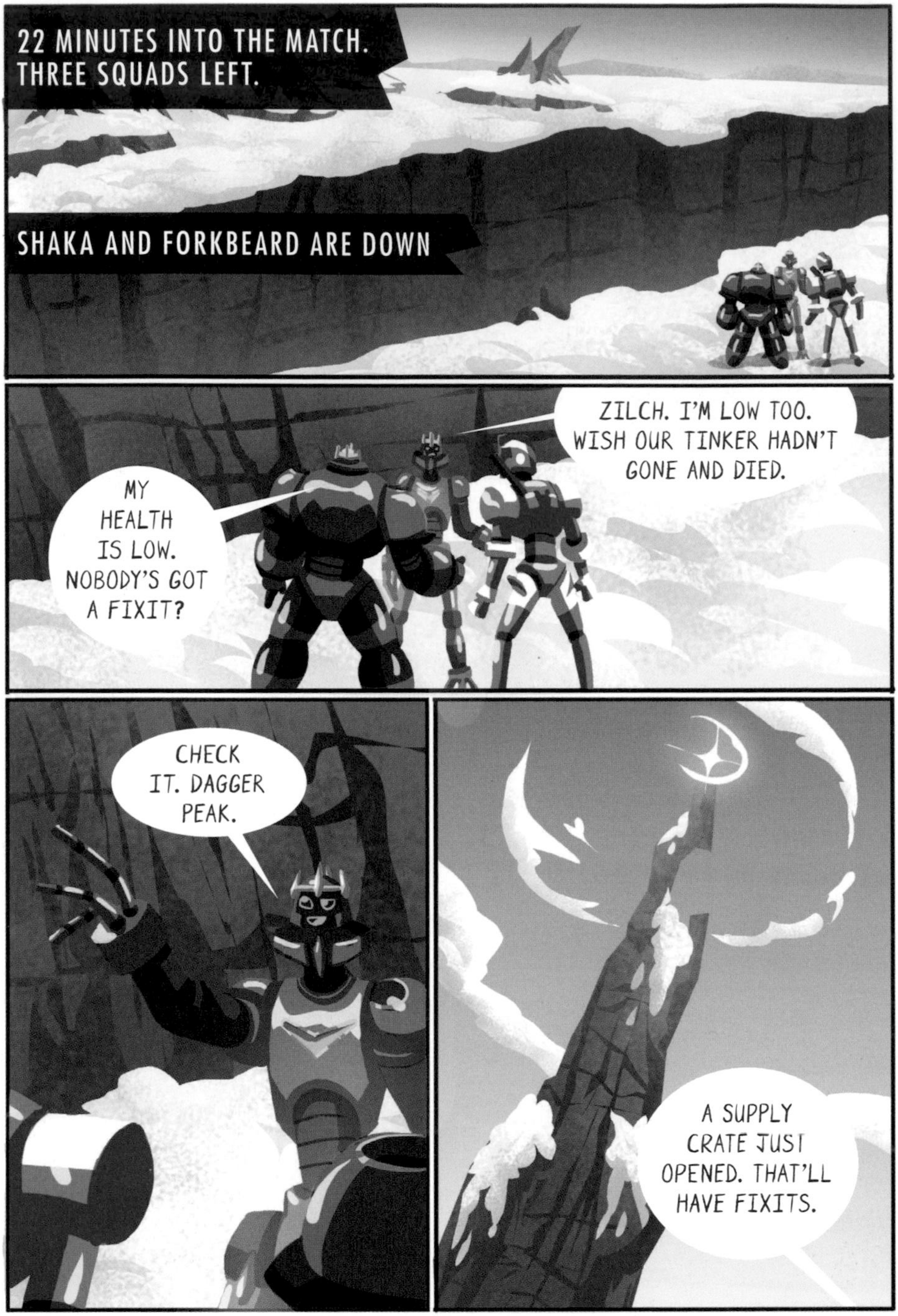
22 MINUTES INTO THE MATCH.
THREE SQUADS LEFT.
SHAKA AND FORKBEARD ARE DOWN
MY HEALTH IS LOW. NOBODY'S GOT A FIXIT?
ZILCH. I'M LOW TOO. WISH OUR TINKER HADN'T GONE AND DIED.
CHECK IT. DAGGER PEAK.
A SUPPLY CRATE JUST OPENED. THAT'LL HAVE FIXITS.

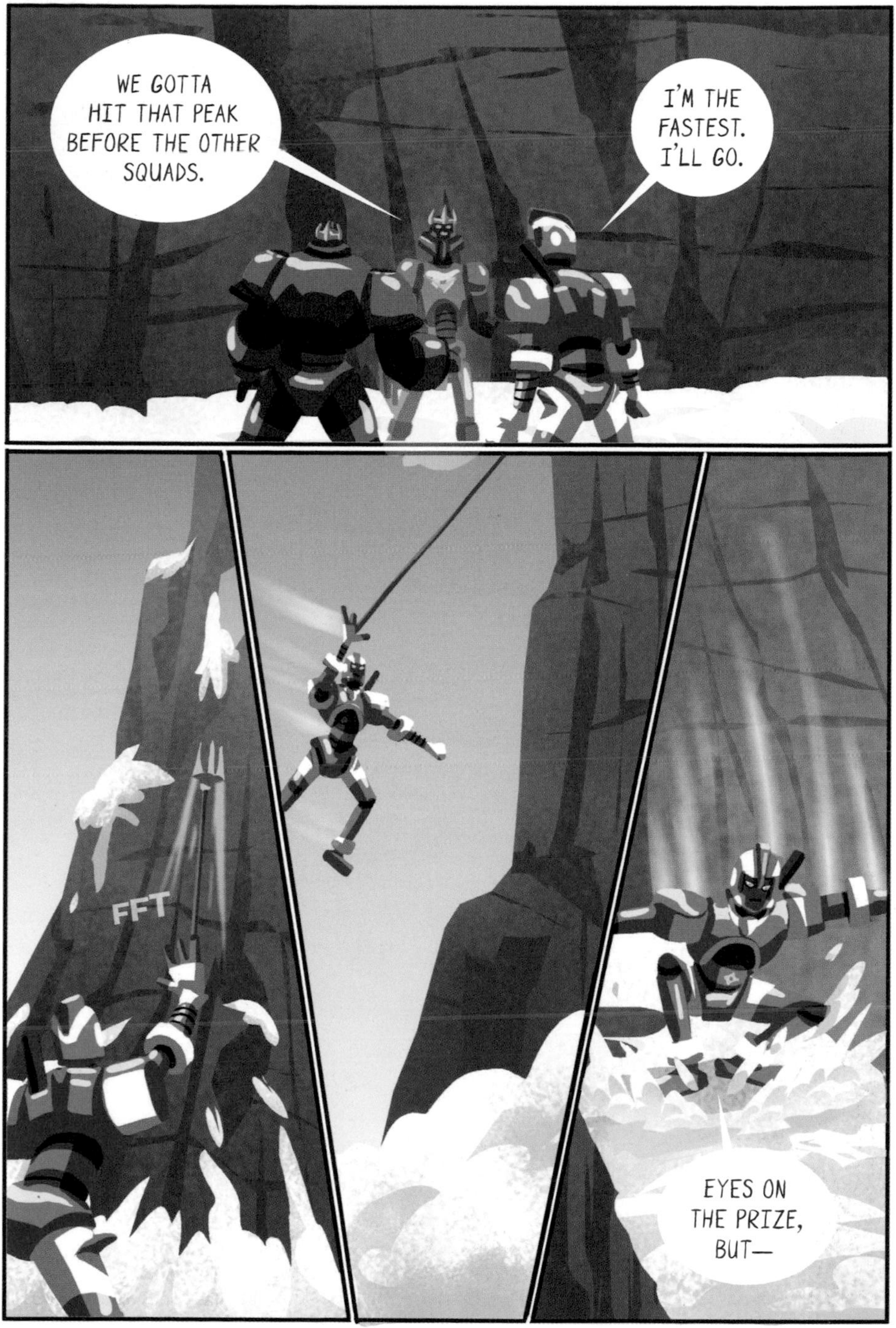
WE GOTTA HIT THAT PEAK BEFORE THE OTHER SQUADS.
I'M THE FASTEST. I'LL GO.
FFT
EYES ON THE PRIZE, BUT—

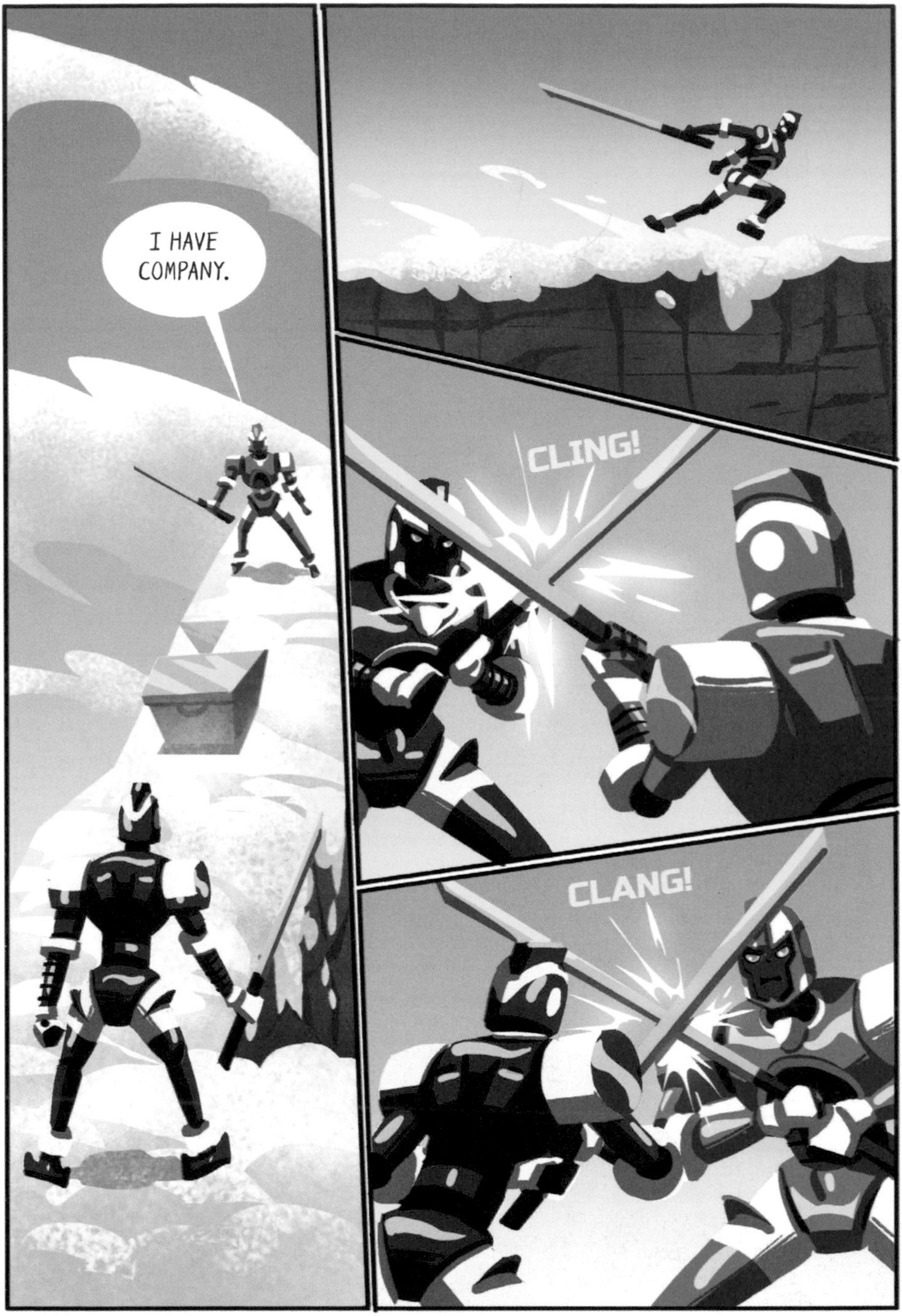
I HAVE COMPANY.
CLING!
CLANG!

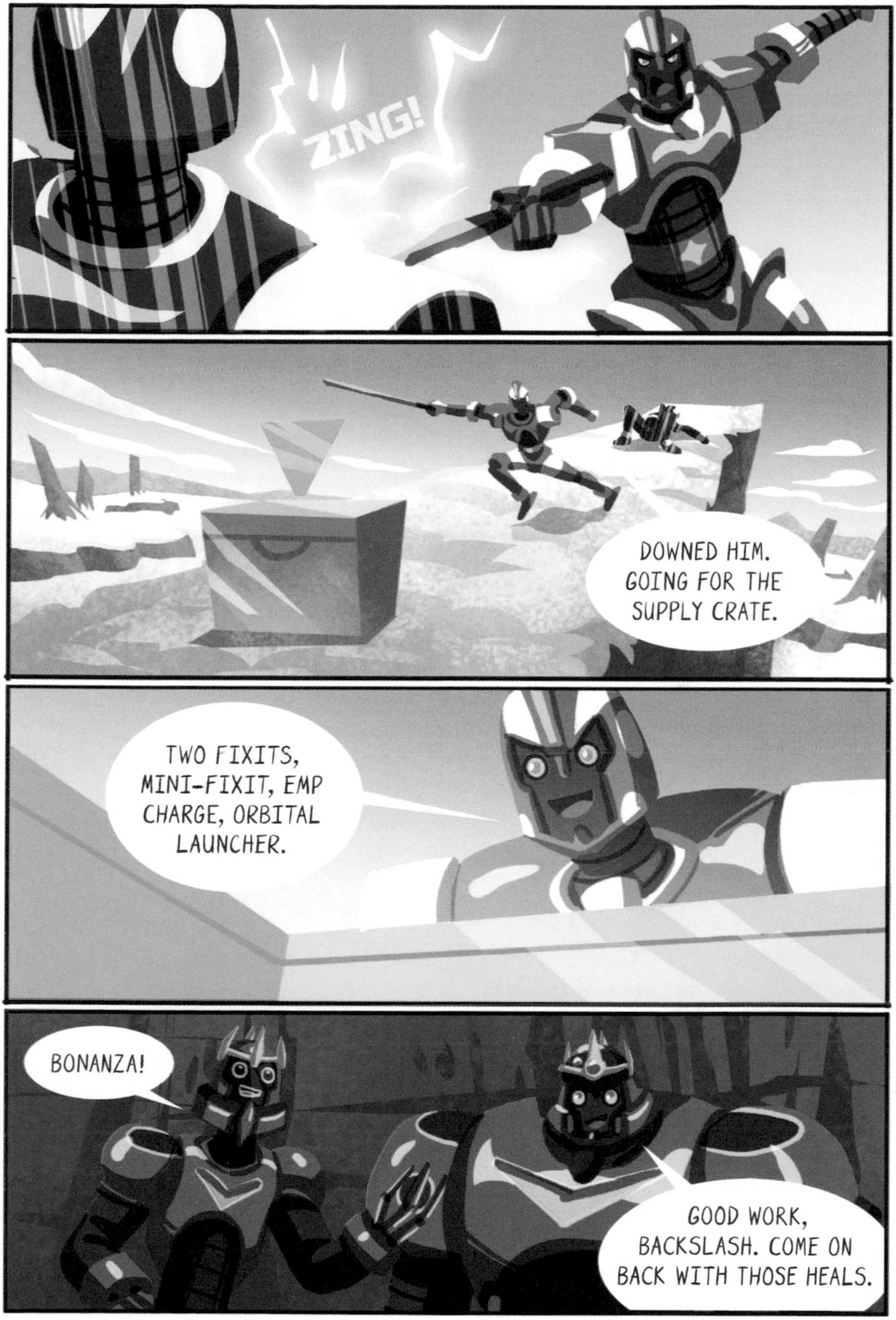
ZING!
DOWNED HIM. GOING FOR THE SUPPLY CRATE.
TWO FIXITS, MINI-FIXIT, EMP CHARGE, ORBITAL LAUNCHER.
BONANZA!
GOOD WORK, BACKSLASH. COME ON BACK WITH THOSE HEALS.

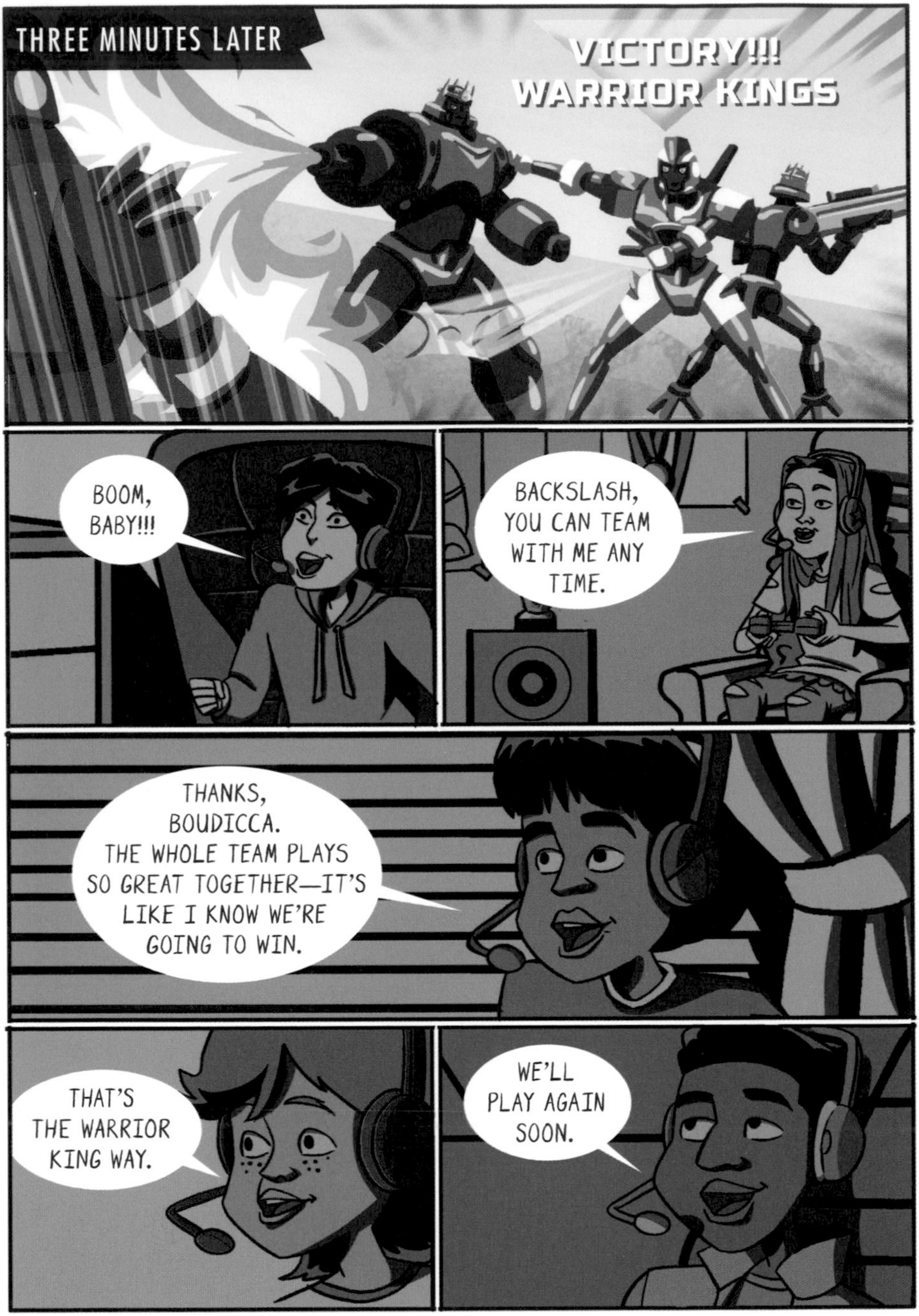
THREE MINUTES LATER
VICTORY!!!
WARRIOR KINGS
BOOM, BABY!!!
BACKSLASH, YOU CAN TEAM WITH ME ANY TIME.
THANKS, BOUDICCA. THE WHOLE TEAM PLAYS SO GREAT TOGETHER—IT'S LIKE I KNOW WE'RE GOING TO WIN.
THAT'S THE WARRIOR KING WAY.
WE'LL PLAY AGAIN SOON.

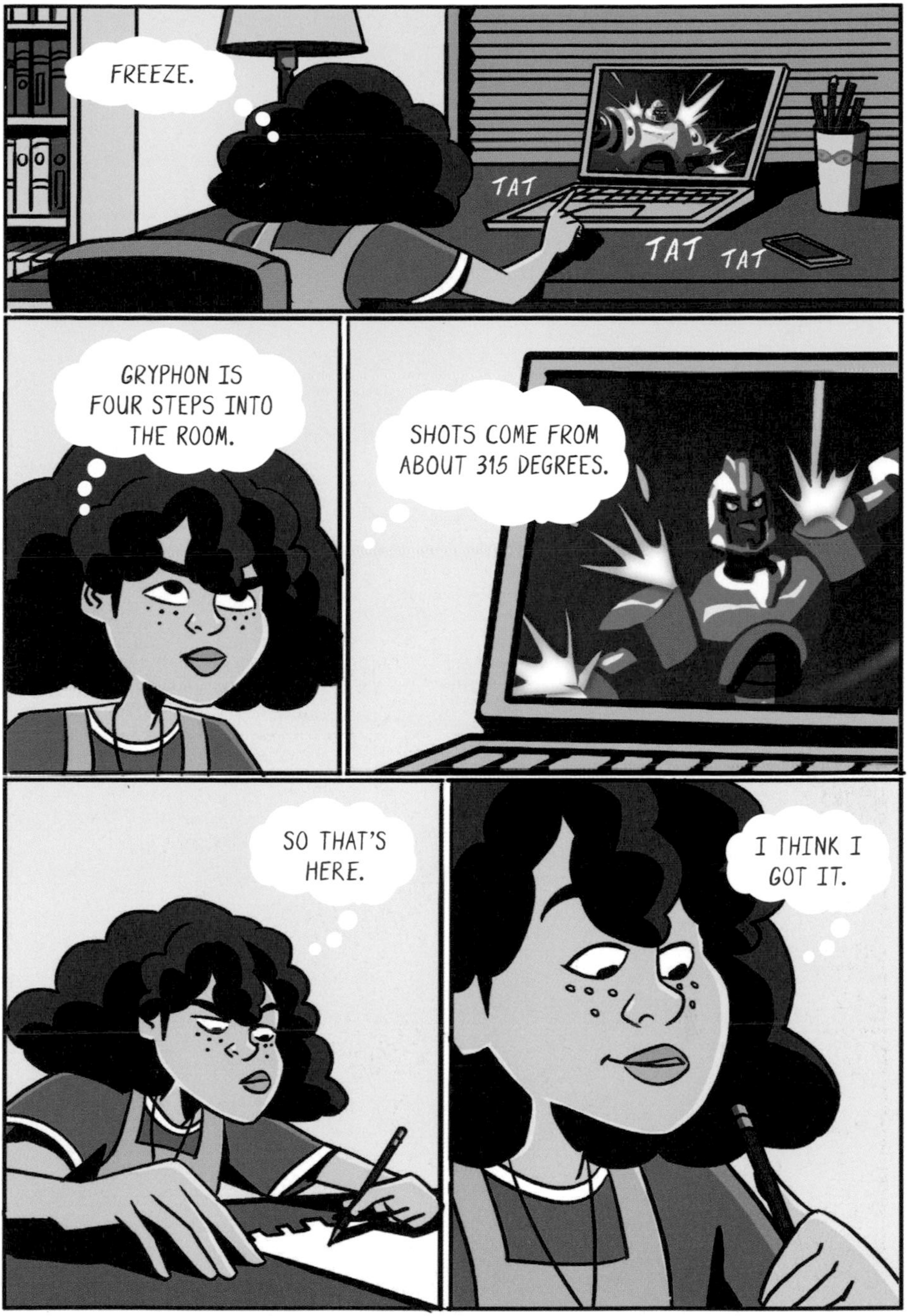
FREEZE.
TAT
TAT
TAT
GRYPHON IS FOUR STEPS INTO THE ROOM.
SHOTS COME FROM ABOUT 315 DEGREES.
SO THAT'S HERE.
I THINK I GOT IT.

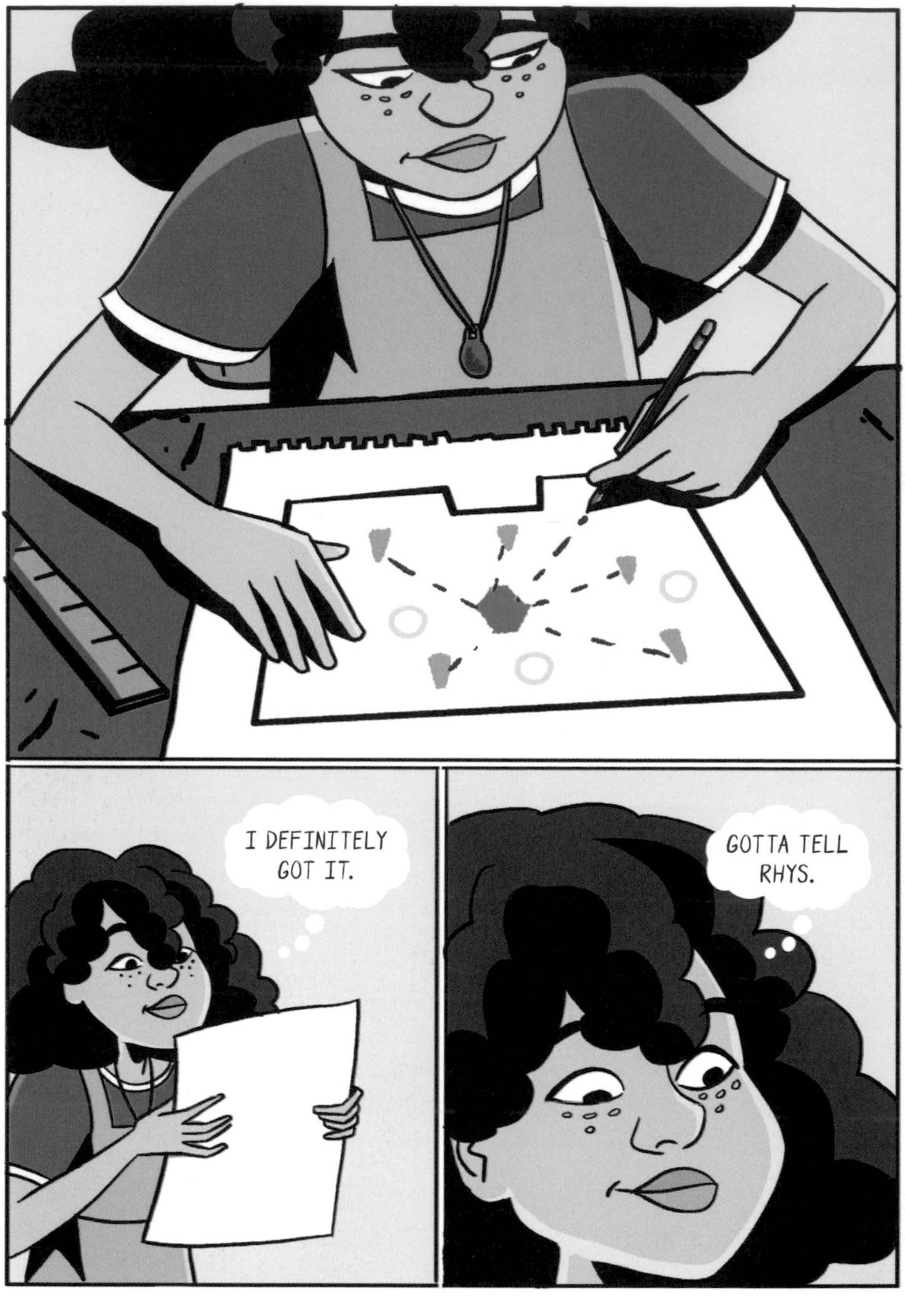
I DEFINITELY GOT IT.
GOTTA TELL RHYS.

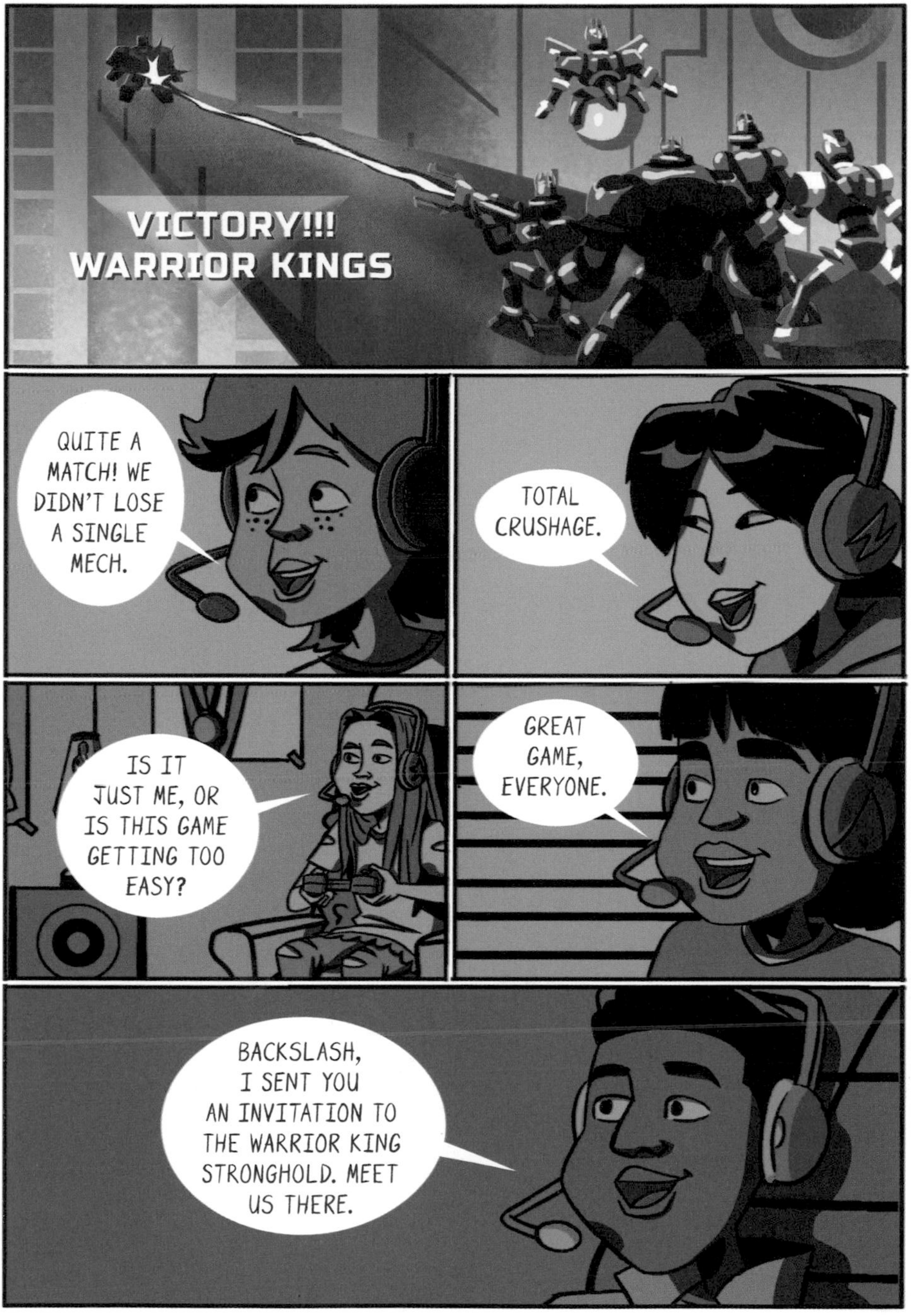
VICTORY!!!
WARRIOR KINGS
QUITE A MATCH! WE DIDN'T LOSE A SINGLE MECH.
TOTAL CRUSHAGE.
IS IT JUST ME, OR IS THIS GAME GETTING TOO EASY?
GREAT GAME, EVERYONE.
BACKSLASH, I SENT YOU AN INVITATION TO THE WARRIOR KING STRONGHOLD. MEET US THERE.

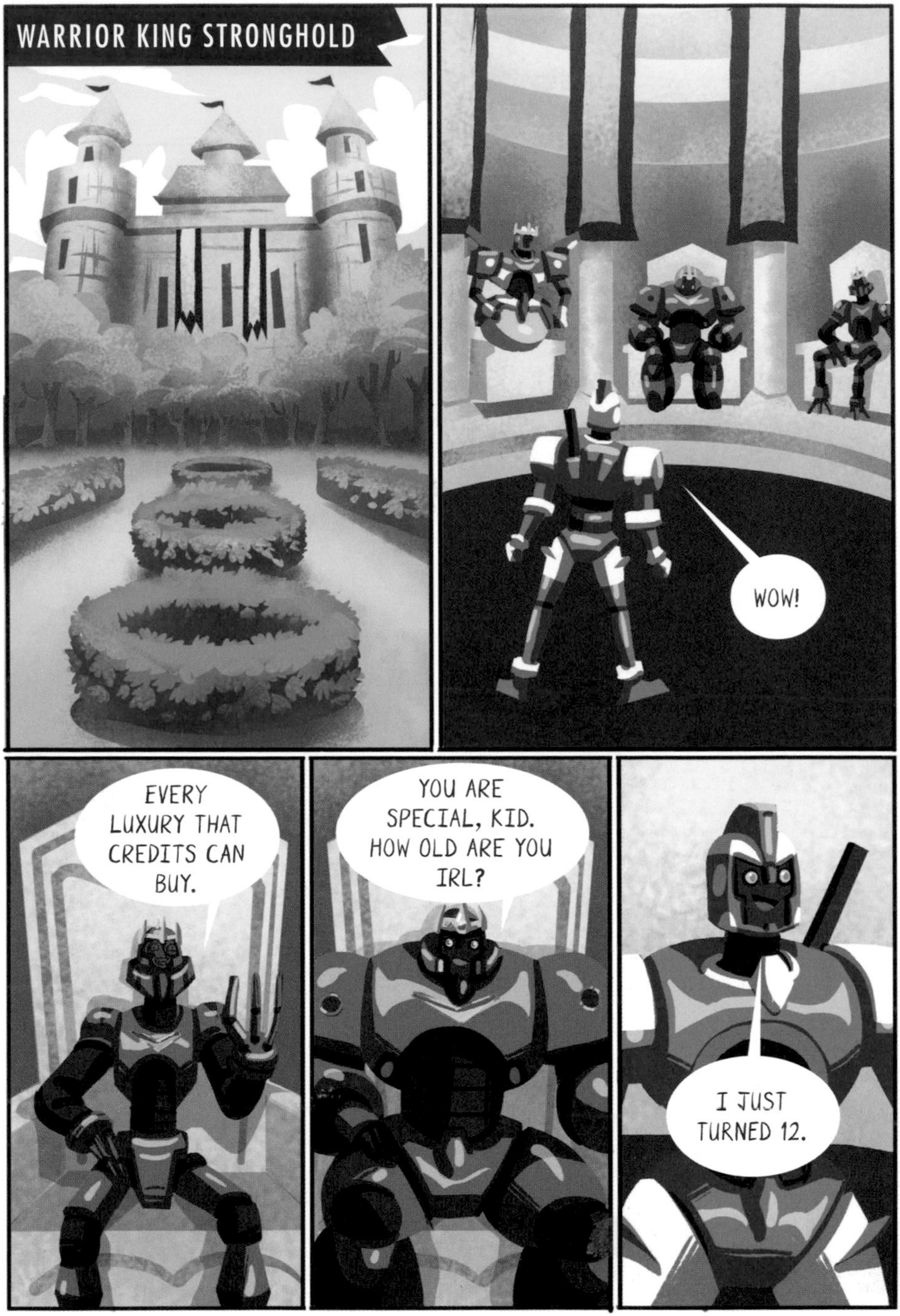
WARRIOR KING STRONGHOLD
WOW!
EVERY LUXURY THAT CREDITS CAN BUY.
YOU ARE SPECIAL, KID. HOW OLD ARE YOU IRL?
I JUST TURNED 12.

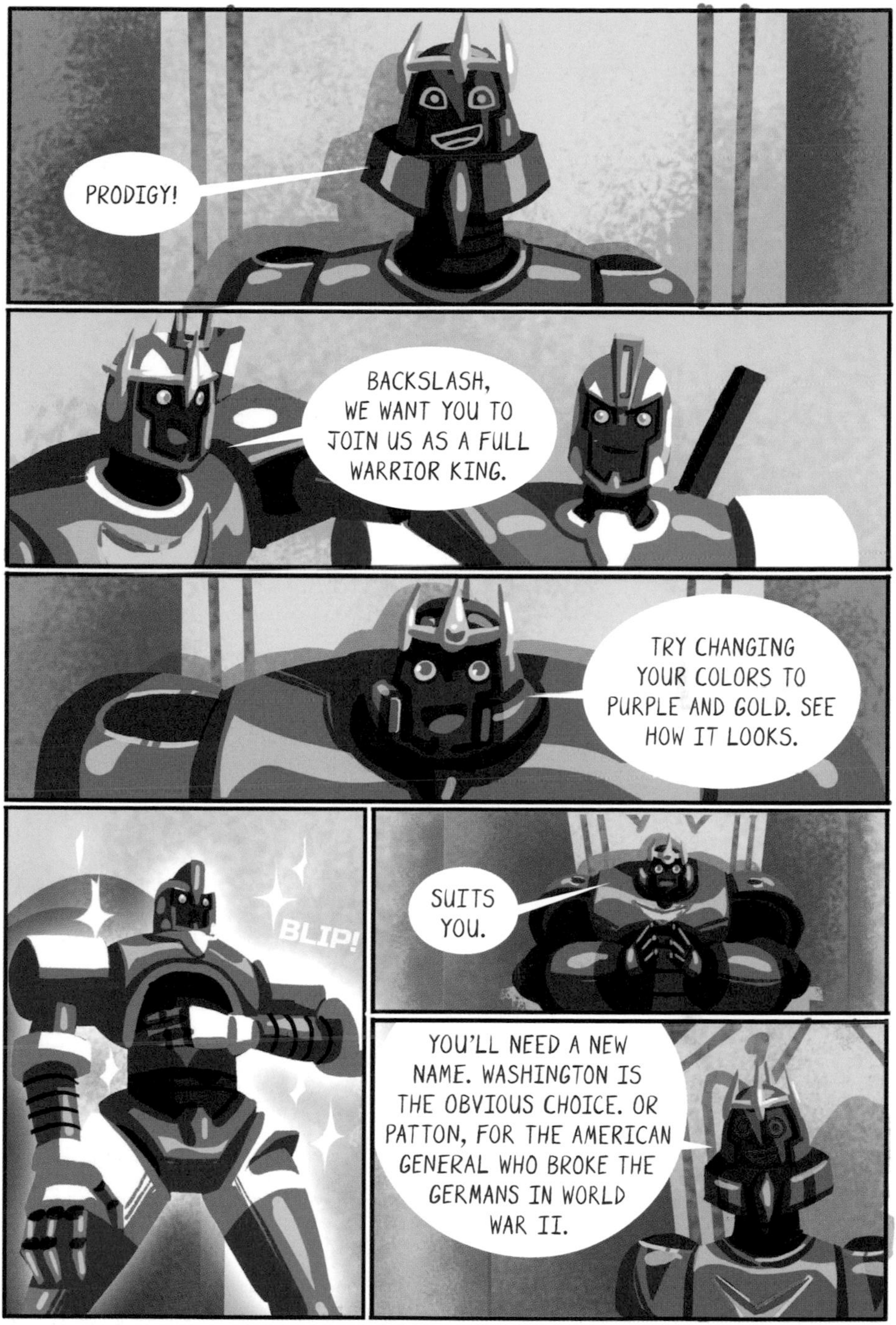
PRODIGY!
BACKSLASH, WE WANT YOU TO JOIN US AS A FULL WARRIOR KING.
TRY CHANGING YOUR COLORS TO PURPLE AND GOLD. SEE HOW IT LOOKS.
BLIP!
SUITS YOU.
YOU'LL NEED A NEW NAME. WASHINGTON IS THE OBVIOUS CHOICE. OR PATTON, FOR THE AMERICAN GENERAL WHO BROKE THE GERMANS IN WORLD WAR II.

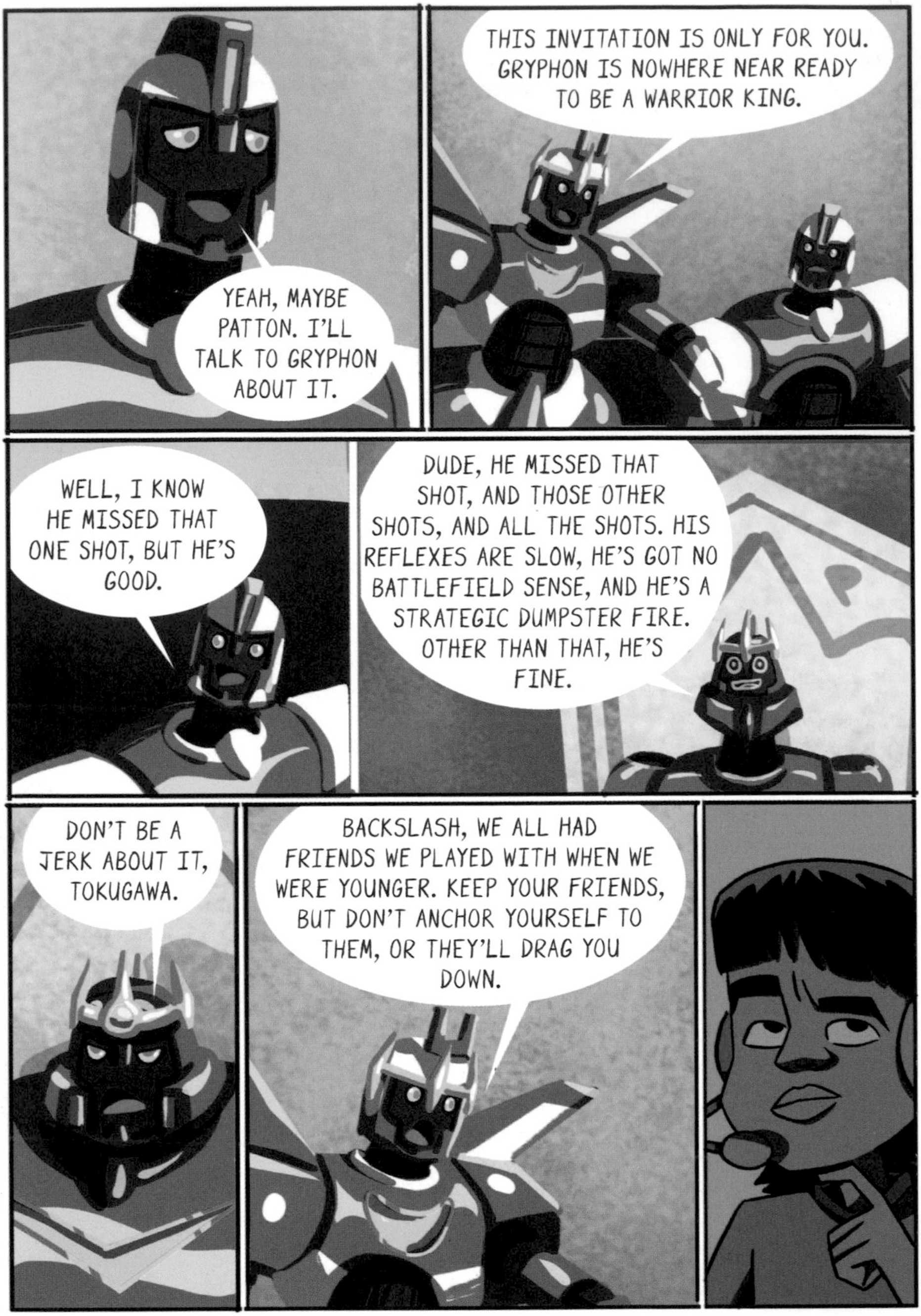
YEAH, MAYBE PATTON. I'LL TALK TO GRYPHON ABOUT IT.
THIS INVITATION IS ONLY FOR YOU. GRYPHON IS NOWHERE NEAR READY TO BE A WARRIOR KING.
WELL, I KNOW HE MISSED THAT ONE SHOT, BUT HE'S GOOD.
DUDE, HE MISSED THAT SHOT, AND THOSE OTHER SHOTS, AND ALL THE SHOTS. HIS REFLEXES ARE SLOW, HE'S GOT NO BATTLEFIELD SENSE, AND HE'S A STRATEGIC DUMPSTER FIRE. OTHER THAN THAT, HE'S FINE.
DON'T BE A JERK ABOUT IT, TOKUGAWA.
BACKSLASH, WE ALL HAD FRIENDS WE PLAYED WITH WHEN WE WERE YOUNGER. KEEP YOUR FRIENDS, BUT DON'T ANCHOR YOURSELF TO THEM, OR THEY'LL DRAG YOU DOWN.

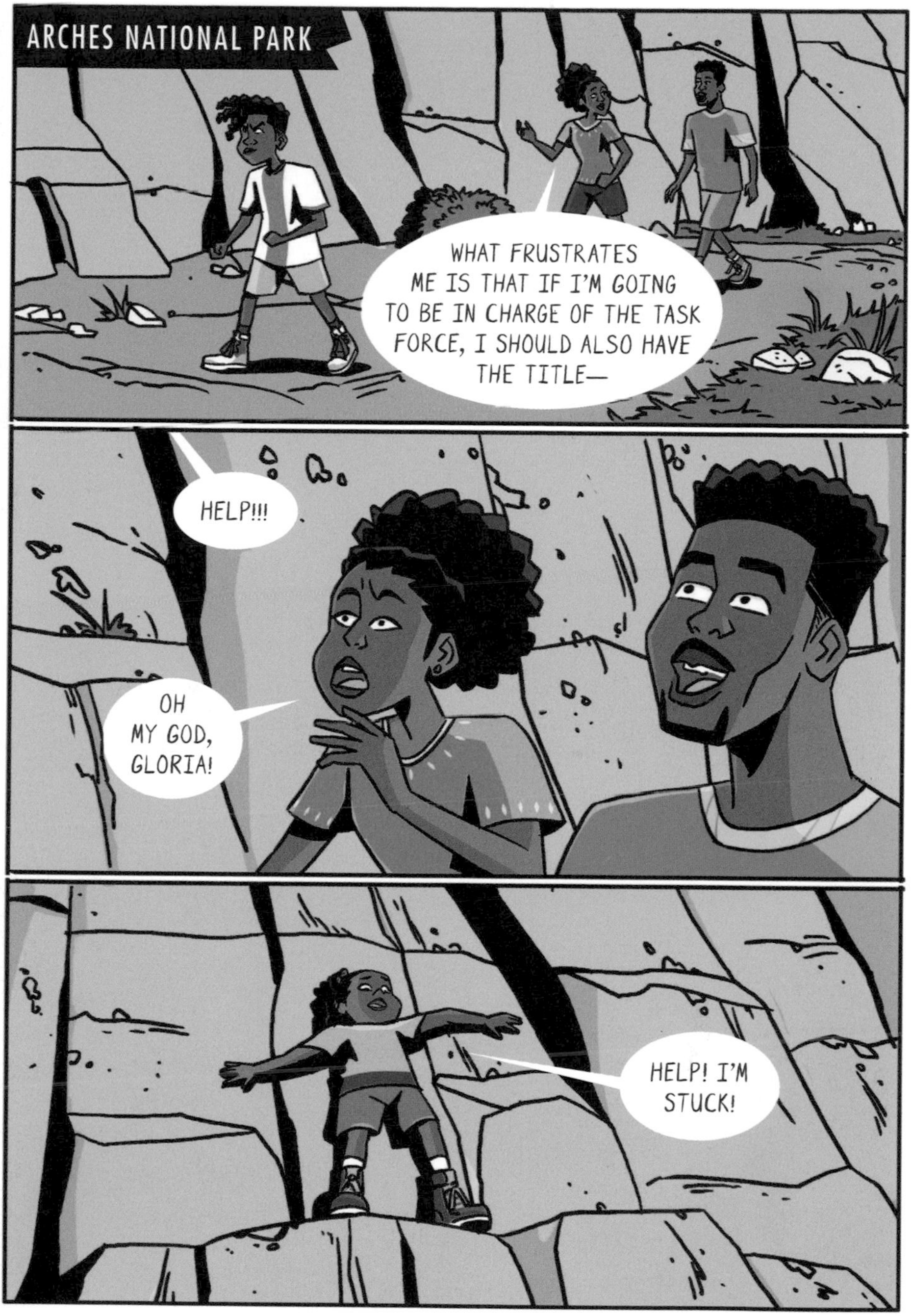

ARCHES NATIONAL PARK
WHAT FRUSTRATES ME IS THAT IF I'M GOING TO BE IN CHARGE OF THE TASK FORCE, I SHOULD ALSO HAVE THE TITLE—
HELP!!!
OH MY GOD, GLORIA!
HELP! I'M STUCK!

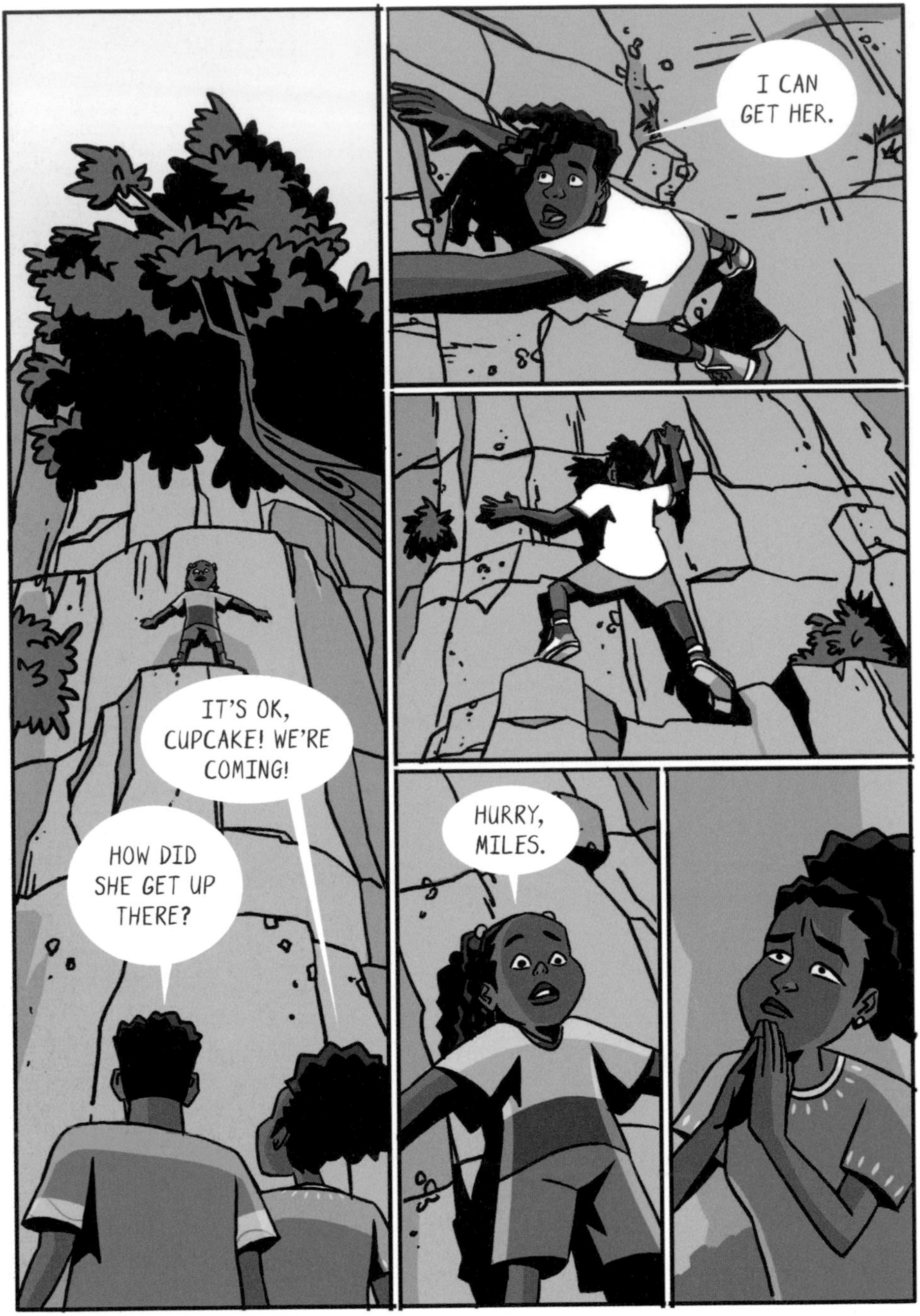
IT'S OK, CUPCAKE! WE'RE COMING!
HOW DID SHE GET UP THERE?
I CAN GET HER.
HURRY, MILES.

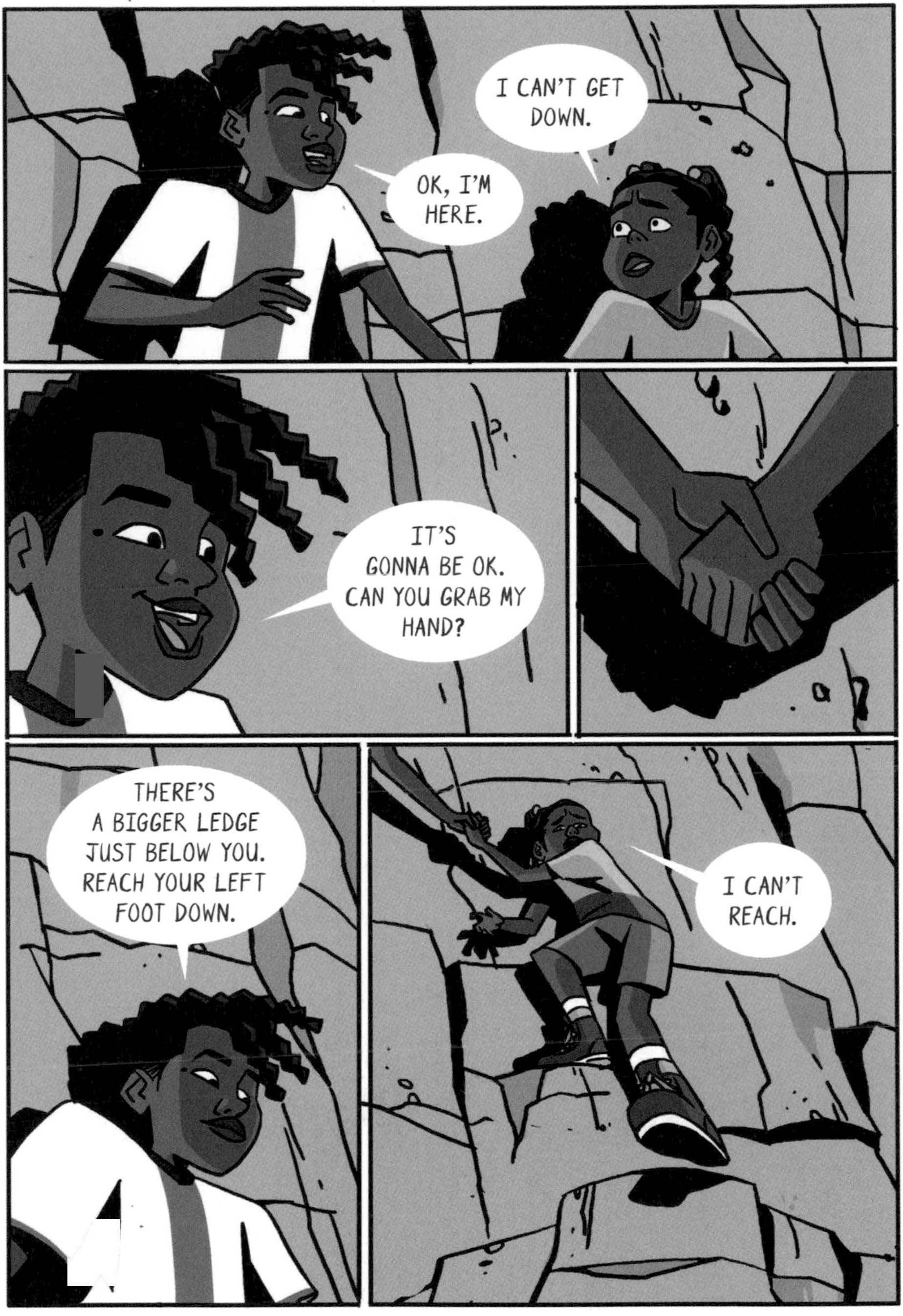
I CAN'T GET DOWN.
OK, I'M HERE.
IT'S GONNA BE OK. CAN YOU GRAB MY HAND?
THERE'S A BIGGER LEDGE JUST BELOW YOU. REACH YOUR LEFT FOOT DOWN.
I CAN'T REACH.

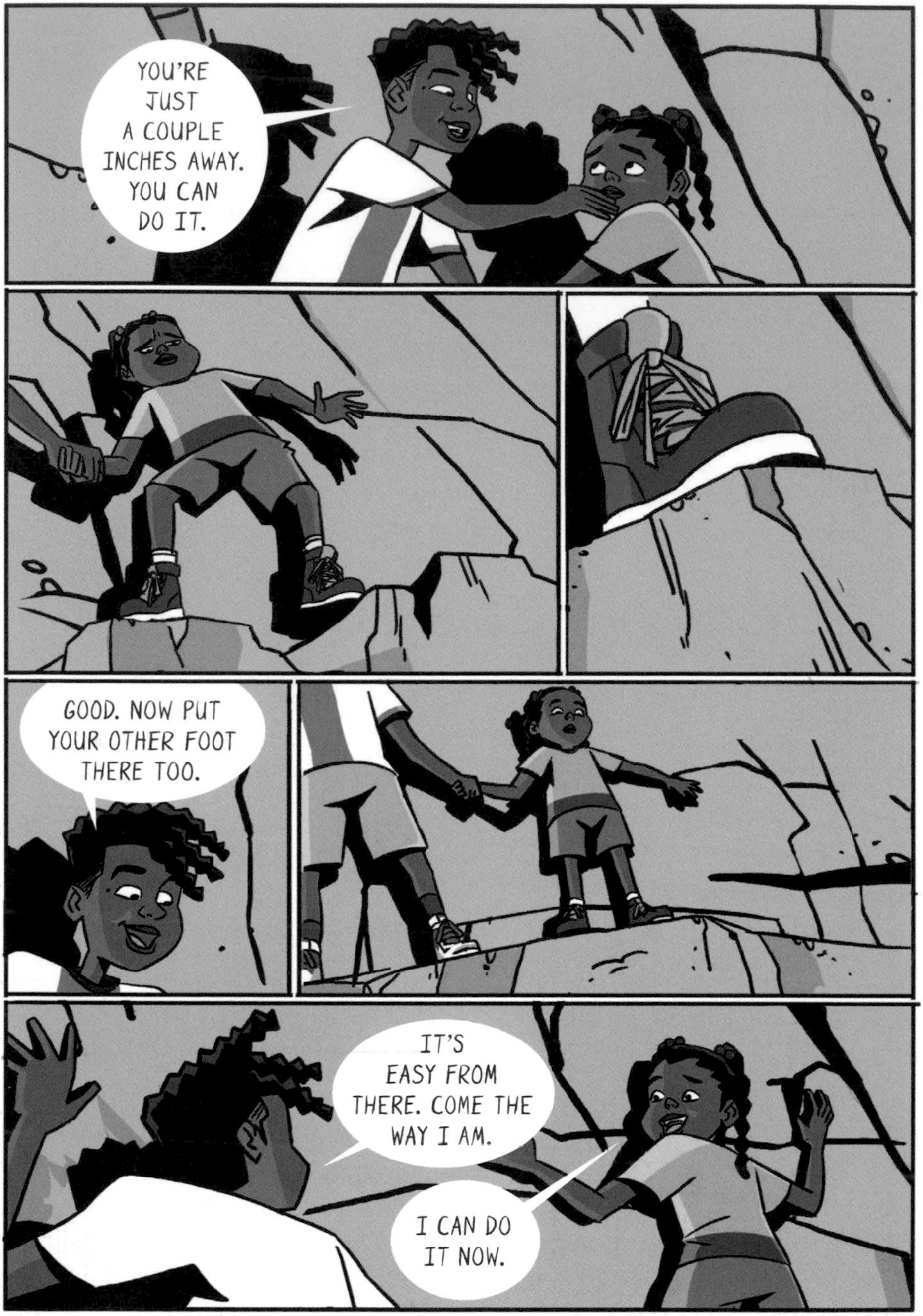
YOU'RE JUST A COUPLE INCHES AWAY. YOU CAN DO IT.
GOOD. NOW PUT YOUR OTHER FOOT THERE TOO.
IT'S EASY FROM THERE. COME THE WAY I AM.
I CAN DO IT NOW.

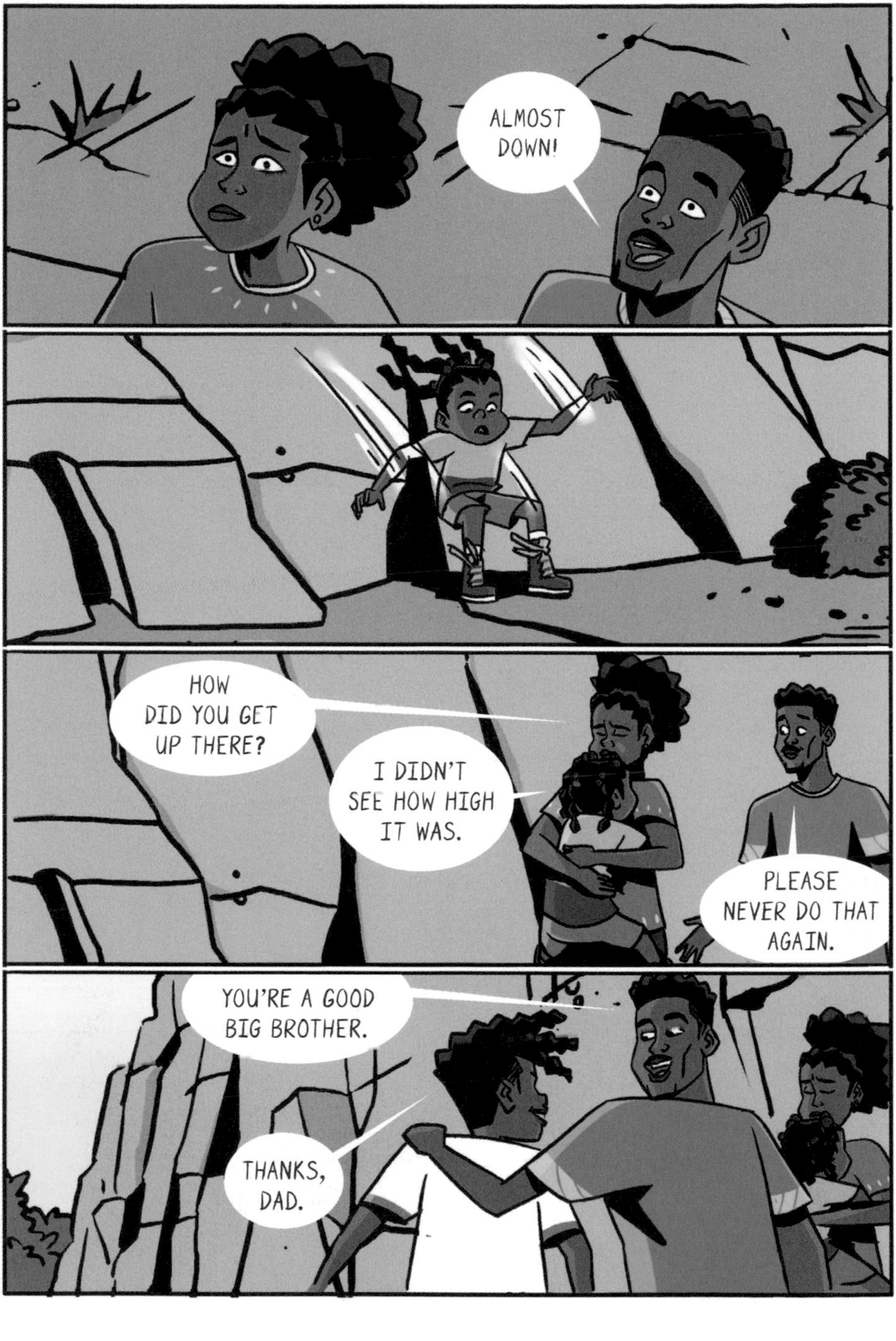
ALMOST DOWN!
HOW DID YOU GET UP THERE?
I DIDN'T SEE HOW HIGH IT WAS.
PLEASE NEVER DO THAT AGAIN.
YOU'RE A GOOD BIG BROTHER.
THANKS, DAD.

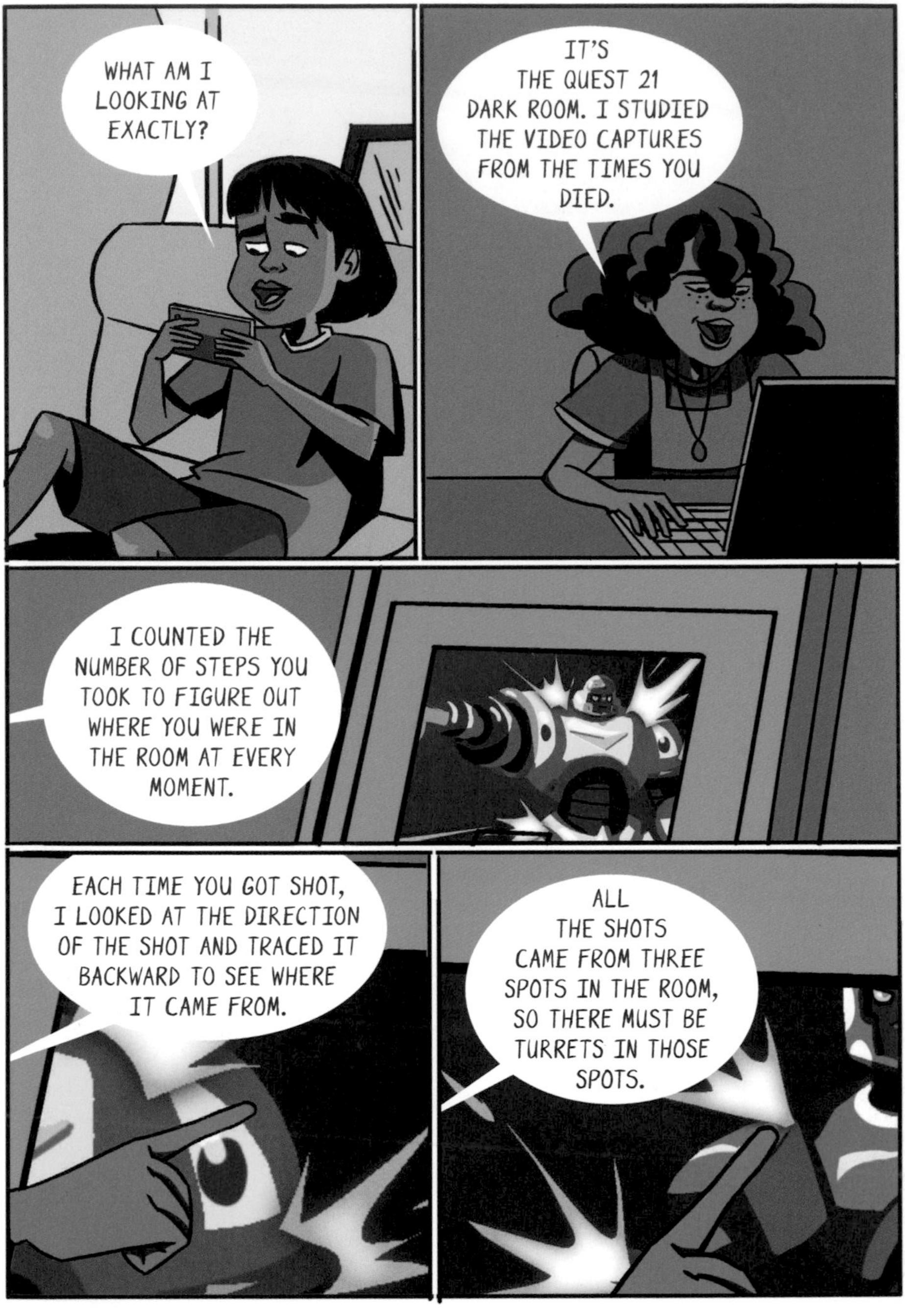
WHAT AM I LOOKING AT EXACTLY?
IT'S THE QUEST 21 DARK ROOM. I STUDIED THE VIDEO CAPTURES FROM THE TIMES YOU DIED.
I COUNTED THE NUMBER OF STEPS YOU TOOK TO FIGURE OUT WHERE YOU WERE IN THE ROOM AT EVERY MOMENT.
EACH TIME YOU GOT SHOT, I LOOKED AT THE DIRECTION OF THE SHOT AND TRACED IT BACKWARD TO SEE WHERE IT CAME FROM.
ALL THE SHOTS CAME FROM THREE SPOTS IN THE ROOM, SO THERE MUST BE TURRETS IN THOSE SPOTS.

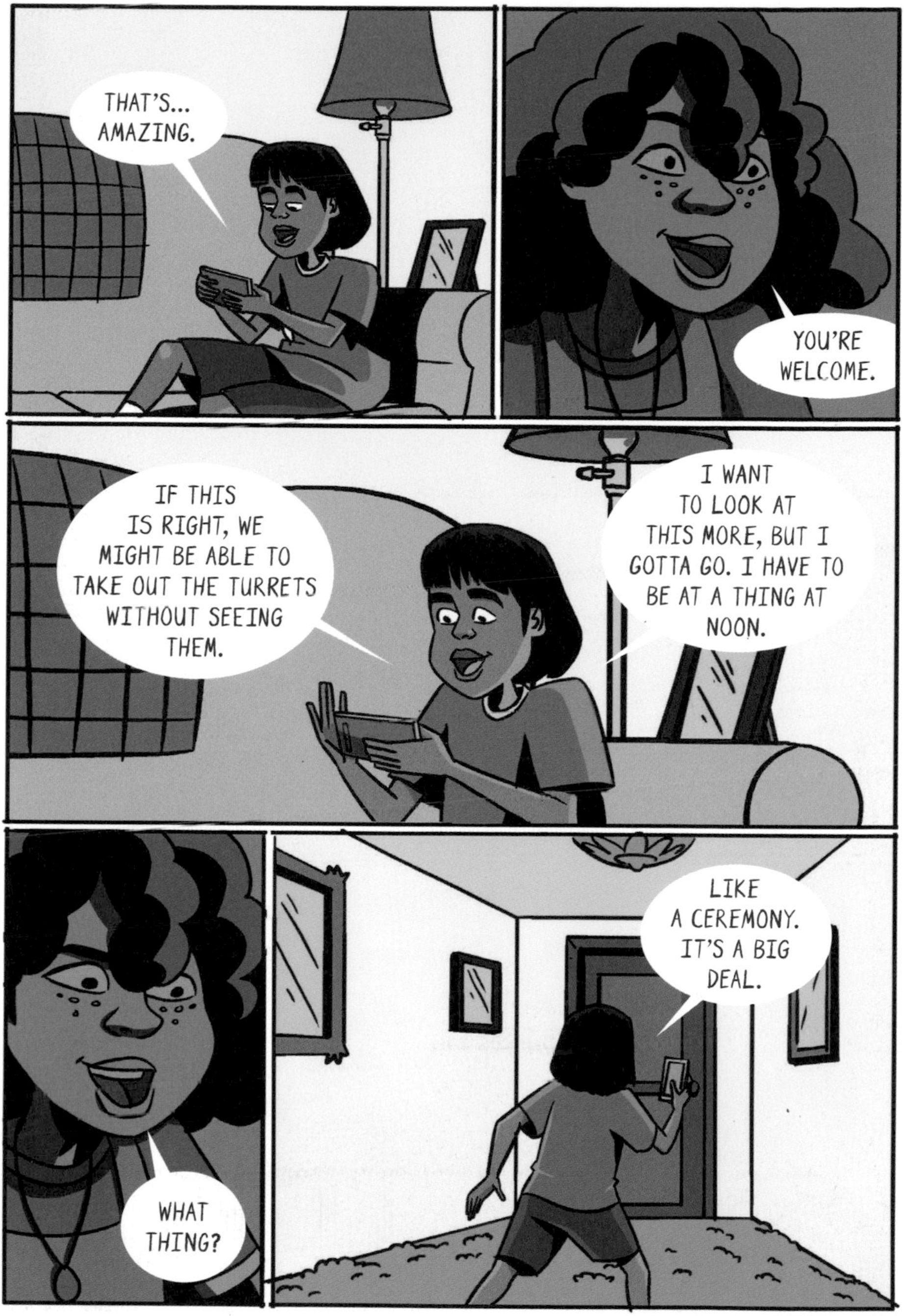
THAT'S... AMAZING.
YOU'RE WELCOME.
IF THIS IS RIGHT, WE MIGHT BE ABLE TO TAKE OUT THE TURRETS WITHOUT SEEING THEM.
I WANT TO LOOK AT THIS MORE, BUT I GOTTA GO. I HAVE TO BE AT A THING AT NOON.
WHAT THING?
LIKE A CEREMONY. IT'S A BIG DEAL.

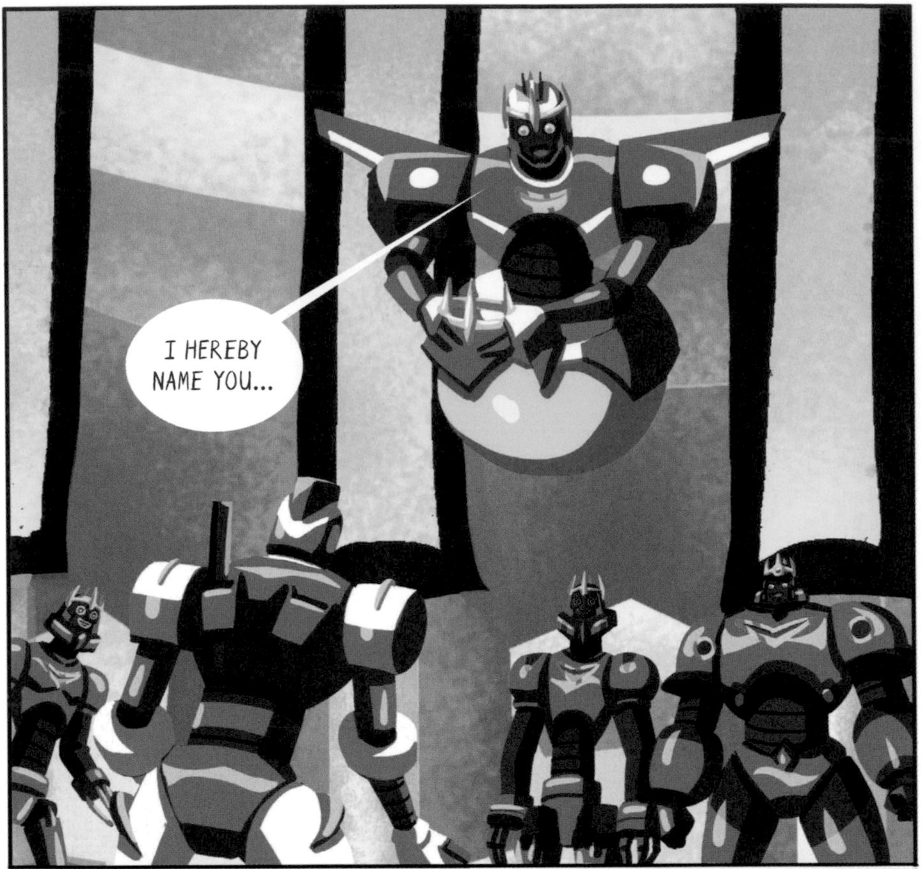
I HEREBY NAME YOU...

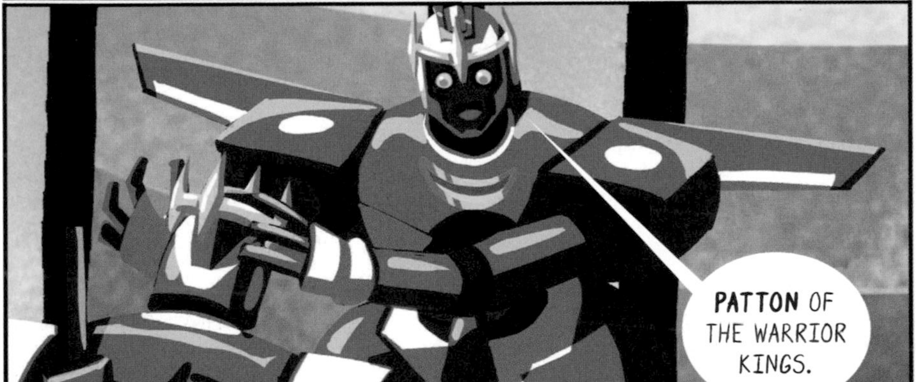
PATTON OF THE WARRIOR KINGS.

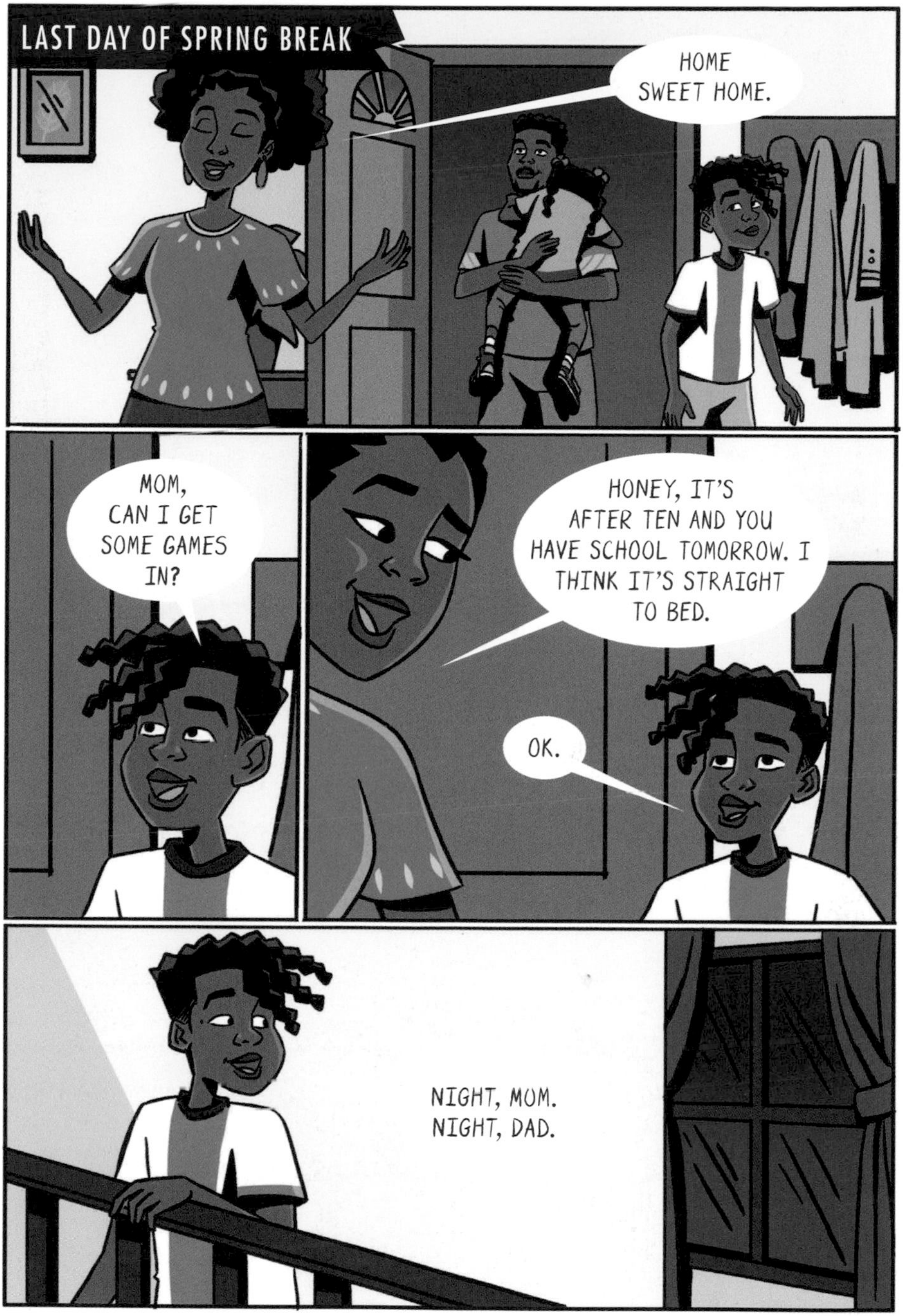
LAST DAY OF SPRING BREAK
HOME SWEET HOME.
MOM, CAN I GET SOME GAMES IN?
HONEY, IT'S AFTER TEN AND YOU HAVE SCHOOL TOMORROW. I THINK IT'S STRAIGHT TO BED.
OK.
NIGHT, MOM. NIGHT, DAD.

CHAPTER 11

BROKEN

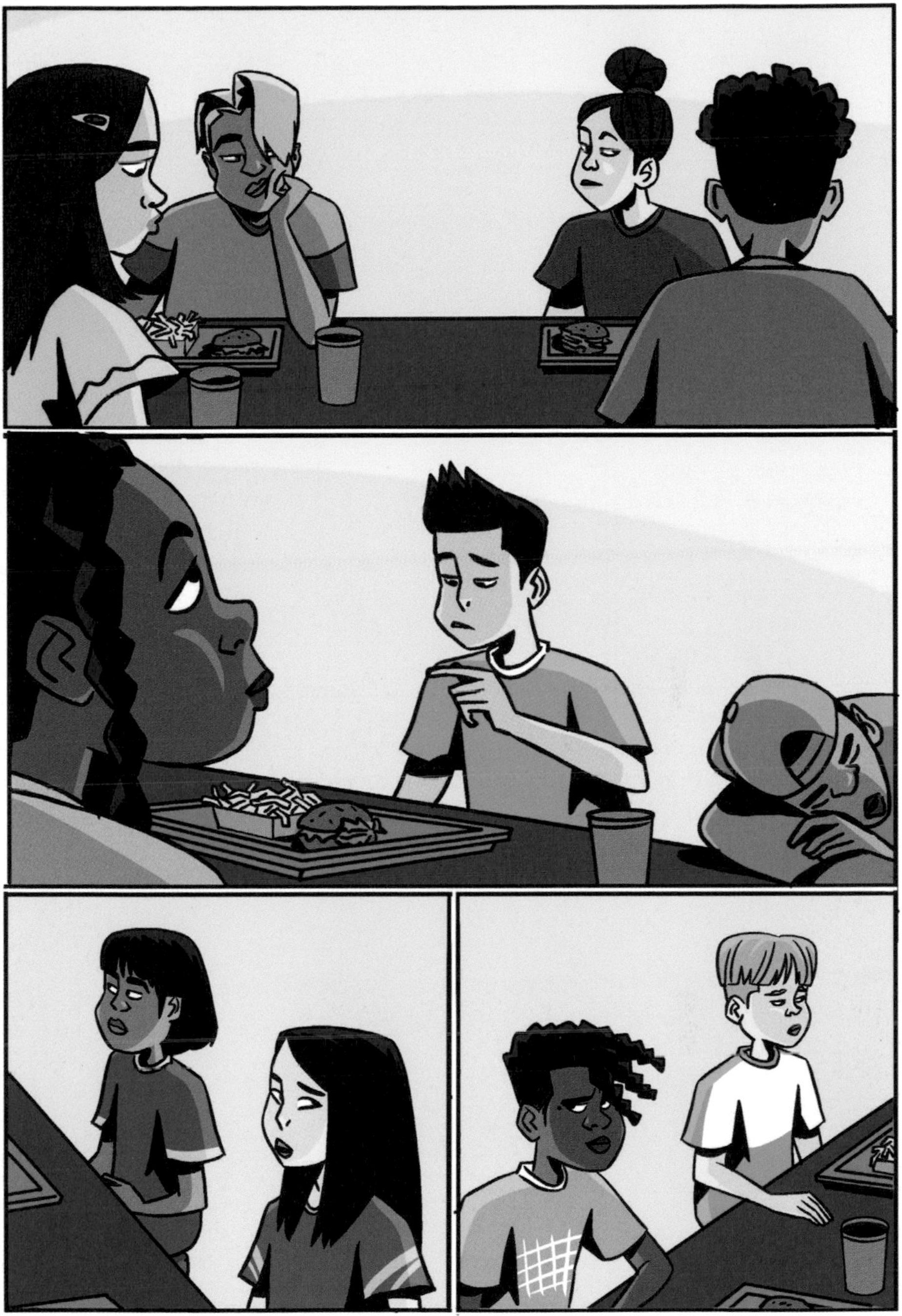

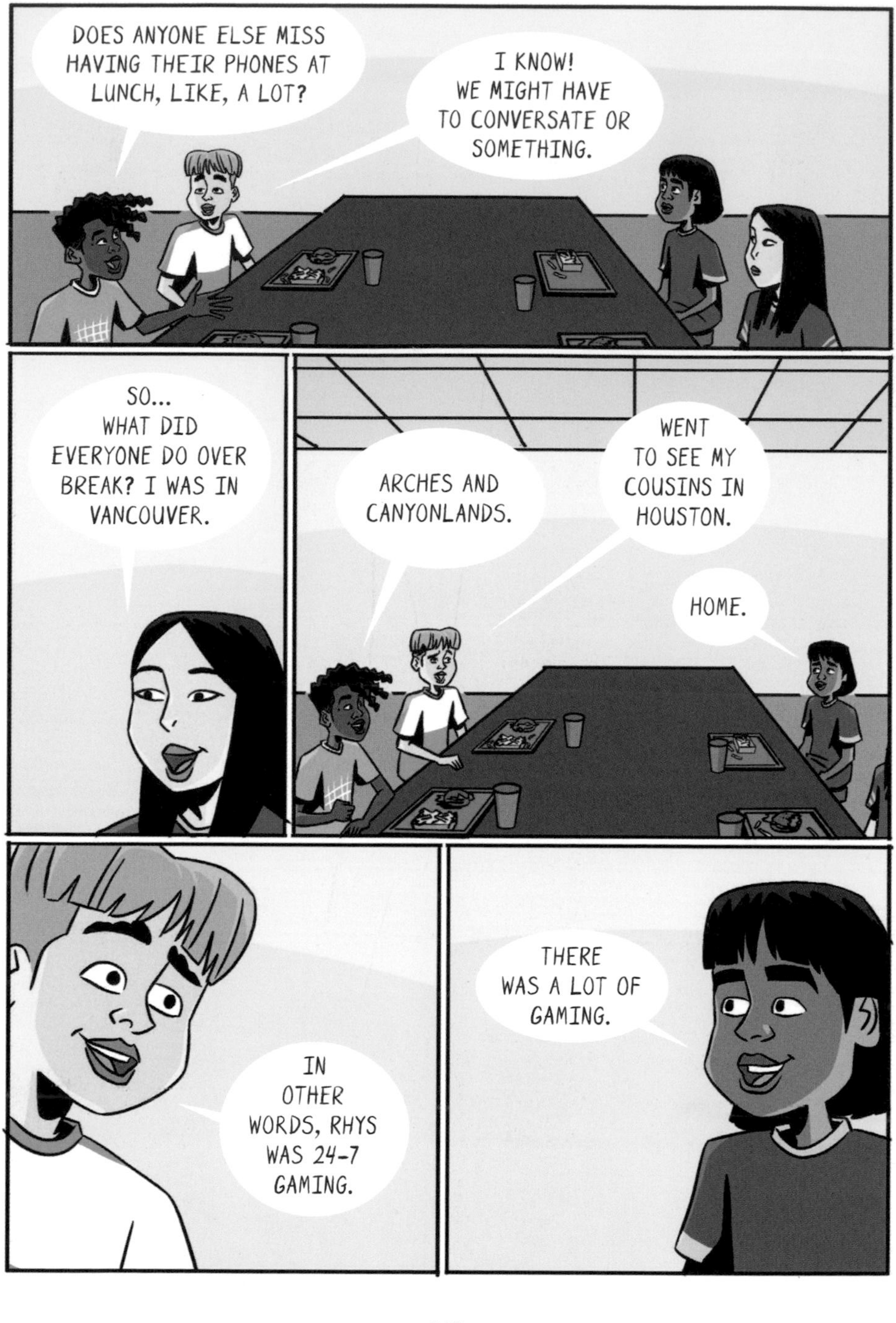
DOES ANYONE ELSE MISS HAVING THEIR PHONES AT LUNCH, LIKE, A LOT?
I KNOW! WE MIGHT HAVE TO CONVERSATE OR SOMETHING.
SO... WHAT DID EVERYONE DO OVER BREAK? I WAS IN VANCOUVER.
ARCHES AND CANYONLANDS.
WENT TO SEE MY COUSINS IN HOUSTON.
HOME.
IN OTHER WORDS, RHYS WAS 24-7 GAMING.
THERE WAS A LOT OF GAMING.

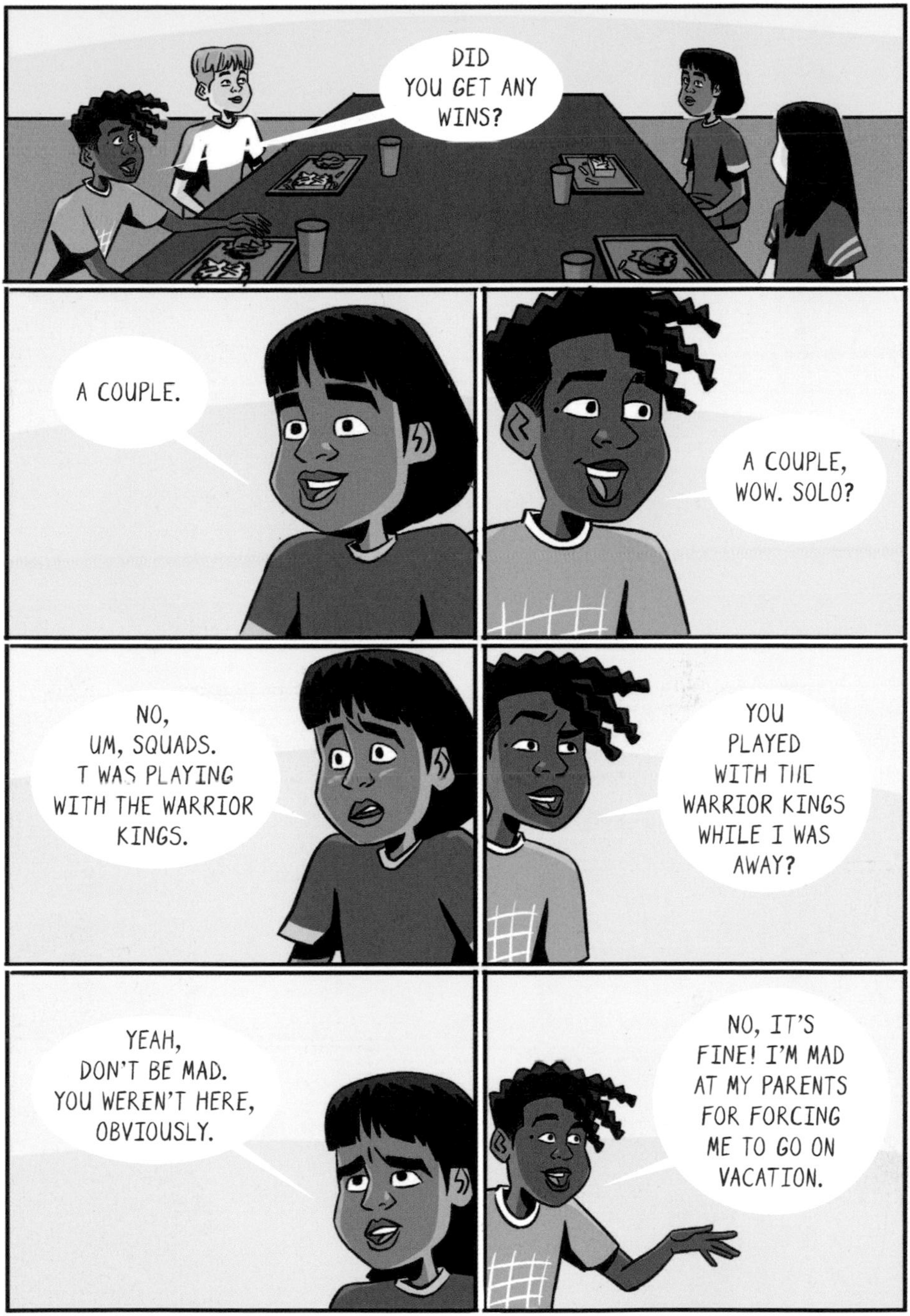
DID YOU GET ANY WINS?
A COUPLE.
A COUPLE, WOW. SOLO?
NO, UM, SQUADS. I WAS PLAYING WITH THE WARRIOR KINGS.
YOU PLAYED WITH THE WARRIOR KINGS WHILE I WAS AWAY?
YEAH, DON'T BE MAD. YOU WEREN'T HERE, OBVIOUSLY.
NO, IT'S FINE! I'M MAD AT MY PARENTS FOR FORCING ME TO GO ON VACATION.

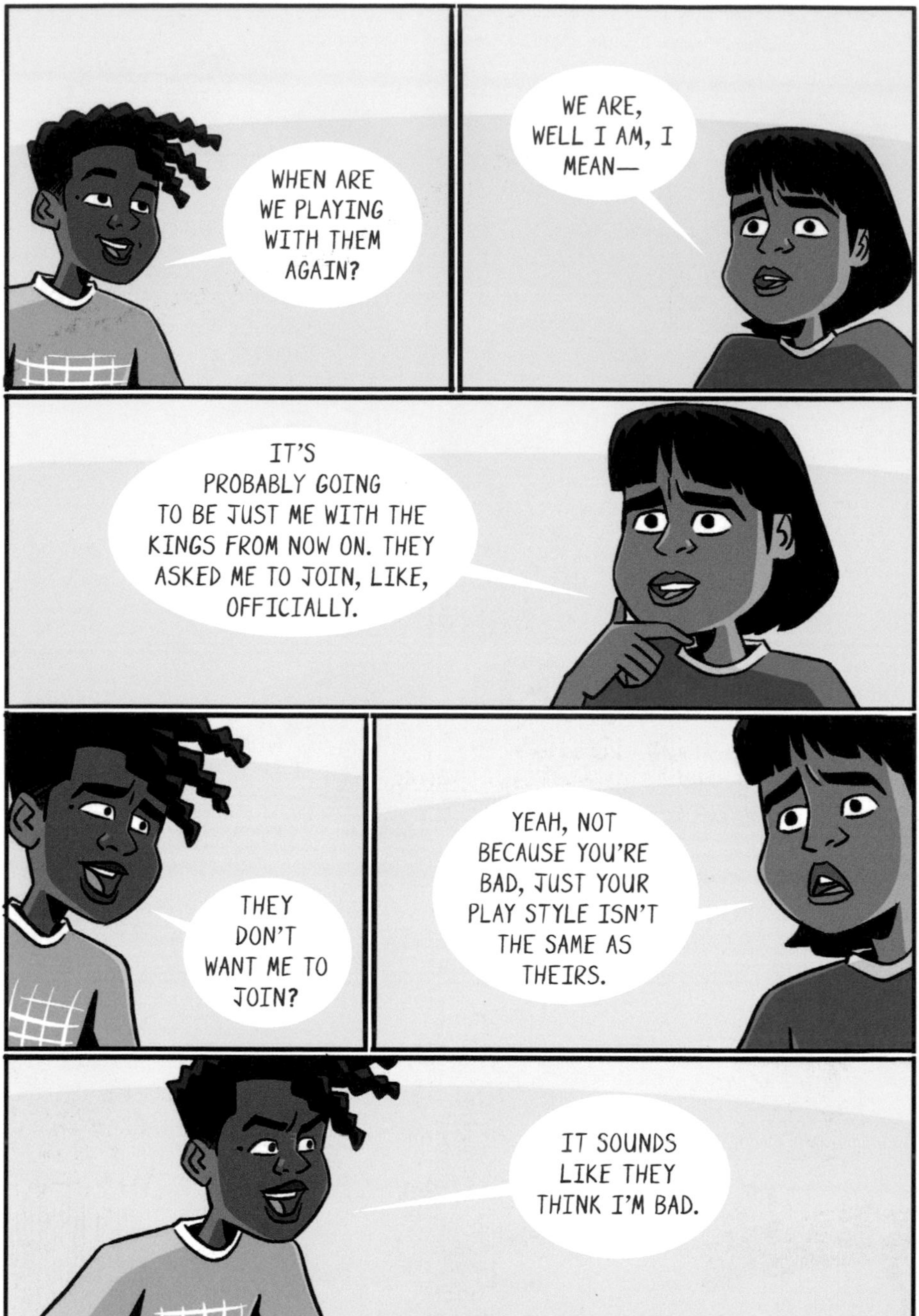
WHEN ARE WE PLAYING WITH THEM AGAIN?
WE ARE, WELL I AM, I MEAN—
IT'S PROBABLY GOING TO BE JUST ME WITH THE KINGS FROM NOW ON. THEY ASKED ME TO JOIN, LIKE, OFFICIALLY.
THEY DON'T WANT ME TO JOIN?
YEAH, NOT BECAUSE YOU'RE BAD, JUST YOUR PLAY STYLE ISN'T THE SAME AS THEIRS.
IT SOUNDS LIKE THEY THINK I'M BAD.

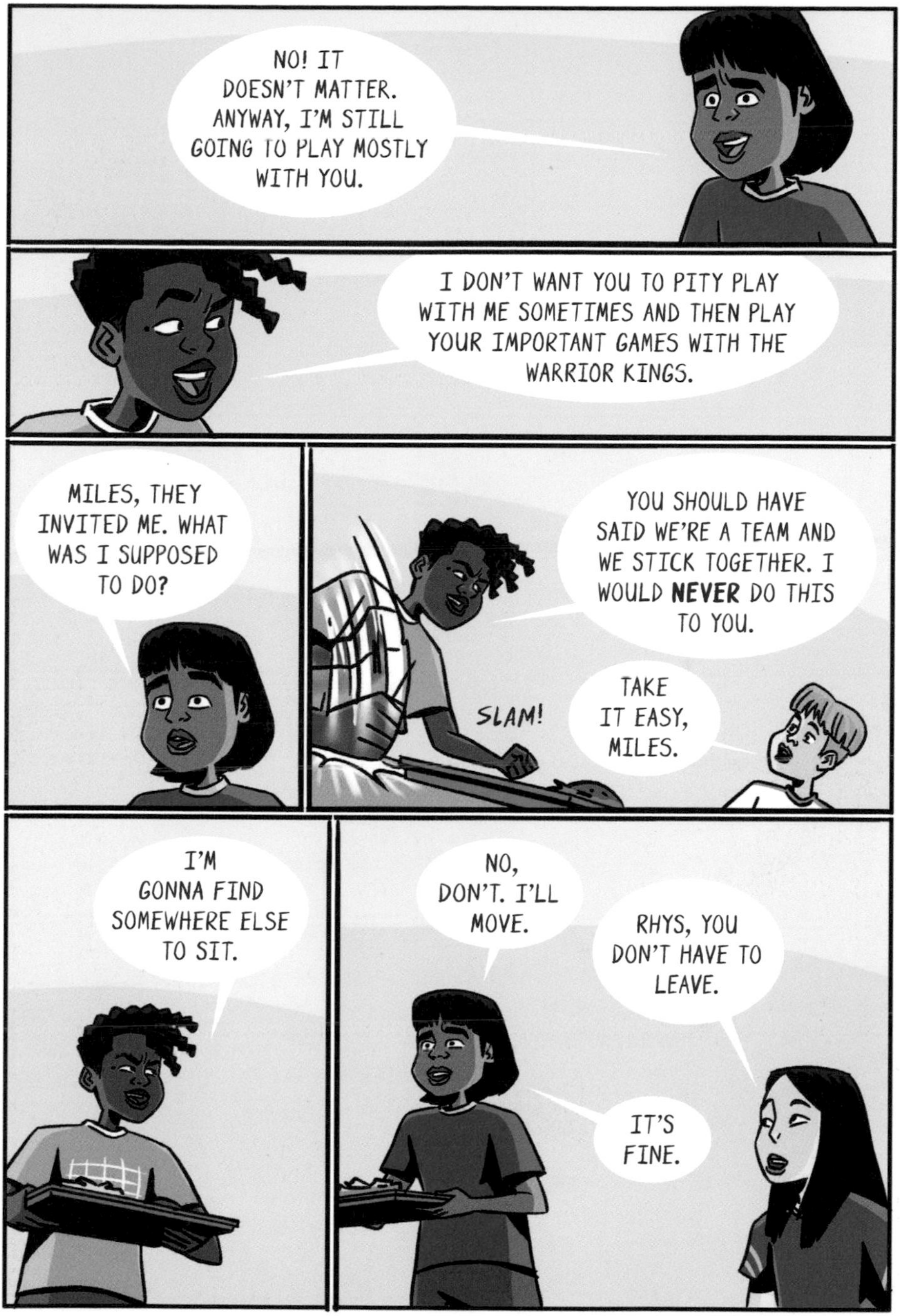
NO! IT DOESN'T MATTER. ANYWAY, I'M STILL GOING TO PLAY MOSTLY WITH YOU.
I DON'T WANT YOU TO PITY PLAY WITH ME SOMETIMES AND THEN PLAY YOUR IMPORTANT GAMES WITH THE WARRIOR KINGS.
MILES, THEY INVITED ME. WHAT WAS I SUPPOSED TO DO?
YOU SHOULD HAVE SAID WE'RE A TEAM AND WE STICK TOGETHER. I WOULD **NEVER** DO THIS TO YOU.
SLAM!
TAKE IT EASY, MILES.
I'M GONNA FIND SOMEWHERE ELSE TO SIT.
NO, DON'T. I'LL MOVE.
RHYS, YOU DON'T HAVE TO LEAVE.
IT'S FINE.

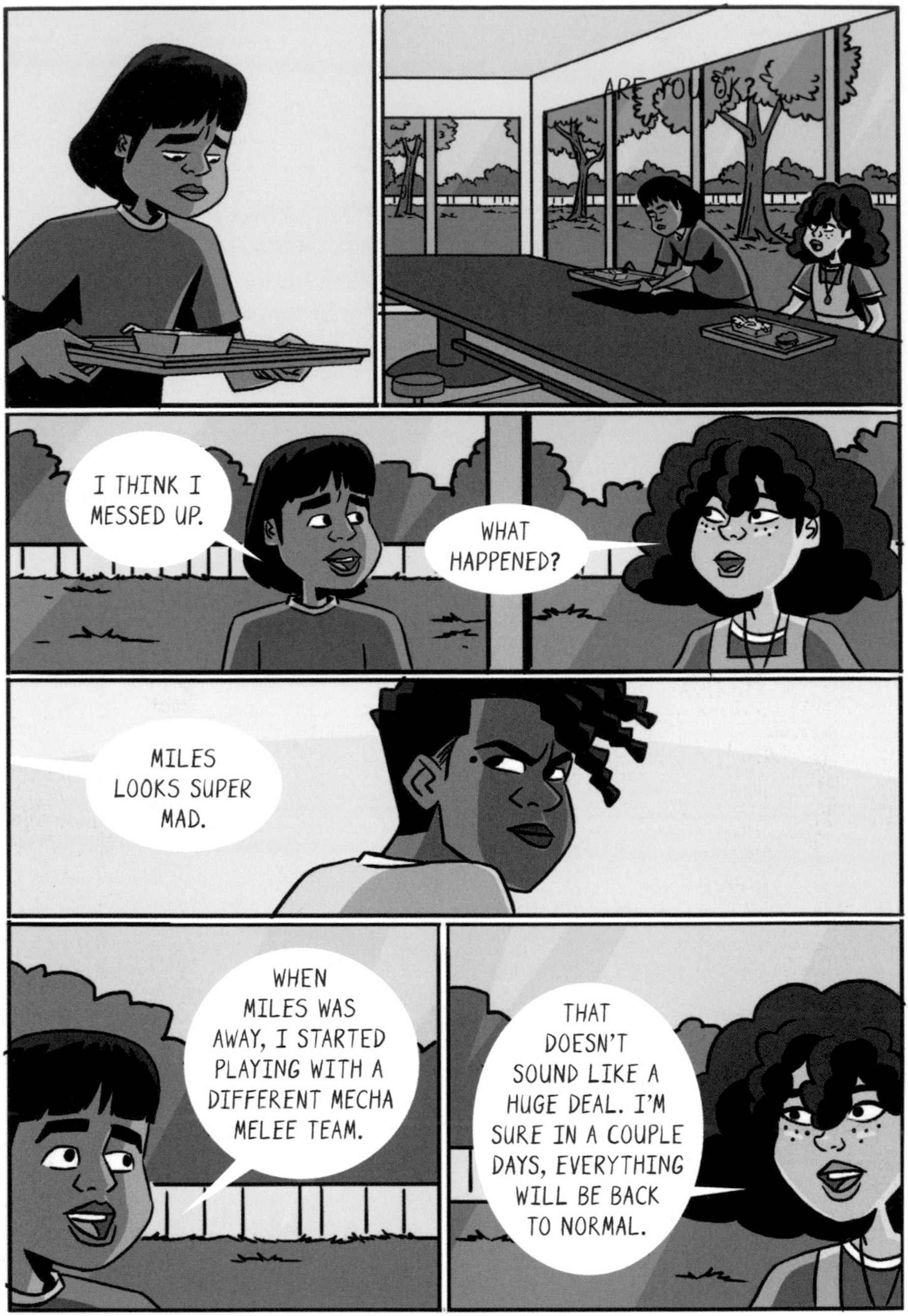
ARE YOU OK?
I THINK I MESSED UP.
WHAT HAPPENED?
MILES LOOKS SUPER MAD.
WHEN MILES WAS AWAY, I STARTED PLAYING WITH A DIFFERENT MECHA MELEE TEAM.
THAT DOESN'T SOUND LIKE A HUGE DEAL. I'M SURE IN A COUPLE DAYS, EVERYTHING WILL BE BACK TO NORMAL.

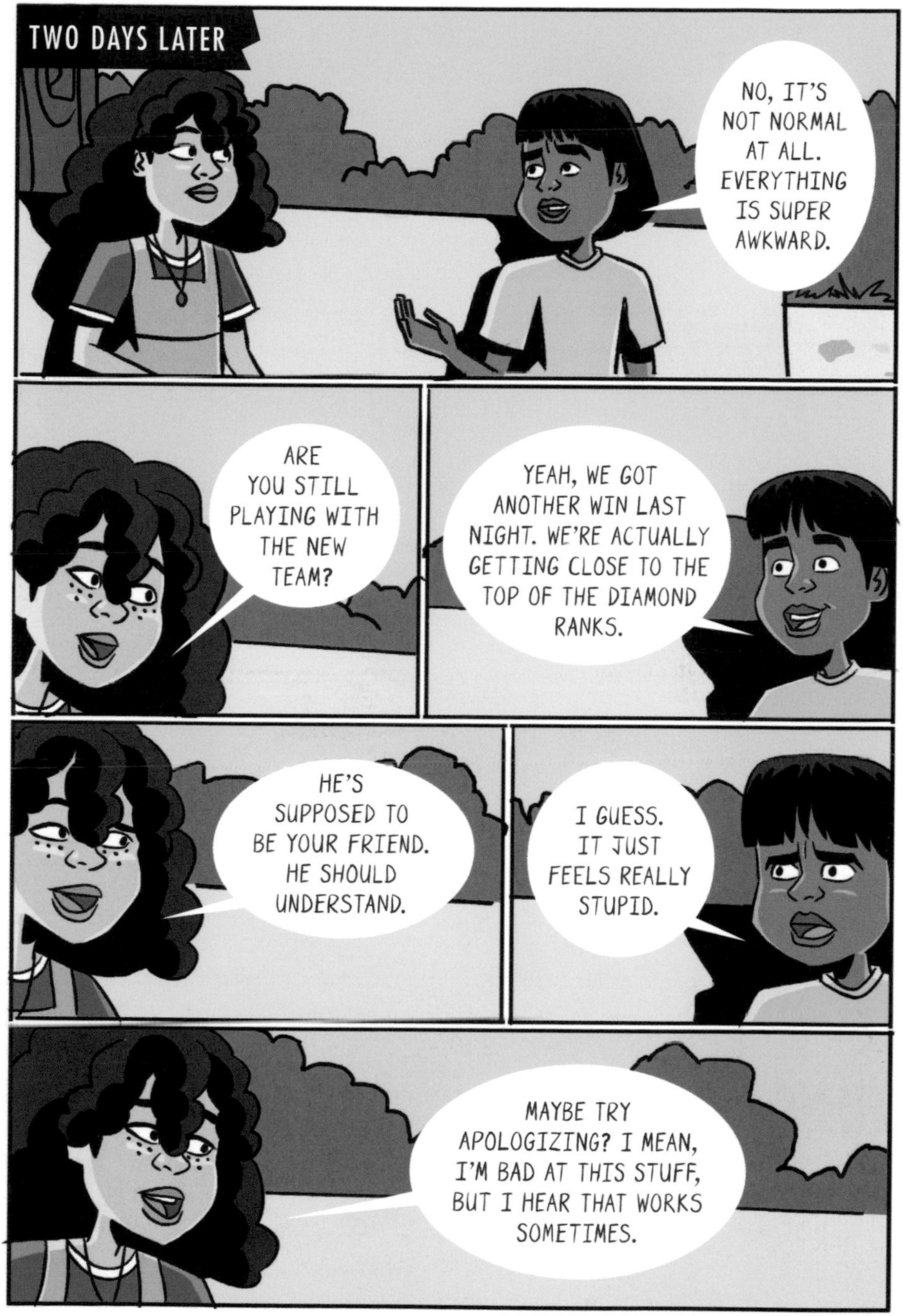
TWO DAYS LATER
NO, IT'S NOT NORMAL AT ALL. EVERYTHING IS SUPER AWKWARD.
ARE YOU STILL PLAYING WITH THE NEW TEAM?
YEAH, WE GOT ANOTHER WIN LAST NIGHT. WE'RE ACTUALLY GETTING CLOSE TO THE TOP OF THE DIAMOND RANKS.
HE'S SUPPOSED TO BE YOUR FRIEND. HE SHOULD UNDERSTAND.
I GUESS. IT JUST FEELS REALLY STUPID.
MAYBE TRY APOLOGIZING? I MEAN, I'M BAD AT THIS STUFF, BUT I HEAR THAT WORKS SOMETIMES.

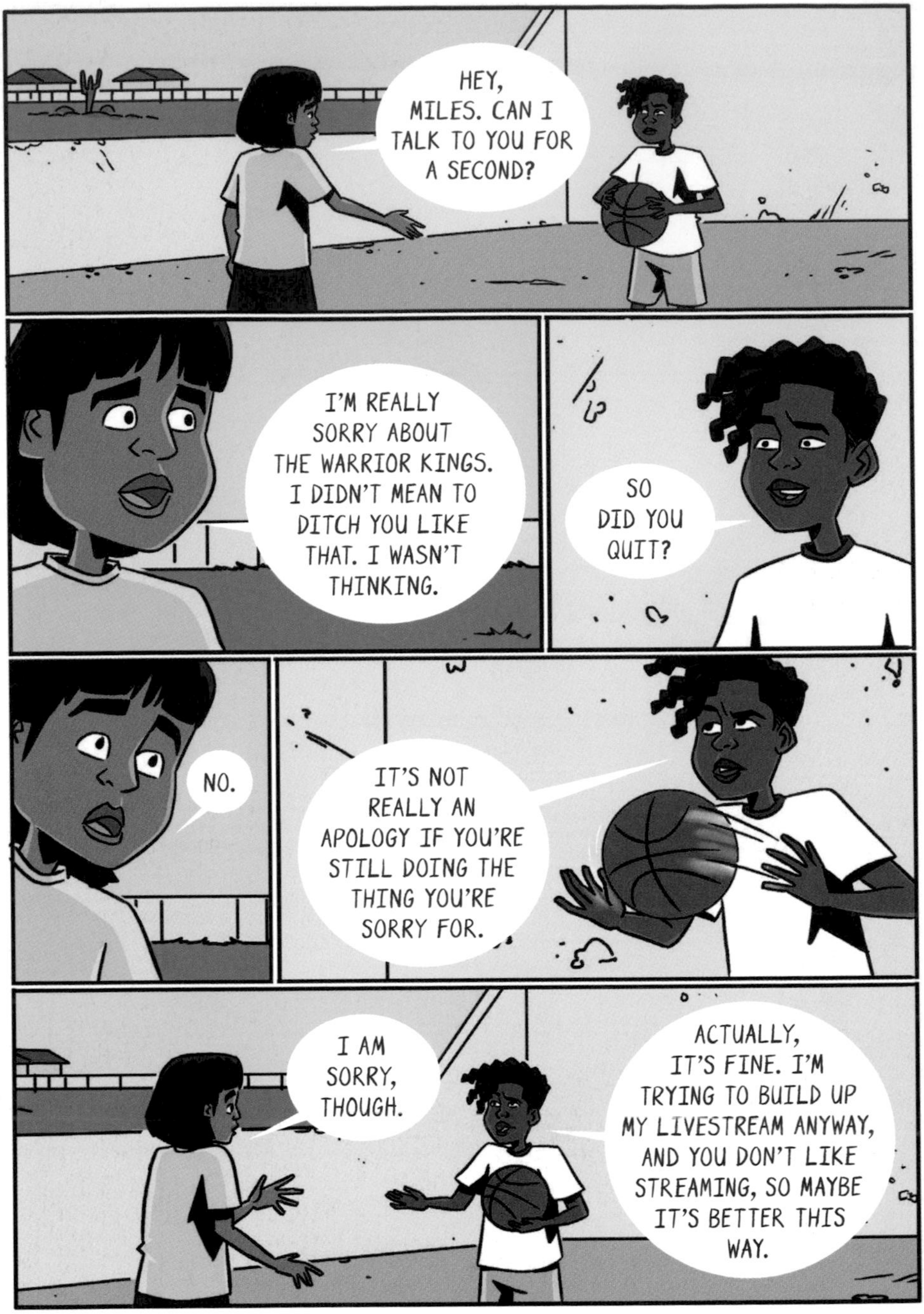
HEY, MILES. CAN I TALK TO YOU FOR A SECOND?
I'M REALLY SORRY ABOUT THE WARRIOR KINGS. I DIDN'T MEAN TO DITCH YOU LIKE THAT. I WASN'T THINKING.
SO DID YOU QUIT?
NO.
IT'S NOT REALLY AN APOLOGY IF YOU'RE STILL DOING THE THING YOU'RE SORRY FOR.
I AM SORRY, THOUGH.
ACTUALLY, IT'S FINE. I'M TRYING TO BUILD UP MY LIVESTREAM ANYWAY, AND YOU DON'T LIKE STREAMING, SO MAYBE IT'S BETTER THIS WAY.

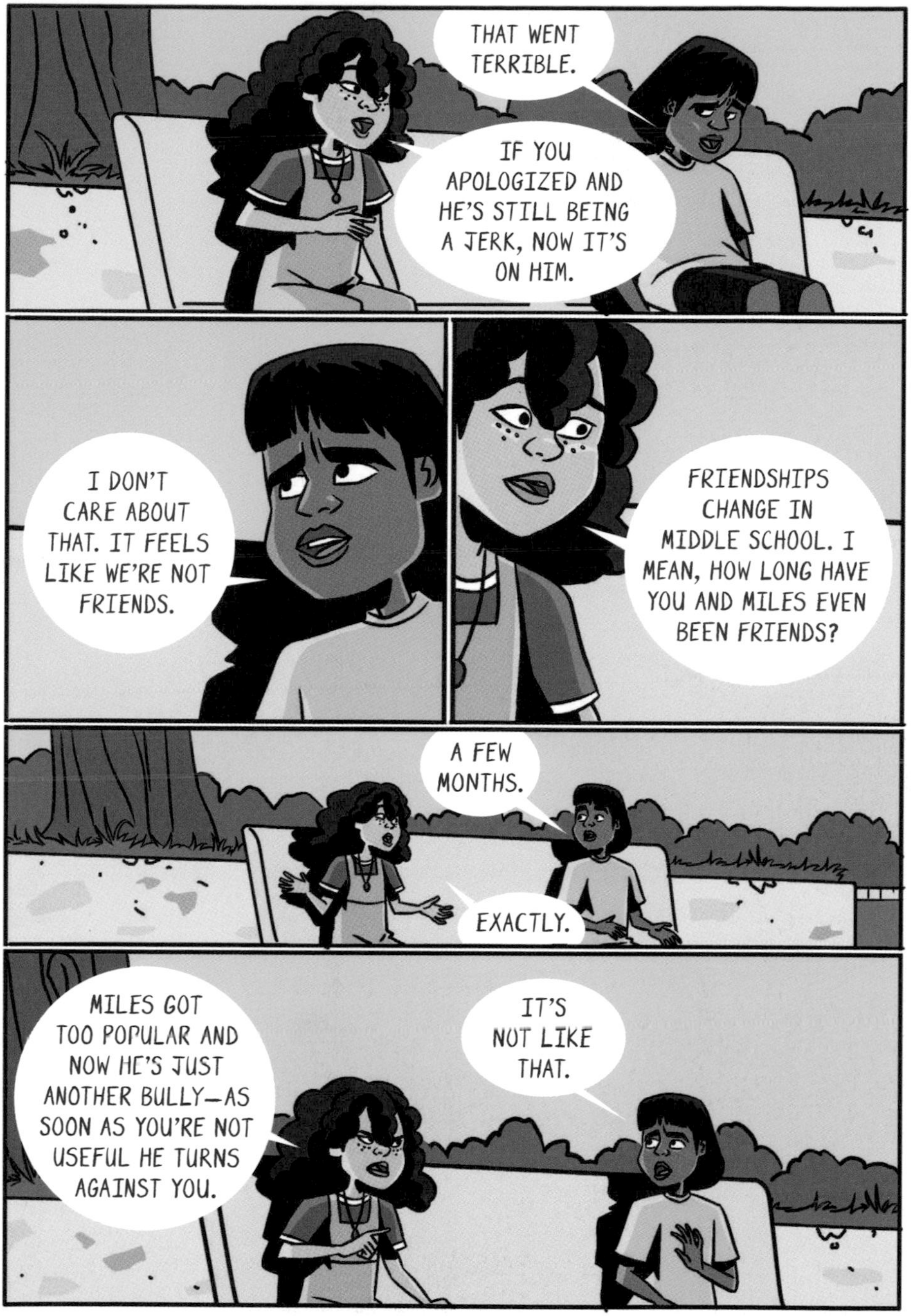
THAT WENT TERRIBLE.
IF YOU APOLOGIZED AND HE'S STILL BEING A JERK, NOW IT'S ON HIM.
I DON'T CARE ABOUT THAT. IT FEELS LIKE WE'RE NOT FRIENDS.
FRIENDSHIPS CHANGE IN MIDDLE SCHOOL. I MEAN, HOW LONG HAVE YOU AND MILES EVEN BEEN FRIENDS?
A FEW MONTHS.
EXACTLY.
MILES GOT TOO POPULAR AND NOW HE'S JUST ANOTHER BULLY—AS SOON AS YOU'RE NOT USEFUL HE TURNS AGAINST YOU.
IT'S NOT LIKE THAT.

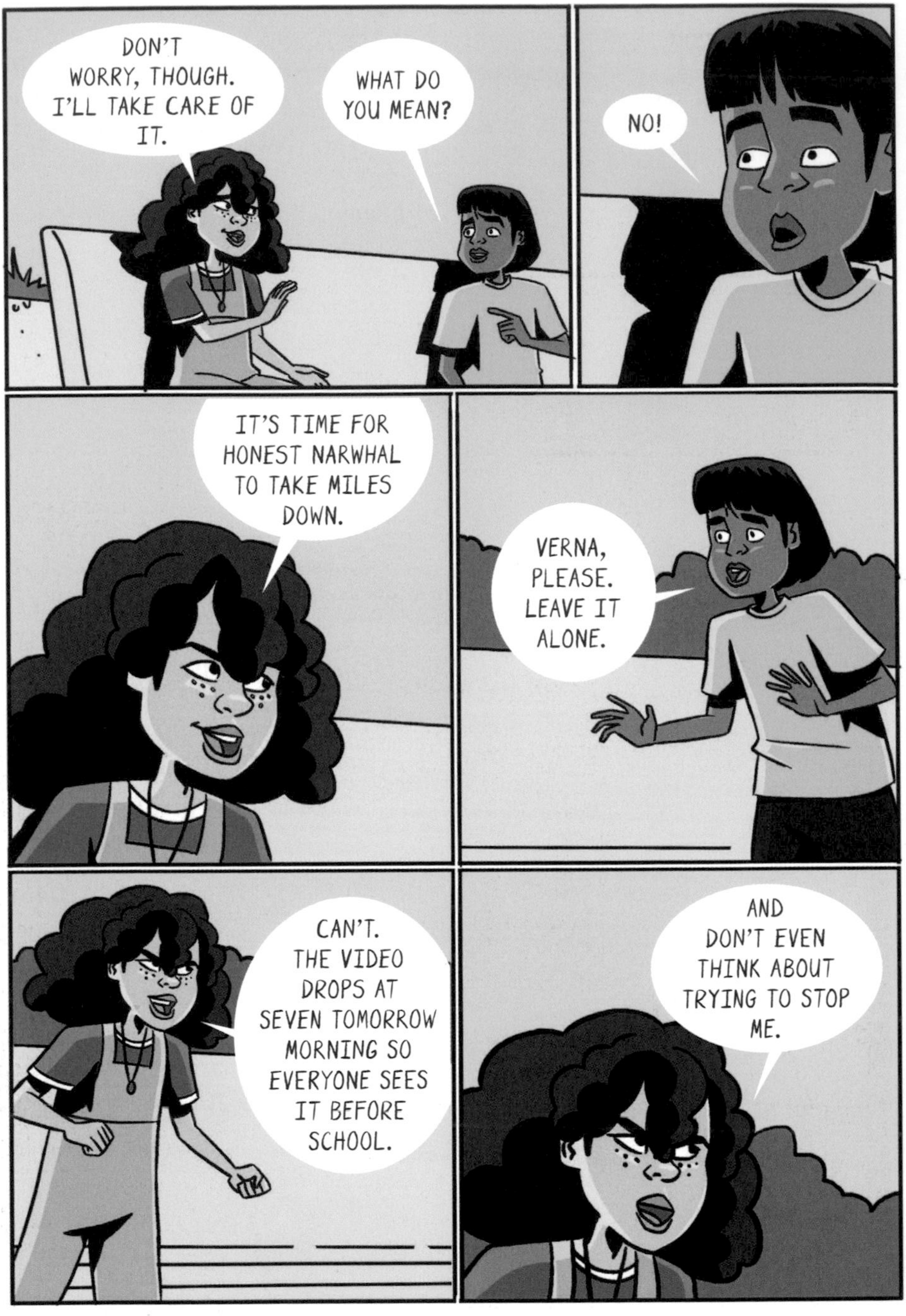
DON'T WORRY, THOUGH. I'LL TAKE CARE OF IT.
WHAT DO YOU MEAN?
NO!
IT'S TIME FOR HONEST NARWHAL TO TAKE MILES DOWN.
VERNA, PLEASE. LEAVE IT ALONE.
CAN'T. THE VIDEO DROPS AT SEVEN TOMORROW MORNING SO EVERYONE SEES IT BEFORE SCHOOL.
AND DON'T EVEN THINK ABOUT TRYING TO STOP ME.

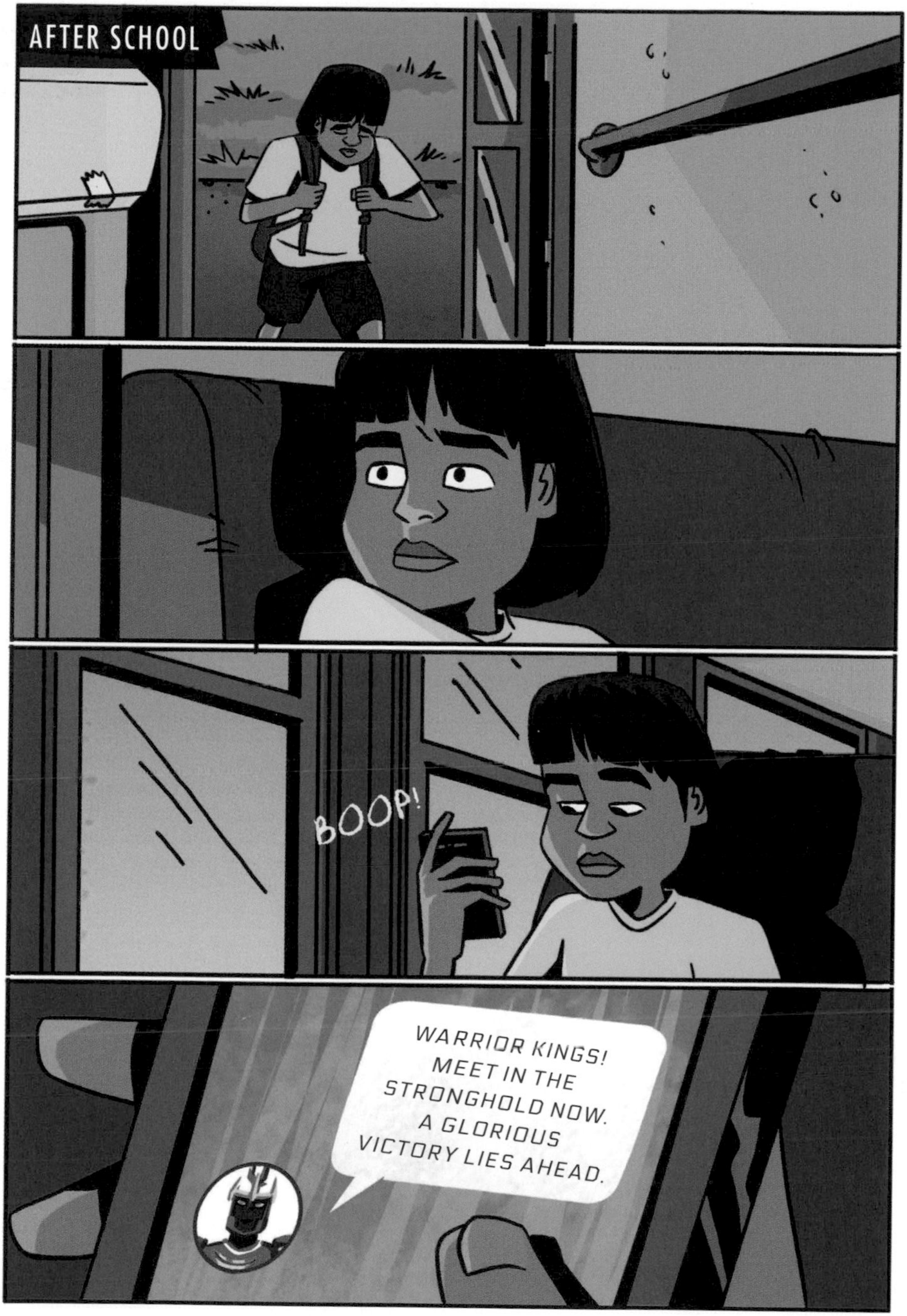
AFTER SCHOOL
BOOP!
WARRIOR KINGS! MEET IN THE STRONGHOLD NOW. A GLORIOUS VICTORY LIES AHEAD.

CHAPTER 12
GLORIOUS VICTORY

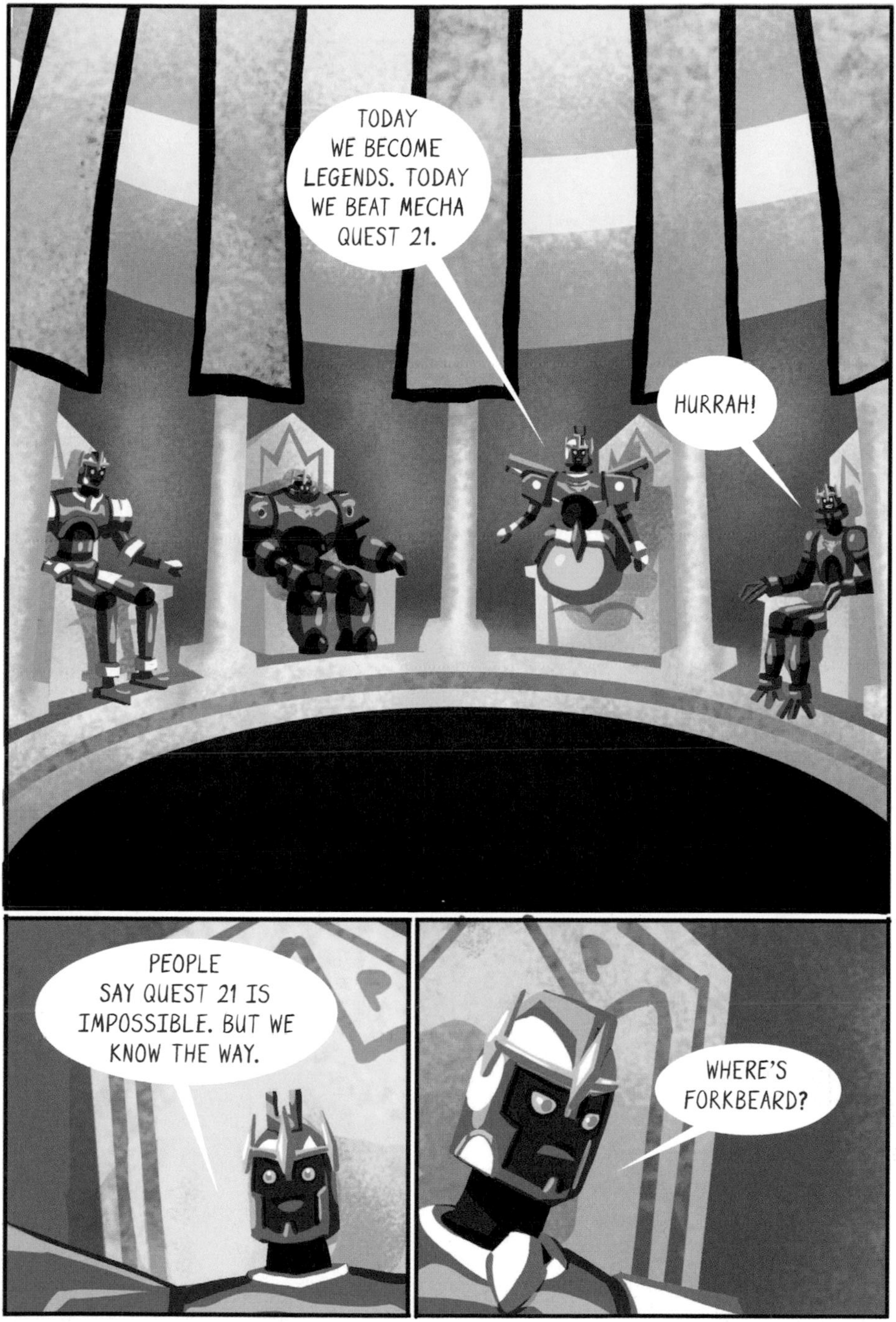
TODAY WE BECOME LEGENDS. TODAY WE BEAT MECHA QUEST 21.
HURRAH!
PEOPLE SAY QUEST 21 IS IMPOSSIBLE. BUT WE KNOW THE WAY.
WHERE'S FORKBEARD?

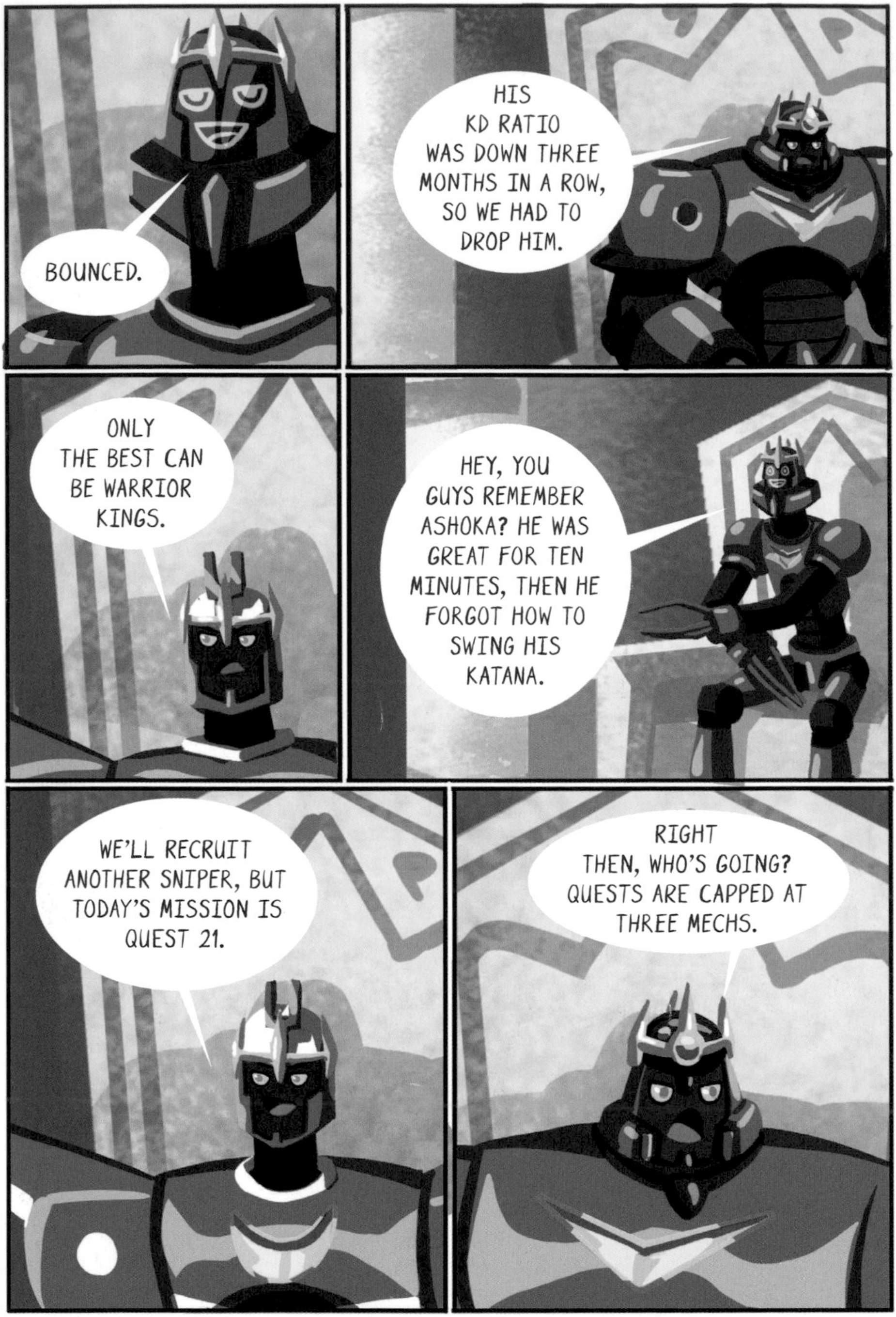
BOUNCED.
HIS KD RATIO WAS DOWN THREE MONTHS IN A ROW, SO WE HAD TO DROP HIM.
ONLY THE BEST CAN BE WARRIOR KINGS.
HEY, YOU GUYS REMEMBER ASHOKA? HE WAS GREAT FOR TEN MINUTES, THEN HE FORGOT HOW TO SWING HIS KATANA.
WE'LL RECRUIT ANOTHER SNIPER, BUT TODAY'S MISSION IS QUEST 21.
RIGHT THEN, WHO'S GOING? QUESTS ARE CAPPED AT THREE MECHS.

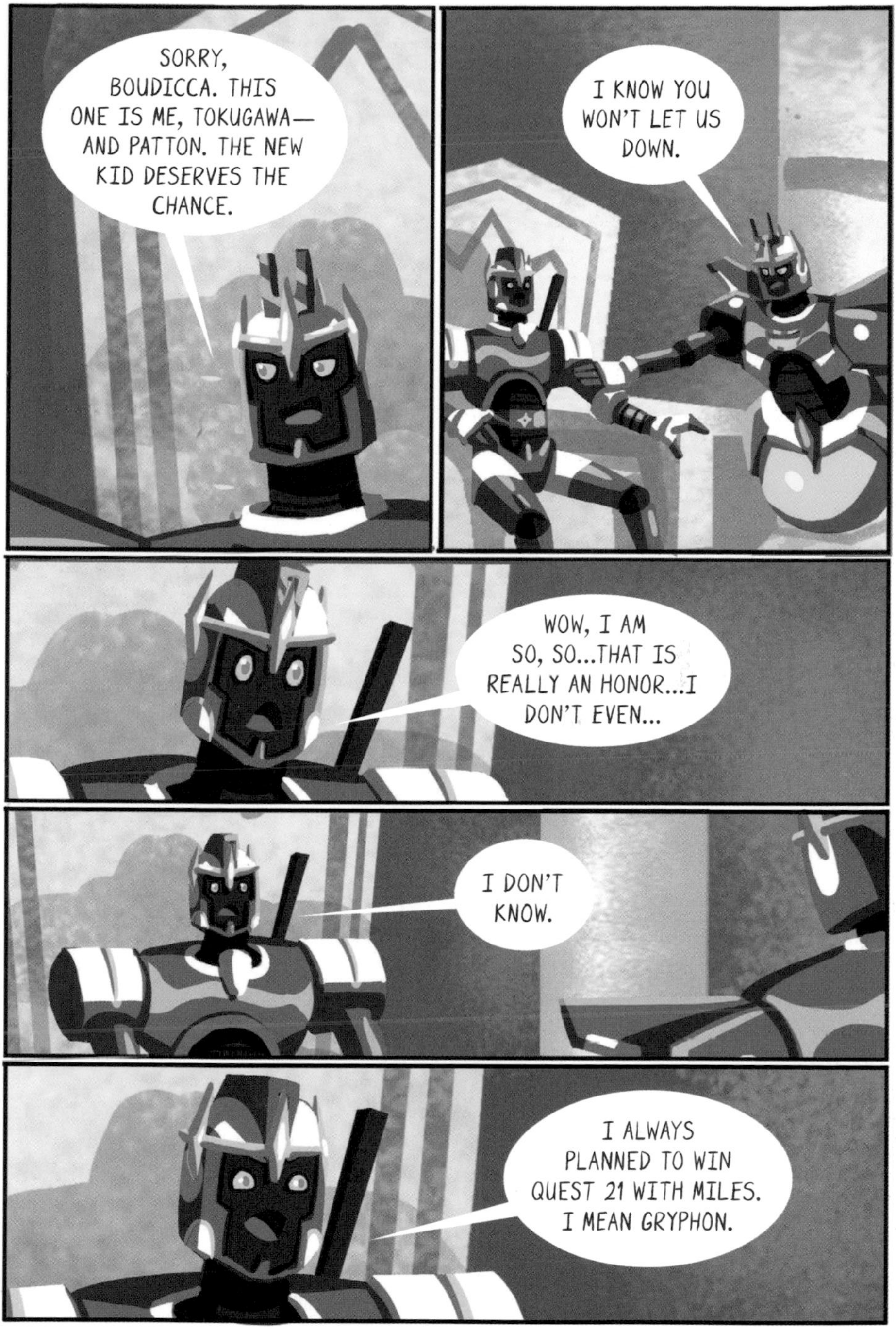
SORRY, BOUDICCA. THIS ONE IS ME, TOKUGAWA— AND PATTON. THE NEW KID DESERVES THE CHANCE.
I KNOW YOU WON'T LET US DOWN.
WOW, I AM SO, SO...THAT IS REALLY AN HONOR...I DON'T EVEN...
I DON'T KNOW.
I ALWAYS PLANNED TO WIN QUEST 21 WITH MILES. I MEAN GRYPHON.

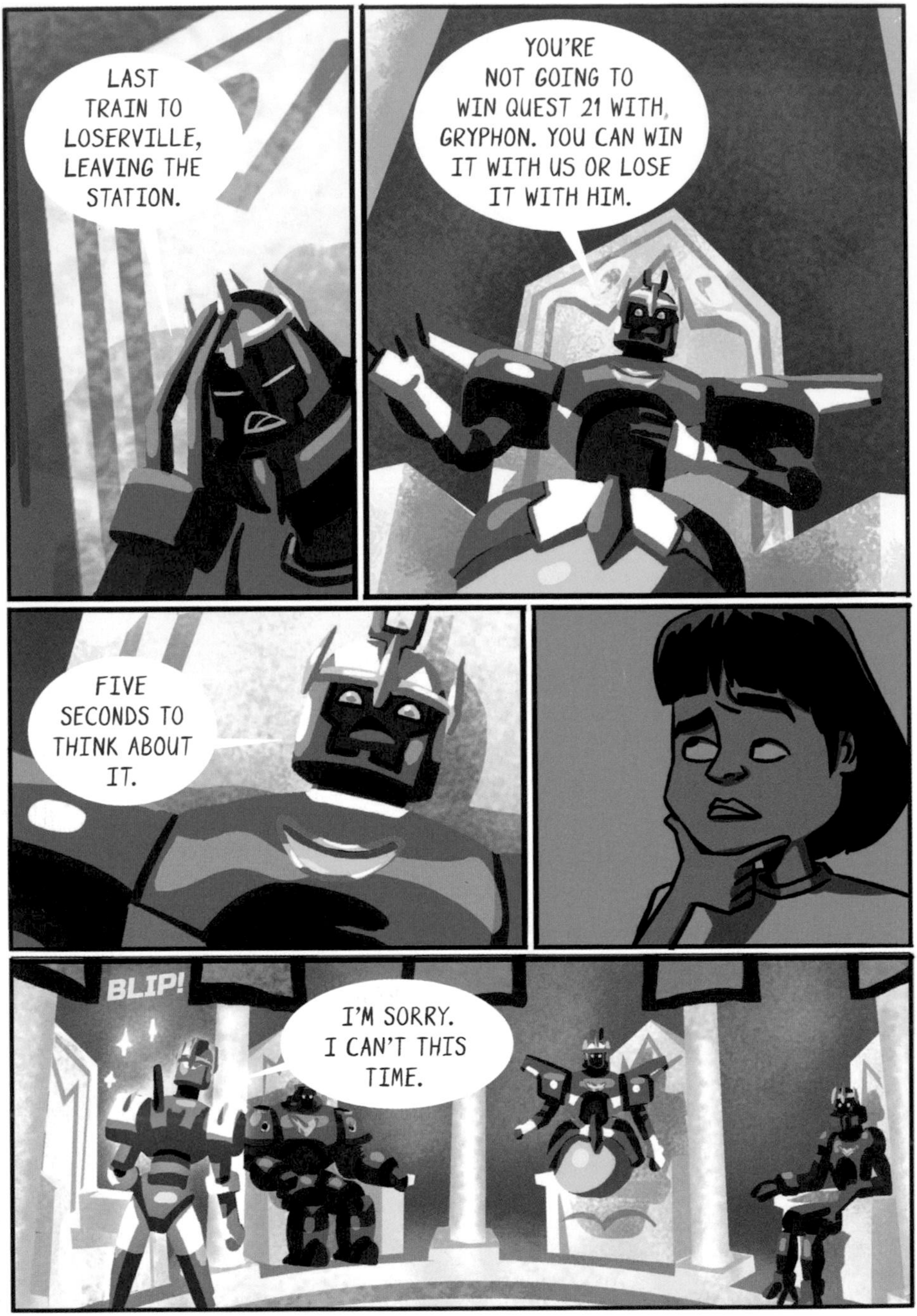
LAST TRAIN TO LOSERVILLE, LEAVING THE STATION.
YOU'RE NOT GOING TO WIN QUEST 21 WITH GRYPHON. YOU CAN WIN IT WITH US OR LOSE IT WITH HIM.
FIVE SECONDS TO THINK ABOUT IT.
BLIP!
I'M SORRY. I CAN'T THIS TIME.

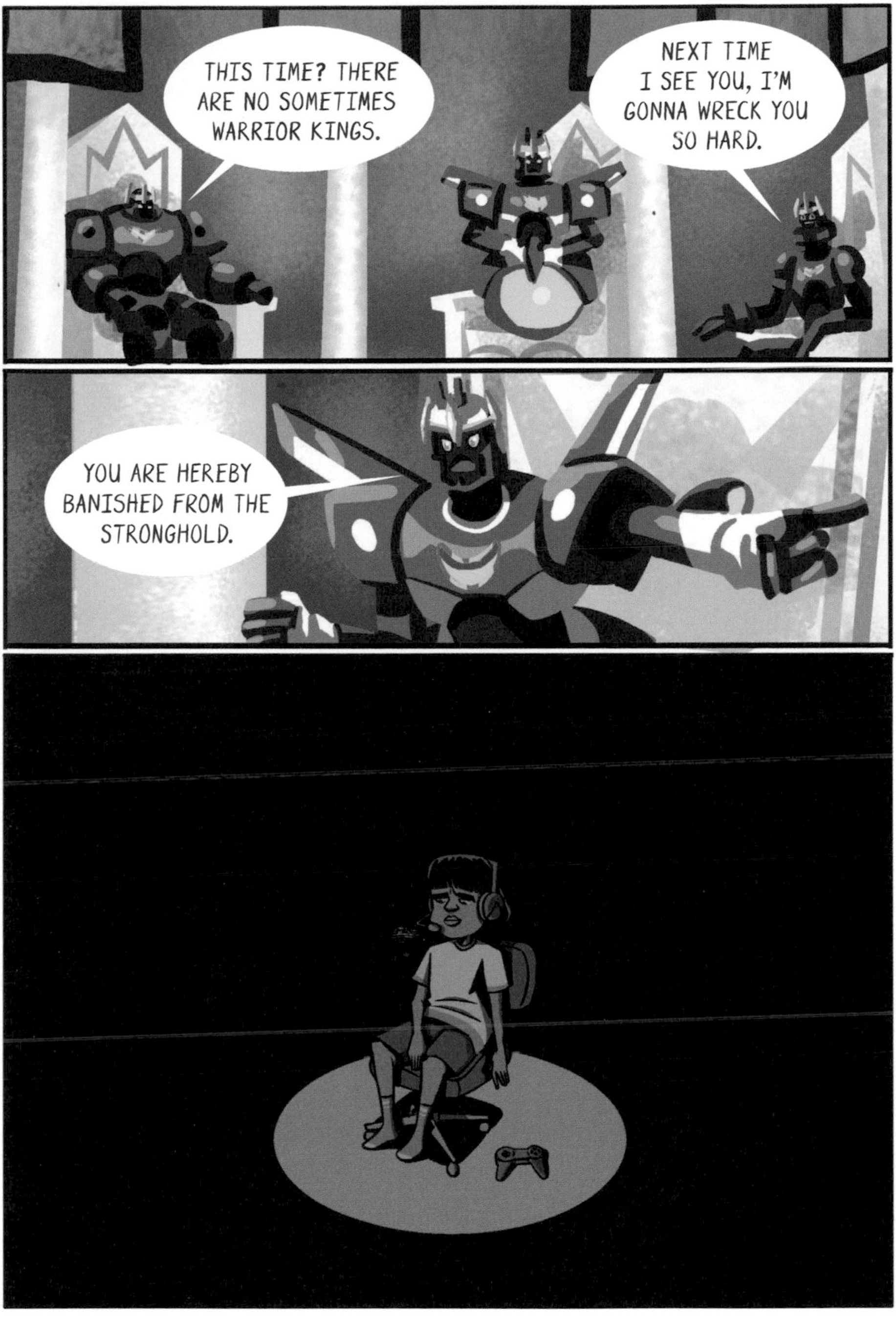
THIS TIME? THERE ARE NO SOMETIMES WARRIOR KINGS.
NEXT TIME I SEE YOU, I'M GONNA WRECK YOU SO HARD.
YOU ARE HEREBY BANISHED FROM THE STRONGHOLD.

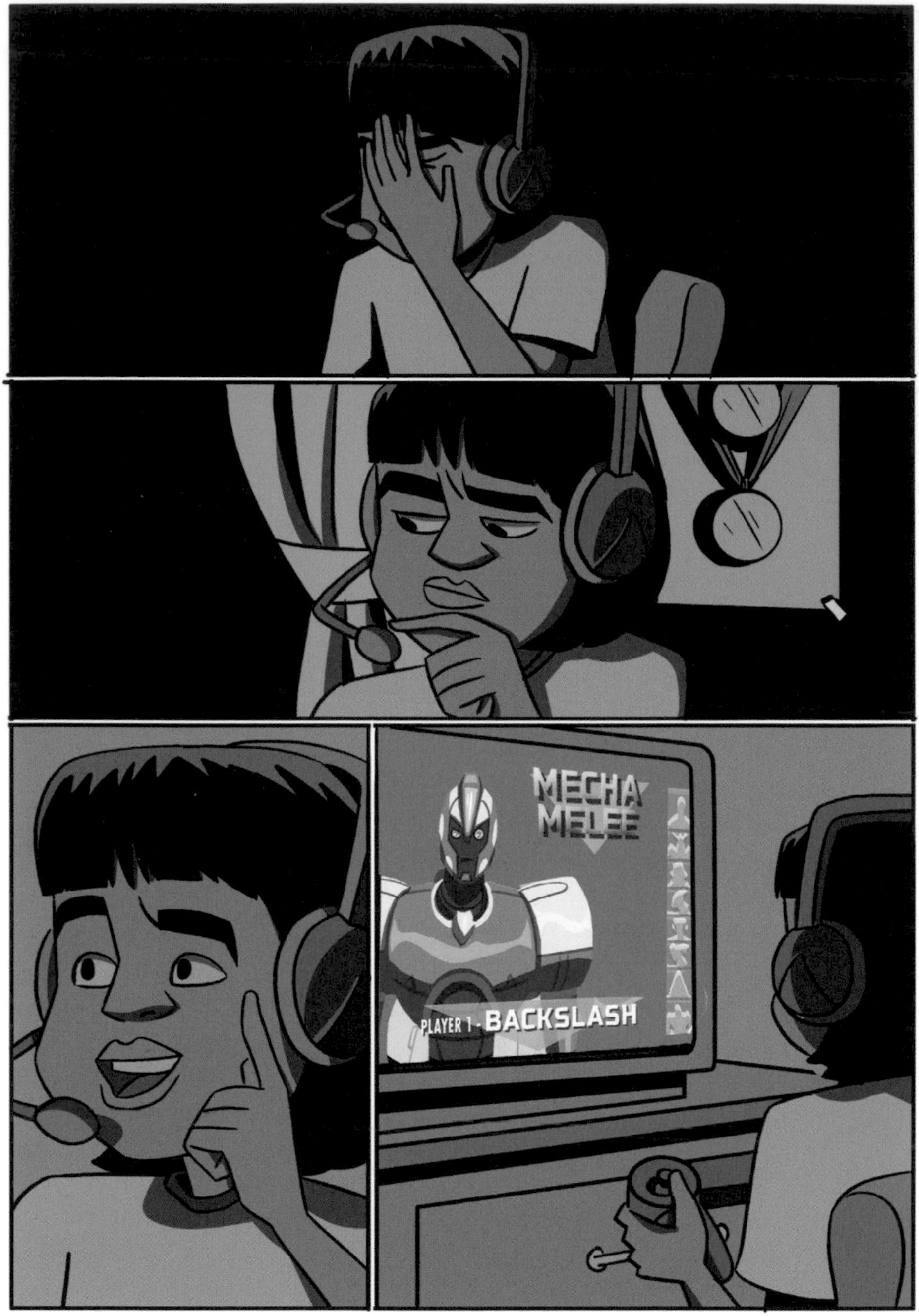
MECHA MELEE
PLAYER 1 - BACKSLASH

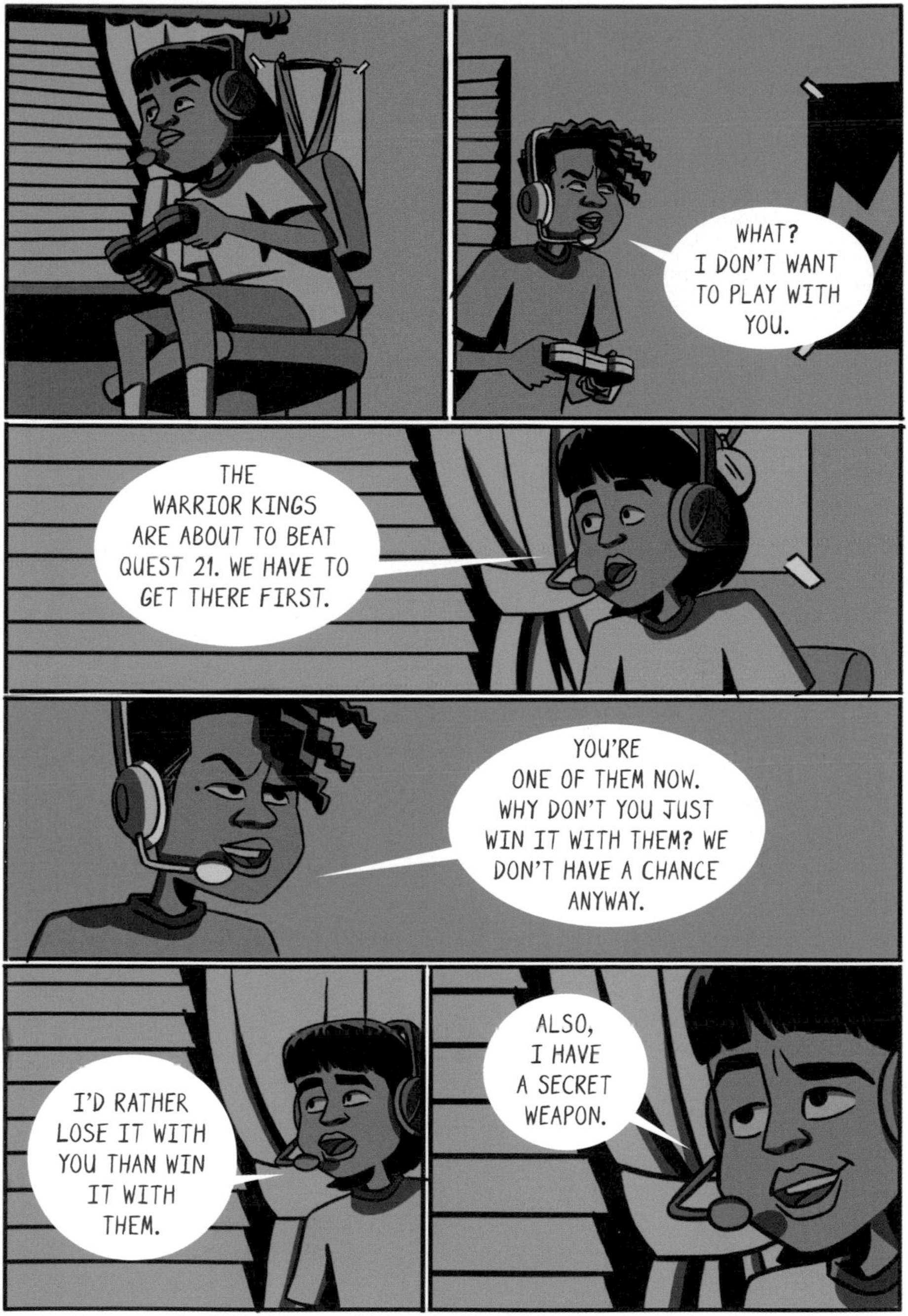
WHAT?
I DON'T WANT
TO PLAY WITH
YOU.
THE
WARRIOR KINGS
ARE ABOUT TO BEAT
QUEST 21. WE HAVE TO
GET THERE FIRST.
YOU'RE
ONE OF THEM NOW.
WHY DON'T YOU JUST
WIN IT WITH THEM? WE
DON'T HAVE A CHANCE
ANYWAY.
I'D RATHER
LOSE IT WITH
YOU THAN WIN
IT WITH
THEM.
ALSO,
I HAVE
A SECRET
WEAPON.

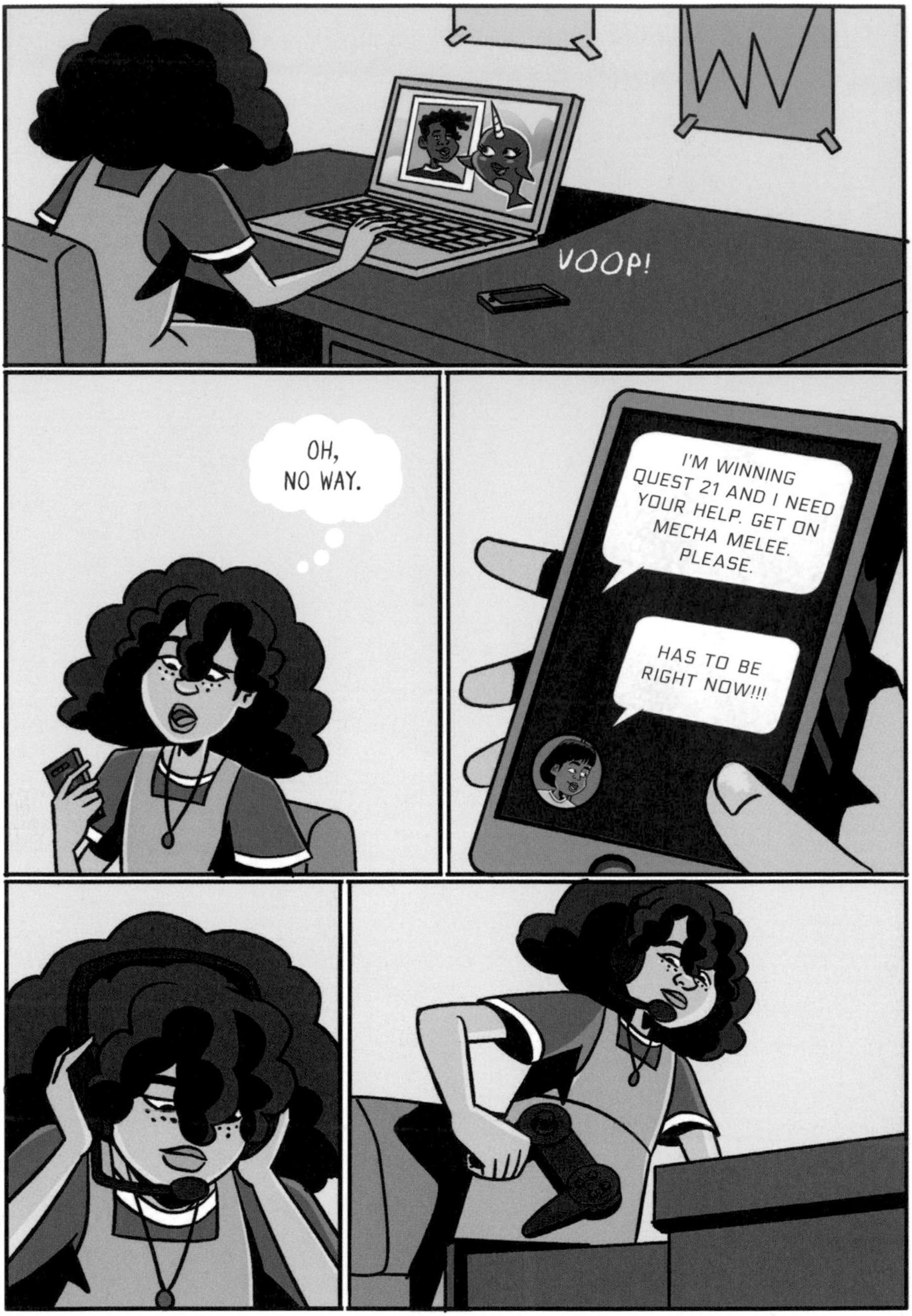
VOOP!
OH, NO WAY.
I'M WINNING QUEST 21 AND I NEED YOUR HELP. GET ON MECHA MELEE. PLEASE.
HAS TO BE RIGHT NOW!!!

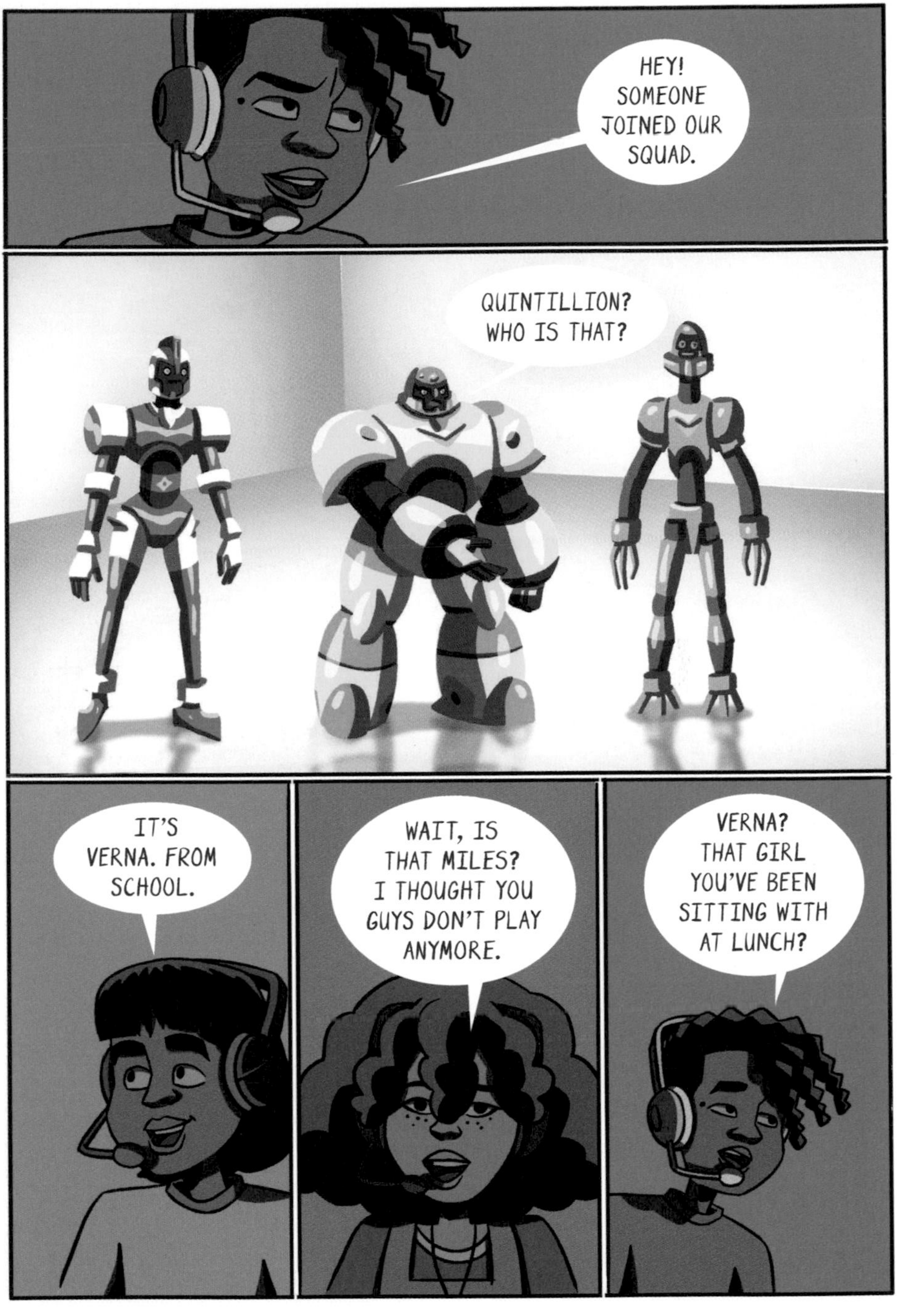
HEY! SOMEONE JOINED OUR SQUAD.
QUINTILLION? WHO IS THAT?
IT'S VERNA. FROM SCHOOL.
WAIT, IS THAT MILES? I THOUGHT YOU GUYS DON'T PLAY ANYMORE.
VERNA? THAT GIRL YOU'VE BEEN SITTING WITH AT LUNCH?

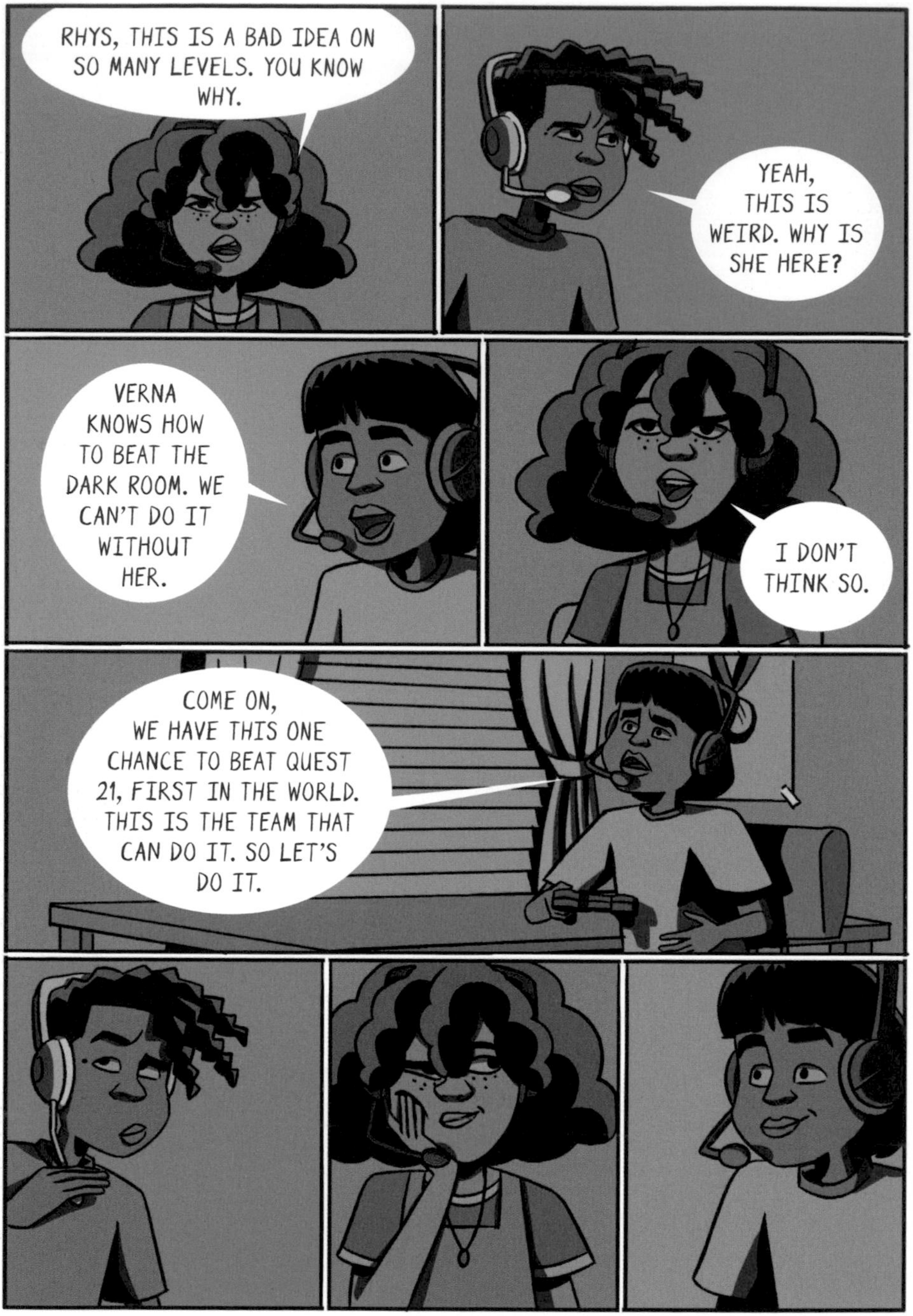
RHYS, THIS IS A BAD IDEA ON SO MANY LEVELS. YOU KNOW WHY.
YEAH, THIS IS WEIRD. WHY IS SHE HERE?
VERNA KNOWS HOW TO BEAT THE DARK ROOM. WE CAN'T DO IT WITHOUT HER.
I DON'T THINK SO.
COME ON, WE HAVE THIS ONE CHANCE TO BEAT QUEST 21, FIRST IN THE WORLD. THIS IS THE TEAM THAT CAN DO IT. SO LET'S DO IT.

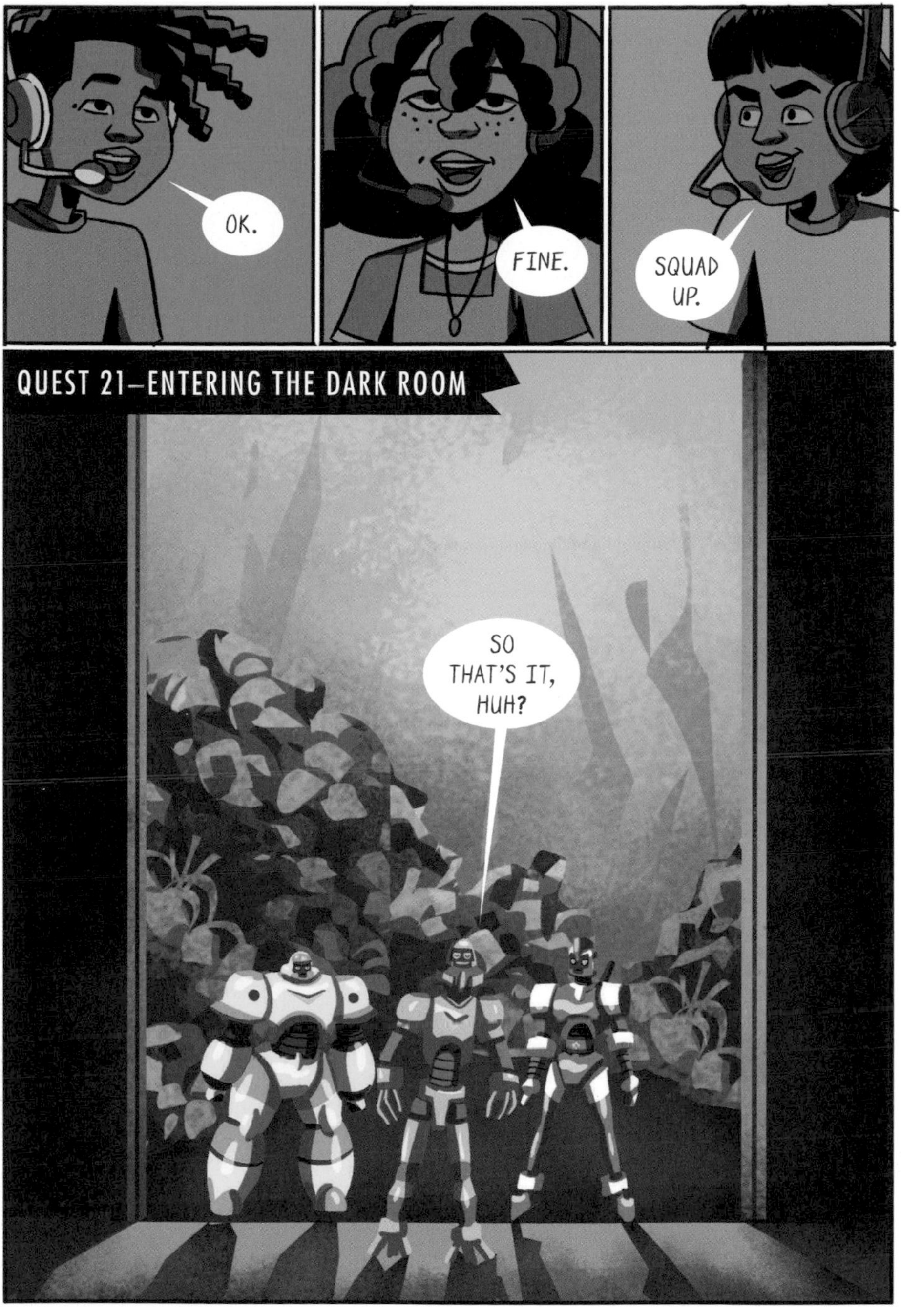
OK.
FINE.
SQUAD UP.
QUEST 21—ENTERING THE DARK ROOM
SO THAT'S IT, HUH?

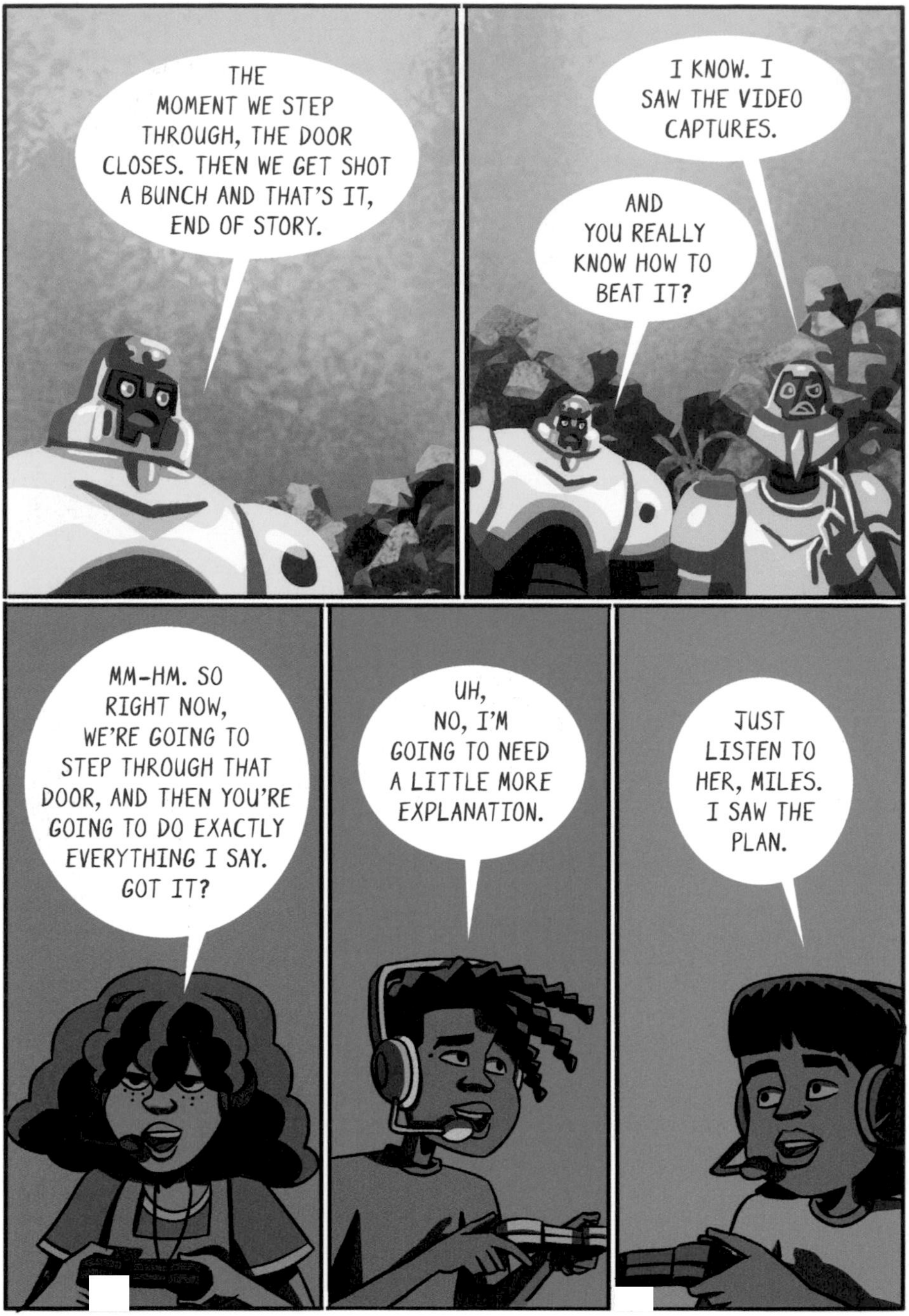
THE MOMENT WE STEP THROUGH, THE DOOR CLOSES. THEN WE GET SHOT A BUNCH AND THAT'S IT, END OF STORY.
I KNOW. I SAW THE VIDEO CAPTURES.
AND YOU REALLY KNOW HOW TO BEAT IT?
MM-HM. SO RIGHT NOW, WE'RE GOING TO STEP THROUGH THAT DOOR, AND THEN YOU'RE GOING TO DO EXACTLY EVERYTHING I SAY. GOT IT?
UH, NO, I'M GOING TO NEED A LITTLE MORE EXPLANATION.
JUST LISTEN TO HER, MILES. I SAW THE PLAN.

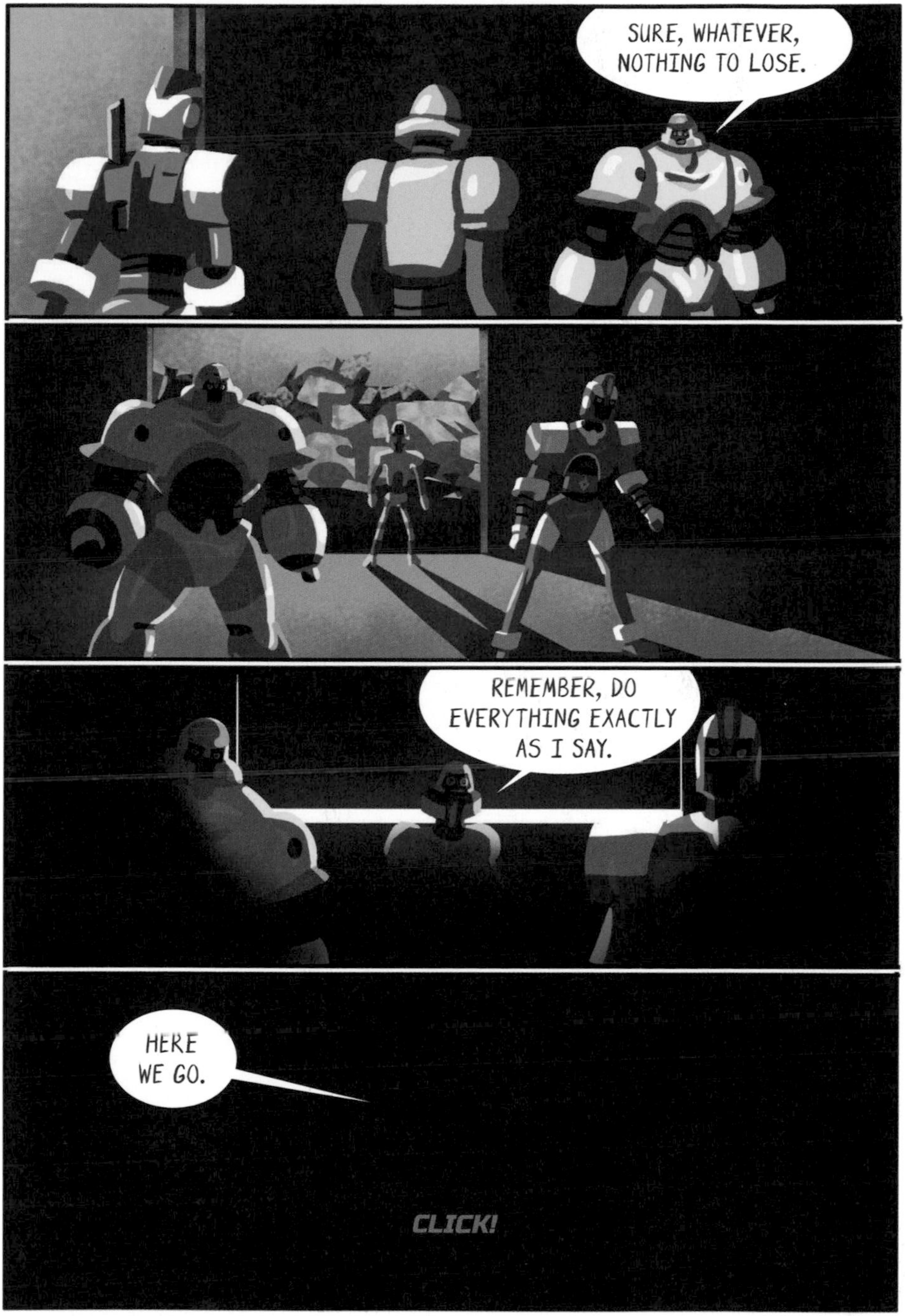
SURE, WHATEVER, NOTHING TO LOSE.
REMEMBER, DO EVERYTHING EXACTLY AS I SAY.
HERE WE GO.
CLICK!

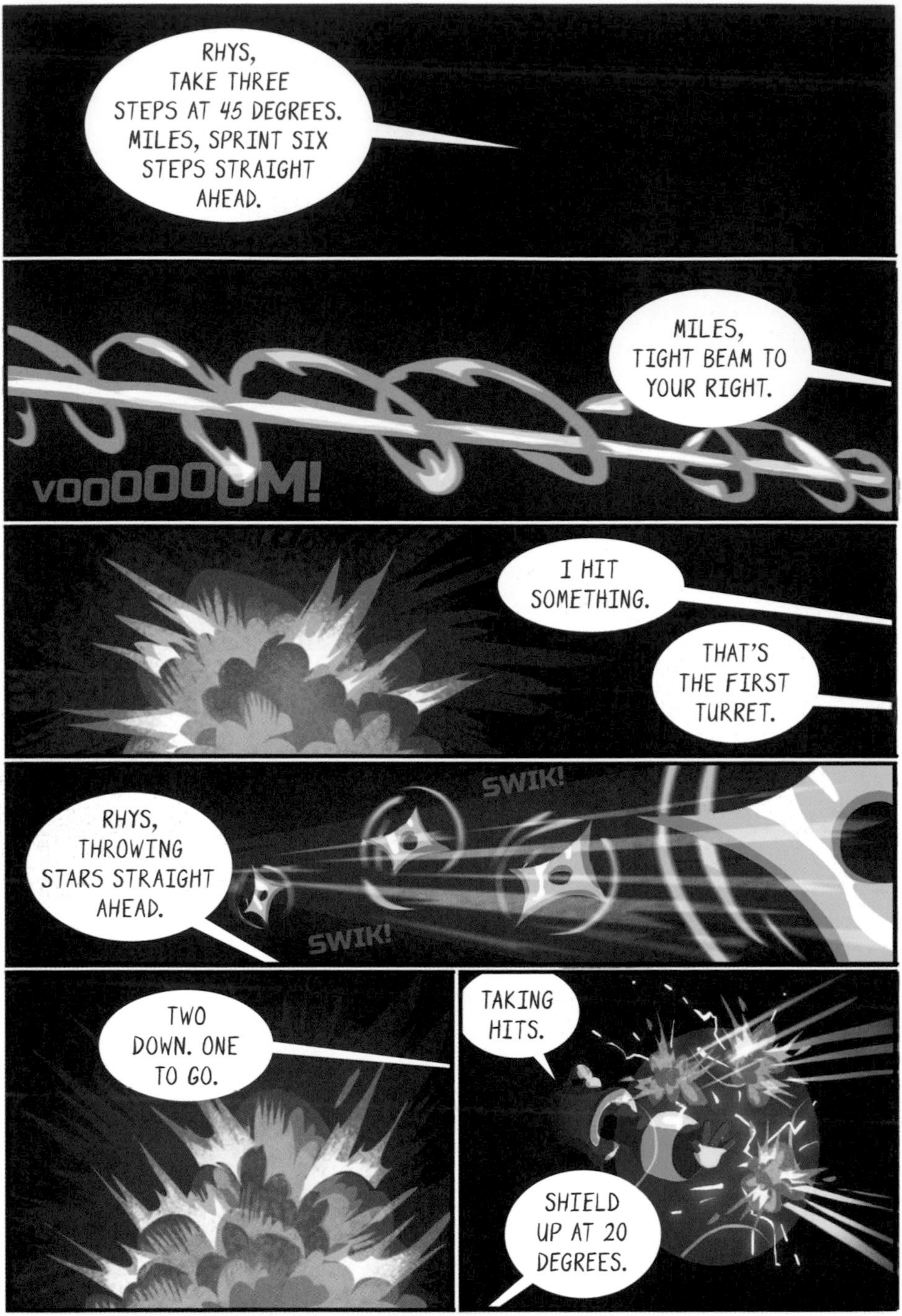
RHYS, TAKE THREE STEPS AT 45 DEGREES. MILES, SPRINT SIX STEPS STRAIGHT AHEAD.
MILES, TIGHT BEAM TO YOUR RIGHT.
VOOOOOOM!
I HIT SOMETHING.
THAT'S THE FIRST TURRET.
RHYS, THROWING STARS STRAIGHT AHEAD.
SWIK!
SWIK!
TWO DOWN. ONE TO GO.
TAKING HITS.
SHIELD UP AT 20 DEGREES.

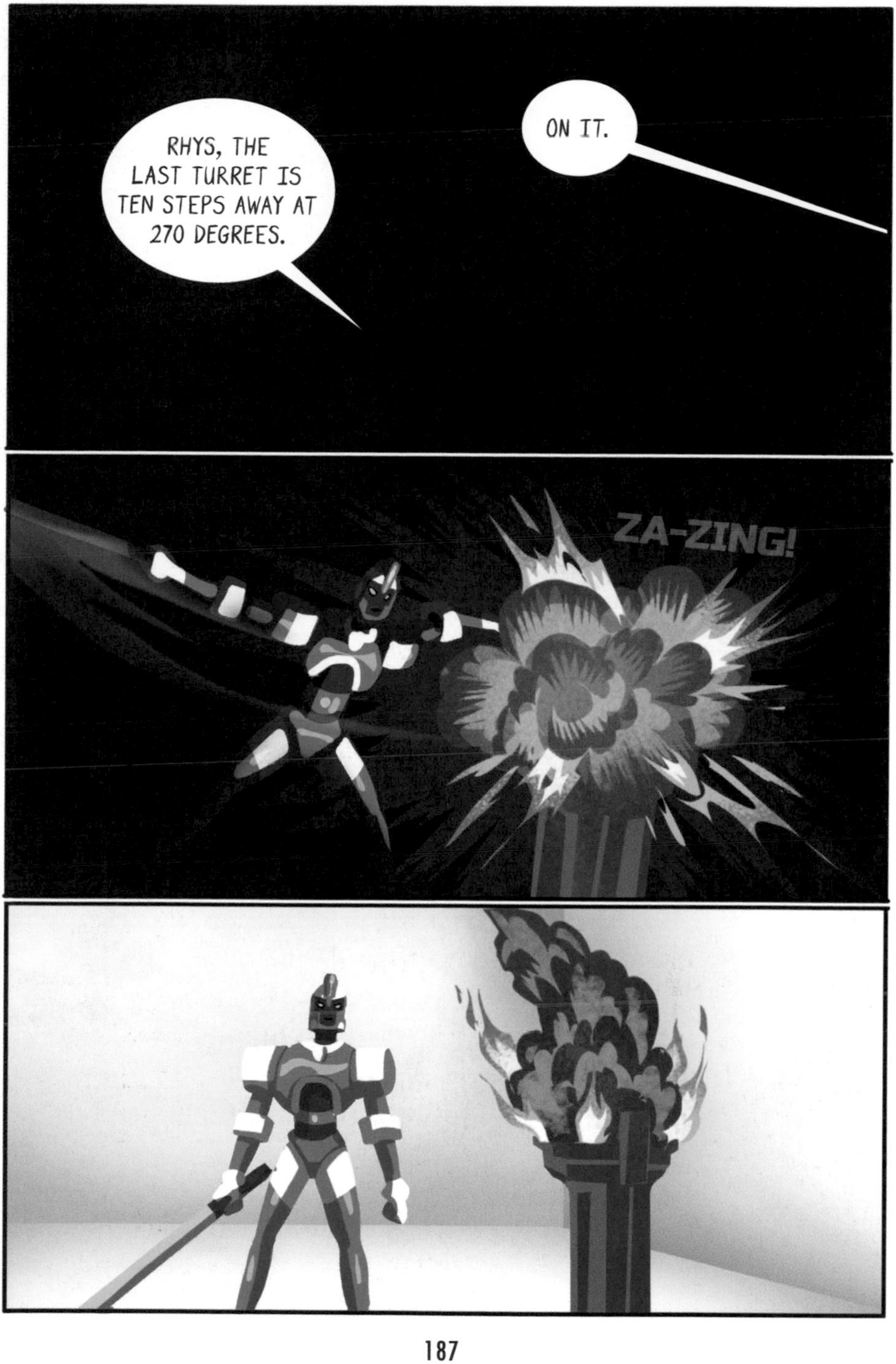
RHYS, THE LAST TURRET IS TEN STEPS AWAY AT 270 DEGREES.
ON IT.
ZA-ZING!

THAT WAS AMAZING!

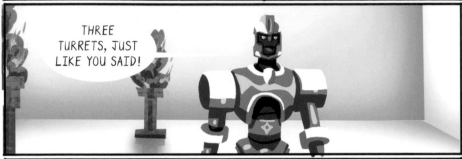

THREE TURRETS, JUST LIKE YOU SAID!

I WASN'T EVEN SURE IT WOULD WORK. NOT ONLY MY CALCULATIONS, YOU GUYS HAD TO DO EVERYTHING PERFECT AND—

WOOM

HELLO. WOW.

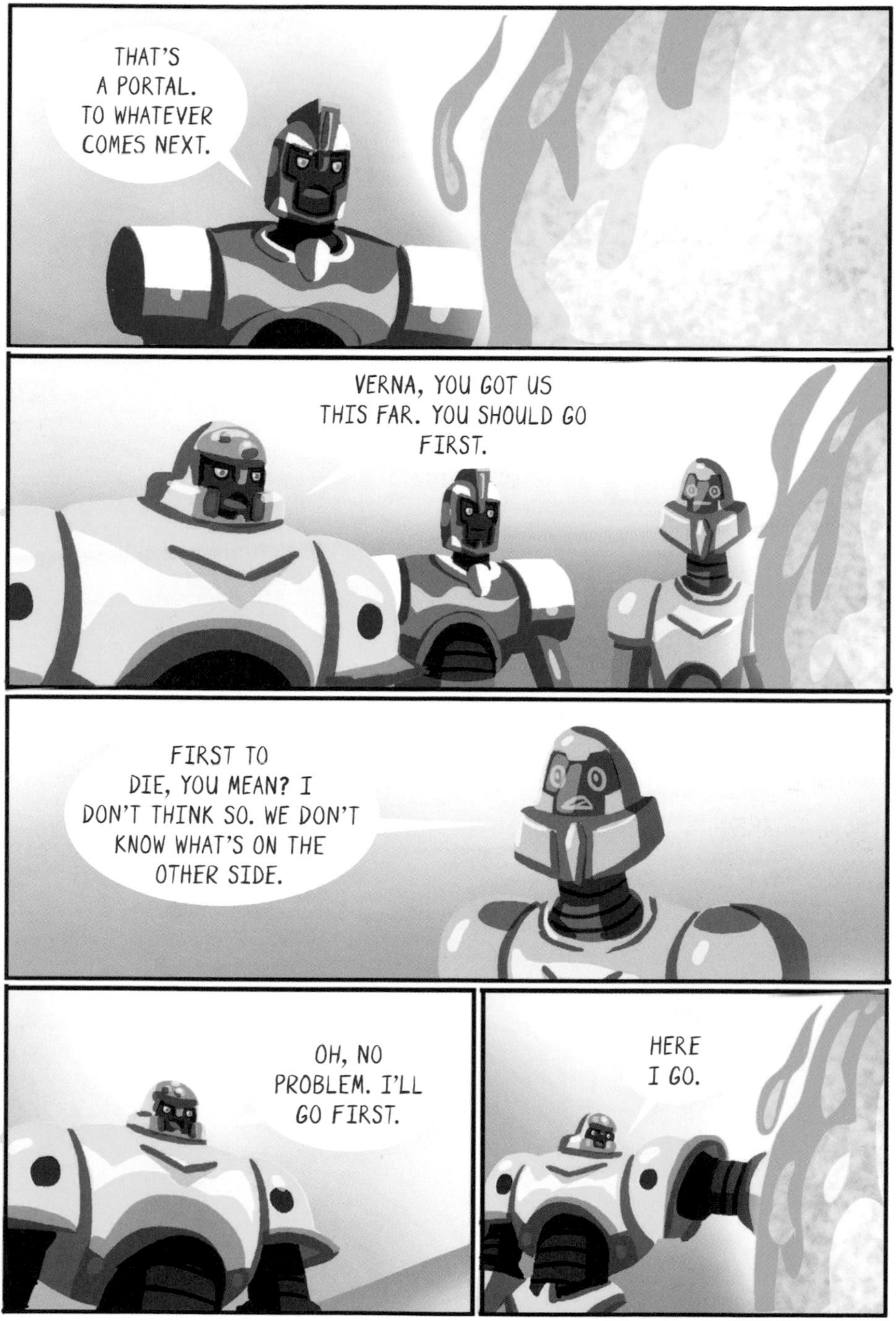
THAT'S A PORTAL. TO WHATEVER COMES NEXT.
VERNA, YOU GOT US THIS FAR. YOU SHOULD GO FIRST.
FIRST TO DIE, YOU MEAN? I DON'T THINK SO. WE DON'T KNOW WHAT'S ON THE OTHER SIDE.
OH, NO PROBLEM. I'LL GO FIRST.
HERE I GO.

CHAPTER 13
CLUTCH

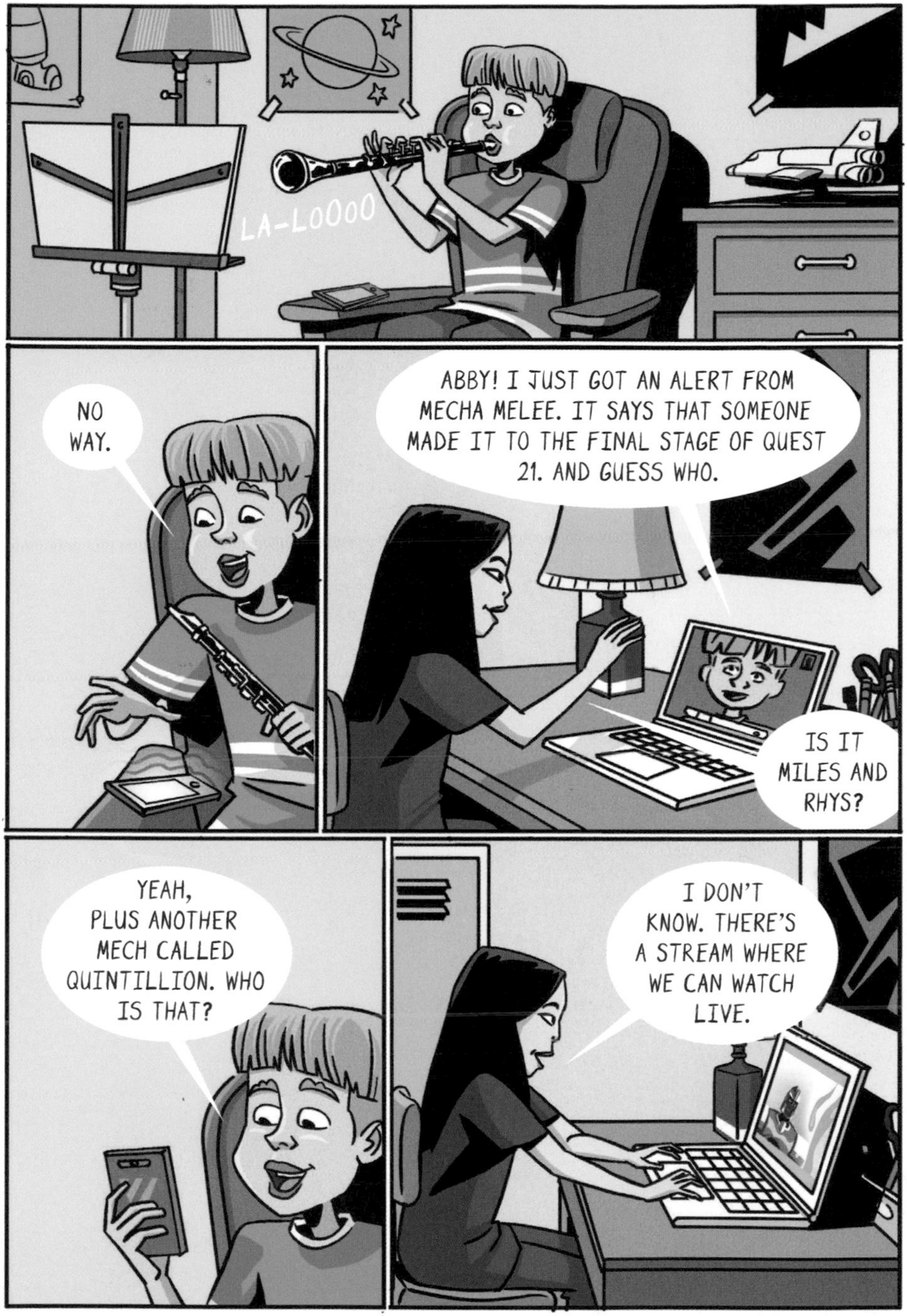
LA-LOOOO
NO WAY.
ABBY! I JUST GOT AN ALERT FROM MECHA MELEE. IT SAYS THAT SOMEONE MADE IT TO THE FINAL STAGE OF QUEST 21. AND GUESS WHO.
IS IT MILES AND RHYS?
YEAH, PLUS ANOTHER MECH CALLED QUINTILLION. WHO IS THAT?
I DON'T KNOW. THERE'S A STREAM WHERE WE CAN WATCH LIVE.

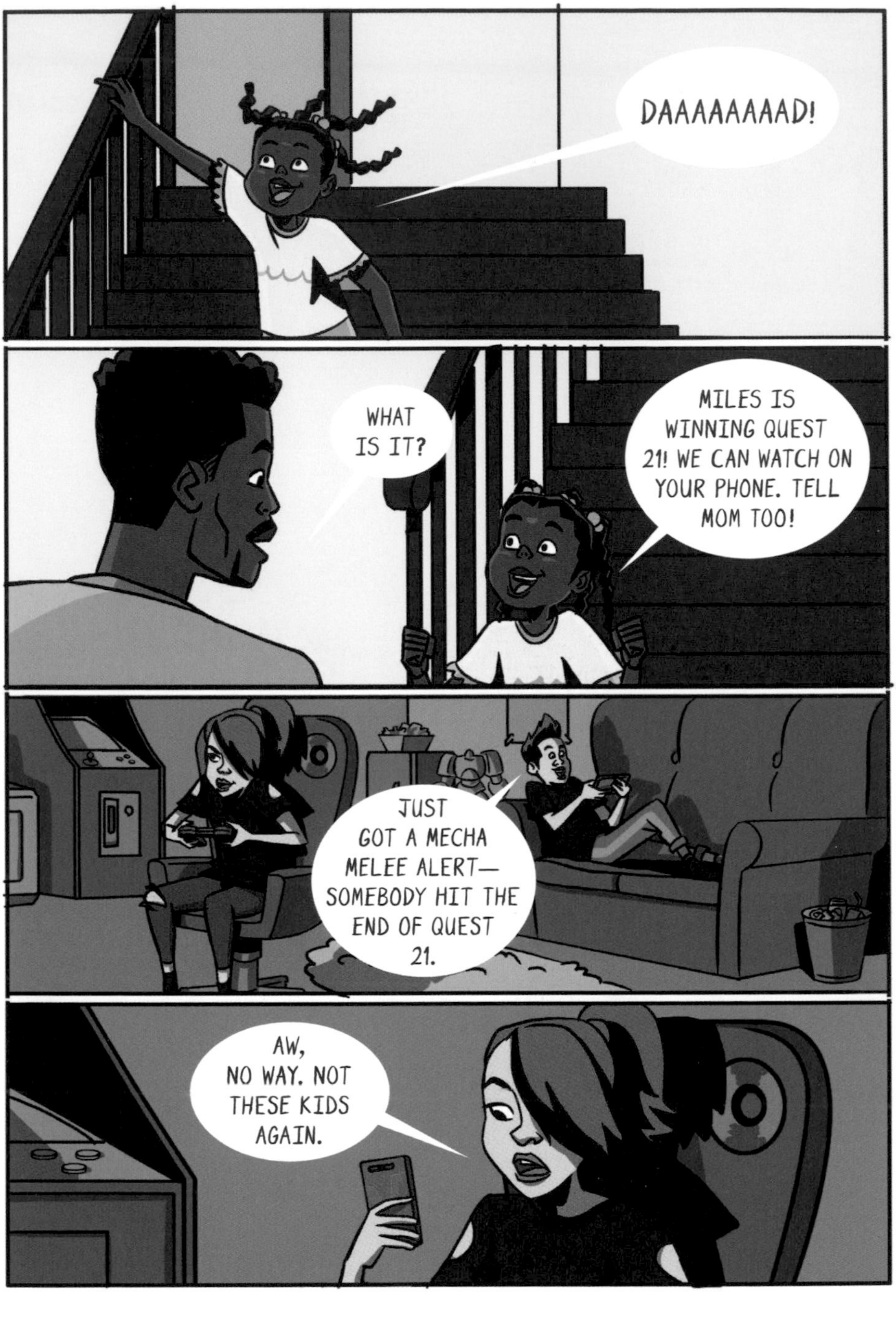
DAAAAAAAAD!
WHAT IS IT?
MILES IS WINNING QUEST 21! WE CAN WATCH ON YOUR PHONE. TELL MOM TOO!
JUST GOT A MECHA MELEE ALERT— SOMEBODY HIT THE END OF QUEST 21.
AW, NO WAY. NOT THESE KIDS AGAIN.

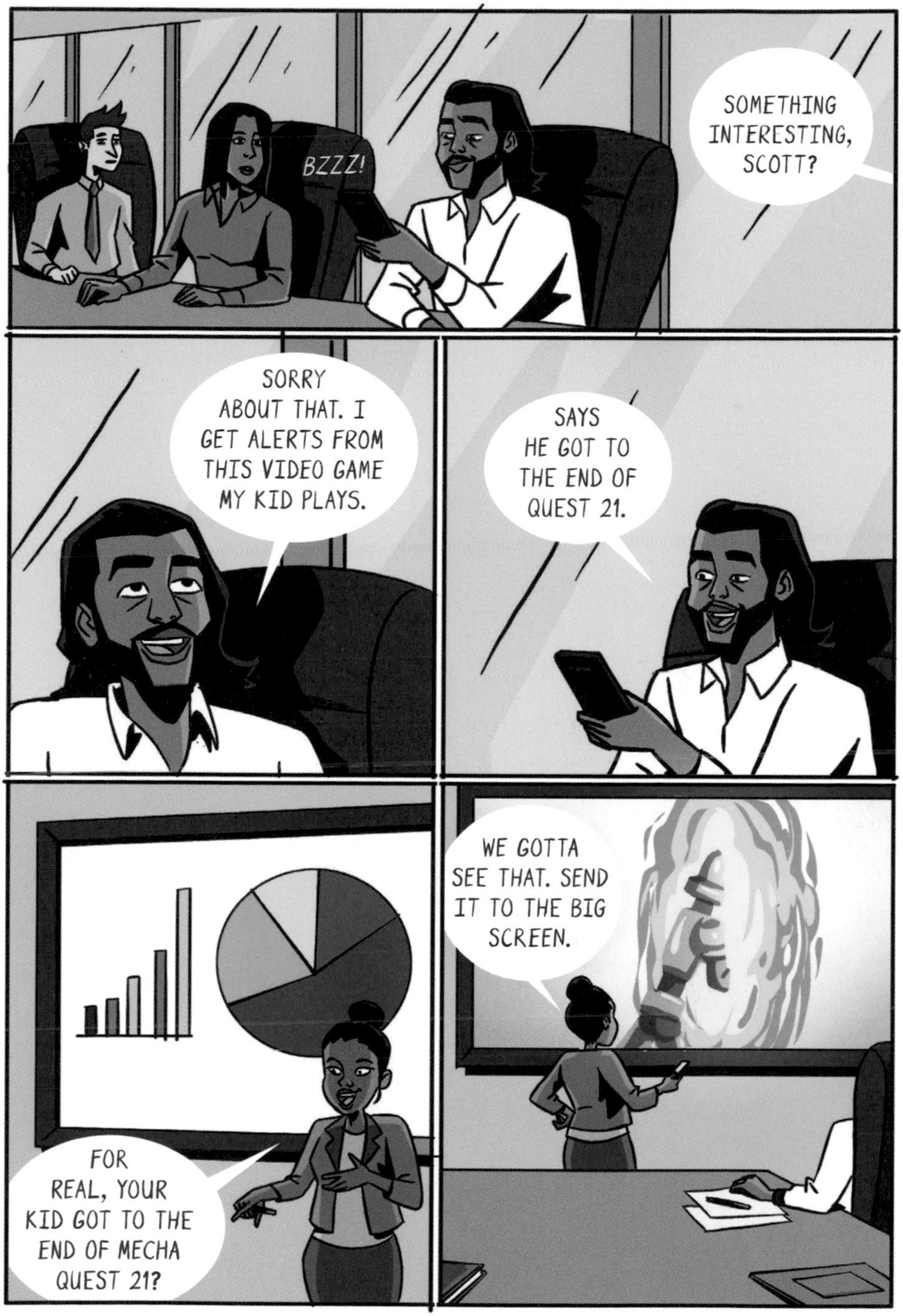
BZZZ!
SOMETHING INTERESTING, SCOTT?
SORRY ABOUT THAT. I GET ALERTS FROM THIS VIDEO GAME MY KID PLAYS.
SAYS HE GOT TO THE END OF QUEST 21.
FOR REAL, YOUR KID GOT TO THE END OF MECHA QUEST 21?
WE GOTTA SEE THAT. SEND IT TO THE BIG SCREEN.

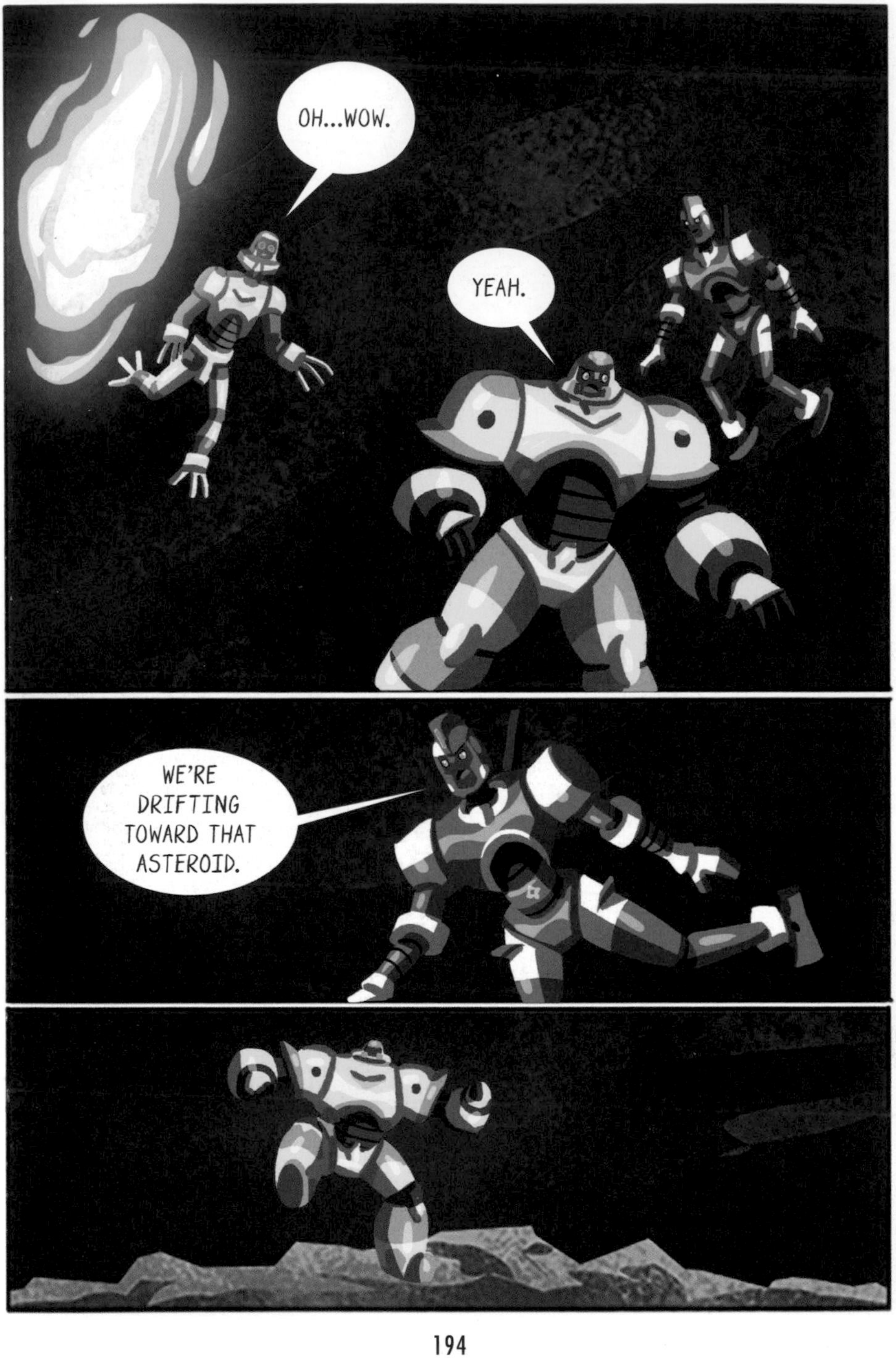
OH...WOW.
YEAH.
WE'RE DRIFTING TOWARD THAT ASTEROID.

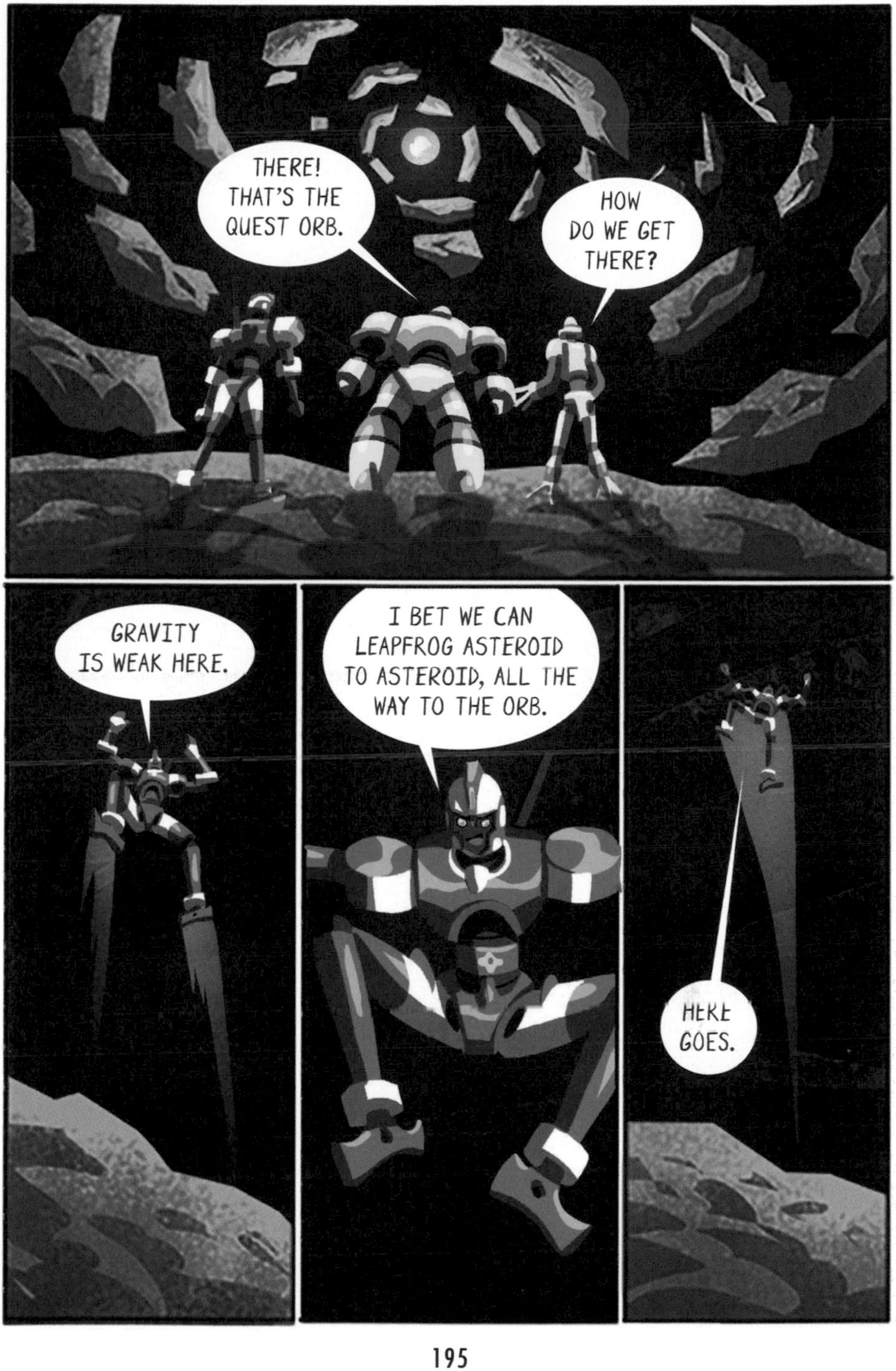
THERE! THAT'S THE QUEST ORB.
HOW DO WE GET THERE?
GRAVITY IS WEAK HERE.
I BET WE CAN LEAPFROG ASTEROID TO ASTEROID, ALL THE WAY TO THE ORB.
HERE GOES.

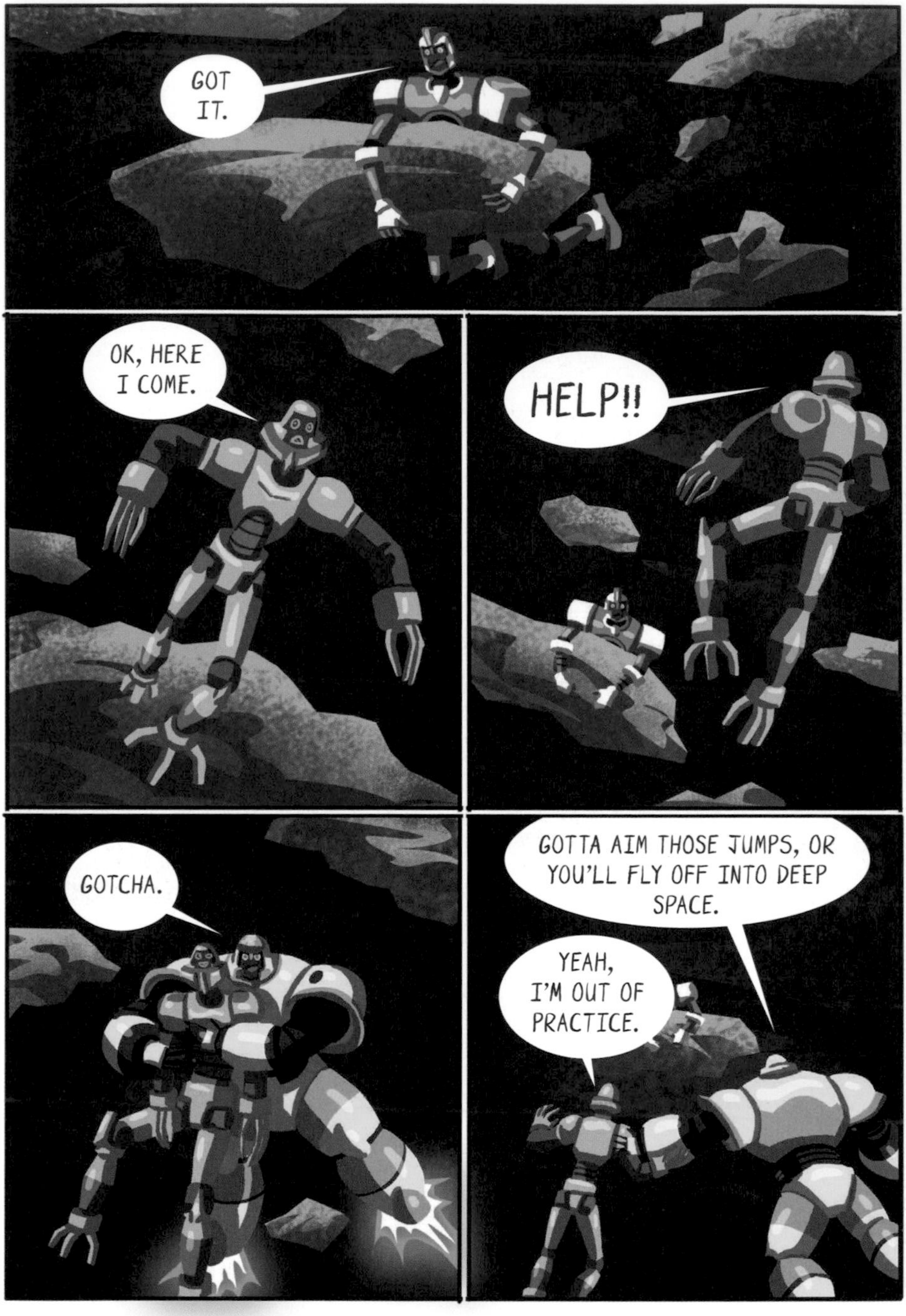
GOT IT.
OK, HERE I COME.
HELP!!
GOTCHA.
GOTTA AIM THOSE JUMPS, OR YOU'LL FLY OFF INTO DEEP SPACE.
YEAH, I'M OUT OF PRACTICE.

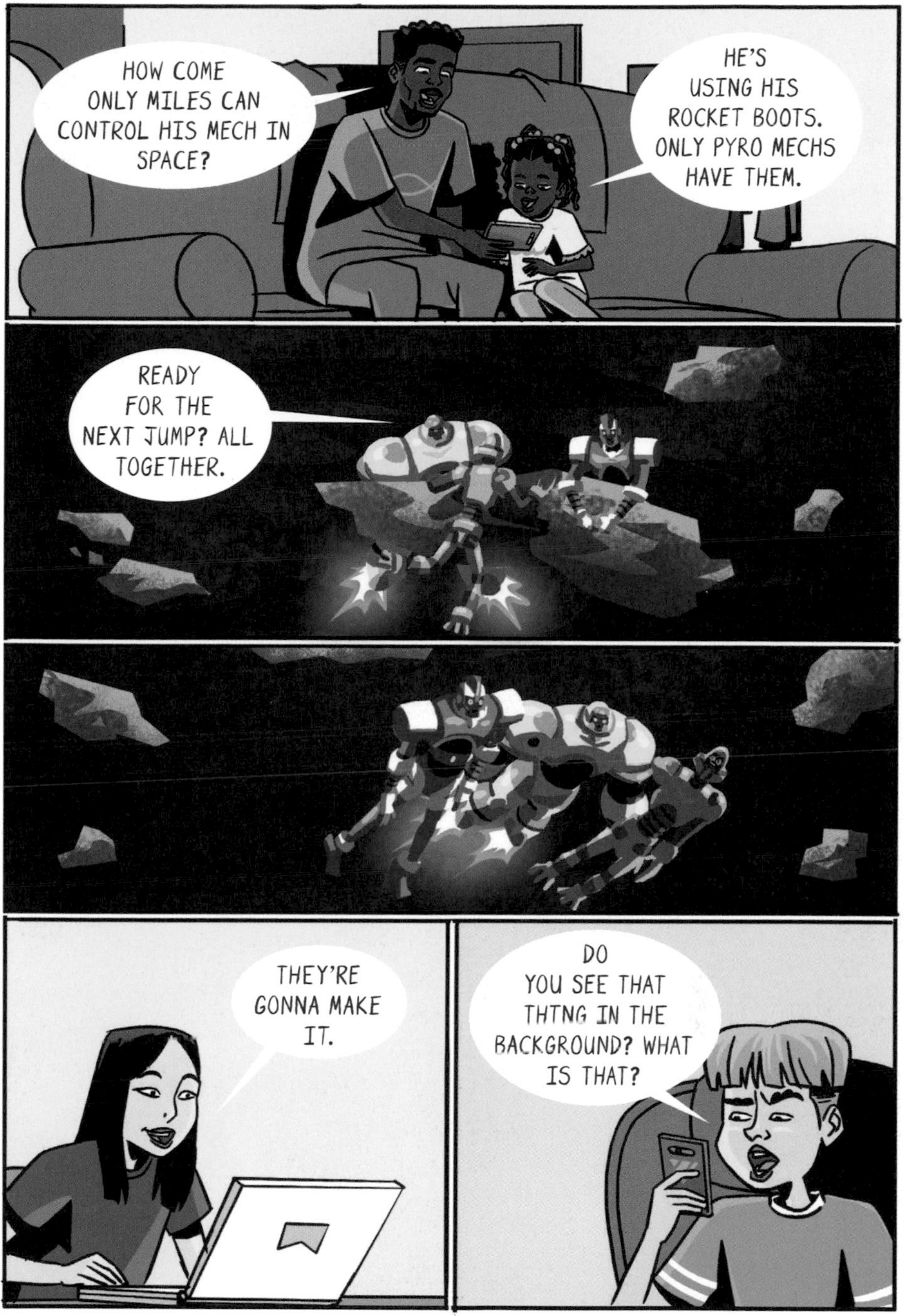
HOW COME ONLY MILES CAN CONTROL HIS MECH IN SPACE?
HE'S USING HIS ROCKET BOOTS. ONLY PYRO MECHS HAVE THEM.
READY FOR THE NEXT JUMP? ALL TOGETHER.
THEY'RE GONNA MAKE IT.
DO YOU SEE THAT THING IN THE BACKGROUND? WHAT IS THAT?

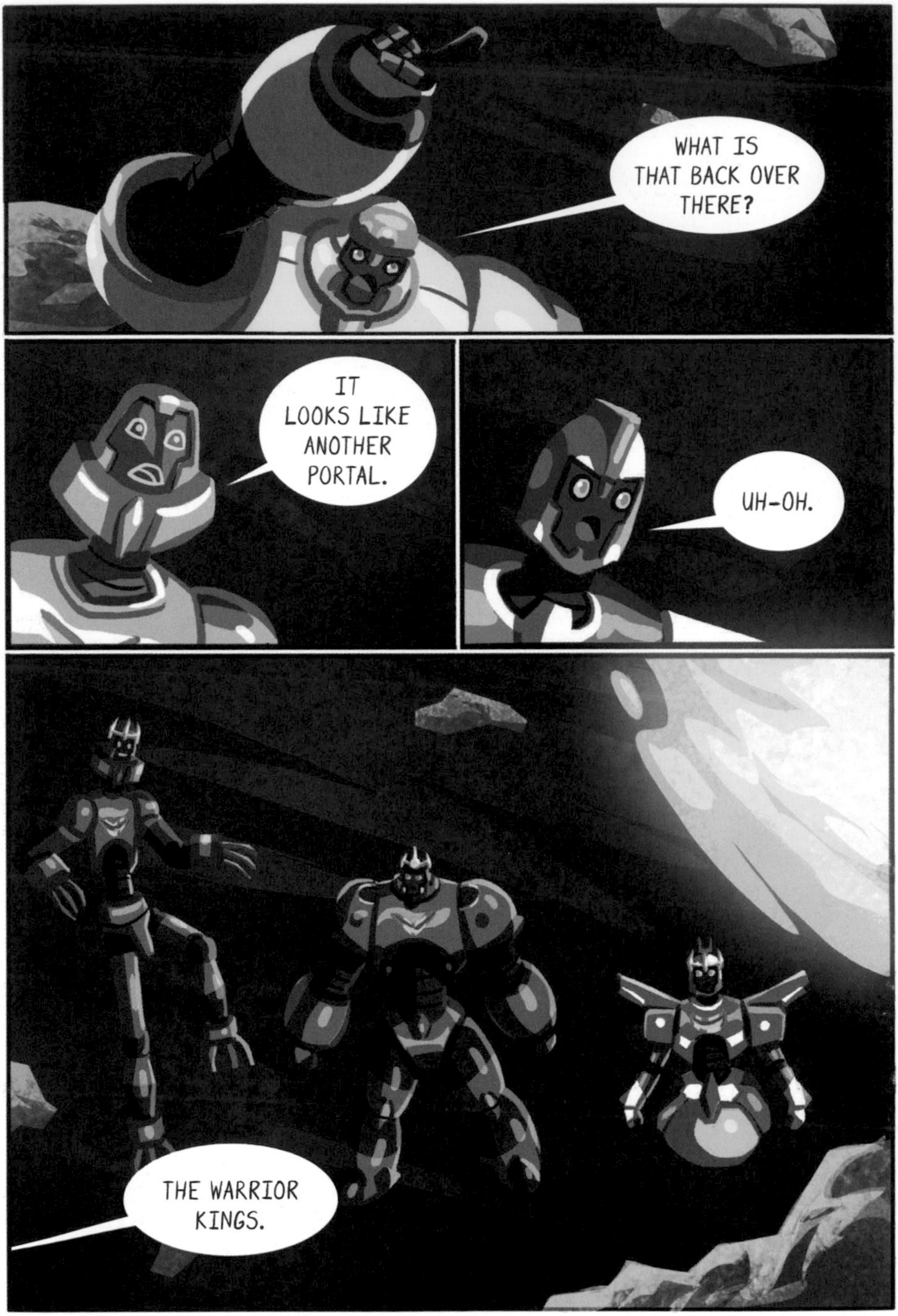
WHAT IS THAT BACK OVER THERE?
IT LOOKS LIKE ANOTHER PORTAL.
UH-OH.
THE WARRIOR KINGS.

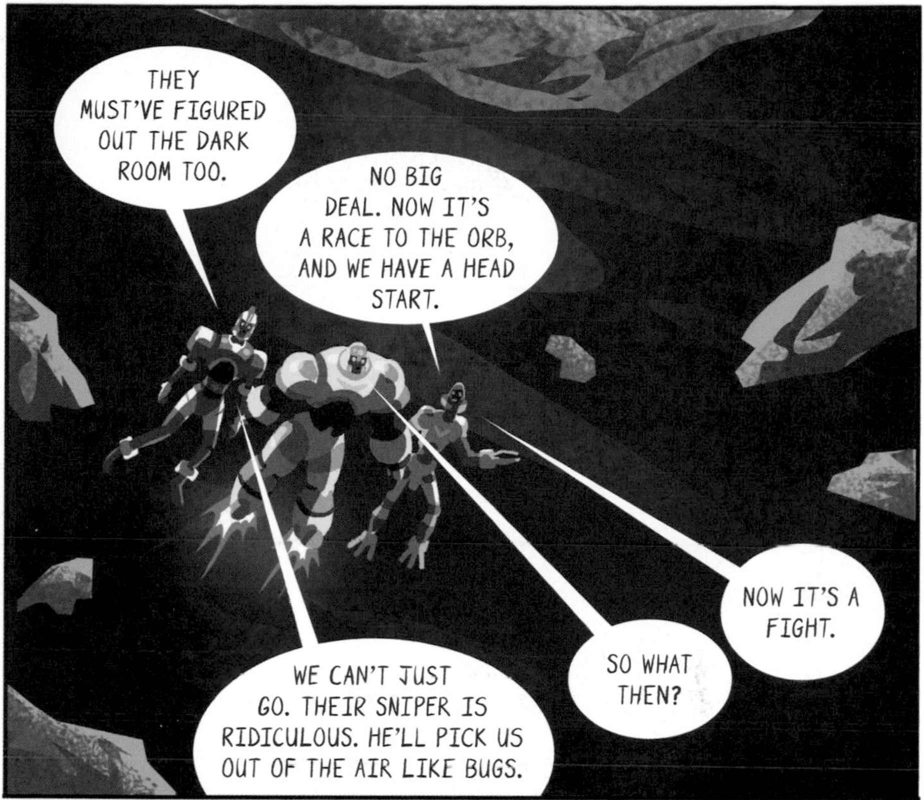
THEY MUST'VE FIGURED OUT THE DARK ROOM TOO.
NO BIG DEAL. NOW IT'S A RACE TO THE ORB, AND WE HAVE A HEAD START.
WE CAN'T JUST GO. THEIR SNIPER IS RIDICULOUS. HE'LL PICK US OUT OF THE AIR LIKE BUGS.
SO WHAT THEN?
NOW IT'S A FIGHT.

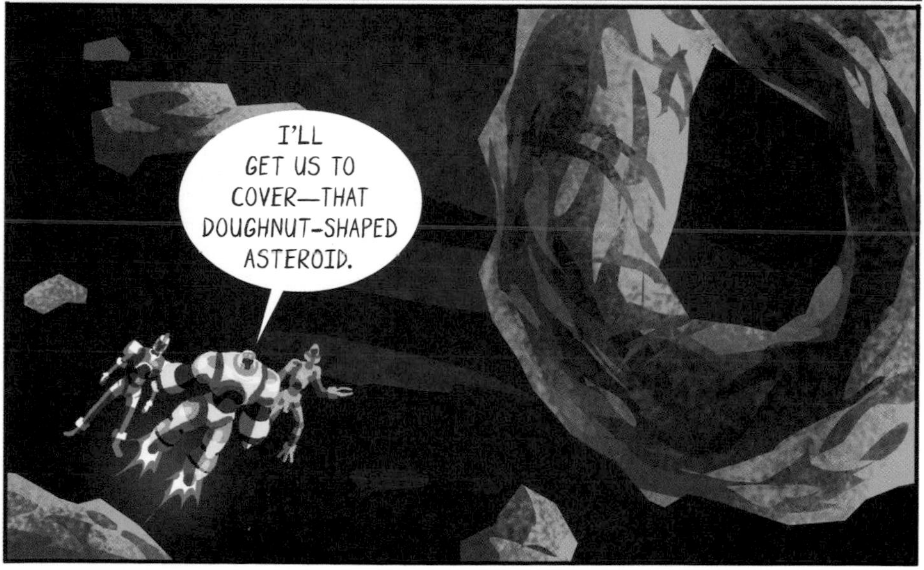
I'LL GET US TO COVER—THAT DOUGHNUT-SHAPED ASTEROID.

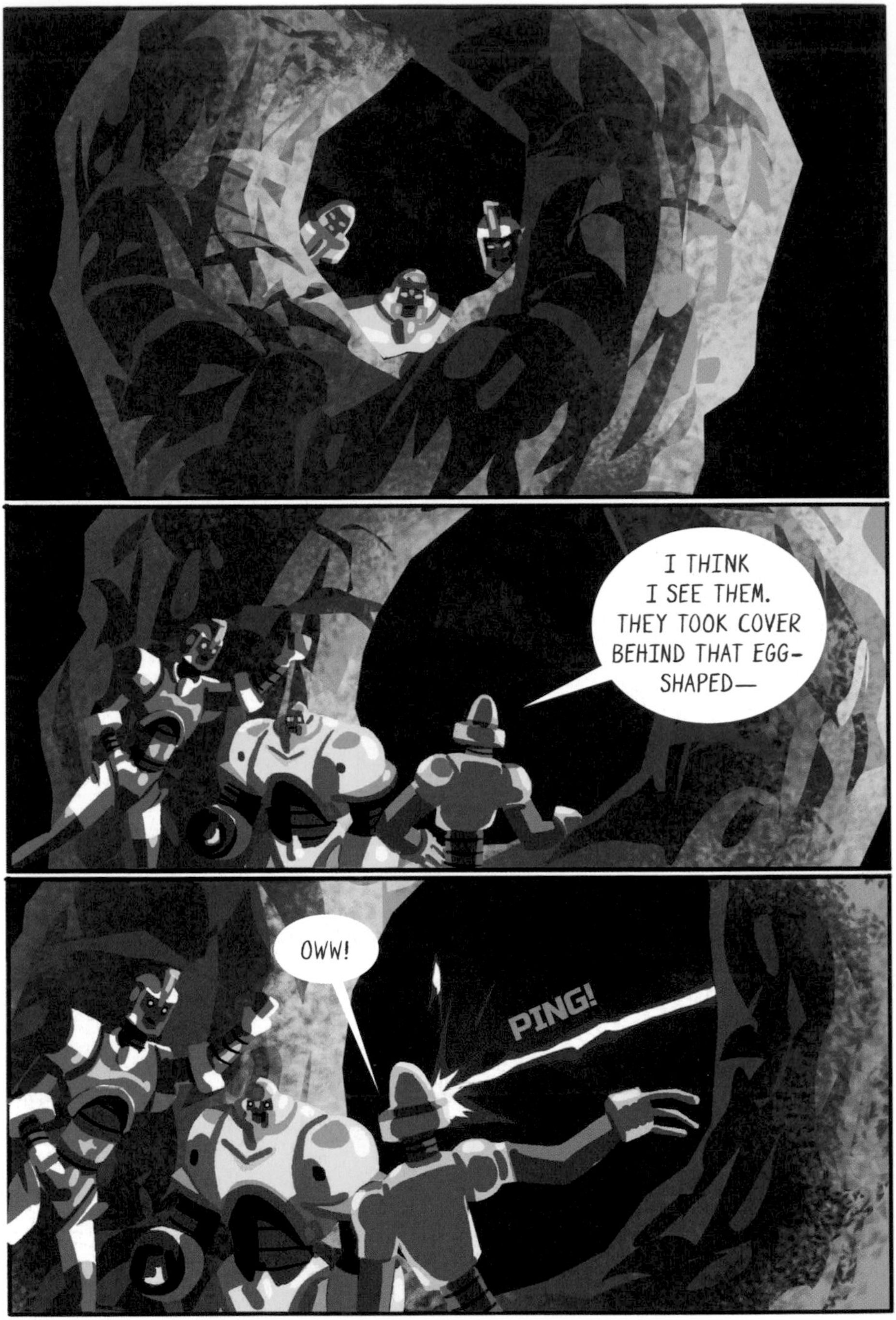
I THINK I SEE THEM. THEY TOOK COVER BEHIND THAT EGG-SHAPED—
OWW!
PING!

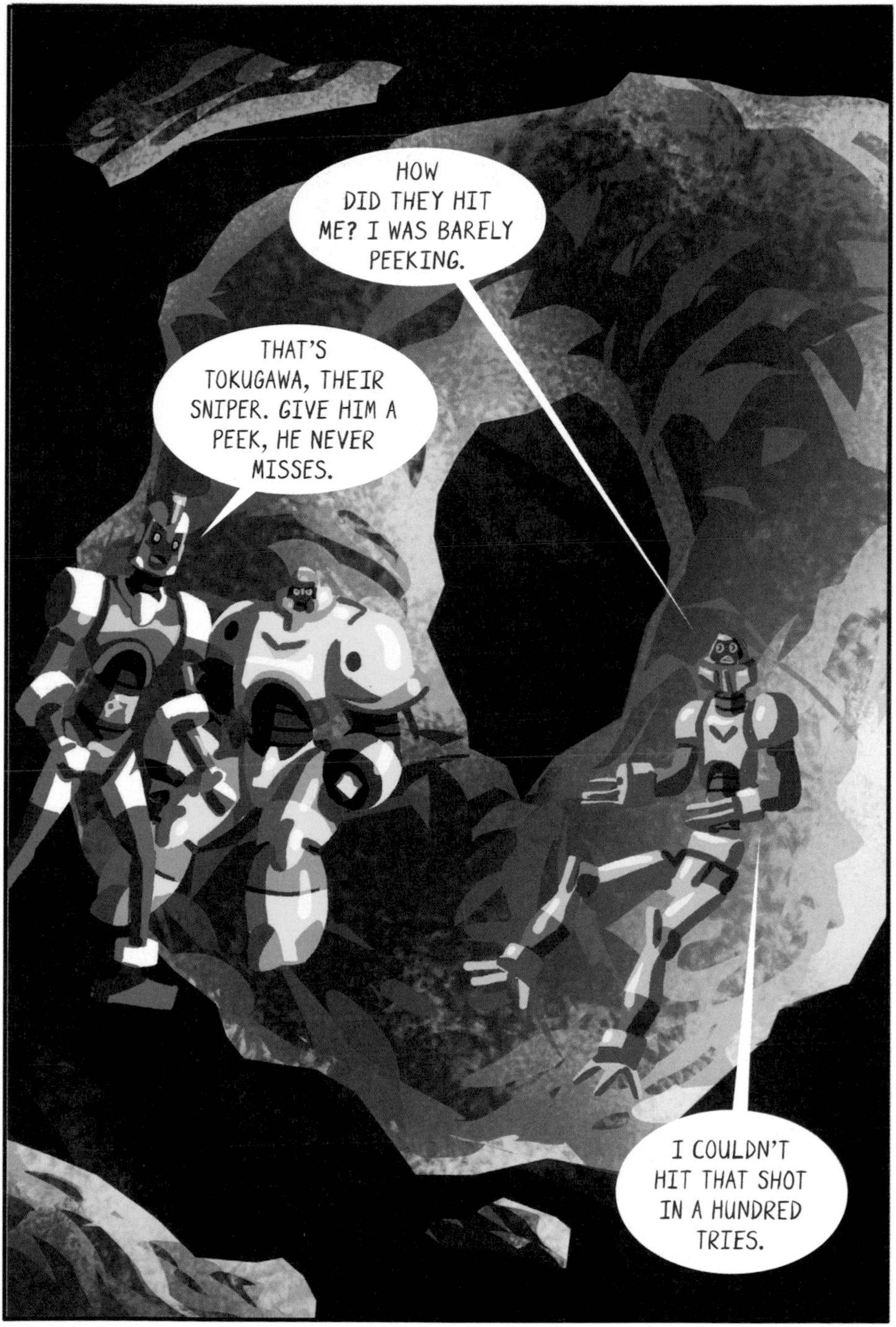
HOW DID THEY HIT ME? I WAS BARELY PEEKING.
THAT'S TOKUGAWA, THEIR SNIPER. GIVE HIM A PEEK, HE NEVER MISSES.
I COULDN'T HIT THAT SHOT IN A HUNDRED TRIES.

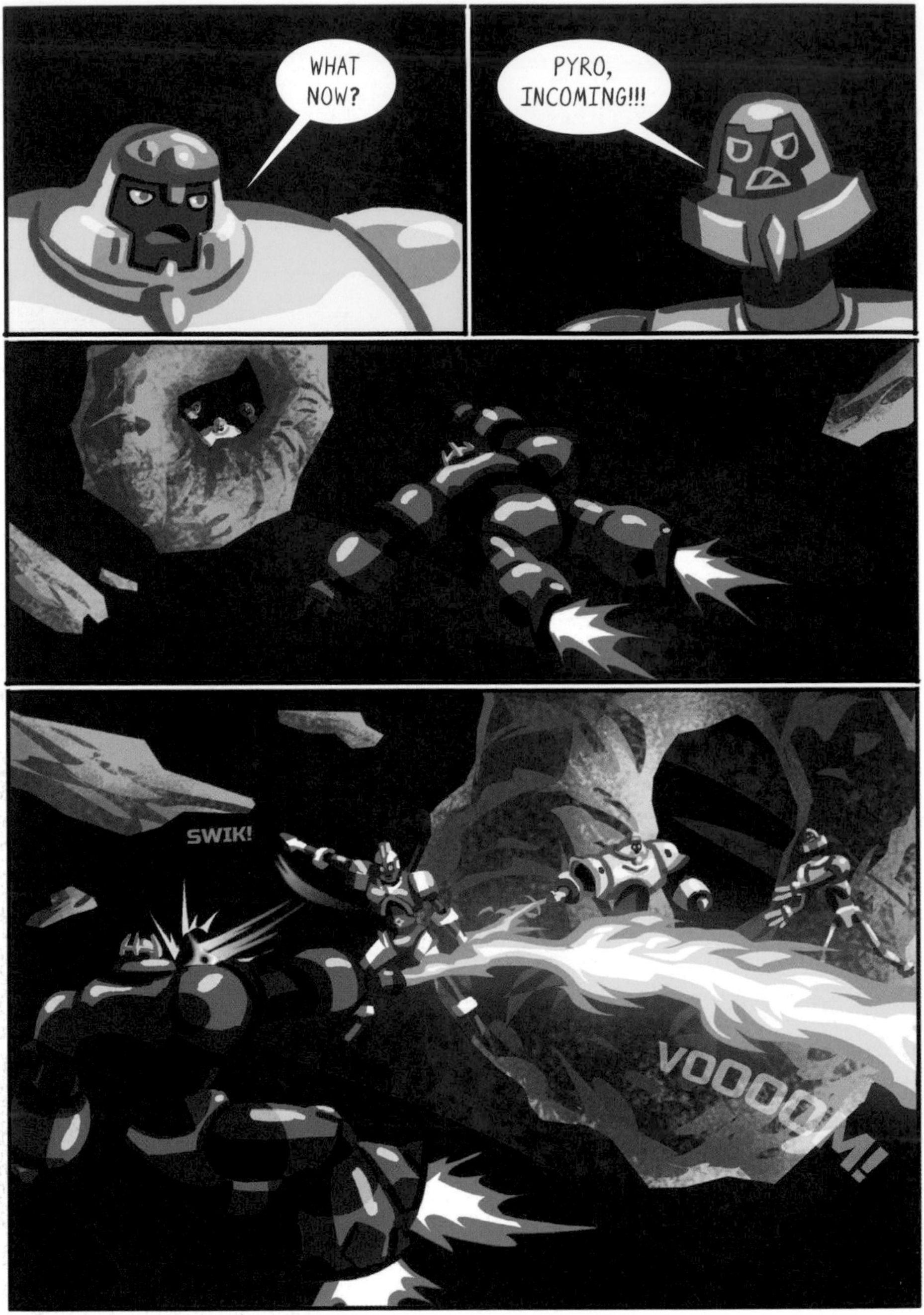
WHAT NOW?
PYRO, INCOMING!!!
SWIK!
VOOOOOM!

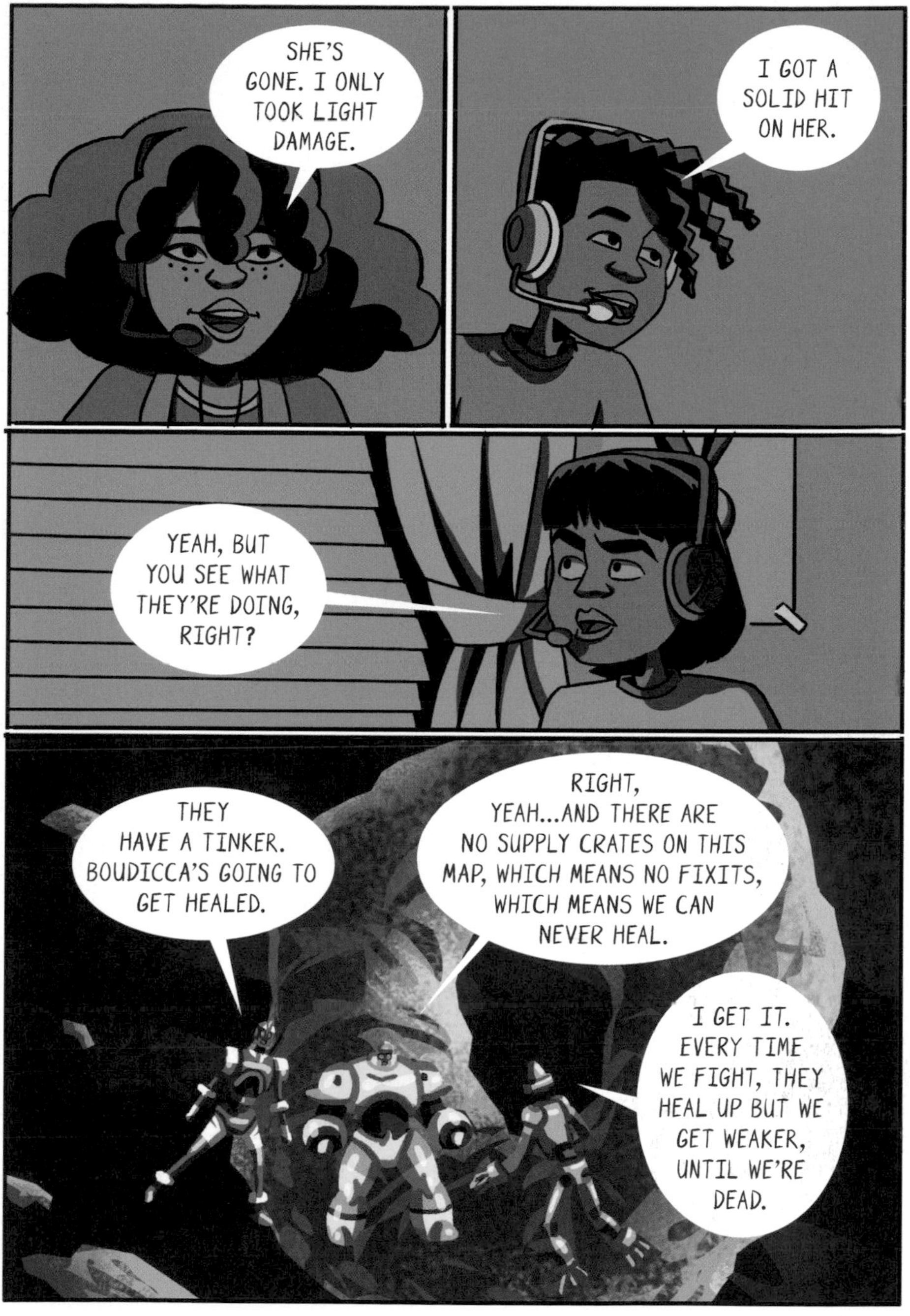
SHE'S GONE. I ONLY TOOK LIGHT DAMAGE.
I GOT A SOLID HIT ON HER.
YEAH, BUT YOU SEE WHAT THEY'RE DOING, RIGHT?
THEY HAVE A TINKER. BOUDICCA'S GOING TO GET HEALED.
RIGHT, YEAH...AND THERE ARE NO SUPPLY CRATES ON THIS MAP, WHICH MEANS NO FIXITS, WHICH MEANS WE CAN NEVER HEAL.
I GET IT. EVERY TIME WE FIGHT, THEY HEAL UP BUT WE GET WEAKER, UNTIL WE'RE DEAD.

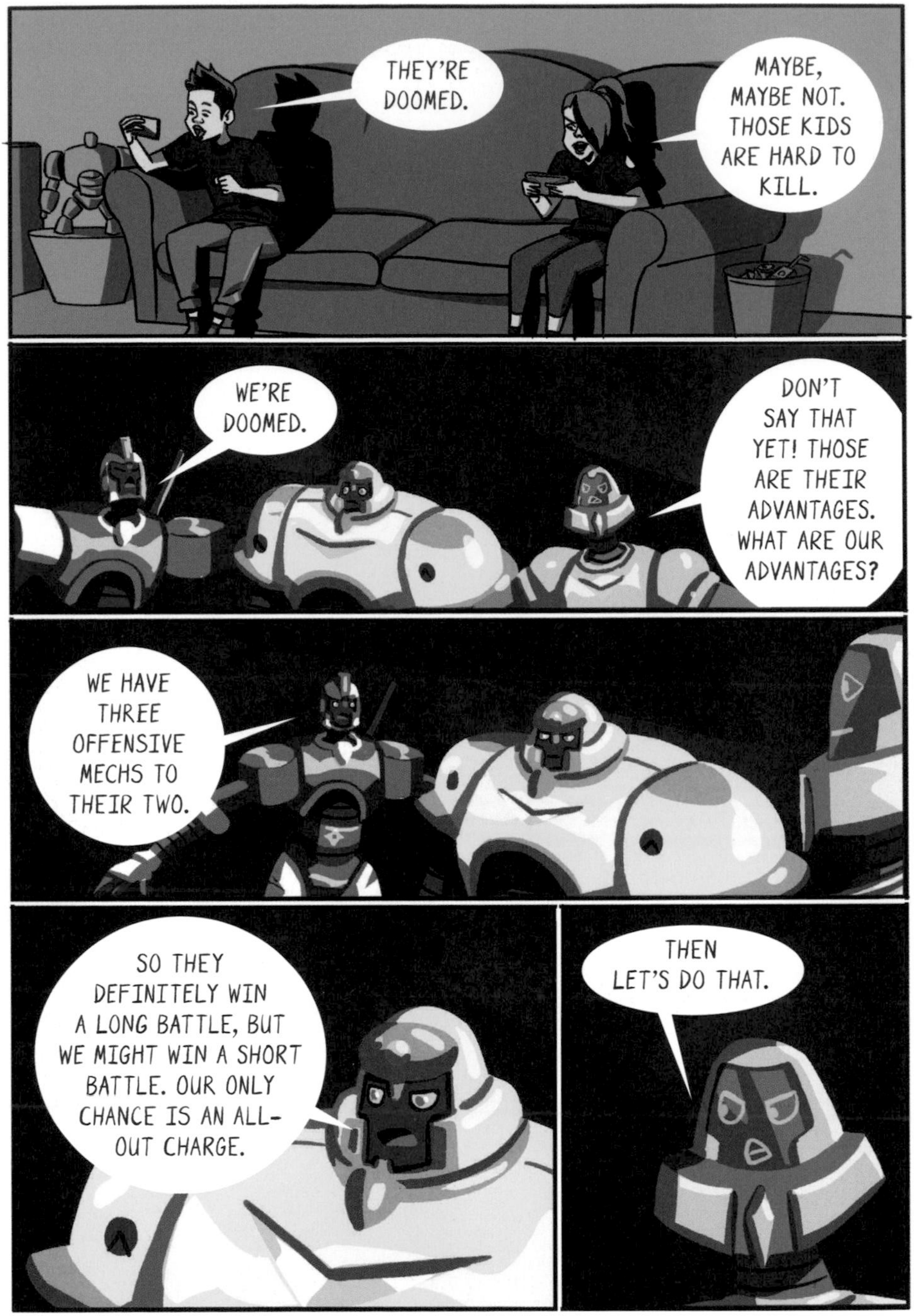
THEY'RE DOOMED.
MAYBE, MAYBE NOT. THOSE KIDS ARE HARD TO KILL.
WE'RE DOOMED.
DON'T SAY THAT YET! THOSE ARE THEIR ADVANTAGES. WHAT ARE OUR ADVANTAGES?
WE HAVE THREE OFFENSIVE MECHS TO THEIR TWO.
SO THEY DEFINITELY WIN A LONG BATTLE, BUT WE MIGHT WIN A SHORT BATTLE. OUR ONLY CHANCE IS AN ALL-OUT CHARGE.
THEN LET'S DO THAT.

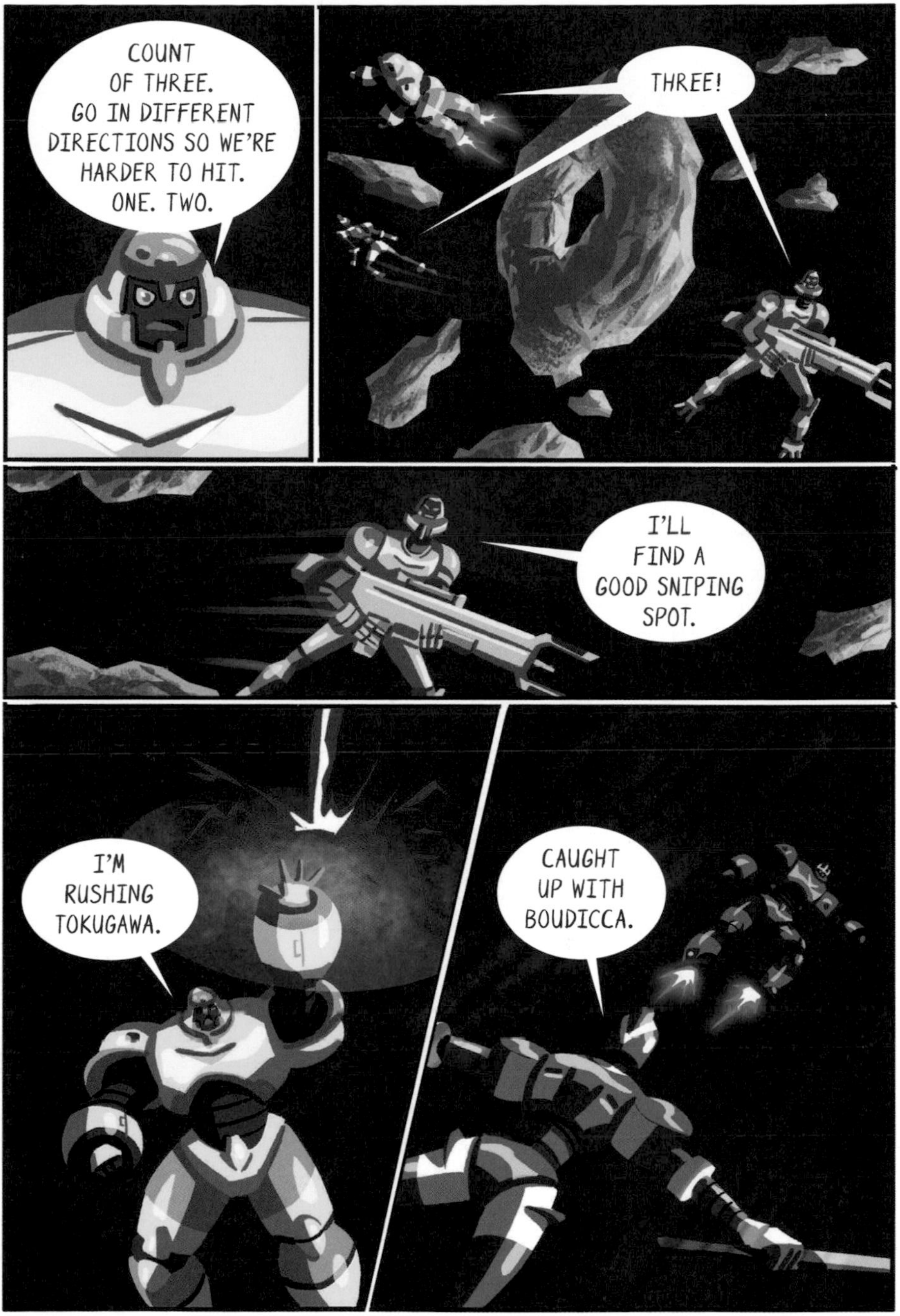
COUNT OF THREE. GO IN DIFFERENT DIRECTIONS SO WE'RE HARDER TO HIT. ONE. TWO.
THREE!
I'LL FIND A GOOD SNIPING SPOT.
I'M RUSHING TOKUGAWA.
CAUGHT UP WITH BOUDICCA.

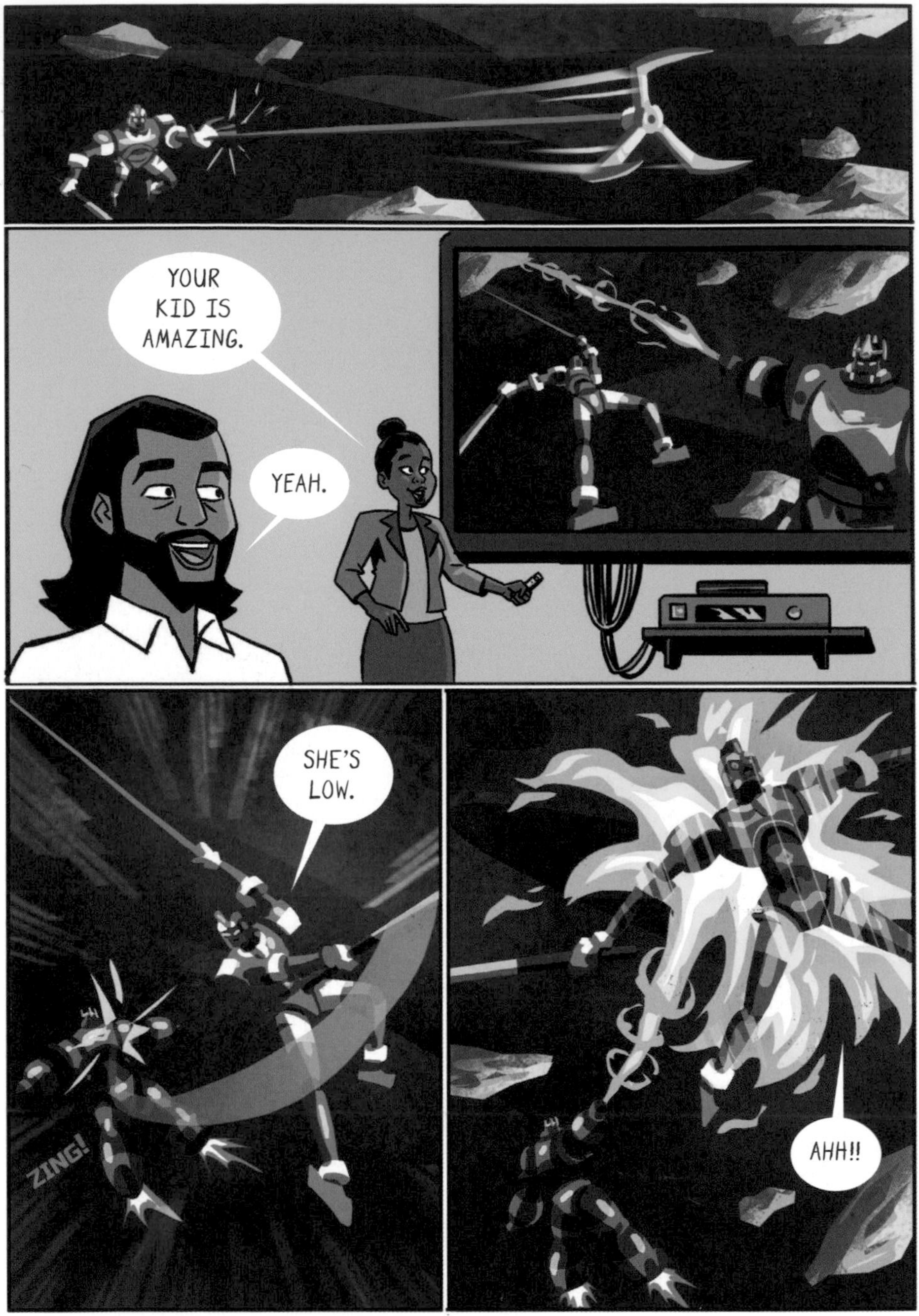
YOUR KID IS AMAZING.
YEAH.
SHE'S LOW.
ZING!
AHH!!

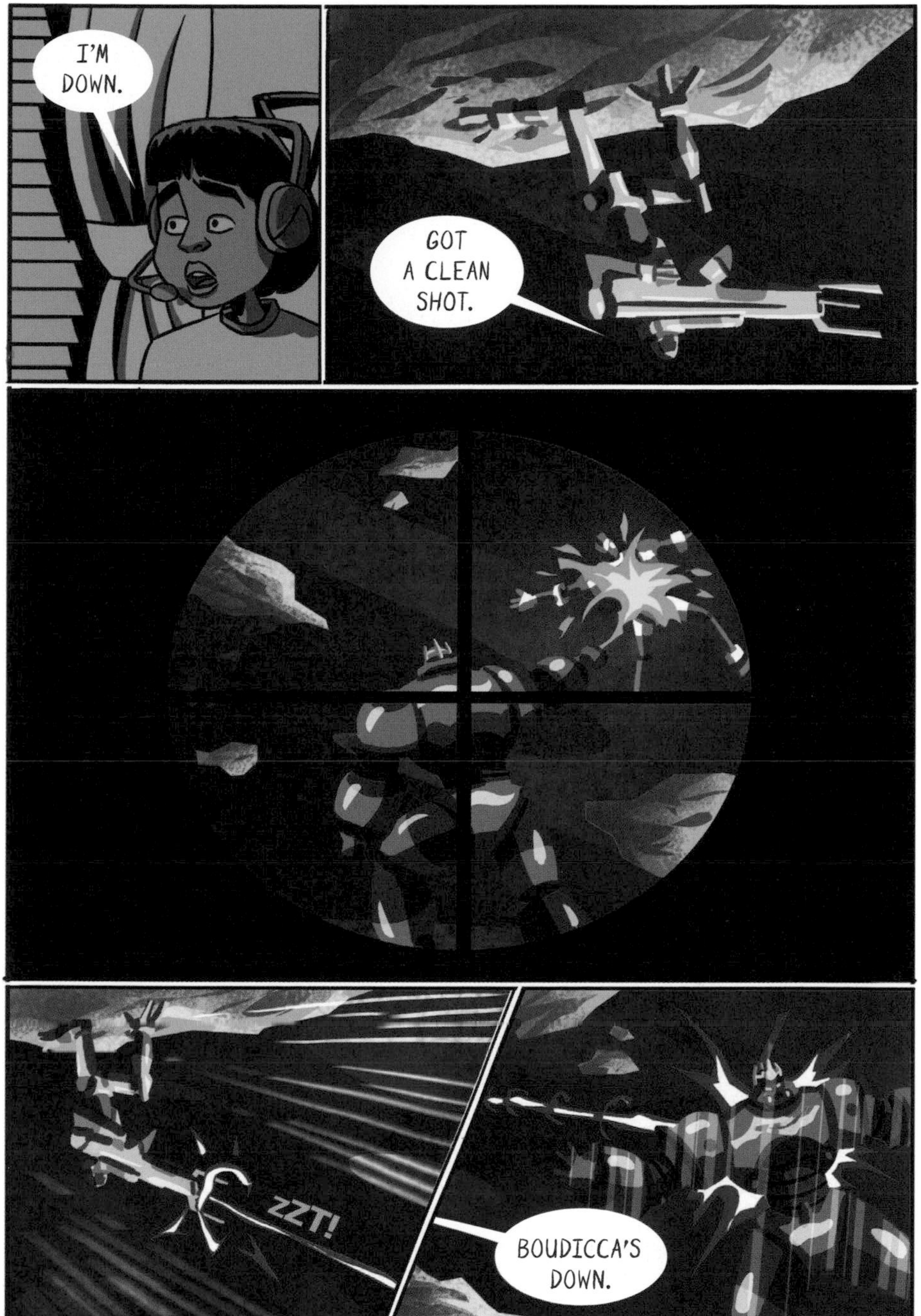
I'M DOWN.
GOT A CLEAN SHOT.
ZZT!
BOUDICCA'S DOWN.

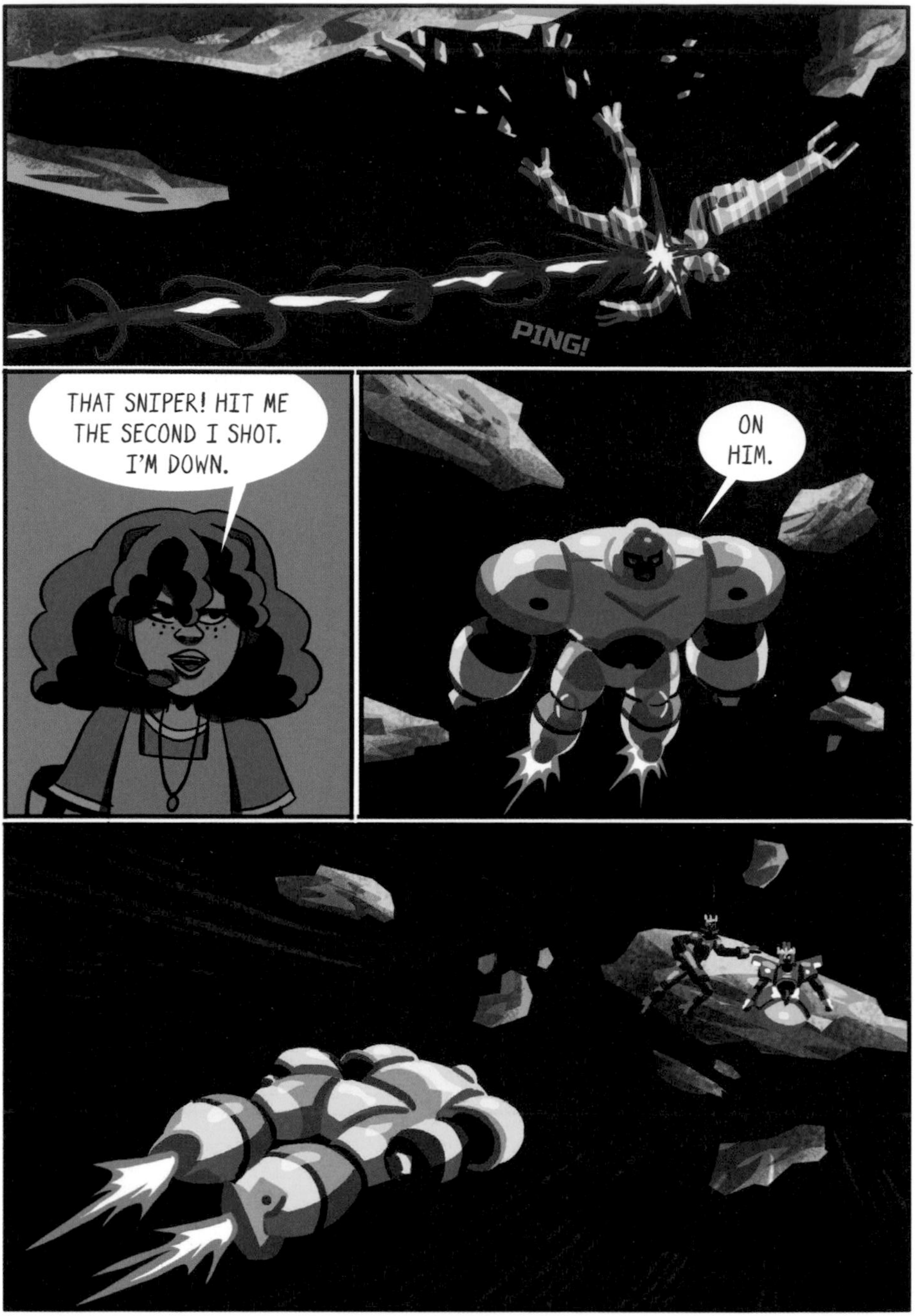
PING!
THAT SNIPER! HIT ME THE SECOND I SHOT. I'M DOWN.
ON HIM.

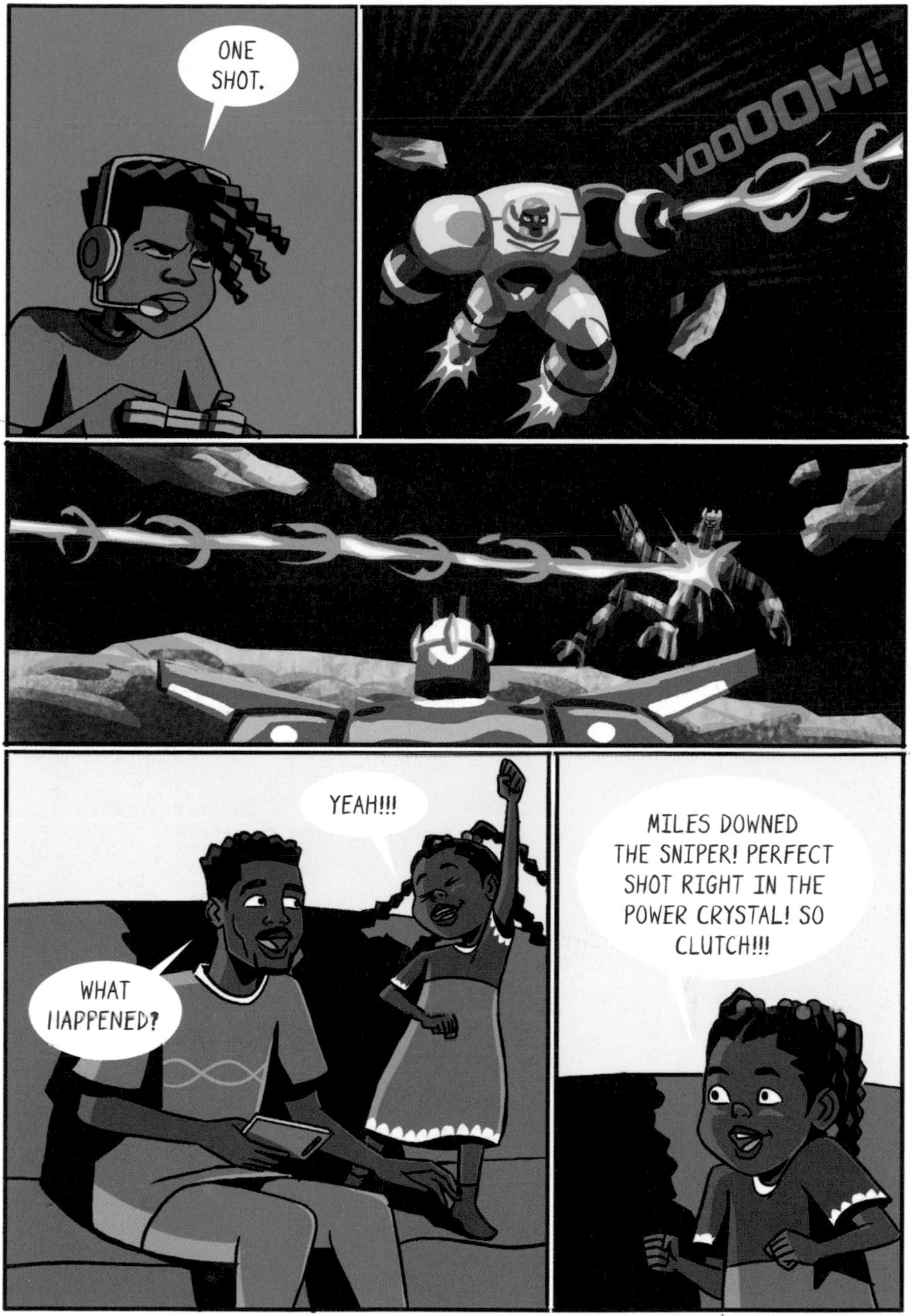
ONE SHOT.
VOOOOM!
YEAH!!!
WHAT HAPPENED?
MILES DOWNED THE SNIPER! PERFECT SHOT RIGHT IN THE POWER CRYSTAL! SO CLUTCH!!!

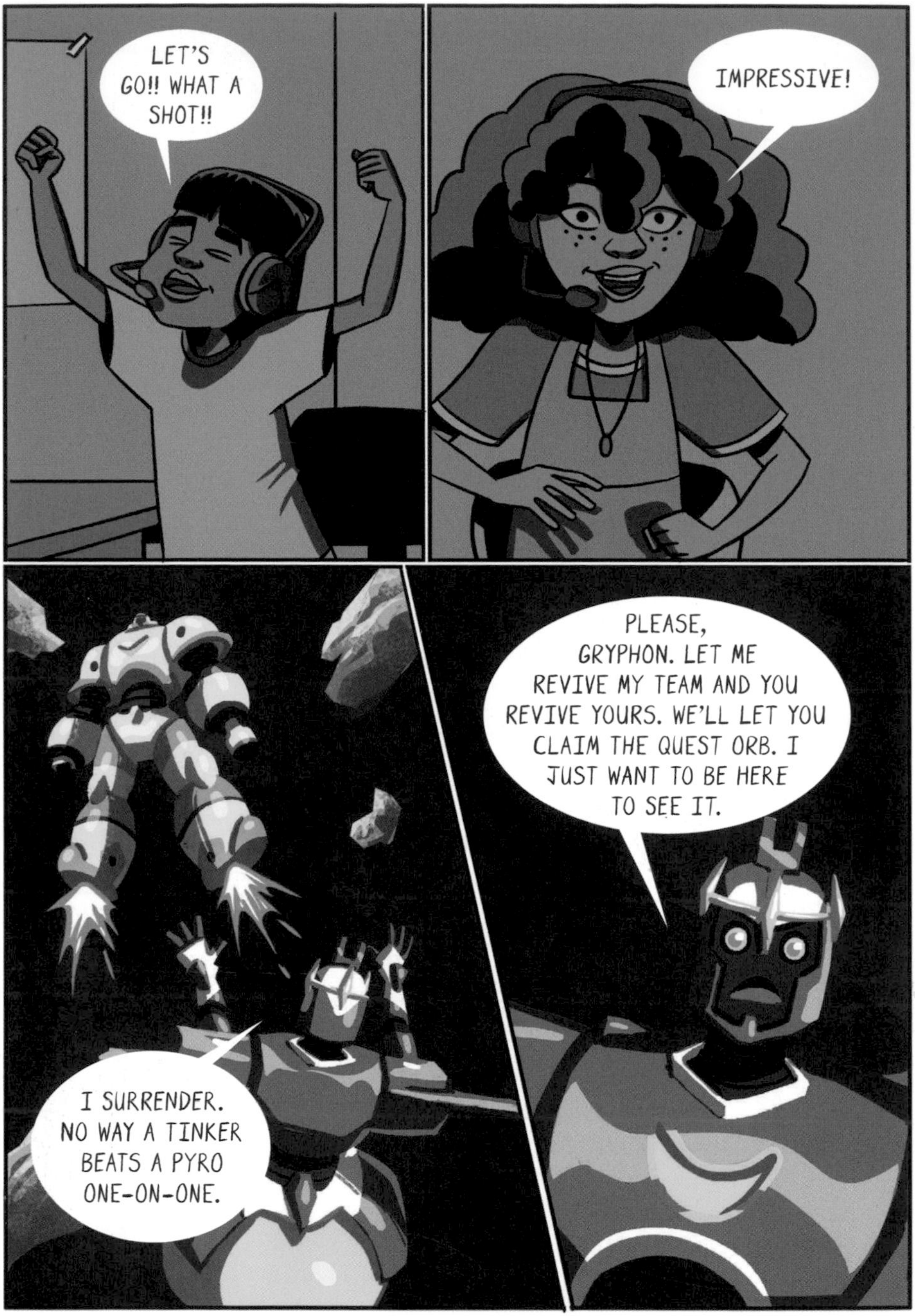
LET'S GO!! WHAT A SHOT!!
IMPRESSIVE!
PLEASE, GRYPHON. LET ME REVIVE MY TEAM AND YOU REVIVE YOURS. WE'LL LET YOU CLAIM THE QUEST ORB. I JUST WANT TO BE HERE TO SEE IT.
I SURRENDER. NO WAY A TINKER BEATS A PYRO ONE-ON-ONE.

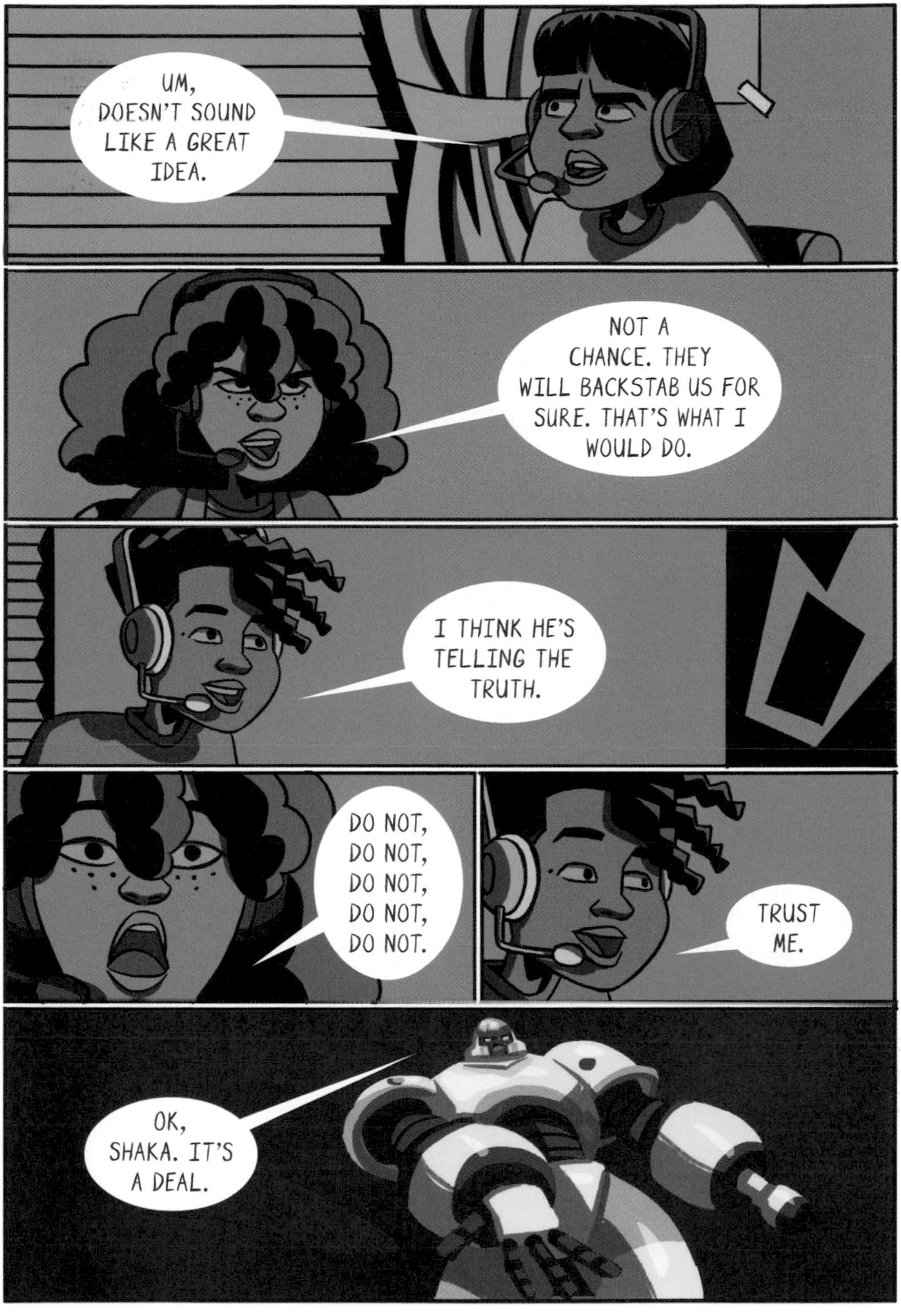
UM, DOESN'T SOUND LIKE A GREAT IDEA.
NOT A CHANCE. THEY WILL BACKSTAB US FOR SURE. THAT'S WHAT I WOULD DO.
I THINK HE'S TELLING THE TRUTH.
DO NOT, DO NOT, DO NOT, DO NOT, DO NOT.
TRUST ME.
OK, SHAKA. IT'S A DEAL.

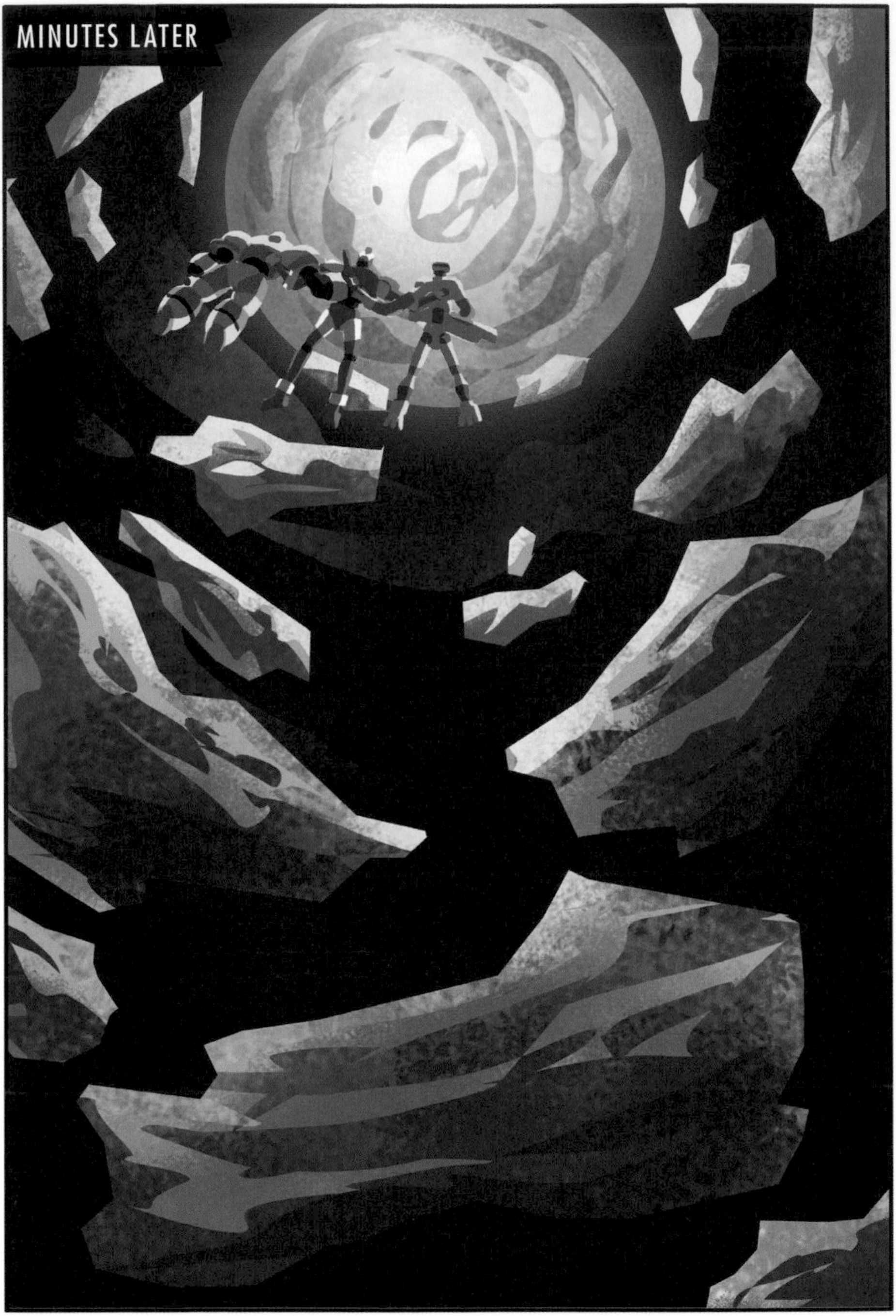
MINUTES LATER

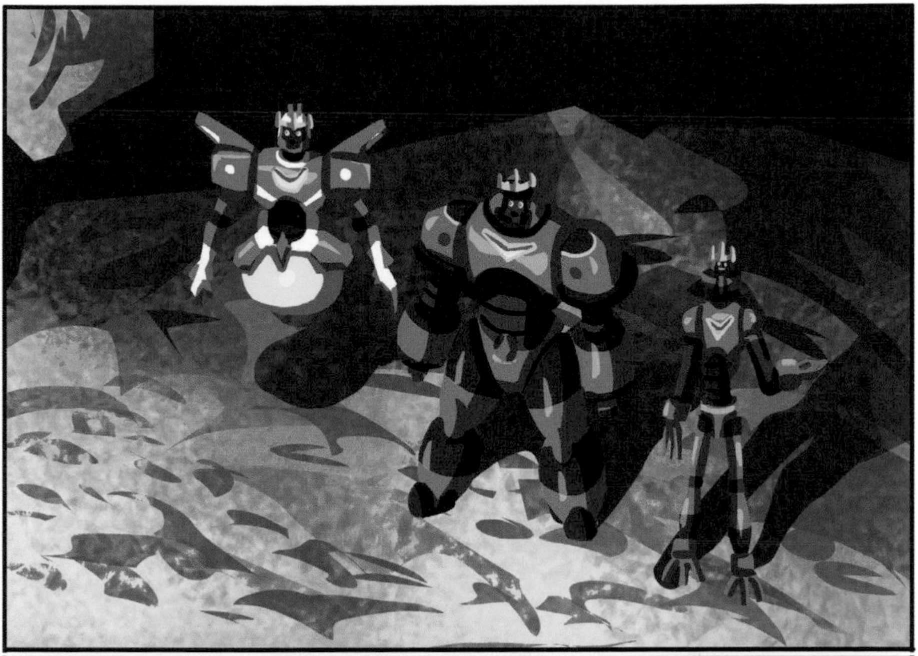

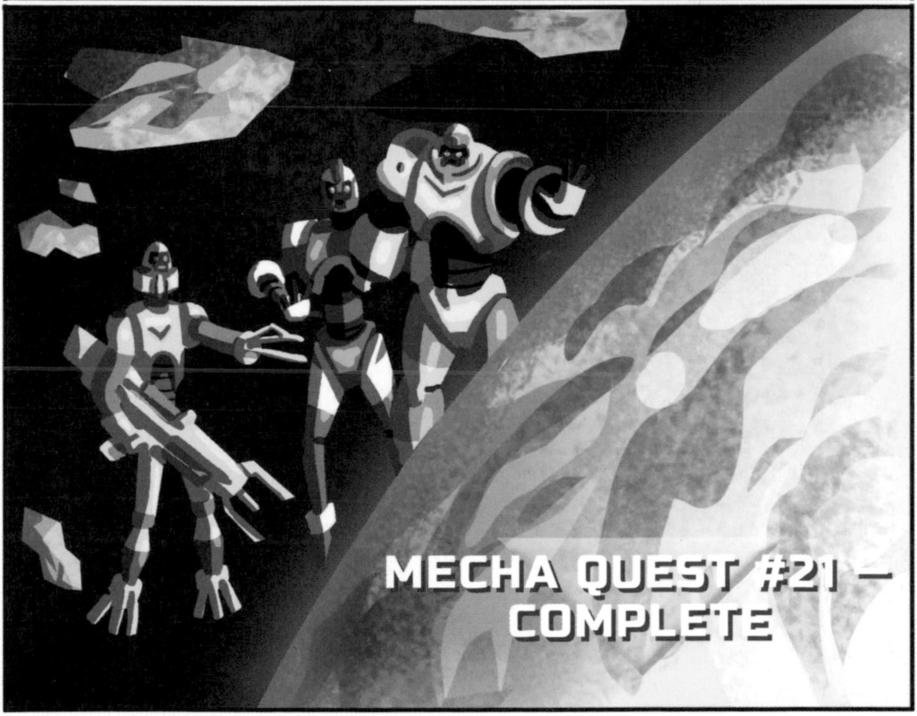
MECHA QUEST #21 —
COMPLETE

CHAPTER 14
LATER

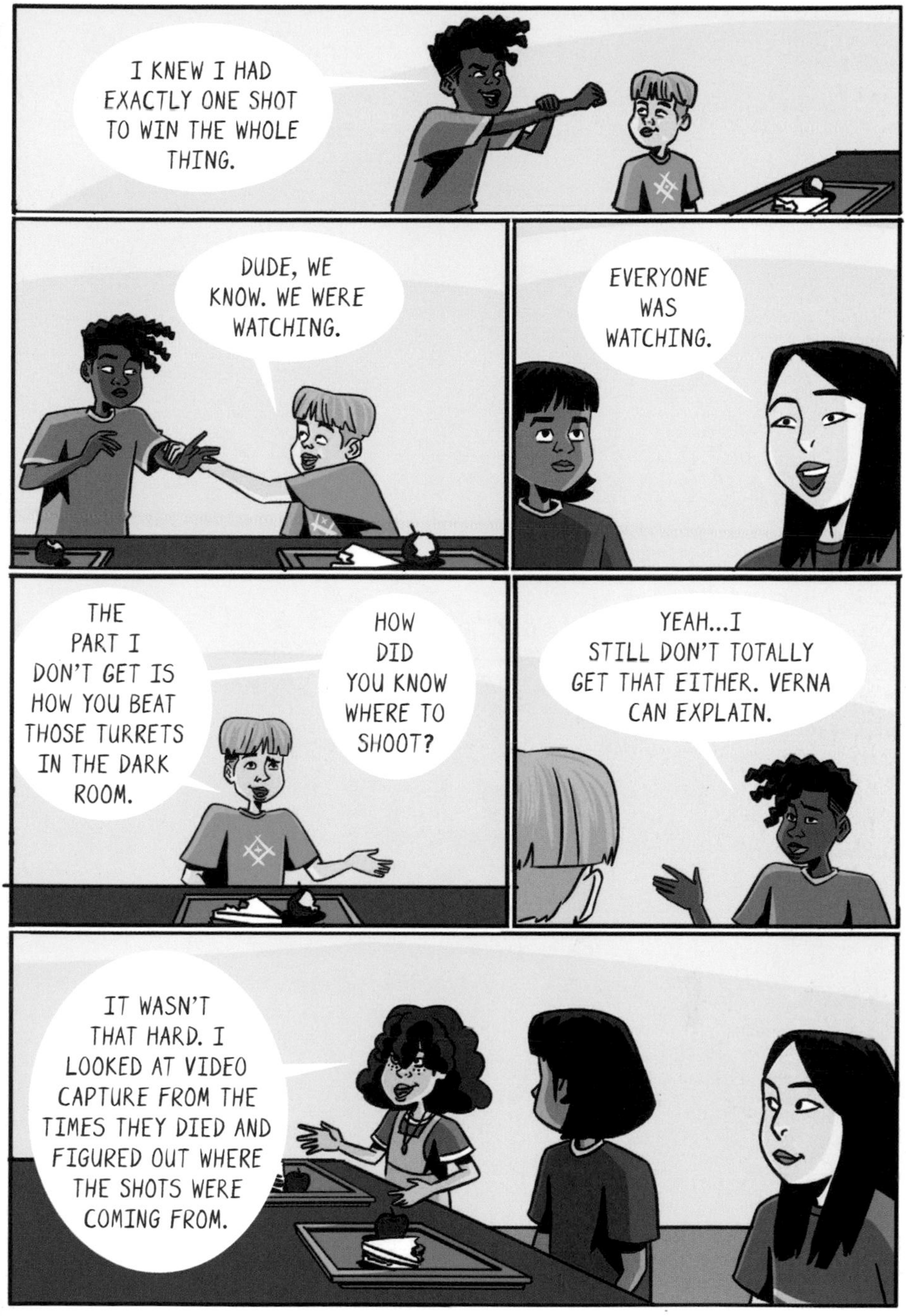
I KNEW I HAD EXACTLY ONE SHOT TO WIN THE WHOLE THING.
DUDE, WE KNOW. WE WERE WATCHING.
EVERYONE WAS WATCHING.
THE PART I DON'T GET IS HOW YOU BEAT THOSE TURRETS IN THE DARK ROOM.
HOW DID YOU KNOW WHERE TO SHOOT?
YEAH...I STILL DON'T TOTALLY GET THAT EITHER. VERNA CAN EXPLAIN.
IT WASN'T THAT HARD. I LOOKED AT VIDEO CAPTURE FROM THE TIMES THEY DIED AND FIGURED OUT WHERE THE SHOTS WERE COMING FROM.

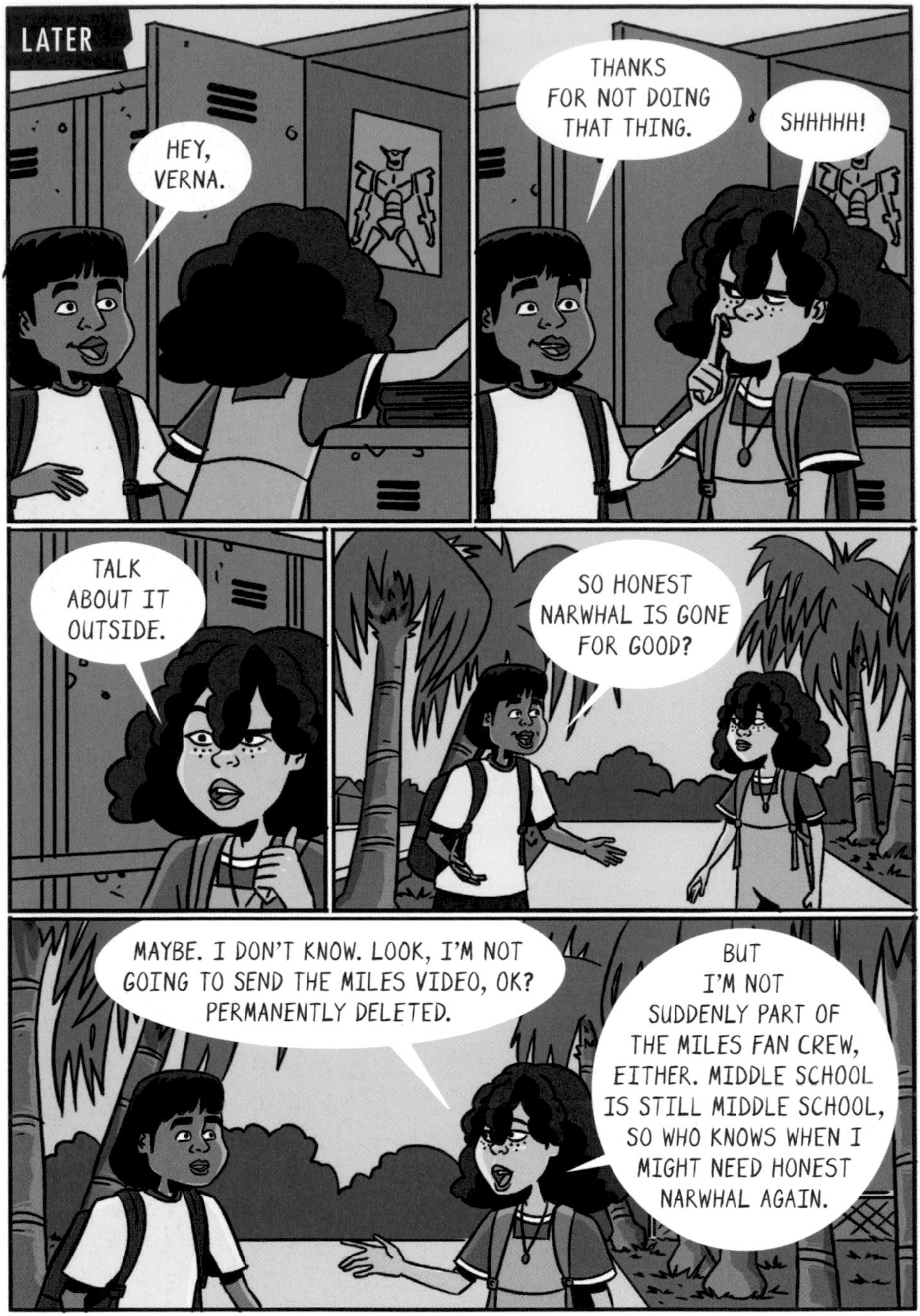
LATER
HEY, VERNA.
THANKS FOR NOT DOING THAT THING.
SHHHHH!
TALK ABOUT IT OUTSIDE.
SO HONEST NARWHAL IS GONE FOR GOOD?
MAYBE. I DON'T KNOW. LOOK, I'M NOT GOING TO SEND THE MILES VIDEO, OK? PERMANENTLY DELETED.
BUT I'M NOT SUDDENLY PART OF THE MILES FAN CREW, EITHER. MIDDLE SCHOOL IS STILL MIDDLE SCHOOL, SO WHO KNOWS WHEN I MIGHT NEED HONEST NARWHAL AGAIN.

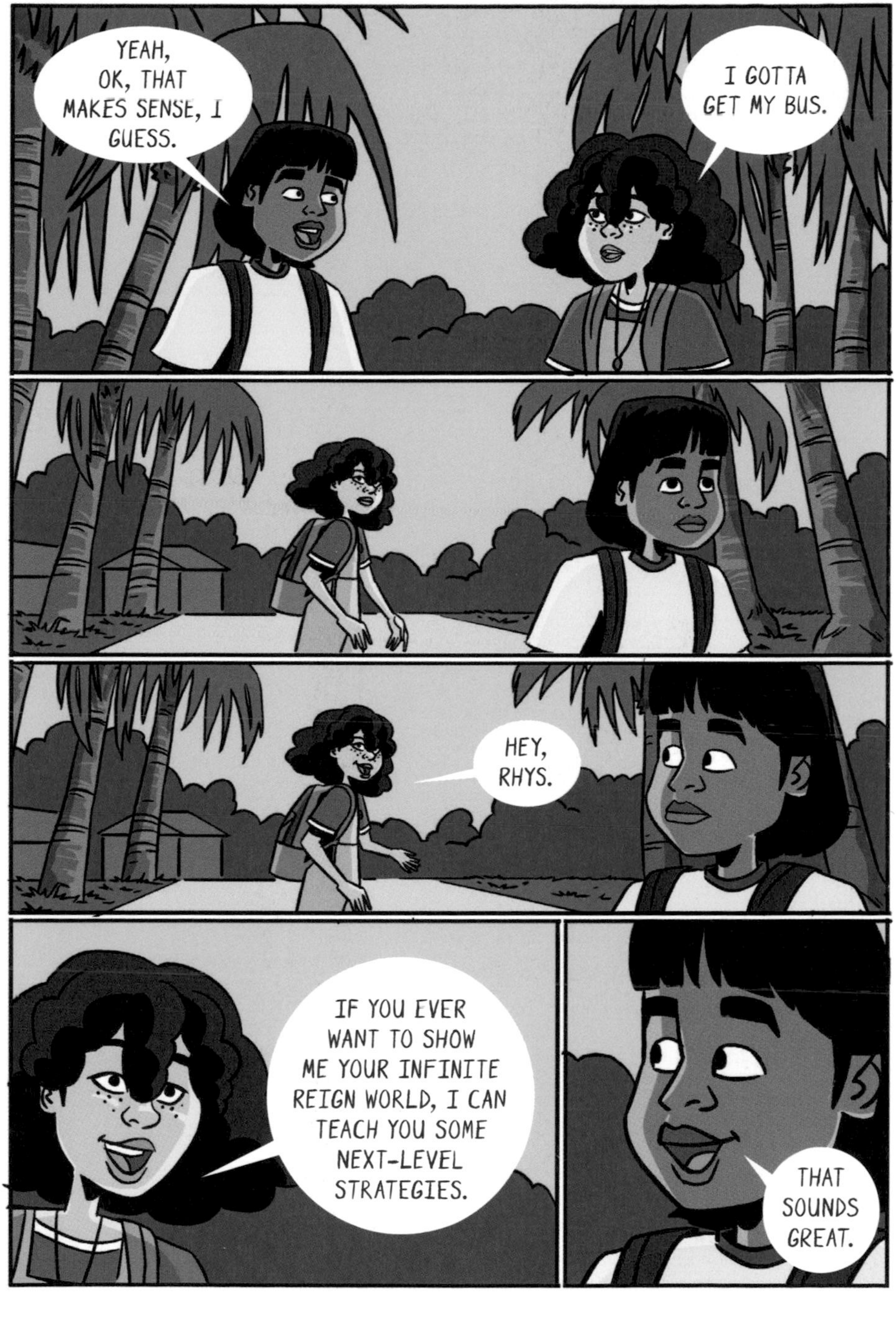
YEAH, OK, THAT MAKES SENSE, I GUESS.
I GOTTA GET MY BUS.
HEY, RHYS.
IF YOU EVER WANT TO SHOW ME YOUR INFINITE REIGN WORLD, I CAN TEACH YOU SOME NEXT-LEVEL STRATEGIES.
THAT SOUNDS GREAT.

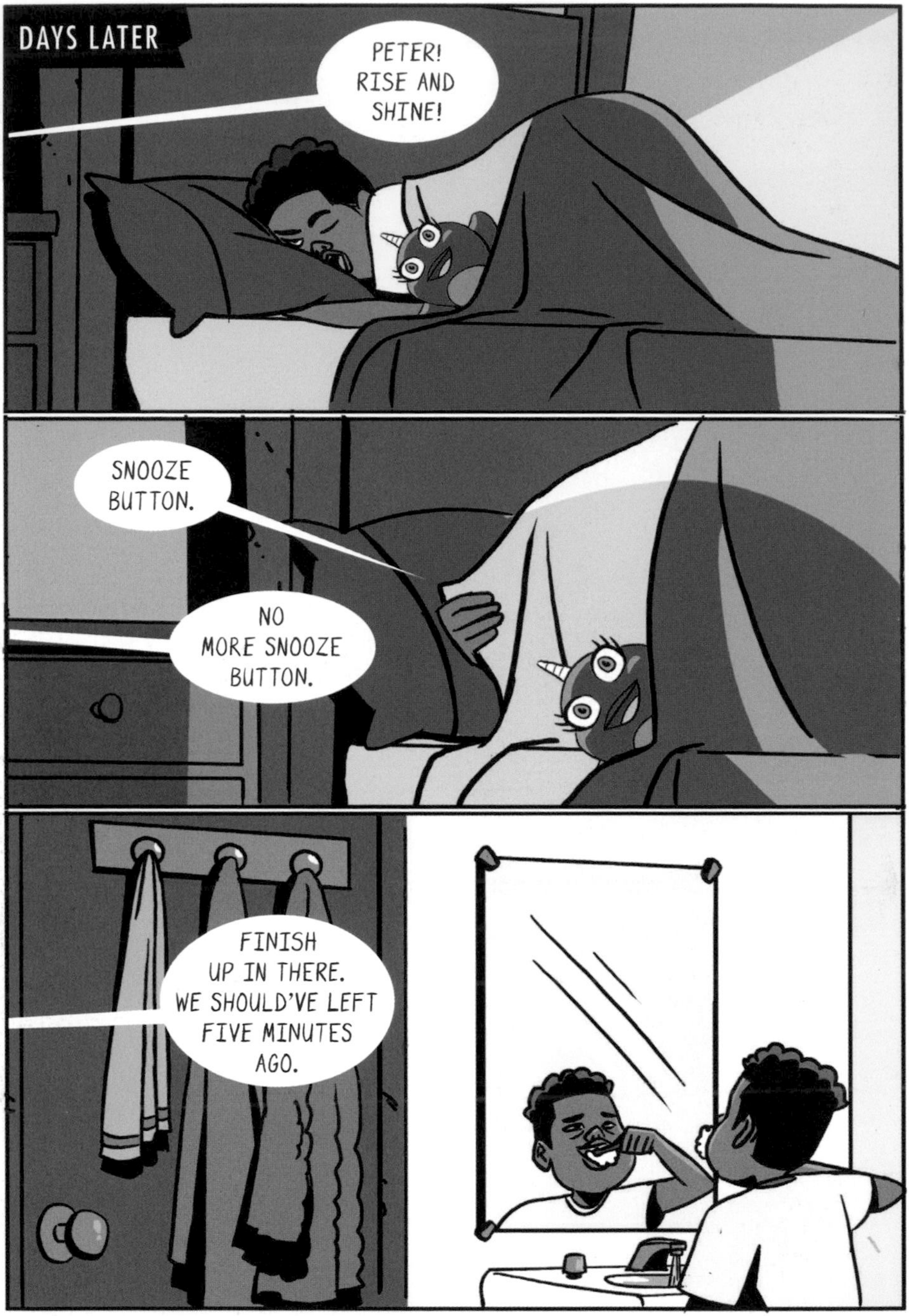
DAYS LATER
PETER! RISE AND SHINE!
SNOOZE BUTTON.
NO MORE SNOOZE BUTTON.
FINISH UP IN THERE. WE SHOULD'VE LEFT FIVE MINUTES AGO.

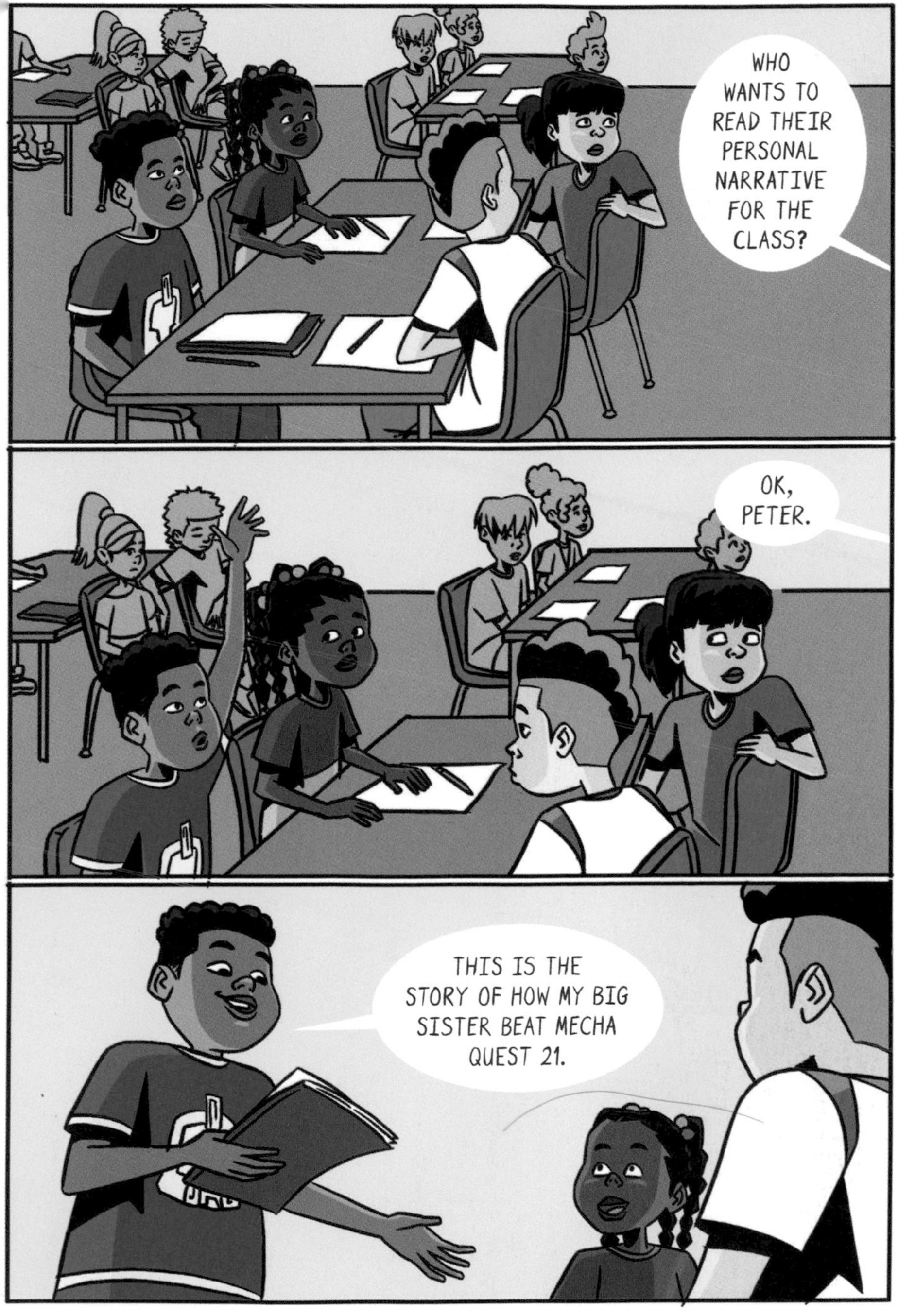
WHO WANTS TO READ THEIR PERSONAL NARRATIVE FOR THE CLASS?
OK, PETER.
THIS IS THE STORY OF HOW MY BIG SISTER BEAT MECHA QUEST 21.

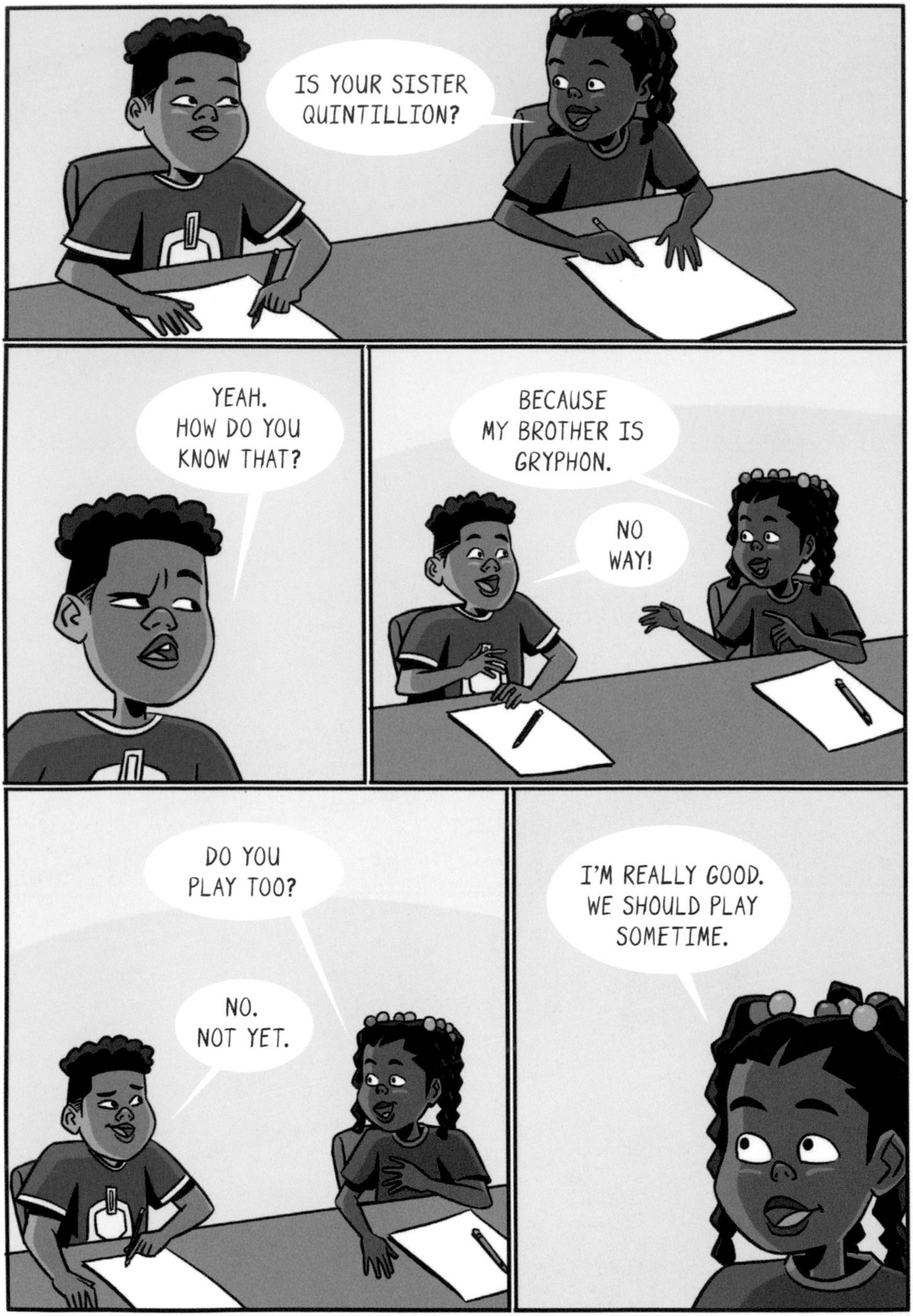
IS YOUR SISTER QUINTILLION?
YEAH. HOW DO YOU KNOW THAT?
BECAUSE MY BROTHER IS GRYPHON.
NO WAY!
DO YOU PLAY TOO?
NO. NOT YET.
I'M REALLY GOOD. WE SHOULD PLAY SOMETIME.

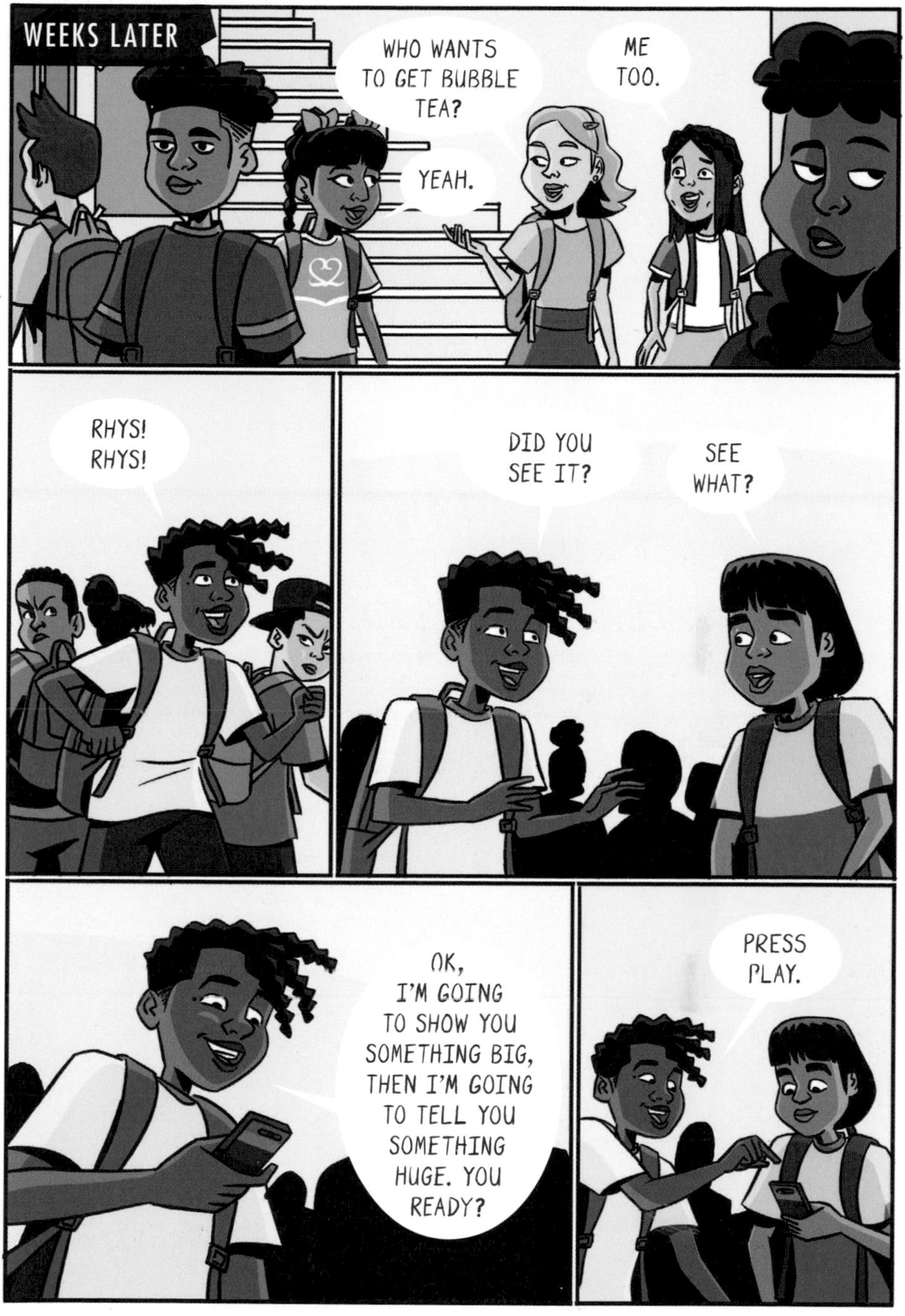
WEEKS LATER
WHO WANTS TO GET BUBBLE TEA?
YEAH.
ME TOO.
RHYS! RHYS!
DID YOU SEE IT?
SEE WHAT?
OK, I'M GOING TO SHOW YOU SOMETHING BIG, THEN I'M GOING TO TELL YOU SOMETHING HUGE. YOU READY?
PRESS PLAY.

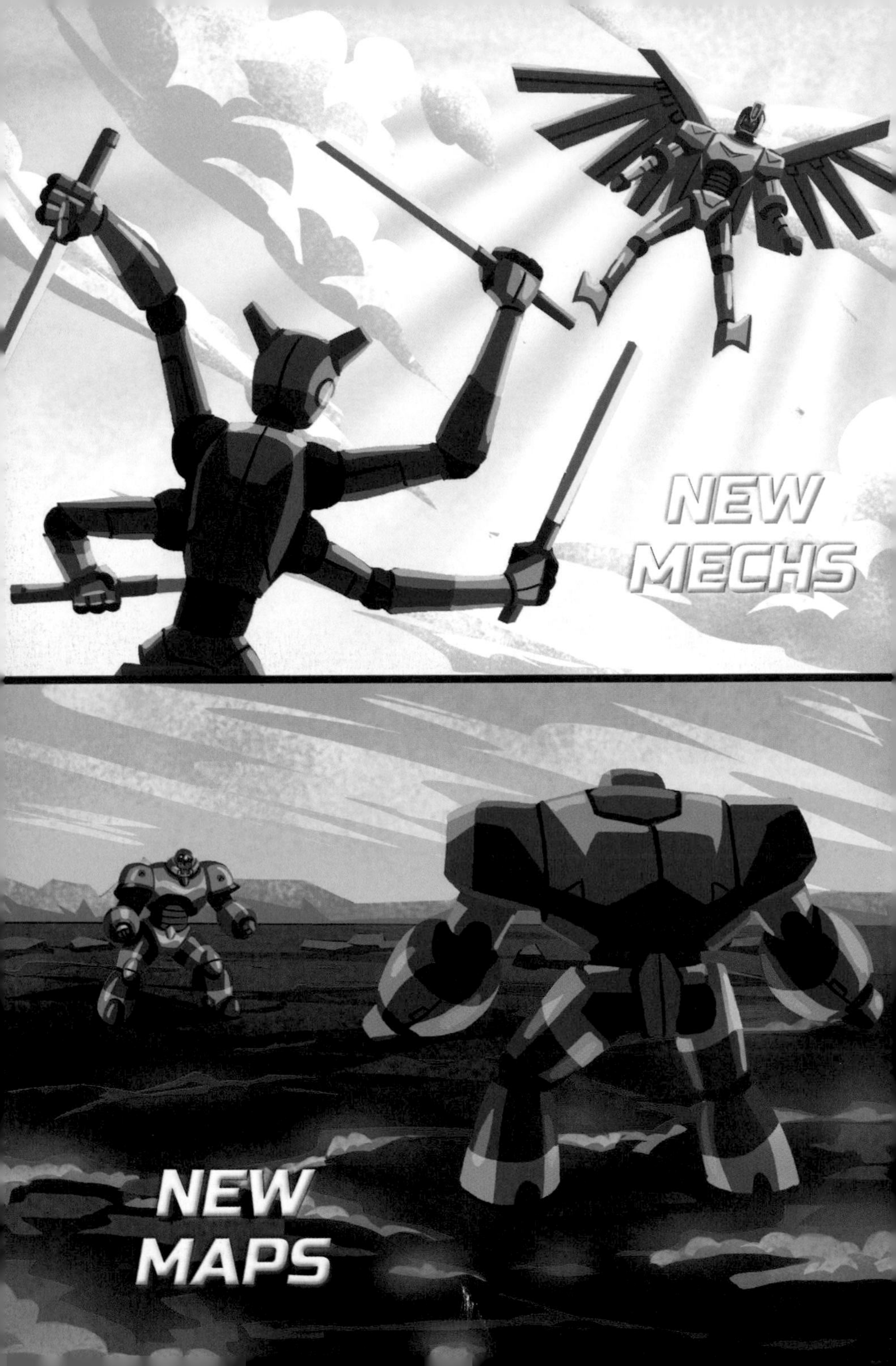
NEW
MECHS
NEW
MAPS

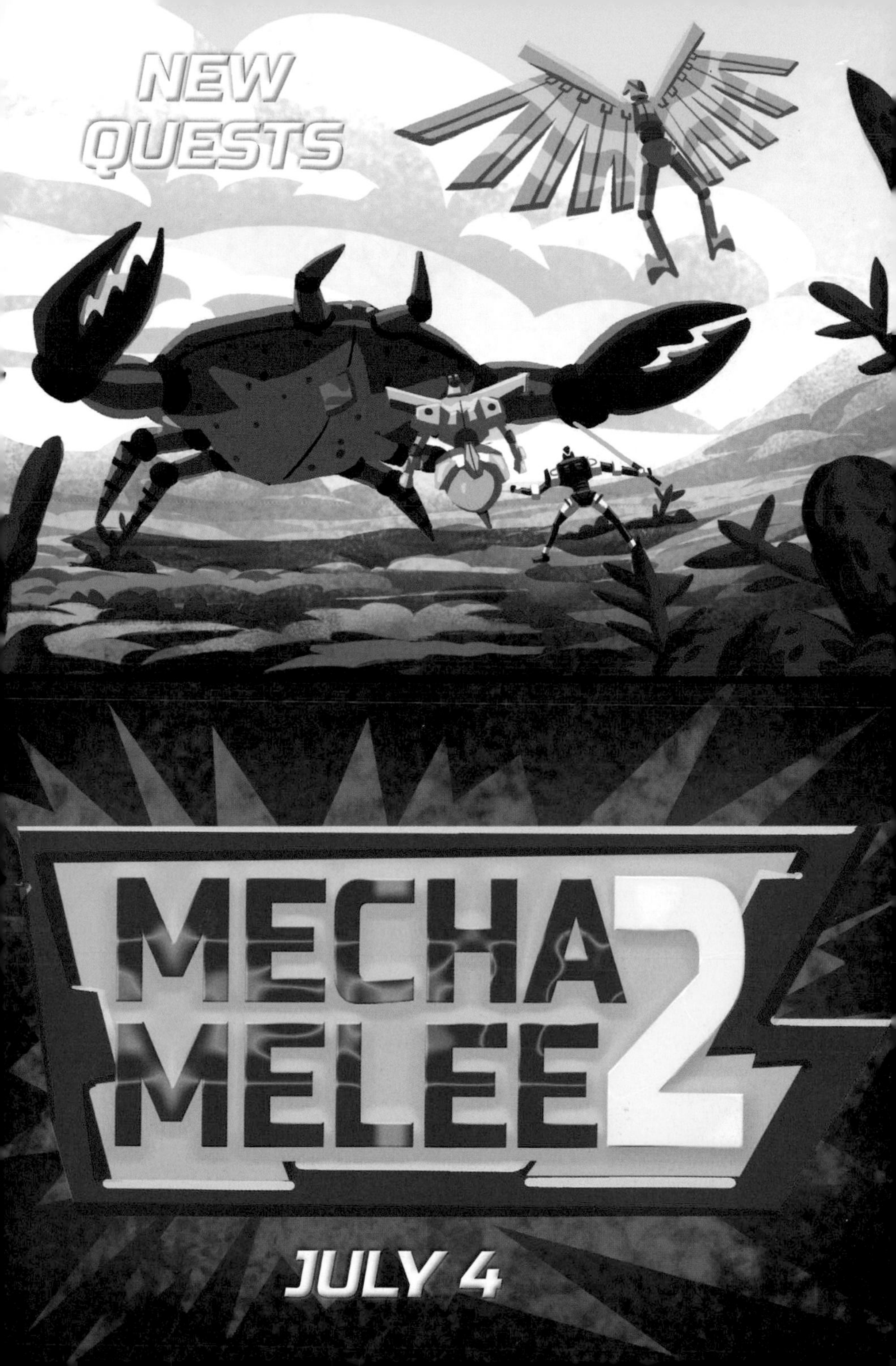
NEW
QUESTS
MECHA
MELEE 2
JULY 4

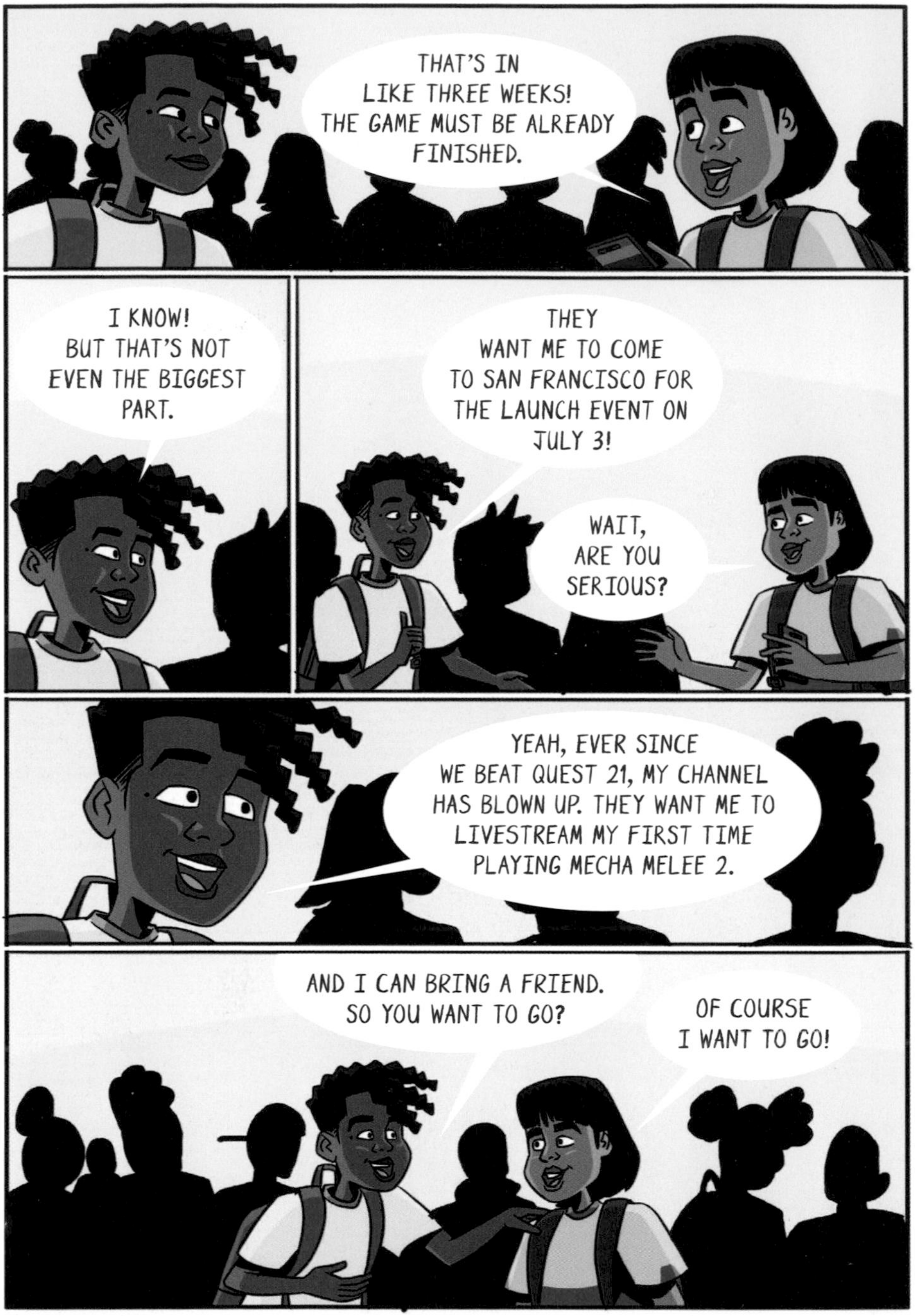
THAT'S IN LIKE THREE WEEKS! THE GAME MUST BE ALREADY FINISHED.
I KNOW! BUT THAT'S NOT EVEN THE BIGGEST PART.
THEY WANT ME TO COME TO SAN FRANCISCO FOR THE LAUNCH EVENT ON JULY 3!
WAIT, ARE YOU SERIOUS?
YEAH, EVER SINCE WE BEAT QUEST 21, MY CHANNEL HAS BLOWN UP. THEY WANT ME TO LIVESTREAM MY FIRST TIME PLAYING MECHA MELEE 2.
AND I CAN BRING A FRIEND. SO YOU WANT TO GO?
OF COURSE I WANT TO GO!

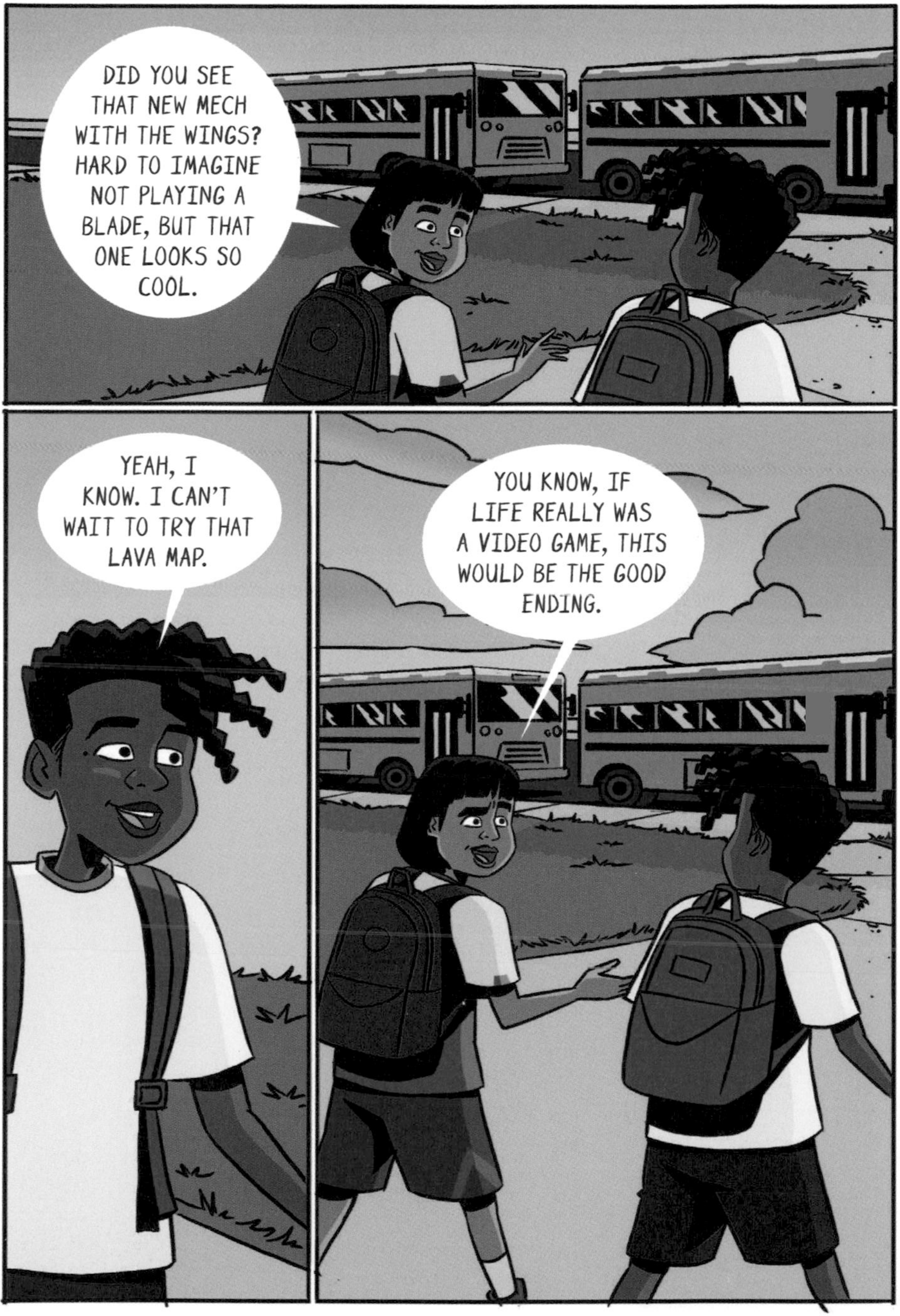
DID YOU SEE THAT NEW MECH WITH THE WINGS? HARD TO IMAGINE NOT PLAYING A BLADE, BUT THAT ONE LOOKS SO COOL.
YEAH, I KNOW. I CAN'T WAIT TO TRY THAT LAVA MAP.
YOU KNOW, IF LIFE REALLY WAS A VIDEO GAME, THIS WOULD BE THE GOOD ENDING.

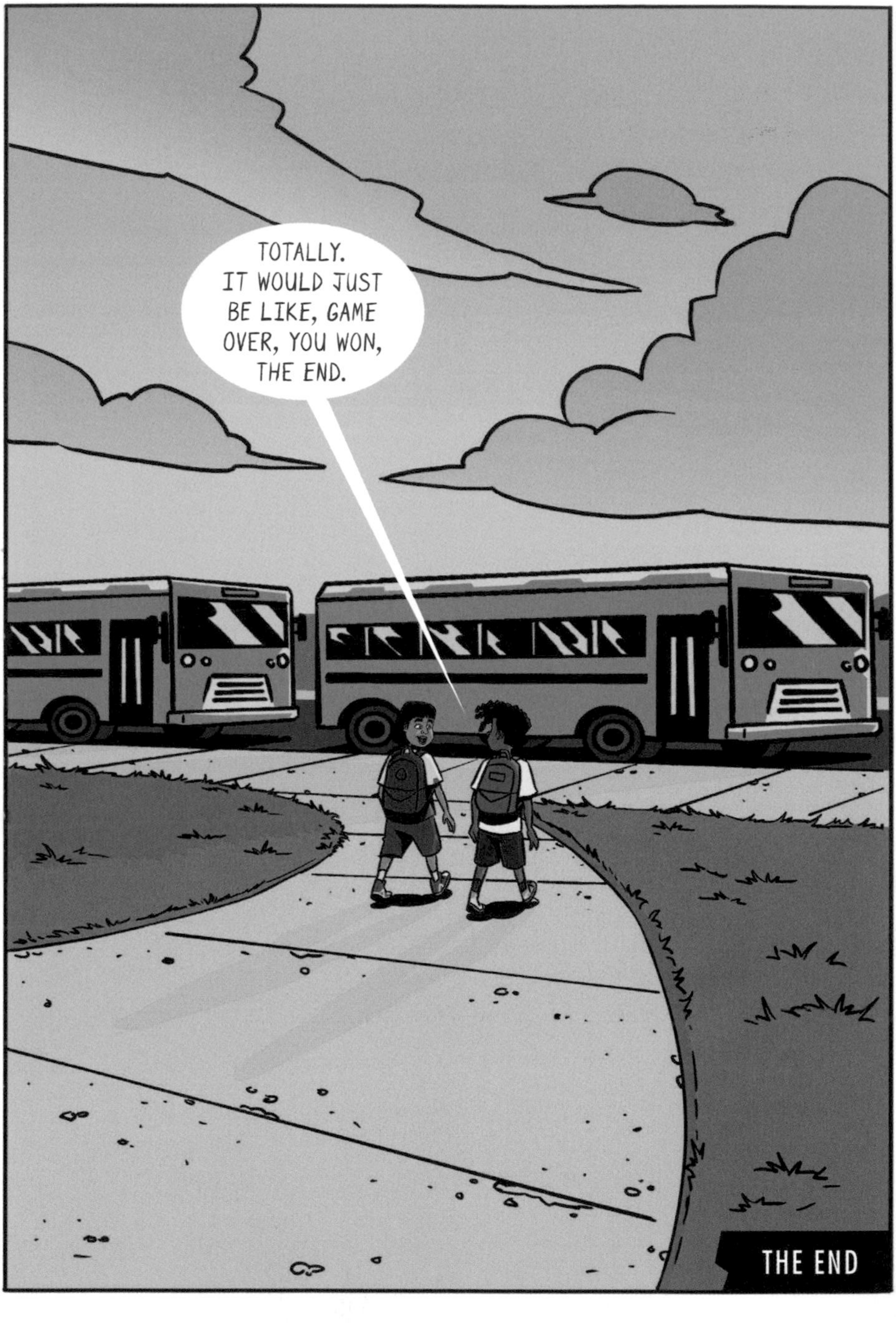
TOTALLY.
IT WOULD JUST
BE LIKE, GAME
OVER, YOU WON,
THE END.
THE END

A BEHIND-THE-SCENES LOOK AT THE MAKING OF *POWER UP* AND *SQUAD UP* WITH AUTHOR AND ILLUSTRATOR SAM NISSON AND DARNELL JOHNSON

HOW DID YOUR LOVE OF GAMES AND COMICS INSPIRE YOUR WORK?

SAM: I've been a total video-game guy since I was five years old, starting with Atari 2600, playing just "one more turn" of Civilization in my twenties, and now watching my kids play. They play almost all the time, online with their friends. For me, gaming was a solitary refuge. Now it's a whole social sphere—like a town square—and it's so interesting to watch them interact there. Sometimes you're a better version of yourself where you're bolder or more confident. And sometimes you're a worse version, and you're meaner because it's so abstract. I wanted the stories to probe that dynamic, which is such a big part of growing up right now. These books show both the good and the bad of video games.

DARNELL: My childhood experience of video games was right before the whole online console video-game systems. But I did play a lot of video games and looked at a lot of comics. I didn't get comics to read them. I got them to look at the art. A lot of what I saw in comics and the video games I played definitely influenced the designs of the characters and the worlds that [Miles and Rhys] enter, and impacted my way of creating art for *Power Up* and *Squad Up*.

SAM, WHAT INSPIRED YOU WHEN YOU WERE CREATING THE VIDEO GAMES IN THIS BOOK, AND WHICH DO YOU WISH WERE REAL SO YOU COULD PLAY THEM?

My mental exercise was to imagine a preview or "coming soon" feature for a game that I would be so excited to play and that my kids would be

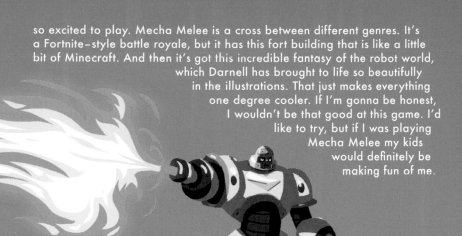

so excited to play. Mecha Melee is a cross between different genres. It's a Fortnite-style battle royale, but it has this fort building that is like a little bit of Minecraft. And then it's got this incredible fantasy of the robot world, which Darnell has brought to life so beautifully in the illustrations. That just makes everything one degree cooler. If I'm gonna be honest, I wouldn't be that good at this game. I'd like to try, but if I was playing Mecha Melee my kids would definitely be making fun of me.

DARNELL, CAN YOU SHARE A LITTLE BIT ABOUT YOUR PROCESS FOR DESIGNING THE CHARACTERS AND GAMES?

Some of them, I already had an idea just by reading the description and I said "Yeah, okay, I know how this character's going to look." But then there were other characters where I had to go through probably three or four iterations. A lot of times, when I nail down the face, which is the first thing that we all look at when we meet somebody, everything else just falls into place. I looked back at my childhood friends and acquaintances and tried to pull from their personalities for the characters in the story. It was fun! I would say I enjoy characters emoting and having them have these wild, crazy, silly expressions. And for the robots that was a challenge. Just trying to figure out how to make them more humanlike, to do a lot of the human movements and still look believable as robots.

WHAT'S YOUR FAVORITE MOMENT OR SCENE IN THE BOOKS AND WHY?

SAM: There's a point where Miles gets to step up in the game in *Power Up*, and he has this selfless, really heroic moment that's super dramatic in the illustrations. And, I won't give anything away, but one of the things I really like about it is that he gets to be a hero in the game, and it's how he wants to be in his life but he's not quite there yet. So it's this really good, joyous moment that resonates in his journey through the book.

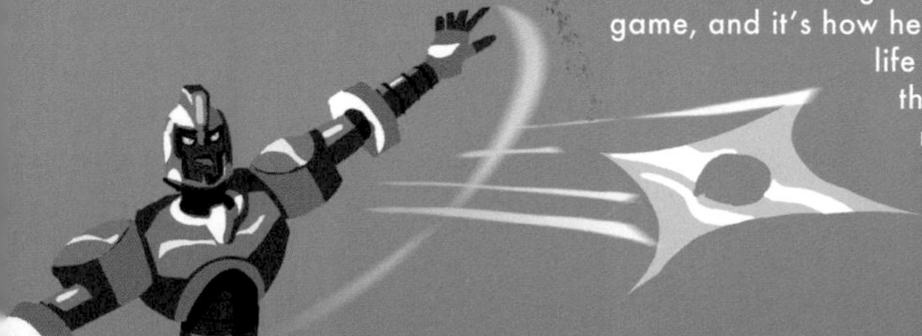

DARNELL: For me, I really enjoy the in-game scenes, for some of the points that Sam brought up. The fact that Miles and Rhys are able to be different people within the game, but they aspire to be those same characters outside in the real world. The action scenes were my favorite because, well, who doesn't like action scenes and action movies? I just enjoyed illustrating those and, as I was illustrating, wondering how the kids who are reading will be drawn into it and, hopefully, how I can inspire some of the next generation of artists.

WHAT DO YOU HOPE READERS WILL TAKE FROM THESE BOOKS?

SAM: First and foremost, I hope they close the book and just say, "Oh, that was a great story." But I also hope that they read it and they feel like it's a representation of an aspect of their life that's very true and that maybe they haven't seen much in books before. I hope they feel like the book gets how video games are in their lives.

DARNELL: I would like the young readers to take some of the life lessons that are being expressed in the book and apply them to their lives, and just love on people more and appreciate people and celebrate what makes them different. Be a kind person, a loving person, and just stop all the hate. I think the book does a great job expressing that you have to have love for others, and appreciate and value them.

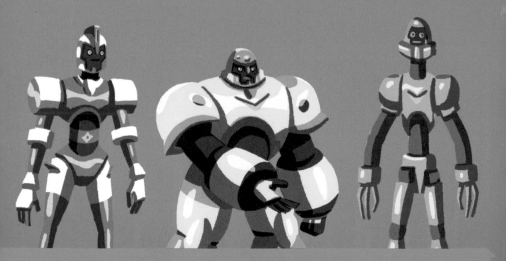

ACKNOWLEDGMENTS

First, I want to thank my kids, Roy, Nora, and Thomas, who helped me brainstorm the plots for these stories based on their own gaming lives. A lot of the language in the book comes from their happy shouts as they game online with friends. Thank you to my wife, Beth, for more things than I can name.

A special thanks to my mom, Diana Amsterdam, who was an accomplished author and playwright and taught me to love writing from the time I could write.

A shout-out to my ten favorite video games of all time: Baldur's Gate II, The Legend of Zelda: Breath of the Wild, Out of the Park Baseball, XCOM 2, Hearthstone, Mass Effect 2, God of War, Persona 5, BioShock, and Portal 2.

And finally, thank you to the Power Up team. I'm amazed by Darnell Johnson's illustrations, how he brought both North Mesa Middle School and the Mecha Melee game world to vivid life. Thank you to Phil Caminiti, for his outstanding design. Thank you to our editor, Bethany Vinhateiro, for her big ideas, her extraordinary sense of plot and character arcs, and for tying the whole endeavor together. It's been a joy.

—Sam Nisson

DON'T MISS MILES AND RHYS'S FIRST ROUND:

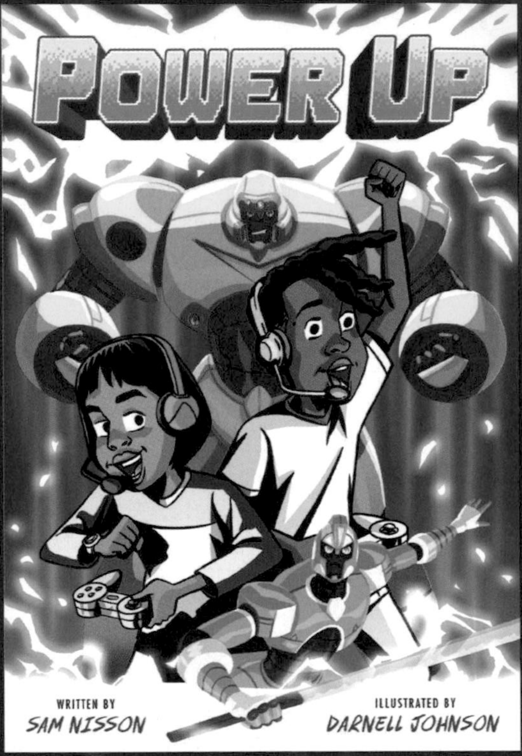
POWER UP
WRITTEN BY
SAM NISSON
ILLUSTRATED BY
DARNELL JOHNSON